OIL AND DUST

THE ELEMENTAL ARTIST

JAMI FAIRLEIGH

KITSUNE
PUBLISHING

Oil And Dust

Published by Kitsune Publishing
23515 NE Novelty Hill Rd, STE B221-309
Redmond, WA 98058
www.kitsunepublishing.co

The Library of Congress has catalogued the hardcover edition as follows:

Fairleigh, Jami, author
Oil and Dust / Jami Fairleigh - First edition
ISBN 978-1-955428-03-3 (hardcover)
ISBN 978-1-955428-01-9 (paperback)
ISBN 978-1-955428-02-6 (lrg. print paperback)
ISBN 978-1-955428-00-2 (ebook)
ISBN 978-1-955428-04-0 (audiobook)

For Dougla

Everything you can imagine is real.
  Pablo Picasso

CHAPTER ONE

I wished I'd been born two hundred years ago.

Before technology died.

Before the world died.

What would it have been like to ride in an autocraft, to float in a mechanical bubble out of the sun and rain and insects? Even when I closed my eyes, I couldn't imagine traveling so fast you could cross a landscape in hours and days instead of months and years.

If I'd been born two hundred years ago, if I'd been born into the world of technology, I'd know who and where my parents were. More importantly, they'd know me. It was what I couldn't wrap my mind around—the family-shaped gaps in my mind and heart. With luck, I'd find my answers, but it didn't feel like they were coming soon.

The gray sky darkened my mood, and glancing up, I urged my horses into a faster walk. If I didn't reach the lake soon, I'd have no chance of booking passage on a ship before the onset of rough weather.

It had taken ten arduous days to pick our way through the wilderness of the White Mountains, and I was eager to talk with the traders who sailed the lake. Reliable news was always scarce, but as the year slipped into fall, the flow of information stopped while travelers over-wintered, nestling into cozy communities.

No one wanted to be in the wilderness once a New England winter began.

In the tales from *Before,* people had enjoyed instant access to news the planet over. Legend said if an earthquake happened at the far reaches of the globe, the entire world tuned in to discuss the deaths, destruction, and impact.

Honestly, I wasn't sure if I believed in such things.

If I had access to an endless stream of information, how would I choose what to focus on? I'd find the world's problems too distracting —any artist would.

Once you learned to restructure reality, the itch to fix or control the chaos was strong.

After graduation, I'd chosen to search for my family instead of accepting a residency in a community. While I hadn't been my own man long enough to regret my decision, the memory of the roar of disapproval from the masters and other students at the abbey still made me flush with shame.

Nevertheless, I loved being on the road. Despite the hardships, the past five months had solidified my desire to continue traveling. For the first time in my life, I determined where I went, and when, and how far. Responsible for only myself, my dog, and my two horses, my job was as simple as filling our bellies and finding a place to sleep.

"The unknown awaits us around the next bend in the road, eh, Charcoal? We are men of action."

Charcoal barked once in agreement, trotting alongside Oxide, my riding horse.

Oxide quickened his pace, his saddle creaking and buckles jangling—a sure sign we were approaching people. Magnesium, my packhorse, crowded forward, and I twitched the rope to warn him back. He ignored my warning, and Oxide pinned his ears and snaked his head to the side, hip twitching as he kicked with his rear foot.

Magnesium snorted as Oxide's foot thumped into his chest, shaking his head with displeasure.

"I warned you," I said to the packhorse as he fell back into line.

Rounding a bend, I glimpsed buildings through the trees and whistled for my dog to heel. I needn't have bothered. Charcoal typically had better manners than the people I met on the road.

Finding a community on the edge of the wilderness was disappointing. The courtesy of the road demanded I stop to share news and gossip, and leaving would be difficult once they knew who I was.

I hated being the center of attention.

Although adept at entertaining a small family, I found interacting with a large group draining. After the solitude of the abandoned lanes and byways, and the peaceful company of whirring insects and chattering birds, human voices were grating. I didn't make it past the trees before the first cries began.

"Traveler! Traveler!"

Sighing, I halted Oxide. Meeting communities was always the same, and I gathered my energy. As we waited at the edge of the wood, Oxide tensed beneath me. Like me, he preferred the quiet emptiness of the road.

People hurried toward us, shouting for others to join. Everyone greeted all travelers thus, but when they learned I was an artist, I knew the community would buzz with excitement.

A teenager with a shock of curly hair was the first to reach us, sweat glistening on his forehead from his haste. "Are you the artist?"

My eyes widened, and I nodded. "Yes, I'm—"

The lad left before I finished, racing toward a squat house on the corner of the green. How had he known to expect me?

"Heya, Traveler," said a breathless woman, her face flushed.

"Heya, Lady." I pointed at the lad who'd reached the squat building. "He scarpered as soon as I—"

"Confirmed you're the artist?" she interrupted. "He's gone to get Administrator Oldham. She'll be glad to see you at last. Here she comes now."

At last?

A large lady bustled toward me, her expression both expectant and cross. I'd not yet met the woman, and somehow, I'd already annoyed her. Dismounting, I straightened my coat, feeling like a schoolboy.

"Artist, please meet Victoria Oldham of—"

"Of Hamilton," Oldham snapped.

"Pleasure," I said with a small bow. "Well met, Ms. Oldham. I'm Matthew Sugiyama."

"Administrator Oldham," she said, narrowing her eyes. "Administrator of *Hamilton*."

I scrambled to find the proper words. "How lovely to find you here at the edge of the wilds."

Lovely it was not proving to be.

"Young man, I am quite put out."

"Why?"

"Why? We expected you Tuesday *last*."

"Me? But why?" What did she mean? I was traveling for myself; I had no itinerary, no specific destination.

"They didn't provide you with the name of our community?"

"Provided with... by whom?" My mind raced as I tried to make sense of her words.

"The headmaster at Popham Abbey."

My stomach churned. "I beg pardon, Administrator, but I've never heard of Hamilton."

"*Outrageous.* You've accepted our commission and are to be our artist of residence."

Though I knew she was mistaken, a sour taste filled my mouth. "I've accepted no commissions."

"*You have.* Here, I have the letter." Theatrically, she pulled a letter from her clutch and opened it with a flourish. The people crowded closer to listen, and I fought the urge to push them away from me.

"My dear Administrator Oldham," she read, "I am pleased to

inform you Artist Sugiyama accepts your commission. He should reach you by the 22nd of September. As discussed, he will stay for five years upon which he will be free to extend his commission or choose another. Yours faithfully, Headmaster T."

What?

"May I see it?" I held out my hand.

Administrator Oldham stared at me before extending the document. The crowd leaned in, and again, I tamped the urge to wave my arms and reestablish my personal space.

The paper, thick and oily, shook as I skimmed the document. Astonishment rising over my ire, I read it again, the words trembling on the page.

"We prepared our finest dwelling for you and planned a welcome ceremony. You're an entire week late."

Swallowing, I willed my pulse to slow. "I'm afraid I know nothing about this."

She snatched the letter back. "Is there another Artist Sugiyama?"

Oxide tossed his head, and I patted his muscled neck, grateful for the distraction.

"Not at Popham. Perhaps you corresponded with another abbey?" I kept my voice measured, reasonable, and confident.

"I did not! Young man, I'm losing my patience. Are you saying you will not be living in Hamilton?"

"Quite."

"But the letter! Your headmaster *promised*."

"Headmaster Sinclair runs Popham Abbey. There's no master with a 'T' surname. It looks like someone has played a trick."

"A nasty trick," murmured a woman. "Come, Victoria, let me get you some water."

"Maybe a chair," said Administrator Oldham. "I'm feeling faint."

My mind galloped, searching for answers. "Administrator, I'm sorry for the confusion."

Why was I apologizing? I wasn't sorry; it was *my* life someone

5

was trying to commandeer. But why? Were they trying to stop me from finding my birth family?

"Will you reconsider? You could make a pleasant life for yourself here in Hamilton."

Absolutely not.

My refusal to join a community had created an uproar at the abbey. Headmaster Sinclair had been furious when I refused to consider the commissions offered...

"You ARE NOT A MINSTREL!" HEADMASTER SINCLAIR HAD shouted. "Artists do not wander."

Astonished by the venom in his voice, I'd lost mine.

Headmaster Sinclair was a mild-mannered man, soft-spoken and thoughtful, and his display of temper unnerved me. His voice thundered in the stone room, reverberating off every surface, muting the crashing waves outside.

"Tell me who my family is," I said, determined to stay calm, attempting to muster authority. I was failing, and the large breakfast I'd eaten sat uneasily in my gut.

Salt and bile rose in my throat.

Headmaster Sinclair spluttered. "Your recalcitrance—the cheek! It is not within my power to say more."

After years of asking about my family, I hadn't expected to learn anything today, but his refusal disappointed me. "Fine. I'll find them myself."

"What? How?"

I glanced around the familiar office, seeking answers. This could be the last time I would visit the room where I'd spent many happy hours drawing. A room which smelled like my boyhood—salt and books and stone. "I shall travel."

"To where? Please, Matthew, be sensible. These are marvelous commissions—communities blessed with sense and situation."

6

"I cannot settle until I find my people. When I find my family, I'll know who I am. Only then will I entertain offers and commissions. *Not before.*"

He stalked to the window, blocking the light.

I shivered. "Are my things my own?"

"How will you travel?"

"I'll need horses and equipment."

"Ah." Headmaster Sinclair nodded, sinking into a chair. A cloud of dust spiraled in the light from the window. "Yes, and you have neither."

Tasting freedom, I continued, "I'll procure what I need."

"Preposterous. How?"

"I'll trade my skills."

"You'd peddle your art? Are you mad? It's not what we've trained you for!"

"I've decided, Headmaster. With respect, I leave at week's end."

"My boy, you're making a dreadful mistake. I'm afraid the world will not live up to your expectations."

I kneeled before him, placing my hand on his knee, bony and frail beneath his heavy robes. "Won't you reconsider, Headmaster? I need to know who my family is, where I come from."

He seemed to waver. His lips parted and his chin wobbled. "We'll miss you, Matthew."

This was it. I'd chosen my fate.

My chest flooded—sorrow and wild excitement battling with heart-thumping knocks. I'd done it. I'd broken the yoke of my training.

Until I learned where I came from and why they'd abandoned me, I refused to settle.

I deserved the whole truth.

7

VICTORIA OLDHAM STARED AT ME.

Chilled and hungry, I'd hoped for an offer of hospitality. A night off the road would have meant a bath and fresh horses in the morning.

It would also give me a chance to reexamine the letter.

However, I didn't want to rekindle their hopes they could induce me to stay.

"I'm sorry, Administrator Oldham, but I must continue my journey. I'm on my way to meet my friend, Liang Zhen."

Until I'd said it out loud, I hadn't had a plan, but why not visit Zhen? He'd graduated the year before, and I was curious what the last year had been like for him.

"I had such plans," she said faintly, as if I'd woken her from a beautiful dream. "What is to become of Hamilton?"

"Are you sure you won't stay awhile, Artist Sugiyama?" asked a man. "We had a feast planned in your honor."

Their hopeful faces tugged at my heart. I hated to disappoint them, but I couldn't eat and leave them empty-handed. My stomach grumbled, and I reached for a compromise.

"Why don't you give me a tour of your community? If I find a project I have time to help with, I'll paint for you and stay for the feast. Otherwise, I'll be on my way. Agreed?"

The people nodded, their eyes lighting with hope.

I relaxed, releasing tension I hadn't realized I was holding. My mouth watered at the anticipation of a hot meal. A *feast*, the man had said. Still, out of prudence, I checked, "You understand I'll decide how much aid to provide?"

Victoria Oldham lifted her chin. "Artist Sugiyama, we understand how the world works."

"Very well, lead on."

Leaves crunched underfoot as we walked, the *snick-snick* reminding me of autumns past. Hamilton wasn't large, and the tour didn't take long. Twenty dwellings wrapped around three sides of the center green. Larger buildings sat on the north side, the three nearest scorched. The charred-wood smell was acrid and clung to the air, making me feel even more grimy.

"Our smithy," said Oldham. "Such a shame. I'm not sure we'll manage repairs before winter arrives."

A quick glance at the sky told me how much daylight I had left. "Mmm. Lucky you stopped the spread of flame. I have time to restore the damaged buildings."

Oldham's eyes widened, and murmurs rustled around me.

"All three? Very generous, Artist Sugiyama. We're honored."

I bowed. "At your service, Administrator. I'll set up my easel here."

CHAPTER TWO

Eager young men unsaddled my stock and set the panniers near me, their quick smiles reassuring.

I examined the buildings as I assembled my easel. If I could repair them quickly, I might yet have time to study the letter before supper.

Could there be others? If I impressed Administrator Oldham, maybe she'd let me examine *all* the correspondence she had received from 'T'.

Upon leaving the abbey, I'd learned art was the most valued currency in the world. For a boy who'd grown up surrounded by artists, this was a revelation. During my travels, they had offered me supplies, food, lodging, houses, and once, shamefully, the company of a young woman.

I accepted the expectation for travelers to stop and trade services and news for meals, board, and supplies. Where I could, I tried to pitch in and help, completing small paintings even when I needed nothing. It made me welcome and kept me well-treated and fed.

Digging through my supplies, I extracted an unassembled canvas. My audience watched and discussed my every action as I prepared it.

This was a show.

I carried several prepared linens with me, rolled carefully to protect the sizing and gesso.

At the abbey, we'd wrinkled our noses the first time we prepared our canvases with gesso made from rabbit glue. First, we learned to skin rabbits—a gruesome task. We sent the meat to the kitchens, but boiled the bones and hides ourselves. Initially, the bubbling vats smelled like soup, but as the lime worked on the bones and skin, the scent turned into a nauseating mix—grease, blood, fur, and sinew. We mixed the hot glue with chalk to create gesso.

I learned early in my travels to prepare canvases ahead of time; applying gesso was a perfect rainy-day activity, and communities were happy to provide me with glue and linen if it meant I'd spend more time with them.

Testing the prepared canvas, I checked to make sure none of the gesso had flaked off. I could have painted the scene on unprepared linen, but I knew the people of Hamilton would treasure the painting, and I didn't want it to crumble and yellow.

It was important to me that my art and artwork be well remembered.

While I worked, my mind returned to the letter. Surely it was a mistake; some other artist had agreed to a living in Hamilton. In truth, I didn't know why any artist would agree to a commission in a community like this. As far as I could tell, Hamilton enjoyed neither sense nor situation.

As I placed the canvas on the easel, the crowd hushed, and the air trembled with expectation. I breathed deeply, emptying my mind.

Moving quickly, I sketched the fire-gnawed buildings with a fine charcoal pencil to capture the perspective of the scene.

The people watched, their attention feeding energy into the ritual.

Unrolling the stiff cloth in which I stored my brushes, I selected my three favorites. Why I carried so many was a mystery even to me; I rarely used any but these three.

I rinsed them in turpentine, the sharp sting of pine overpowering the scent of char. My eyes rarely left the buildings as I mixed my pigments, my mind focusing on the texture, shape, and shadow of the structures.

The crowd sighed with expectation.

Time to get to work. Time to shut out all distractions and focus on what mattered: my artwork. Through it all, I could sense the people peering at me, sizing me up, eyes wide and mouths agape.

Shut it out. Shut it all out.

Dabbing the brush into the first paint, I added pigments to the sketch on the canvas to build the color, layering them and working toward hyper-saturation.

As I worked, my thoughts cleared and focused. The past and the future faded from my mind, and unencumbered, I captured texture and shadow on my canvas.

The last step of the painting was to catch the light and reflection. I added the sense of late afternoon sun and painted shine on the broken glass of the windows. When finished, I stepped back and examined my work.

The buildings in my painting were almost a photo-real capture of the ruined buildings, illuminated by an artificial October sun, their outlines bent and ashamed.

Time to create art.

I closed my eyes and pictured the buildings again, only this time, seeing them repaired. Cementing the image in my mind, my eyes snapped open. Focused on the outcome I would produce, I stepped forward, crackling with energy. Moving my brush over the canvas again, I painted my mind's image over the ruins depicted on my canvas.

Here was something I could control and master.

As I concentrated on my work, a familiar tingle spread through my hands. I didn't need to look at the actual buildings to know they were changing.

The people watching me gasped when the wooden timbers

moaned and shrieked as I reordered them. The murmurs of the crowd didn't slow my work; I'd painted in front of people often enough to expect reactions. With a dab here, a flick there, a swirl of brush, a layer of pigment bleeding and blending with the previous, I worked methodically.

Painting the new roofs, the *flap-flapping* of the new slate shingles moving into place filled me with a sense of peace.

Order from chaos; beauty from ruin.

My hand cramped around the slender paintbrush, but I continued to paint, adding a cobblestone road in front of the workshops. I added the dark tones between each cobble, where the dust of the street would come to settle, kicked up by carts and horses and scurrying feet. I painted their grooves clean, their edges nicely rounded and beveled, no chips or fractures.

"Now," I said, looking up, "what improvements can I make?"

An older man spoke, his words a croak. "Nothing, lad. They're just as they were."

I cocked my head. "You want nothing more?"

He cleared his throat and looked around. "A rain barrel would be handy."

Easy.

The addition of the barrel broke the crowd's hesitance, and they continued to suggest minor improvements.

When I finished the last addition, the people stood as if frozen.

I stepped back and stretched. "There. What do you think?"

I'd erased all traces of the fire.

The previously derelict structures appeared brand new. Gone were the blackened and brittle beams, the giant cracks in the surrounding scorched earth, and all signs of the ashes and debris. Instead of char, the fragrance of new wood and fresh paint perfumed the air.

Victoria Oldham's eyes shone. She opened her mouth and closed it, saying nothing.

"Is it real?" asked a lad.

Twisting, I smiled at the boy. "Go see."

The crowd surged forward.

"Mercy! Mercy!" a woman bawled as she staggered toward me. "I never, no I never!"

She rushed at me, and instinctively, I spread my arms to protect the still-wet painting. My reaction was illogical; I manifested changes in the physical world through the artwork, not the finished art. They could destroy the painting without affecting the buildings.

The crying woman flung her arms around me and sobbed into my chest. "I never, I mean, never!"

My palms were sweaty, and anxiety coiled in my gut as her hot tears soaked my shirt. I patted her back in what I hoped was a soothing gesture and thought about the letter from 'T' again.

"Look!" screeched children racing around the green.

Chickens squawked and scrambled out of the way, loose feathers flying.

Charcoal raced after them, enjoying the mania and enthusiastically barking.

That dog. Such a sucker.

The woman wailed louder into my chest. "And I mean, I NEVER!"

I continued to pat her as I watched people examine my work. A quiet pride bloomed each time I helped someone, and I never tired of it. Back at the abbey, I'd been an exemplary student, but my work had benefited no one. Here, I'd effected a genuine change, improving their lives and community.

Shuddering, the woman pulled back and gave me a watery smile. "I suppose we should get started on the feast. One masterpiece deserves another."

Giving her hand a gentle squeeze, I tried to pull mine away, squirming as she continued to gush. I'd grown up with little physical contact, and displays like this made me uneasy. My neck flushed, and I tried to edge away.

"Dorothy, let him go," ordered Administrator Oldham. "He

hardly needs you weeping all over him. We'll host you in the yellow dwelling for the night, sir. I'll have a lad fetch you when supper's ready."

Her manner toward me had changed. Emboldened, I asked, "Administrator Oldham, were there other letters? Other correspondence with 'T'?"

"Yes, two. Would you like to see them?"

"Very much, thank you."

"We're in your debt." Administrator Oldham shoed the community members away, shouting orders as she marched toward the dwellings, her skirts billowing as she went.

Packing away my equipment, I grinned, relieved to have a moment alone. My tear-soaked shirt was rapidly cooling in the deepening afternoon chill, making my hands clumsy and dull. My stomach rumbled as I finished stowing my gear.

I hoped the women of Hamilton could cook.

CHAPTER THREE

My eyes widened at the picture before me. They had set up long tables draped with white clothes on the green and hung lanterns from strings. The candles flickered in the evening dark, and the air was fragrant with the smell of roasting meat and fresh bread, punctuated by the tang of fruit.

At my best, I was a poor cook, and after enduring days of my ill-prepared food, my mouth wetted, and I couldn't wipe the grin from my face.

Victoria Oldham and a group of elders were sitting at the head table. Seeing me, she beckoned. The elders looked up, their jaws set and eyes determined.

A procession of people walked toward the tables, carrying steaming dishes.

Victoria beckoned again, and my stomach rumbled. If I sat with her and the elders, I suspected we'd argue about my departure. But if I sat elsewhere, would she withhold the letters from 'T'?

She had *promised*, and I had fixed up the buildings.

Children giggled at a table set near the edge of the festivities.

With a grin, I pulled out a chair there and chuckled as it sank into the soft grass under my weight.

"This is the kids' table," whispered a girl with blonde braids.

"I know," I whispered back. "Can we eat with you?"

I'd ask to read the letters after the meal. For now, I only wanted feeding.

Charcoal stood on his hind legs and surveyed everyone's faces. He looked like a waif, with his short blue-gray coat and intelligent eyes. Tonight, his plaintive expression melted the blackest heart.

The children ducked their heads conspiratorially before agreeing.

Smiling women brought food to our table, and we oohed and aahed over a stewed chicken, brown and aromatic, swimming in a thick gravy with dumplings. We clapped for the bowl of succotash with corn, white beans, tomatoes, and peppers.

An elder with a face like a dried apple set a dish of pickles and a crock of white butter in the center of the table. Last, an older boy brought a basket piled high with fluffy biscuits.

"I'll take those," I said with authority. Eying the children, I hugged the basket to my chest. "All mine."

"You must share!"

"Must not. I'm the guest of honor."

"We'll make you sit with the grownups," said the girl with the braids.

"You win," I said, and the children cheered. I juggled two of the hot biscuits and held my plate out to the oldest girl at the table.

"Here you go," she said, piling the plate with sliced chicken, dumplings, and gravy.

Wind sighed through the treetops, and stars glimmered and winked through the waving branches. The clinks of forks and soft laughter from other tables reminded me of the dining hall at Popham Abbey, but instead of being homesick, I felt free.

Digging into my supper, I tasted the chicken, smiling as its salty-rich flavor swam over my tongue. The multihued succotash tasted of the harvest, rich and sun-toasted. The pickles, sweet and crunchy, made my tongue curl. Mopping up the gravy on my plate with a biscuit, I watched Charcoal circle the table, accepting treats and handouts from the children who passed tidbits in secret. I pretended not to notice.

Waiting for a second serving, I cleared my throat. "Dinner is a marvel. I don't eat this well often, Hamilton. Thank you."

The children swelled with pride. "We helped!"

Several children squirmed in their chairs, struggling to stay quiet. The oldest girl smiled at them. "Do you mind?" she asked me.

"Not at all. Ask away."

"Is it magical paint?"

"How did you do it?"

"What happens if the painting rips?"

"Are you a wizard?"

"Do you travel all the time?"

"Will the changes last forever?"

"Can you paint me a pony?"

"Can anyone be an artist? How many artists are there?"

Their questions tumbled out, each springing forth before the last had settled.

Sated and content, warm and safe, I was ready to entertain them. I'd given this speech many times while on the road. I took a long swallow from my water glass and waited until their questions slowed.

"They sent me to an abbey as a young lad to train as an artist. A master later told me I'd taken an aptitude test, though I don't remember it. The abbey was my home and school. There are many abbeys, but I've only visited one other than where I grew up."

The children listened with rapt faces and enormous eyes. From the elder's table, Administrator Oldham glowered.

"What else did you... ah, yes. No, destroy the painting and nothing happens to the buildings. The paint isn't magical, and I'm not a wizard. Have you learned quantum physics?"

They nodded.

"Good, then you know matter is made from whirling bits of energy." I knocked on the plank table. "Even this."

I paused, breaking my third biscuit open. "Just as your body can take apart the food you eat and use the energy to build what your body needs, they teach artists to work with the energy of matter to change it through our artwork." I took a bite of the biscuit, enjoying its crisp, buttery crust and the soft, flaky interior.

A girl nodded knowingly. "You're like an engineer."

"No, dummy!" A large boy gave the girl's shoulder a shove. "An engineer builds out of actual stuff. An artist builds out of energy."

"We're like engineers," I said, hiding a smile as the girl's chest puffed. "Like us, they learn to envision the final product and use the materials at hand to bring their vision into being. But they can't improve the materials."

"So, what about a pony?" asked a boy without guile.

"Jackie!" scolded the oldest girl. "I'm sorry, Artist Sugiyama. We're grateful for the work you've done."

I rubbed my belly. "Please, this dinner is thanks enough. While it's possible to create a pony, it would be much faster to get a mare in foal, raise the foal, and train the pony than to paint one. You'd probably end up with a better-behaved pony, anyway." I winked at the boy and pushed back from the table. "Now, we'll bid you good night."

I held up my hands as the children protested. "We're leaving early."

The children fell silent, lowering their eyes respectfully, and I realized someone was standing behind me.

The feeling of safety fell away in an instant.

"If you leave now, you'll miss the pie, and you must allow us to host a community breakfast," said Administrator Oldham.

Her invitation sounded like an order. Had she been hovering and waiting to pounce? I turned and bowed, ready to argue about the breakfast.

"I'll bring the two additional letters for you to review in the morning."

Blast. She was prepared to hold the letters hostage. Perhaps it had been a mistake not to sit with her and the elders. If I wanted to read the letters, skipping breakfast was now out of the question.

"Sharing another meal with you will be my pleasure, and I'm eager to read the other letters you received from Popham. However, I must leave as soon as we've eaten."

She frowned, but I held my ground. "I've many kilometers to travel before winter comes, and though I've enjoyed your hospitality, I must insist."

Oldham nodded. "Breakfast then, and off you'll go."

I smiled and bade them a good evening. By flirting, I won a large slice of pie and carried it to my borrowed dwelling. The walk was short, and I breathed deeply, enjoying the cool, still air as Charcoal danced around me.

"We leave early tomorrow," I said to Charcoal as I toweled off after my bath. I laid down with a groan, finishing my pie.

Charcoal sighed and snuffled for crumbs before resting his head on my chest.

The bed was soft and pillowy after weeks of sleeping on the ground. "Don't get too used to having a roof," I muttered, unsure if I was talking to myself or the dog.

Settling deeper into the bed, I tried not to obsess about the letters that could provide clues about why someone would want to keep me from my family.

CHAPTER FOUR

The road leading south narrowed and wound lazily, as if to encourage travelers to slow and enjoy the scenery. Although the trees had grown to the edges of the old black-top, I found it picturesque and restful, not cramped and claustrophobic as someone had notated on the last map. The chilly afternoon breeze ruffled the hair at my collar, and I shivered.

Despite our late start, we ambled down the road, lazy and peaceful.

Breakfast had been a bust—a sticky amaranth porridge without honey or syrup, bitter dandelion tea, and grim-faced community elders determined to induce me to stay and settle in Hamilton. They tried to tempt and seduce me with promises of lunch, then with a supper to rival last night's feast, but my urge to continue south bested my unsatisfied appetite.

The letters Oldham brought had offered no additional information. They were administrative in tone and signed by 'T', but provided no further clues.

Determined to stop obsessing about the letters, I slipped into a game I'd made up as a child at the abbey and mentally painted the world around me.

The names of pigments had always felt magical: Purple Madder Alizarin, Manganese Violet, Phthalocyanine Green, Payne's Grey. The red sugar maples, the orange and golds of the beeches, the blazing colors of the white ash suggested Yellow Ochre, Raw Sienna, and Indian Yellow.

Mesmerized by the exhibition of autumnal color, I was unprepared when Oxide veered to the left. I fought to keep my seat—the last thing I needed was to hit the pavement in front of strangers.

Oxide snorted and tossed his head as I resettled myself. He never skipped the chance for a meal, and we'd arrived at a filling station.

I patted his neck and surveyed the premises.

While they had abandoned and left most buildings from *Before* to decay, filling stations had largely survived. This station was stout and made of nondescript, gray concrete blocks with a long rectangular window facing the road and a large opening on the left side of the building. A covered awning stood in front, the roof of which dipped in the middle as if the builders had accidentally put it on upside down.

A woman wearing blue overalls strolled over to meet us, her hand raised in greeting.

"Heya, Traveler," she called.

Magnesium nickered in reply.

"Heya, Keeper." I dismounted, and my left hip protested. "Blast."

"Too long in the saddle?" she asked, taking Oxide's reins.

If I'd been alone, I would have rubbed the pain from my hip. Strangely, I was reluctant to do so in front of her. My eyes roamed over her face, memorizing the planes and shadows.

"Perhaps longer than I intended. Is this Crane's Corner?"

The woman nodded, stroking Oxide's neck. "Would you like a filling for these brutes?"

"Yes. I promised them a meal some time ago."

"And the wee one?"

"The wee—oh, you mean Charcoal." I rubbed my chin and shrugged. "Yes, please. He's traveled as far, with less complaint. Have you a map inside?"

"Sure do." Clucking to Oxide, she walked toward the large door, leading a horse in each hand. "There's a man within to do you up. Name's Earl."

I fought the urge to follow her and opened the door she'd pointed at instead. Unsure of Charcoal's welcome, I stood in the doorway, peering into the gloom.

"Your chap can enter," a voice called.

Charcoal needed no further invitation, and I followed, my eyes adjusting. The dog skirted a large table in the middle of the room, claws clicking against the rough wooden floor. He chose a booth near the back, hopping onto a hide-covered bench to survey the room, as if a valued patron waiting for his usual ale and a pie.

The man behind the counter chuckled. "Will he be ordering, too?"

I smiled and approached the counter. "Heya, Earl, I'm Matthew."

The man raised his hand in greeting, but shook his head. "I'm not Earl. She is," he corrected, jerking his chin at the woman who had entered from a side door.

"Your horses are eating with gusto," she reported. "I loosened their girths but didn't unsaddle. If you're going to stay, I can do so."

I glanced at the clock on the wall. My intention had been to wolf down a meal, pay with a quick update to their map, and get back on the road. Now, I was reluctant to leave. "Good question. I've had unexpected delays recently. My name is Matthew, an—"

"Artist," she interrupted. "I snooped in your bag. The menu today is venison stew, and I have bones for your chap."

This was the first time I'd met anyone who didn't fawn over me upon learning I was an artist. My interest in Earl sharpened, and I considered my options. "Is your map out of date?"

"The last scholar came through five years ago," she answered. "Will you update it?"

They prominently displayed their map on the large central table. I glanced at it, curious about my route options. "Done. I'll unsaddle the horses when I get my kit."

Earl smiled. "I'll check on lunch."

In my history classes, I'd learned that after the world had died, the technologies from *Before* had slowly malfunctioned. When the infrastructure broke, no one had the skill or will to maintain it. The cellular towers had gone first. As they failed, engineers dismantled their metal skeletons and salvaged the materials for new uses. Next, they'd lost the use of telephones and telegraphs.

The masters referred to them as 'land lines' during dinner tales, but I didn't know if they referred to the ropy network of cabling left attached to the great shafts of wood that never rotted, or if the telephones had required a straight line of sight to the person at the other end. We boys had concocted a network of cans and string to share secret messages between our berths when we thought the masters had gone to bed, and those required direct lines.

More interesting to me were the minstrel stories about the autocrafts that ran while they had fuel to burn or batteries to power them. These autocrafts had also decayed once they were no longer operable. I'd seen one or two rusted hulks during my travels and considered improving one to satisfy my curiosity.

As people reverted to horses or human-powered transportation, they'd lost the knowledge the people *Before* had used to navigate large landscapes. Today, we used hand-drawn maps maintained by artists and scholars to provide guidance on passable routes.

Like most maps, a blue star marked the center at my present location. I traced my finger up the Route 153 trunk line, finding Hamilton.

Had I agreed to Victoria Oldham's demands, they would have trapped me for five years in a community stuck at the edge of *nothing*. A lucky escape, and a good reminder that when I was ready to entertain offers, I should check a map of the area before making my decision.

There were few routes through this area, limiting my options.

To reach the lake, I needed to travel southeast, but the primary routes from here were east-west trending. I'd have to take a lesser-traveled road. The lack of options meant if another artist named Sugiyama was traveling locally, he'd have passed this filling station.

The man behind the counter was intently working on something in a wooden box, so I cleared my throat politely. The big man looked up, his right eye enormous behind a thick lens fastened to his head with a leather strap. Surprised by the contraption, I forgot to ask if he'd heard of another artist traveling through the region.

I'd assumed the man behind the counter was a cook, or doing repairs, or completing a housekeeping task, but I could see now he was deep in the intricate innards of a contraption.

Inside the box were gears and levers, each balanced precariously against the next. The innards reminded me of a complicated clock, but timekeepers surrounded every clocksmith I'd met, the clatter of ticking and tocking unmistakable.

"What are you working on?"

The man smiled and wiped his fingers on a linen towel. "A computer."

"A computer?"

"Yes, I'm experimenting with digital computers," the man replied, crossing his arms.

"You're not a craftsman?"

"No, an engineer, though I rarely work on tiny projects."

Behind me, Charcoal huffed, and I turned as Earl entered the room.

She carried a large wooden tray to Charcoal's table and removed a platter holding three raw bones.

Charcoal whined as she bent to set the platter on the floor.

Shrugging, Earl placed the platter in front of the dog.

He stared at the bones, not moving as Earl placed a bowl of water next to the platter. Head ducked, he gazed at her until she nodded, then licked his first bone.

She watched the dog before bringing the tray to me.

"Thank you, Earl."

Steam rose from the bowl in ghostly curls of mushroom and rosemary. The surface of the stew shimmered, and thick chunks of potato and carrots slid in and out of view as I tilted the bowl. Venison, cubed precisely, glistened amongst the root vegetables.

I savored the stew, meaty and earthy, its salt-fat flavors familiar and comforting. The heat of the earthen bowl chased the ache from my hands.

Earl smiled and perched on the stool next to me. She swiveled to look at the dog, who'd wedged a bone between his front paws. "Does he always eat like that?"

"From a plate? Yes, whenever someone will indulge him," I said between bites. "He's done it since he was a pup. He never breaks the crockery or makes a mess, so no one asked him to eat his meals like a dog."

Earl nodded and turned to the box. "Bowman is trying to build a computer—"

"A digital computer," Bowman corrected.

"To calculate weather for the flier," she continued.

"A flier?" I mumbled around a mouthful of stew.

Bowman nodded. He was a large man with short white hair curling around his skull like a wool cap. He was broad across the shoulder and hip, but didn't give the impression of a man sagging into middle age. I estimated him to be in his fifties. He had a broad flat nose and a high forehead sloping back from intelligent eyes. His skin was dark and rich, inky brown with a red undertone.

Bowman looked at Earl. "Where's *my* lunch?"

"Oh! The tray was full. I'll be right back."

I watched her walk through the swinging door.

"She's a looker, our Earl," said Bowman as he rounded the counter to take a seat on an empty stool.

Embarrassed Bowman caught my interest, I nodded.

Earl was a slim woman about my age with pale, nearly translucent skin showing faint veins of muted cerulean blue.

In some ways, she reminded me of a painting, a multiplicity of tones and subtle hues—at first, fragile-looking.

She'd parted her hair in the middle, and long, twin braids hung down each side of her neck. Their color was much the same red-orange as the fall beech trees outside.

I was uncomfortably aware of how attractive I found her as she entered, carrying two more bowls and a basket covered with a red-checked cloth.

"Biscuits!" Bowman's eyes gleamed.

"Maisie baked," Earl replied. "Said the weather had given her the itch."

"There are three of you here?" I asked.

"No, we're twenty-five," said Bowman. He dipped a biscuit in his stew. "Twenty-two," he amended. "Our community is a ten-minute walk away, and we each fill a few labor hours here as keeper. Like most communities, we're self-sufficient, but we like to visit with travelers."

"Travelers bring things to trade. And news," agreed Earl. "We like news."

I nodded.

"Earl's our butcher," Bowman continued. "Best sausages in eastern New Hampshire."

"A particular butcher," I said, a perfect cube of meat balanced on my spoon.

Earl nodded, unembarrassed by the praise.

Wiping my bowl clean with a biscuit, I gave a slight bow to Earl as I set the empty bowl back on the tray. Her lips curved, and time slowed as I watched her smile.

At that moment, I ardently wished I knew how to talk to women. It was a skill I hadn't gained, despite hoping the nuances might seep into my awareness. To be honest, maybe it hadn't mattered enough to me to allow any learning to occur. Not that I'd found much chance to learn. Art had been my obsession—what I thought of as I fell asleep, and what I woke to as the morning's sun rose.

As a student, I'd painted, sculpted, and sketched beautiful women, yet I'd never injected much thought into knowing what lay beneath the outward form of the women modeling.

My mind buzzed with questions, and I discarded one after the next, afraid to make a fool of myself, and loathe to waste too much time on them in case it led to nothing.

I cleared my throat to clear my thoughts. "I made a quick sketch of the map at Brownfield Depot and have updates from my travels too. Have you local changes to add?"

"Yes, we have a list," said Bowman.

"Good. I'll get my kit." Pleased to be of service, the pull of the road receded. Besides, I had plenty of time to reach the lake before winter arrived.

My heart raced when Earl put down her own half-finished bowl and rose.

"I'll come with you."

Charcoal watched us walk to the door but didn't move from his bench. He grinned at me, his tongue hanging out of his mouth. Like always, the dog had known I'd stay before I did.

Acutely aware of Earl's proximity, I yanked on the door.

"Push," she said, her voice musical.

The door opened easily, and a flush crept up my neck.

CHAPTER FIVE

B efore Earl and Bowman had finished their meals, I'd completed the primary map updates. Though no one had built routes since the world had died, our maps still required attention.

Earthslides, land tremors, and even heavy winters buckled and broke the old roads, making them dangerous at best, and at worst, impassible. We also lost routes when rivers changed course, and the ancient bridges, left over from *Before*, gave way.

Human-directed activities could change the landscape, too; low areas were drained or flooded by dams. Communities often sprang up at a crossroad if the land was open, creating diversions for travelers with new connections and wagon-ways.

Besides the routes and community names, we annotated the maps with known hazards, potable water sources, good campsites with forage for stock, and the approximate time to walk from a cross-road to the next community, crossroad, or depot.

Map editors often annotated points of interest. It lent a personal touch, and each editor had their own favorite things to add. I liked to add the names of hosts with whom I'd enjoyed staying. With my finest brush, I scripted 'Hamilton.'

"Who's there?" Earl asked.

"The community who hosted me last night. They set a terrific dinner." I finished the lettering and stood back to let it dry. "What's the makeup of your community?"

"Oh, I should think we're much like any other," Bowman answered. "We have an engineer in Star Creek, though."

I chuckled; this was the most fun I'd experienced in weeks. Though I needed to get back on the road, I didn't want to leave. "A complete community."

Earl shrugged, a smile tugging at her mouth. "As complete as you can be without an artist, scholar, or minstrel."

"Good luck with that," I said with a wry smile. Small communities could only extend offers to scholars if they had resources to spare and could rarely entice an artist to join them, even if their resources were bountiful. Minstrels too were notoriously hard to keep, even for large communities. Minstrels thrived on change and liked to be the center of attention, with a regularly refreshed crowd to play to. While a good minstrel could keep a community in thrall for a season with their news, songs, and stories, interest eventually waned.

They grew bored by the same faces—and it was mutual. There were only so many times you could hear the same tale or joke. Minstrels were the only people who traveled frequently.

Other than me.

"What changes should I add?"

"There's a new bridge here, and the community of Stone is finishing a dam here," said Bowman, pointing at the map.

Earl raised an eyebrow. "Are you sure?"

"Yes, they came and consulted me. They've been working with another engineer, but they wanted to know if I thought there'd be any trouble in expanding Long Pond into a reservoir."

Earl frowned at the news. "It means fewer beavers, which means less fur traders traveling through."

"I saw the dam myself last week when I was testing the flier," said Bowman.

I glanced at him. "Flier? You mentioned it earlier."

"Bowman built a flier," said Earl, collecting our dishes. "It's a great, delicate thing."

"It works?"

Earl chuckled. "Of course it works. He *is* an engineer, and a good one."

I tried to imagine what an engineer-built flier would look like. A dragonfly? A bird?

My mind's canvas remained blank.

Bowman beamed. "Anyone who can pedal can fly."

"What's the computer for?"

"Ha!" Bowman said. "You remembered. The flier's gears work well in a light breeze, but wind speed and direction can be problematic. The computer—"

"If it works," interrupted Earl.

"*When* it works, will calculate the best gearing for wind speed and direction."

My mind burned with a single question. A question I shouldn't ask, a question which would mean a longer delay. "May I see it?"

Earl and Bowman grinned, their smiles identical. They'd hoodwinked me, tempting me with the flier to entice me to stay.

No matter.

Anticipation flooded over me; I'd dreamed of seeing things like fliers since I was a small boy listening to stories of the world *Before*.

"I can stay and mind the station until Duncan comes," said Earl.

A pang rushed through my chest; I'd assumed she'd come with us.

Bowman grinned and packed his computer into the crate. "Thanks, Earl. Let's go as soon as you're finished," he said, stowing the crate under the counter. "It is a thing of wonder."

"Leave your stock," Earl said.

"Thanks much." I put my sketching pencils into their pouch and stacked them on top of the leather portfolio. Shrugging into my coat, I looked at Charcoal's empty booth.

He stood next to the door, the last marrow bone in his mouth. Obviously, he wanted to see the flier too.

Bowman opened the door and called to Earl, "I'll see if Duncan will come early to relieve you."

The walk to the community passed quickly, the leaves crunching beneath our boots, and the chilly autumnal air flushing our cheeks. We chatted as though we'd known each other for years.

I tossed a stick for Charcoal. "Have you lived in Star Creek long? What do you like about it?"

Unwilling to drop his bone, Charcoal ignored the stick.

Bowman held a branch back for me. "Fifteen years. I like the size; we have eighteen inhabited buildings besides the filling station. But what I like best are the people."

In most communities, the green was a central place where they held festivals, market days, and community meetings. Some communities paved a portion of the green while others decorated the borders with masses of flowers and shrubs, kept purely for decoration.

When Star Creek came into view, I stopped and inhaled, the smell of freshly cut pine sharp and bracing, mingling with wood smoke and moldering leaves. Gloriously, instead of decorations, the community of Star Creek had a flying machine standing in the middle of their green.

WITH RELATIVE EASE, WE GLIDED HIGH ABOVE THE GROUND. The fabric of the flier luffed above me with rhythmic slaps, and the air smelled of ice. I could see to eternity, and yet, though we were near the great Atlantic, I couldn't see a hint of the big water.

How large the world is.

Charcoal's nails dug painfully into my thighs, making pedaling troublesome. Uncomfortable, I shifted, trying to calm the anxious animal as we floated above the world.

"We'll wait until Bowman finishes his computer and installs another seat before you and I fly together again," I muttered to the squirming dog.

We followed Route 153 as it sinuously wound through fall foliage, a breathtaking blanket awash in a riot of colors. The deep green of the needled trees anchored the purples, reds, scarlets, and golds of the rest.

To the north, the White Mountains looked benign and easily crossed. It had taken me more than a week to pass through them, but I judged I could pedal the distance in a half-day with favorable winds.

At the abbey, the masters had counseled us to rise above our subjects and circle them in our minds, examining color, light, and shadow from every angle.

Now, I'd *literally* risen above, and my mind ached to capture the gorgeous sight, to memorize the shape and texture of clouds so close I could almost touch them.

I'd heard the people who had lived *Before* had access to great flying machines, traveling around the globe with a minimum of fuss. How backward our world would appear to them.

Modern travel was arduous and required the goodwill of the people a traveler passed.

Since leaving the abbey, I'd faced storms, hunger, and the interminable insects pestering and plaguing us. While I wasn't ready to give up the road, I could better understand the lure of community, of settling in a single location, and the luxury of weaving relationships with the other members.

Travel could be lonely and difficult, but also exciting and liberating.

And, at times like this, it could be incredibly awkward.

As soon as I spotted the community members waiting to congratulate me on my nascent flight, I knew they would offer me a commission in Star Creek.

Although my intention was to travel until I found my family, the idea of settling here wasn't as terrifying as it ought to be.

If I left, there were no guarantees I'd find what I was looking for. What if I never found my family? Never found out why they'd abandoned me at the abbey? Would I relinquish my quest after a lifetime of searching and find I'd missed my chance at a life?

For the first time since leaving the abbey, I could imagine settling in a community. I'd relish the chance to fly again, to deepen my affinity with Bowman, and to pursue my attraction to Earl. But would I grow to resent them for tempting me from my path?

As far back as I could remember, I'd carried an ache inside me, a deep-seated need to know who I was and where I came from. Without solving my mystery, I'd never feel complete.

I landed with my decision made. My resolve only faltered when I caught sight of Earl watching me with her deep jade eyes.

The walk back to the filling station was unbearably long.

Bowman and I struggled to find a neutral subject after he'd insinuated Earl was interested in me as a *man*. He'd even hinted she'd issue her own offer if I changed my mind and stayed. Furious with him for using her as a commodity, and for putting the thought of nights with Earl in my mind, I'd retrieved my horses in stony silence.

Even now, after riding for several hours, I was conflicted, torn between my desires to turn around and to continue forward. In truth, I'd never known the love of a woman.

Worse, I wasn't sure I'd be much good at loving one. The thought of leaving a woman like Earl unsatisfied in bed made me squirm. My cowardice had contributed to my decision to decline. But would I regret my choice? Did I regret it already?

Rounding a bend in the road, screams of terror and rage pulled me from my fears of the future and rooted me in the present. The hairs on the back of my neck rose, and I froze. Oxide, unnerved, danced sideways. Magnesium snorted, eyes wide and ears pricked.

Charcoal stood statuesque, hackles raised, a low growl rumbling.

Another scream broke my stasis, and I kicked Oxide forward.

There, at the bank of the next curve, two figures struggled.

Drawing nearer, I saw a man had a woman pinned to the trunk of a broad oak. With his free hand, he was pulling at her heavy skirt, one knee already wedged against her leg. She lashed out with her free leg, trying to kick him, her body bucking against his.

My nausea churned; this was an assault. I'd never seen violence before nor imagined a person could treat another thus.

The man struck the woman hard against the side of her face, and she crumpled forward, her struggle over.

Without thinking, I was off my horse and running toward the couple, bellowing. Sharp stones bit into my boots, and my blood pulsed hot and loud in my ears.

The man whirled to face me, releasing the woman, and unsheathing a knife in a single motion.

My brain mired in mud. I was forty meters away and closing fast, but didn't know what I'd do upon reaching them.

I only knew I had to *stop* him.

My breathing ragged, I hoped my face didn't show my anxiety.

The man swore, vaulting onto a nervous-looking white horse. He kicked it savagely, and it sprang forward.

The horse was upon me before I could alter my course. Too late, I tried to spin out of the way, but the rider's knee struck my cheek.

Oh!

I hit the road as the fleeing horse reached Oxide and Magnesium. White pain bloomed in my face, and I tasted copper. Dazed, I watched my horses whirl and spring apart. Magnesium wasn't quick enough, and the galloping horse bowled him over. He whinnied in alarm, tumbling under the white horse's hooves.

My vision grayed, and my mind screamed as my horse rolled off the edge of the road.

CHAPTER SIX

A sound like a groaning door woke me.

I cracked my eyes and squinted at Charcoal's nose, inches from my own. Weakly, I patted the dog and tried to sit up.

The world spun.

I thrust an arm behind me and shut my eyes to counteract the whirl. When it slowed, I opened one eye, peering around.

The woman sobbed at the base of a tree, knees hugged into her chest, her hair covering her face.

Oxide grazed nearby, his reins tangled around a hoof. An impatient whinny shattered my head.

Whining, Charcoal padded to the side of the road and peered over the edge.

I turned too quickly, and the spinning resumed.

Squeezing my eyes shut, I shifted onto my hands and knees. Moving as though I might shatter, I raised one knee and rested before standing. My mouth watered as nausea gripped me. I gasped for air, bending forward, resting my hands on my thighs.

Charcoal pressed against my calf, his whine anxious.

"Are you okay?" I croaked, trying not to vomit from the strain.

The woman sobbed.

Had she heard me?

My head throbbed in time to my heartbeat. I held my breath and tried standing again. This time, my stomach lurched less, and my head cleared a little.

"Miss?"

The woman pulled her legs tighter against her chest and continued to sob.

Woozy, I turned my attention to Oxide.

Normally, I'd pick up his front foot to free his leg from the leather reins, but unsure I could lean forward, I unbuckled the bridle, letting it slide down his face. Freed, Oxide snorted and wandered several steps to graze.

I pointed at the discarded bridle. "Give."

Charcoal obediently picked it up and handed it to me before returning to the edge of the road.

Unsteady, I joined the dog. Magnesium was standing in a narrow gully about five meters below. A small creek trickled through the gully, winding around rocky outcroppings.

The horse nickered.

Waves of fatigue broke over me. I didn't have the energy or balance to scramble down the slope to help him out of the gully.

"Charcoal, go get him."

The dog launched from the road and slid down the steep incline. Reaching the bottom, he circled the horse as Magnesium stamped his foot in warning. Charcoal moved behind him and snapped his teeth, then feinted left and snapped again. Magnesium pinned his ears and kicked. With an urgent yip, Charcoal ducked and rushed forward to snap at the horse again.

"Enough. Leave it," I called. If the horse could escape, Charcoal would've had him moving.

The dog scrambled to me and hung his head in failure.

"You did fine. He can't climb the slope." I ruffled his head and surveyed the area, unsure what to do next. My stomach lurched, and I swallowed hard. Even if I could abandon my packhorse, I was too dizzy to ride. With some relief, I noticed it would soon be dark.

"We camp here tonight," I announced with as much authority as I could muster.

No one answered me.

The steel gray skies had lowered and hung heavy.

If I didn't construct a shelter, we'd likely wake in a downpour. Moving as quickly as I dared, I slid my saddle from Oxide, letting it lie where it fell. I tied hobbles around his front legs to keep him from wandering away and rested for several minutes. Rising, I wobbled like a sick drunkard, panting, my head throbbing.

When the nausea passed, I tossed a line over a branch and anchored it to a root stub on the uphill side of the road. Unfurling a canvas tarpaulin, I tried to toss it over the taut line. It took me four attempts—and even longer to tie two corners of the tarpaulin to the stakes I pounded into the packed earth. To save time and effort, I tied the last two corners to small trees. When finished, I had a shelter of sorts, one side sloping steeply toward the road.

I dug through my gear, looking for the sack of food Bowman had given me. It wasn't here. My head hurt, but I kept pulling everything out of my saddlebags. Frustrated, I tossed my water canteen on the ground.

Water.

Blast. The food was in the panniers. And the panniers were on Magnesium, who was stuck in the gully.

I wanted to sit and cry, too.

If the woman hadn't been present, I might have and skipped supper entirely, but what would she think of me if I crawled under the shelter and went to sleep?

Sighing, I snapped my fingers at Charcoal. "Let's go."

I slid and scrambled down the slope, heart thumping. When I reached the bottom, Magnesium rubbed his forehead vigorously on my chest as I unclipped his cotton lead. Moving to his side, I lost my balance and fell into the stream. I sat for a miserable moment, the cold water rushing over my legs. I looked at the horse and up toward the road's edge. From here, the slope looked even steeper.

"You're spending the night here."

Lunging out of the water, I caught the edge of a pannier to steady myself. My hands clumsy, I unbuckled each one, setting them on the side of the bank. I unlashed the cinch and pulled the packsaddle from Magnesium. He shook vigorously and sauntered along the bottom of the gully, investigating the browse.

"Charcoal, I need you." I fashioned a harness for the dog with Magnesium's cotton lead and tied one pannier to it. Dragging the other pannier, I staggered toward the hill, grasping for bits of brush to help me climb. Thorny shrubs tore at my hands as I crawled up the slope.

Charcoal stood at the bottom, watching me.

"Come on, you've got to pull it."

Gasping, I reached the top of the slope and half-carried, half-dragged the pannier underneath the tarpaulin shelter. Charcoal scrambled over the edge of the ledge and lay down, panting. I untied the dog and dragged the second pannier near the first.

Exhausted, I peered into the sack Bowman had given me—more of Maisie's biscuits and a dozen uncooked sausages wrapped in linen. I pulled out three, re-wrapping the rest.

"We need firewood."

Charcoal sat without moving.

"Give stick!"

Charcoal left to investigate the brush at the side of the road while I pulled a frying pan from a pannier and found a steel bowl and long wooden spoon.

The dog returned with a stick and dropped it at my feet, his tail stub wagging.

"Sorry, chap, we're not playing. Give stick!"

The dog fetched another stick. He would play this game all day—

and it was a good thing because now he'd assumed a responsibility I couldn't handle.

I continued to set up camp, asking for a new stick each time the dog returned. By the time I was ready to start the fire, Charcoal had provided an impressive pile of firewood.

Thankfully, the fire caught quickly.

After building it up, I approached the woman. She was no longer sobbing but sat with her arms wrapped around her knees, head down and obscured by long, dark hair.

"Heya, Lady, come sit by the fire." When she didn't answer or move, I tugged on her elbow.

She snatched her arm back, trembling.

I sighed and returned to the shelter. "Go get her," I instructed the dog.

Charcoal walked to the edge of the road where the horse waited.

"Charcoal, no. Go get *her*," I said, pointing at the woman.

The dog cocked his head to the side but trotted toward the woman.

I pushed the blazing sticks out of my way and set the pan on the glowing coals. When the pan had heated, I added the sausages and water from my flask. Waiting for the sausage to cook, I chopped an onion and a carrot, glancing up to gauge Charcoal's progress.

He had nudged his muzzle under her arms, burying his head under the woman's hair. As I watched, his tail stub wiggled. He was winning their battle of wills.

Adding the vegetables to the pan, I stirred, breaking the sausage into chunks. The woman stroked Charcoal's face, and they seemed to have an earnest discussion.

When I judged the food ready, I whistled, and the dog whirled, bounding toward me. I gave him a stern look, and he melted back into the night, reappearing with the woman in tow. Feeling strangely proud of myself for making camp and preparing a supper, I smiled in welcome.

"Welcome, Traveler," I said, handing a bowl of stew to the woman.

"Thank you, Keeper," she murmured. Instead of taking a seat across the fire as I expected, she skirted it and sat to my left.

Charcoal followed her and sat to her left.

Traitor.

"For him," I said with a jerk of my chin.

The woman took the saucer I held out and set it in front of Charcoal.

He looked at the plate and back at me, as though judging the meal.

I filled my bowl and took a tiny bite, willing my stomach to remain calm. The stew had little flavor, and the larger chunks of carrots were hard and uncooked. The broth was thin and smelled of onion but tasted of scorched fat.

Not the worst thing I'd cooked.

"Blast." Setting my bowl down, I rose and retrieved the sack. Ignoring the reignited pounding in my head, I handed it to her. "We have biscuits."

She chose one for herself and put one on Charcoal's saucer before handing it back.

Head reeling, I sat again. "If the meal is poor, blame the chef. I have it on good authority the sausages are the best in New England."

The woman ate mechanically, saying nothing.

"You cannot judge me on the biscuits either. Maisie baked them, and though I don't know Maisie, based on her biscuits, I imagine her as a great warm woman in possession of... powerful hands."

I stole a glance at the woman, who stared at the fire as she ate. Who was she? The silence was making me twitchy, so I tried again, unable to stem my flurry of words.

"Maisie, as a proper baking master, has a terrible side, too. When no one is looking, she beats her apprentice for not cutting kindling sticks to an exact length. She may also frighten the children who collect the eggs, saying that one cracked shell—just one, mind you— could mean no cake for Christmas."

"She will hoard the vanilla and spices collected from depots," the woman murmured.

Relief flooded through me; she was talking. "And keep all the baked beauties on the shelves while passing out the uglies to her least favorite folk."

"She will put salt instead of sugar into a child's birthday cookie, and—"

"Bake the smallest puppy into a pie," we said in unison, bursting into laughter.

"Well met, Lady. I'm Matthew." I was making a fool of myself, but at least she was talking.

"Josephine. Well met, Matthew."

We ate, occasionally tossing a quick smile at the other. When we'd finished, I collected the bowls and stood with a groan. My back was stiff, and my head ached. I rinsed the dishes and put them in a mesh bag to hang.

"There is a small creek in yonder gully. I'll give these things a proper wash in the morning."

The thought of the horse stuck in the gully gave me a twinge of guilt. I walked to the edge of the road and called down into the dark, "I'm sorry, chap. I promise I'll figure out a way to release you in the morning."

A faint nicker answered.

"Who's down there?" whispered Josephine.

"A horse who had the misfortune of meeting a white mare today."

"Seraph."

"Pardon?"

"The mare. Her name was Seraph."

"She was yours?"

Josephine nodded. "All my things were in her bags."

We walked back to the shelter, and I waited for her to continue.

"We were traveling when she began limping, each step a hop. I got off and tied her rein to a branch." She stopped and stared into the darkness. "I don't know where he came from. He said 'Heya' as though well met, and I assumed he was coming to help."

I poked the fire and added branches. Did I want to hear this?

"I knew in mere moments. There was something... strange about him. His smile never reached his eyes." Her voice trailed off, and she shuddered. "Then you arrived."

I had no words and remained quiet.

She looked around the makeshift shelter. "Now, I have nothing."

"Tonight, you'll sleep in my bedroll." I held my hands up and continued before she could protest. "I'll sleep here on this side of the fire. In the morning's light, we'll figure out what's next."

Josephine chewed her bottom lip and nodded. Saying nothing further, she walked to the bedroll and kneeled, patting it straight.

Relieved, I walked out of the tent to check on Oxide and give Josephine a few moments of privacy. I wanted to make amends to her. Why? Because I was a man and therefore culpable? Because she needed help?

Because I was a fool trying to act the gallant?

Strangely, I was also pleased. I'd stopped an assault, erected a shelter, and helped a stranger—all on my own.

When I returned, Josephine was in my bedroll. I added more sticks to the fire and lay on my side, head propped on my right arm.

Charcoal slid to the ground behind me, leaning heavily against my back.

What a day. What would tomorrow bring?

CHAPTER SEVEN

A light breath teased the hairs around my neck, and a gentle tugging on my earlobe brought me back from slumber. Had Earl joined me in the night?

Another gentle tug, this time on the upturned collar of my coat. I opened my eyes.

Instead of the pale beauty of Earl, I found thick, rubbery gray lips covered in whiskers. I pushed Oxide's head away in annoyance and sat up. The horse took a step backward and bobbed his head in greeting. The dog grumbled when I moved, glaring at us both.

I peered across the shelter, but the predawn light didn't illuminate the shadowed corner where Josephine lay.

Oxide had made his way beneath the shelter and stood near where Charcoal and I were.

"Thanks for not trampling us," I whispered.

Oxide looked at me kindly and swished his tail.

I stood, scratching under his chin. Oxide closed his eyes and wiggled his lips, and I stifled a chuckle. I patted him and walked to the edge of the road, my body aching.

Magnesium lay at the bottom, legs curled tightly beneath him.

44

After last night's rain, he shivered and looked miserable. I squatted on my heels and pushed away the aches and pains from yesterday as I considered my options.

The slope leading from the road's edge to where Magnesium lay was steep. Farther down the road, the slope was less steep but strewn with boulders. I could climb the boulders, but the horse couldn't follow.

I walked in the other direction. Here, the edge of the road retreated into a thicket of impenetrable brush. Returning, I stared at Magnesium, considering the situation.

He gazed back at me.

Before leaving the abbey, I'd walked into the community of Phippsburg to find traveling supplies. I'd envisioned traveling in relative comfort, out of the weather, in a fine carriage. Of the carriage, I'd no concerns; my skills were enough to turn a humble wagon into a vehicle befitting an artist. But I soon learned a carriage was out of the question because, to my astonishment, no one wanted to travel with me.

During my years at the abbey, I'd never needed to look after myself. The food they provided was delicious and plentiful. They kept my room immaculate and my clothing promptly laundered. The staff even addressed Charcoal's needs. How could I harness a team, drive a carriage, make camp each night, and cook for myself?

I settled for traveling by horseback and chose Oxide, assuming a single horse could carry me and my equipment. Laden with art supplies and an excessive amount of food, Oxide and I staggered out of Popham Abbey. Within a week, I'd tired of walking and was actively searching for a pack animal. Trading an hour's worth of art for Magnesium had allowed me to ride Oxide, increasing our speed and comfort.

The simplest solution now would be to leave the poor creature behind and find another packhorse.

As if he could read my thoughts, Magnesium twitched his ears nervously.

My heart lurched.

I couldn't leave him. Over the months, I'd developed a bond with the silly animal. My horses were partners, not equipment.

Not wanting to disturb Josephine, I retrieved my art supplies as quietly as I could and slowly picked my way down the tumbled field of boulders toward the bottom of the gully.

Charcoal followed, jumping from one to the next.

Near the bottom, I hesitated.

The last drop was two meters onto ground strewn with rounded cobbles. Yesterday's events were punishment enough; I was not eager to give my head another crack.

I kicked at the boulder's edge, dislodging a pebble. It skipped and skittered down the rocky face, landing in the water with a *plop*. I sighed and looked at the horse.

Magnesium waited, tail swishing.

I tossed my leather parcel in a gentle lob toward the steep hillside, halfway between myself and the horse. It landed on the soft dirt and slid toward the bottom of the gully.

Magnesium leaned forward to investigate.

"Leave it alone."

I turned and found purchase for my fingers on the coarse rock. Backing over the edge, I wriggled until my trousers snagged. I struggled until the fabric tore.

I'd be doing some mending later.

Freed, I lowered myself, but while hanging from my fingertips, my right toe slipped from its foothold, and I dropped. My left ankle twisted, and I fell to one knee, biting my tongue.

"Blast!"

Wincing, I pulled up my trouser leg to inspect the knee. Blood oozed from a shallow cut where the skin on the bottom of my kneecap had split.

I stood to test it, and my ankle protested more than the knee. The taste of blood reminded me of yesterday's pain, and I spat.

The dog huffed at me, but I shook my head. "No, stay up there. Make sure Oxide doesn't wander away."

Charcoal sat in protest, issuing a mild whine.

Ignoring him, I turned and nearly ran into the horse. "Hey, boy. How did you get so sneaky?"

The horse bobbed his head and waited. He smelled like rain and wet earth and moss.

Absently, I rubbed behind his ears and examined the hill. From here, I could tell the slope was man-made—likely created from dumping soil over the ledge during construction. Giving him a last pat, I stepped around the horse and retrieved my parcel. Choosing the midpoint of the slope, I slowly moved backward, trying to view the hillside in its entirety. My left foot sank into the creek, and I yelped as cold water rushed into my boot.

Wonderful.

Feet squelching, I continued to back until I could see the whole slope without turning my head. Pulling out my sketchbook, I set to work.

After sketching the hillside, I took a moment to stretch my neck. I closed my eyes, visualizing the changes I wanted to make. Technically, I didn't need to close my eyes, but the ritual helped cement my vision. I sketched from my mental picture, adjusting and shading the drawing, guided by the familiar tingle in my fingers.

Finished, I looked up and grinned.

Where the slope had been featureless and steep, now a narrow trail snaked up from the bottom of the gully up to the road. I'd drawn in a few small trees and rocks at the switch-backed corners to anchor the image and provide perspective.

Magnesium was halfway up the trail, and Josephine stood at the top. The horse reached the road and waited for her to move. When she did, he bobbed his head and continued off the path and out of sight. Oxide knickered a greeting.

Josephine was stowing the bedroll in the drawstring canvas sack by the time I'd gathered my things and trudged up the narrow trail.

Silent, she turned from me and walked down the trail with the dirty dishes.

What had I done?

Perhaps I'd woken her when I stepped in the creek and yelled. I looked at Charcoal and shrugged. "Sorry, boy," I said, though I had no clue what I was apologizing for.

He searched my face before padding after her.

My stomach rumbled as I surveyed the camp. Though I was in a hurry to leave, I didn't want Josephine to feel rushed—especially as the warmth and camaraderie we'd shared last night had evaporated.

Rekindling the fire, I rubbed my hands.

Once warmed, I untied the ropes and was folding the tarpaulin when she spoke.

"You're an artist." Her tone was half-statement, half-accusation.

Clenching my teeth, I turned. "Have I offended you?"

She stared at the ground, water from the dishes dripping down the side of her skirt. A moment later, she squared her shoulders and looked directly at me.

Seeing her full face for the first time, I gasped.

And then the world died.

Josephine had an oval-shaped face with high cheekbones and wide-set eyes. Her hair, loose, was a medium golden-brown with a slight wave. Dark eyes and well-balanced eyebrows enhanced her olive skin tone.

During our portraiture lessons at the abbey, the masters held a mirror to the middle of a subject's face, showing the slight deviations between the left and right sides. The closer a face was to perfect symmetry, the more beautiful it was.

If a mirror double-cast the right side of Josephine's face, the image would be breathtaking. If the mirror double-cast the left side, Josephine would appear monstrous.

Half a dozen scars radiated from the corner of her mouth, toward her ear and jawline. Puckered and crimson, they twisted and wheeled across her cheek. Her left eyelid drooped, and a scar pulled at the skin from the crease of the lid past the corner of her eye. Fainter scars of brown ochre patterned down the side of her nose and followed the curve of the sag under her eye. A deep, sickle-shaped scar adorned her left cheekbone.

She shivered under my scrutiny.

Heat crept up my neck; her face was both horrifying and intriguing. Selfishly, shamefully, I wanted to sketch her.

I dragged my eyes from her ruined face with great effort.

She met my gaze and waited.

CHAPTER EIGHT

I opened my mouth—and right away, closed it again.

Josephine flinched.

Clearing my throat, I took the coward's path. "I *am* an artist, and I'm hungry. If you'll pass those over, I'll start on breakfast," I said, gestured at the dripping pans.

"I'll cook," she said, brushing past me and putting sausages in the pan. Sparks took flight as she slammed the pan onto the rekindled fire.

The tension between us was thick and visceral.

Pretending her deformity hadn't shocked and excited me was gutless, but I didn't know how to handle the situation. At my best, I strove for charming awkwardness.

This was not my best.

Mustering jollity I didn't feel, I said, "Wonderful. While we eat, let's discuss what to do next."

By the time the meal was ready, I'd repaired my trousers and finished packing our camp.

Without a word, Josephine handed me a bowl of sliced sausage and a cold biscuit. The sausage had a hard crust on one side and was within a hair of being raw, despite the foul, scorched odor. The stale biscuit was no better and crumbled when I tried to split it.

I couldn't choke down the food, my stomach knotting at the greasy, burned flavors. "Well," I said, putting the bowl on the ground, "you're no better a cook than I."

Josephine stiffened and set her own bowl down. Instead of straightening, she slumped forward, shoulders heaving.

Her howls made my skin crawl. Why didn't I keep my mouth shut?

She raised her face, tears streaming from her eyes, laughing as she gulped for air.

The absurdity of the situation hit me, and I chuckled.

Charcoal investigated our discarded bowls and backed away, uninterested.

The dog's refusal of the ruined food finished us.

Bellowing, we laughed until we couldn't breathe. We exchanged smiles while gasping for air.

"I'm a scholar, not a cook," Josephine said, following me to the creek. "I was on my way to Rochester Depot to search for records when he attacked yesterday." She stopped. "Only yesterday. How strange."

I scoured the greasy pan with a handful of pebbles. "Rochester Depot? How far is it?"

"With good roads and a reliable horse... two weeks? Not that I'm likely to travel at speed without a horse."

"Why are you traveling alone?"

Josephine shrugged. "I started out with two others heading in the same direction. More soon joined us, and I..." She paused and shook the bowls she had rinsed. "I'm not comfortable in a crowd."

Given my reaction to her face, I could imagine why. "I often choose the less-traveled roads myself. How did you find this one?"

"By accident."

"Did you stop at the filling station?"

She shook her head.

Climbing the trail behind Josephine, I studied her gait. "Have you hurt your leg?"

She nodded. "I didn't think it bad when I wrapped it last night, but now the binding is too tight."

She was limping badly by the time we reached the top and sank to the ground at the edge of the road. I hissed when she lifted her skirt.

The skin bulged between the bindings, purple and blue. Her calf was pale and cold. She winced when I touched her, but let me unwrap the knee. Color quickly returned to her lower leg, but the knee remained hot and swollen.

I sat back, helpless. "What should we do?"

"Perhaps a poultice?"

I shrugged. "I know nothing of healing."

Josephine looked up, surprised. "You didn't apprentice?"

"Apprentice?"

"Children start trial apprenticeships on our tenth year. At fifteen, we chose our future occupation and enter a formal apprenticeship with a master."

I shook my head. "No, they sent me to the abbey when I was three."

"Three? You didn't choose art?"

"I don't think you *choose* to be an artist. Most of the lads are between three and six when they arrive. The oldest I ever saw brought to Popham was seven, but he'd transferred from a different abbey."

"All boys?"

"Yes, they only train boys to be artists."

"How do they know a child has artistic potential?"

"There's an aptitude test. But even if you're admitted, you can fail out if your skill doesn't develop." I finished wrapping Josephine's knee, looser than it had been, but snug enough, I hoped, to provide support.

There was no way she could walk until the knee healed.

Thus far, I'd been careful to remain apart from the people I'd encountered during my travels, but here, I had two choices. One, leave her to heal and continue when she was able. My supplies were adequate; I could leave her a few things to keep her warm, dry, and fed until she could walk.

Two, I could invite her to travel with me or take her to the nearest community. Star Creek didn't have a scholar in residence; surely, they'd jump at the chance to host Josephine while she recuperated. Either choice would slow me down.

About to suggest the first option, the memory of her sobbing last night struck me. "You're not walking, and must ride."

"I have no horse," she protested.

"You'll ride mine until we can find one for you."

"But where were you going?"

"I was..." I stopped.

Good question.

Since Hamilton, I had the vague intention of traveling to visit my friend Liang Zhen.

Impulsively, I said, "The nearest depot for art supplies, so Rochester sounds ideal." There was a finality to my choice. There'd be no chance of speaking with the sailors if I skipped the great lake, but it felt right.

She nodded, satisfied with my answer.

"Tell me about your people while I saddle the horses."

Josephine picked at the cotton lead I'd left tangled in the gorse. "I was born in a mid-sized community near Lake Champlain. My parents are craftsmen—my mother a silversmith and my father a leathersmith. I grew up with brothers who studied healing and engineering. Neither stayed in the community; we weren't close. I apprenticed with a scholar in Warwick."

"Have you visited your parents?" I asked, tightening the girth on Magnesium's packsaddle. I couldn't imagine knowing your family and not wanting to be near them.

"Yes, twice. They replaced us quickly with fosterlings. I didn't feel missed." She'd nearly freed the cotton lead from the prickly shrub.

I evaluated my saddle. "How tall are you?"

"A meter and three quarters. Almost."

"I'm a shade over two meters myself."

As I adjusted the leathers, I could feel Josephine's eyes on me. After spending years practicing self-portraiture, I knew what she saw.

I am a beautiful man, barely twenty, with piercing gray-brown eyes, and long hair tied midway on my head, so the ends curled and brushed my collar. After months on the road, I'd grown a beard I kept close-cut. I could appear watchful and closed, often mistaken for being stern. But I ruined the effect when I smiled; my smile stretched my face, my eyes crinkling into half-moons.

Oxide rubbed his forehead vigorously on me, covering the front of my coat, trousers, and tunic with white hairs.

Josephine laughed.

"Blast," I said, trying to brush them off. Shrugging, I heaved the heavy saddle onto Oxide's back.

The horse grunted and gave me a displeased look.

Josephine hopped to Oxide and bent her good knee.

"Leg up?"

I gave her a quick boost and helped settle her in the saddle. She seemed comfortable enough, though I'd never understood how women rode in heavy skirts.

Josephine murmured to Oxide while I finished saddling Magnesium.

The leather was stiff as I pulled the buckles tight. "Which way should we go? Star Creek is north, and I have friends there."

Josephine shook her head, her dark eyes pleading. "I don't think I can face a crowd. Not now."

"Are you sure? There's a healer in Star Creek."

"I'm... I'm sure. We'll run into another community if we continue south. I don't think—"she shuddered—"that's the direction *he* went."

My knee was sore, and I wanted an excuse to return to Star

Creek. But, I didn't blame her for needing to avoid the northern route. "We go south." I clipped the cotton lead onto Magnesium and tugged. In less than a meter, he balked, stumbling.

I checked him first, then bent and brushed the leaves from the ground. Hidden underneath them were smooth, round rocks, roughly a quarter the size of my palm. While unremarkable on a trail, these were sitting atop the pavement. "Blast. What a scoundrel. He brought stones to hobble horses."

Or people.

Charcoal investigated the rolling rocks as I swept a clear path with my foot.

Once we were clear of the stones, Josephine brought Oxide alongside so we could chat as we walked. Though I typically stumbled in speech, awkward with new acquaintances, it was a pleasure to converse with Josephine.

Charcoal wandered ahead, investigating the roadside brush and flushing grouse. After what had happened to Josephine, I was more grateful than ever for my chap; no one could spring out of the scrub to surprise us with the dog around.

We stopped for a hasty lunch, eating the last of the stale biscuits, two small apples I had in my bags, and the rest of my dried meat. While we ate, I consulted my map, trying to ignore my aching feet.

"If we head east at the next junction, we could be in the community of Porter by late afternoon," I said, tracing the route with my finger.

"What else?"

"There's another filling station five or six hours south, but it'll be dark by the time we arrive."

Josephine chewed her lower lip. "We'll be closer to Rochester Depot if we keep traveling south. The weather has been fine but..."

If I'd been on my own, I would have gone to Porter, but I tried not to let my disappointment show as I stowed the map. "True. Snow is coming, and I'd like to be as far south as possible before it hits. South it is."

CHAPTER NINE

As I'd feared, we arrived at the filling station well past dark. I was footsore after the long walk and wanted nothing more than to fall onto any horizontal surface, but Josephine's reticence with strangers exceeded my own, so I negotiated for both of us.

The keeper agreed to feed and house us in exchange for an update to the station's map and a scholar-scripted letter. Starving, we devoured the provided meal, declaring it the best thing we had ever tasted. In the morning, neither of us could remember what the keeper had served for dinner.

Delighted to be hosting an artist and a scholar, the keeper threw together a breakfast celebration for us, *gratis*.

Sunlight streamed through the dusty windows when we entered the common room in the morning. A chafing dish discharged curls of steam above a mountain of scrambled eggs, sausages, and bacon. My stomach rumbled at the scents of nutty-sweet chicory coffee and maple sugar.

The room was full of chattering people holding steaming mugs. Upon our entry, they turned expectant, smiling faces toward us.

Josephine ducked behind me, but not wanting to face the crowd alone, I escorted her forward. Almost immediately, I regretted my action. She endured the gasps and whispers with a stony face as guilt gnawed at me.

Penitent, I transformed into a jovial guest to draw focus from her.

The locals asked the expected questions. How long were we staying, were we looking for further accommodation, and had we picked a community to overwinter with?

Between mouthfuls, I answered as best I could, speaking for both of us.

They pressed us for news, and my report of the ride I'd taken in Bowman's flier thrilled them. Even Josephine listened with rapt attention.

Why I hadn't brought it up yesterday?

We made our way back to the keeper to clarify what services he wanted in exchange for our stay. From Josephine, he wanted a handwritten letter for a woman he was long-distance courting. Though most people could read and write, a letter written in a scholar's fine penmanship was special. He pointed me toward his map and agreed to trade an additional improvement to his cowshed for spare bedding.

Josephine touched my arm, which I hoped meant she'd forgiven me. "May I borrow a pencil to script the letter?"

"Of course. I'll have the map updated and the cowshed improved within the hour. Do you need longer?"

She shook her head. "Could you ask about a horse, too?"

My feet still hurt from yesterday. "Great idea. I'll paint an improvement if it's easier to trade."

Josephine's smile twisted. "Few would choose scripting over art from a master."

"A master? No, I'm—" But she was right. I *was* a master now. "How odd. I suppose I need to alter my schoolboy view of a master being an abbey instructor."

"Are you traveling to your new community after Rochester Depot?"

"No, I'm... I haven't chosen a community."

She stopped and looked at me. "You haven't accepted a position in *any* community?"

"No."

"Why not?"

Why did I bring it up?

Sweat broke out on my upper lip, and my stomach knotted. This was a conversation to avoid. Inevitably, it led to the other person declaring me selfish and irresponsible.

"Long story. Talk when we're on the road?"

She nodded, a thoughtful look crossing her face.

While I worked on the map, I asked if anyone knew of an available saddle horse. People suggested routes where we might find one, but I'd be walking at least another day.

My chest loosened after we left the station and I shed the false persona. Josephine's smile appeared more natural, too.

We soon found the news of a traveling artist had proceeded us. Farming folk waited alongside the roads, hoping to offer us accommodations. We spoke with each, exchanging the customary greetings and inquiring about a horse.

Expressing regret, each group watched us leave. The day was warm, the air thick with dust and damp. Sticky and tired, the many fruitless conversations did nothing to lift my mood.

Around noon, we reached an overview I'd noticed on the station's map. Josephine waited while I investigated. The footpath wound a half-dozen meters through thick brush and ended at a rocky outcropping. My heart light, I retraced my steps and secured the horses before escorting Josephine to the ledge.

The view was magnificent.

Josephine gasped, releasing my arm, and limping toward the drop-off. The ledge sat on the eastern side of a deep valley overlooking a forest resplendent with golds, purples, scarlets, and crimsons. Towering evergreens anchored the arboreal finery. At the far end, a thin fog crept along the valley floor.

After I helped her sit, she rubbed her sore knee as I dug through the saddlebags for our lunch. The rock was warm and smooth, and I groaned with pleasure as I collapsed.

Munching on bacon sandwiches, we enjoyed the view and tossed morsels of bacon and thick brown bread to Charcoal.

"Josephine, as a scholar, you studied history, right?"

"Mmm. A scholar's primary purpose is to understand the human experience. We study human history to understand what happened *Before* to prevent such a catastrophe from happening again. Did you have history lessons at the abbey? Did they discuss why the world died?"

Nodding, I recited, "Politics, Money, Power, Religion, and Greed. These are the things we never again need. Aren't all children taught this?"

Josephine laughed. "It was more complicated, but yes, that's the general belief. We scholars study to help us understand the impact of politics, the economy, and religion on the people from *Before*."

"The masters didn't go deep into why the world died; they used it as a fulcrum to describe the functions of art *Before*, versus now."

"You're squirming. Is there something specific you're curious about? Go ahead, ask."

I'd always wanted to ask more about the topic. "How did the world die? Sorry for the simple question."

Josephine looked thoughtful as she finished her sandwich. "It's the question we're asked most, so don't feel bad. I'm happy to explain the prevailing theory."

"Theory?"

Josephine sighed. "Yes, based on the documents from that time. Many factors were involved, but at a high level, people stopped exercising empathy."

"What factors?"

"Weak political systems, a rise in nationalism, religious intolerance, social injustices, and economic inequalities. Add in global pandemics and a lack of leadership. These led to a global financial collapse, and the world's most powerful nations devolved, followed by civil wars and revolutions. When the dust cleared, billions had died."

"From wars?"

"Yes, some, but also from despair, famine, illness, and unrest-sparked violence."

Shivering, I tossed the rest of my sandwich to Charcoal. Josephine's explanation was both difficult to wrap my mind around and easy to imagine. "I'm a little sorry I asked."

"Tell me about the flight you took instead. Was it terrifying?"

My hand rasped against my trousers, the repair I'd made barely visible. "I suppose I was more concerned I'd drop the dog or damage the flier than myself. The flying machine was a great, delicate thing."

I leaned back on my hands, rubbing the heel of one boot on the toe of the other. The boots were too snug, and my feet throbbed with my heartbeat. "Bowman made its frame of metal tubing. He covered the wings with a gossamer-like cloth, nearly transparent, stretching fifteen meters to each side. There was a small canard out front—"

Her eyebrow lifted. "Canard? Like a duck?"

"Yes; from the ground, it resembles a duck's head sticking out in front of its body during flight. Bowman told me it's for pitch and roll. Pitch is when the nose moves down or up, and roll is when the wings are level or tilted to one side."

She frowned. "Did the wings flap?"

"No, they were fixed. A large spinning blade propelled the flier. Bowman built it so you sit reclined, like in a granny's armchair, with pedals in front of you."

Josephine dusted off her palms. "Was it fast?"

"Perhaps, if you pedal quickly. Or if you have the wind at your back. I wasn't flying fast."

Charcoal gave me a side-eye look.

"We weren't flying fast."

Josephine tickled under his chin. "What was it like?"

"Imagine a bicycle on this ledge. Have you ridden a bicycle?"

"We had a yearly race between my community and the next when I was an apprentice. I never won, but I was never at the back either."

I clambered to my feet. "Here, let me help you up. Close your eyes, and I'll walk you forward. With your mind, pedal toward the edge. At the edge, your bicycle will dip forward, so pull back on the handlebars. Can you imagine it?"

Josephine, eyes closed, nodded as she took a faltering step.

I moved behind her and steadied her around her waist. "Open your eyes. As you pedal, look around. If you lean too far to either side, the wing will dip and you'll turn, so ride as straight as you can."

She laughed, stretching her arms out to the side like wings.

"You'll feel the chill of the air as you pedal. The cloth above your head flaps with uneven slaps. As you pedal, the flier drops and rises, floating on invisible air currents." I tightened my grip. "Now dip your left wing."

She did, laughing again.

"To land," I murmured, "turn back to the field from where you took off and stop pedaling."

The hairs on my arms stood as the energy between us changed. A sheen of sweat broke out on my forehead, and I swallowed.

She wants something from me.

Josephine turned and faced me.

She stood too close to the edge, so I kept my hands on her waist, though I wanted to step away from her. She looked into my eyes, but uneasy with the intimacy, I examined the valley beyond her.

Did she want me to kiss her? I hoped not. We barely knew each other. Worse, a man had assaulted her two days ago. Heat crept through my stomach.

Charcoal flushed a grouse behind us and broke the moment. I took a cautious step backward, still gripping her waist. Grateful for the interruption, I cleared my throat and released her.

Josephine smiled at me. "How marvelous."

Relieved to talk about anything other than what had just happened, I beamed. "It was. I should have liked to take it out for more sessions. Perhaps I can stay longer if I visit again. We should go."

Helping Josephine mount, I pondered how a lack of empathy had destroyed a civilization. Maybe I should practice patience with the horseless farm families we encountered.

WHILE WE WALKED, I REHEARSED ASKING WHAT HAD HAPPENED to Josephine's face.

"Josephine—"

"Matthew—"

We laughed, our words colliding in mid-air.

"You first," I said.

"You said you'd tell me why you're traveling," she reminded me.

Relieved she hadn't asked what had happened at the ledge, I grinned. "Of course. I wanted to ask about—" I stopped walking and watched Josephine ride up the road. My stomach gurgled, and Charcoal glanced at me.

"You want to know about my scars," she called over her shoulder.

How could I explain my professional curiosity? I twitched Magnesium's lead and hurried to catch up.

The clonk-clunk of his hooves on the road slowed as we caught up with her, and she sighed. "Since we're both reluctant to share, I suppose I'll go first... to repay your kindness. I was seven when I had the accident. My family was moving, and we'd stopped at a community for supplies. My parents left me to mind my younger brother while they negotiated with the administrator."

She stopped speaking, and I waited for her to continue, a lump in my throat. Yesterday, she'd only spoken of older brothers.

"My brother was so little, he shouldn't have been able to unseat the wagon brake, so I thought nothing of it when he climbed up front. He loved to play at driving." She bent her head.

"You were a child." Stealing quick glances, I studied her scars and considered how I'd paint them—an intoxicating challenge.

"I was the elder. The wagon picked up speed so fast; the horses must have been in a panic. We were rocking and bouncing, and I couldn't reach my brother. I yelled at him to jump, but he was crying. We were going so fast."

I waited, the lump in my throat painful.

"I knew I had to go first, so I closed my eyes and counted to three and jumped. A stub of a branch caught me, and I remember the sound of my flesh tearing. I screamed and screamed. My brother heard me shrieking and didn't jump."

She wiped her eyes, and my heart ached.

"I think my screams scared him too much. The horses didn't follow the next bend and ran straight over the edge. They took the wagon and my brother with them."

"I'm sorry." My words were inadequate, and my chest tight. Was it only sorrow for Josephine or guilt for my desire to paint her portrait?

"My mother shattered; she couldn't bear to leave him. By the time my father convinced her I needed an accomplished healer, my scars had set."

I wanted to ask more about her family, and if the accident caused the rift she'd mentioned yesterday, but another group of people waited ahead.

She wiped her eyes. "We'll talk later."

I sighed. "I'd like that."

Raising my hand, I greeted the group. Neither they nor the subsequent families we encountered had a horse to trade, but conversing with each prevented us from rekindling our conversation.

For once, I appreciated the interruptions.

Josephine's tale had drained me, leaving little energy with which to share my story. My mind puzzled over what I'd learned; I'd never considered family estrangement.

Had they sent me away because of a tragedy?

Bands tightened around my chest. Focused on my desire to learn truths about myself and my family, I hadn't considered the implications. For the first time, I wondered if learning my truths would heal or harm me.

CHAPTER TEN

The sun was skimming the tops of the trees when we sighted two men standing on the roadside. If we couldn't find a horse for Josephine, we might not make it to the depot before the snows arrived. The weather would force us to overwinter wherever we were.

We needed a horse.

I didn't want to spend dreary winter months in a tedious community when I could explore the ruined remnants of a city and converse with other travelers in a depot.

"Blast," I growled. Tired of walking, my feet hurt.

Josephine shot me a sympathetic look. "Maybe the twentieth try is the successful one."

"Twenty?"

"Though I stopped counting after twelve," she admitted, "and made up the number. We should find somewhere to stop."

"I know. I think the keeper at the filling station sent us on a turkey chase to gain favor with his neighbors."

"Yes." Her voice low, she asked, "Do we want to stop if they offer?"

"Probably." Stopping for hospitality was the rational thing to do while I had enough daylight left to paint.

The older man stepped forward and raised his hand. "I'm Dean Forshee, and you are the Artist Sugiyama and Scribe Josephine." He paused, beaming.

Forshee was pudgy, with a shock of gray hair springing up and outward as if trying to escape his head. Great, bushy eyebrows loomed over small, squinting eyes. His chin had long since abandoned him, leaving his ruddy face to meet his fleshy neck without introduction.

"*Scholar* Pliny," corrected Josephine.

Forshee continued, as if Josephine hadn't spoken. "You're in luck; I have the saddle horse you're seeking."

Josephine and I exchanged glances.

"Can you describe the animal?" I asked, striving to keep my tone cordial.

The younger man stepped forward. "He's a flash thing, Sir—"

"He's *exactly* what you need," Forshee interrupted. "We can offer you restful accommodations, too." Triumphant, he smiled as though we'd already agreed to his invitation.

My dislike for the man growing, I didn't want to accept. "We must evaluate the animal first."

Forshee frowned.

I pulled my shoulders back and lifted my chin. "If it's artwork you seek, I set the terms. If you want to barter for knowledgeable services, Scholar Pliny will lead negotiations. Agreed?"

The men nodded.

Disappointed, I said, "Right. Lead on."

We followed the men down the way to the edge of a broad, slow-moving creek. The near bank looked steep and slick, but the younger man assured me the ford was well-footed with sand and small gravels. The far bank climbed gently up a slight rise.

Had I known about the knee-high water, I would've declined the obnoxious man's offer.

My toes curled as my boots flooded with icy water, and I glared at Forshee's broad back.

Climbing the far bank, I turned to make sure Josephine wasn't struggling with Oxide. Not fond of crossing water, he often balked when I rode him through creeks.

Josephine had him standing placidly in the middle of the stream, as though there was nowhere he'd rather be.

The woman could ride.

Once Oxide clambered out of the stream, we continued up the drive.

The main yard was fifty meters to the right, and the drive wound down the far side of the hill, toward a barn. They'd neatly mowed the fields, and the fences were in good repair.

The smell of fresh-cut grass and the droning of insects floated on the humid air, giving the false impression of an early summer afternoon.

"Yonder is the beast," Forshee said, pointing and shaking his wet trousers. A chestnut horse trotted back and forth in a small paddock next to the barn.

Josephine squinted at it. "How old is she?"

"He," the younger man corrected. "He's coming on five."

"A wonderful age," Forshee added.

"Is he a good saddle mount?" I asked.

Forshee clapped his son on the shoulder. "Broken by Karl."

Karl had the same wiry hair as his father, but his was dark where his father's was a woolly white. Karl's brows were tamer, framing smiling eyes. His face and neck hinted at a corpulent future.

"Is he a good saddle mount?" I asked again. "We're looking for a well-behaved horse."

Forshee swelled. "Even my youngest son has sat upon him, and he's only nine come spring."

"I'm sure he'll be fine," Josephine said, leaning forward to dismount.

"What sort of work are you looking for?" I asked, distracted. Why hadn't Josephine insisted we look at the horse before negotiating?

"Art, of course!" Forshee laughed.

Struggling to keep my voice even, I asked, "What did you have in mind?"

Forshee oozed false friendliness. "A bridge would be an improvement."

"Yes, I agree." My wet toes splayed inside my boots.

"It would need to be *substantial* and fitting with the character of the place."

Stopping here had been a mistake. Accustomed to being treated as an honored guest, Forshee's attitude made me feel small. Sweat pooled near the waistband of my trousers. "Anything else?"

"Wide enough for a wagon to pass without crowding," Karl suggested.

Forshee nodded in agreement. "Yes, wide and substantial."

It would be an easy enough project, and I weighed my dislike of Forshee against my disinclination to keep walking. "Done. I'll get my things and set up."

Karl took a horse in each hand and hustled down the lane as if to cement the bargain.

"Karl, wait," I called before I could change my mind. I unbuckled the saddlebags containing my art supplies.

"Thanks."

Charcoal crowded my leg.

"You best go with your friends," I said, giving the dog a scratch behind one ear.

"I'll walk him to the barn," Josephine offered. "I'd like to meet the horse. A gelding, right?" she asked, turning toward Forshee.

"Yes, yes, a gelding, fine and true!" Forshee agreed. "But no need to trouble yourself, Lady. Sam! Come here, boy!"

A small boy appeared from the corner of the shed. "Yes, Father?" he asked, with a hint of a lisp.

"Take this dog to the barn."

The boy bobbed his head and looked at Charcoal.

"Go get a length of rope," Forshee said with exaggerated patience, giving us an exasperated wink as Sam turned to obey.

"Sam, wait," his father ordered. Forshee spoke a few words in a low voice to the boy.

I watched Sam slide away and wondered why Forshee was reluctant to let Josephine meet the horse.

"Lady, can I introduce you to my wife?"

"Josephine," she corrected him.

"Yes, er, Lady Josephine. My wife?"

"Josephine will be fine." She cast a wry, perplexed look at me before following Forshee.

I'd nearly finished sketching the stream when the boy joined us.

"Sam, was it?" I asked, studying the crossing.

"Sir, yes," Sam whispered. Body rigid, he stood with a limp rope hanging from his hand and stared at the dog.

"Don't be afraid, he's a nice enough chap. Here." I held out my hand for the rope. "If we twist a loop like this, we can slide it over his ears. There, done!" I handed the boy the end of the makeshift leash. "Kiss to him several times, and he'll walk with you fine."

The boy looked at the dog but took the leash from me. "Thank you, Sir," he said with a ghost of a smile. "I'm scared of dogs, but I can manage this fellow."

"Good lad." I squatted onto my heels and rubbed Charcoal's ears. "I'll see you in the morning. Watch the horses for me."

Charcoal gave me the same look Josephine had, but obediently followed the boy.

"Something *substantial*," I said out loud, "and fitting with the character of the place." Based on Forshee's attitude toward us, I owed him nothing more than exactly what he'd asked for.

I was cleaning my brushes and rinsing the palette when footsteps crunched on the gravel.

Forshee stopped with his left foot in the air to survey the scene.

He finally remembered to put it down and walked toward me, frowning.

I sucked in a grounding breath.

Patience, Artist.

Josephine and another woman followed Forshee.

The woman was slightly taller than Josephine and looked as if she weighed twice as much. She had a wide forehead with a heavy brow, her hooded eyes lively and expressive. She, too, was in danger of losing her chin.

"We've needed a bridge for ever so long," she called with a smile. "Well met, Artist!"

Forshee's silence grew louder.

The crossing had transformed from a ford flanked by two muddy banks to a solid concrete bridge approximately five meters wide, spanning the banks high enough to make the drive relatively flat. I'd painted a single arch through which the stream flowed unrestricted, and I'd added tubular metal handrails to the sides of the bridge.

"Well," said Forshee, still frowning. "Well. I asked for a *bridge*."

"Dean? Honey? This *is* a bridge," the woman said.

Forshee gave her an irritated look and widened his arms. "A *substantial* bridge."

"It was a wonderful idea, Forshee. This is quite an enhancement," Josephine said, her tone bright.

Although I'd intended to annoy Forshee, his reaction disappointed me.

For the first time in my life, my artwork hadn't impressed. Forshee was clearly unhappy with my efforts.

I'd understood what he wanted, and I'd purposely delivered what he'd asked for instead of what he desired. My art had been retributive because I'd been in a foul mood and because he'd bruised my pride. He'd also been rude to Josephine. But using my talent to punish Forshee left me heavy and low.

"It will be ever so much better than wading through the silly old creek. I hope my supper justifies such a welcome improvement," trilled Forshee's wife. She poked Josephine in the ribs. "Your friend cuts a dashing figure. You didn't tell me he was as handsome as the moon." She turned and played the coquette, lifting my spirits.

Josephine blushed. "Matthew, this is Jerri Forshee."

Jerri angled her face at me.

Surprised, I bent and brushed my lips across her smooth cheek.

Jerri giggled again. "Jerri, Jerri Forshee. And no, I have no lisp." She laughed and looked at us, having successfully delivered the joke before.

I smiled, and Jerri blushed.

"Now see here, Artist," Forshee began.

The tone of his voice was the last straw.

My jaw clenched, and determined not to lose my composure, I ignored him. Snapping my palette shut with finality, I slung the saddlebags over my left shoulder and offered my right arm to Jerri with a broad smile.

"Art builds in me a powerful hunger." I crooked my left arm for Josephine.

Jerri simpered and gushed as I escorted the women up the hill toward the house, leaving Forshee standing alone, trying to work out what had happened.

CHAPTER ELEVEN

S am was setting the table when I escorted the women into the house. The dwelling was fragrant with the smells of lamb, garlic, and freshly baked bread. Shy, the child ducked his head and slipped back into the kitchen, but not before I'd noticed a purple shadow over his left eye.

When he returned with a steaming bowl of boiled greens, I asked, "Sam, how did you hurt your face? Not an argument with Charcoal, I trust?"

Sam shook his head and opened his mouth, but shut down when Karl entered.

Karl, Josephine, Jerri, and I enjoyed a lively conversation throughout the meal while Forshee sulked from the end of the table and heaved great sighs. He glowered at his wife as she brightly asked us for news and shared tidbits of local gossip. She continued to chatter, undeterred by his taciturn refusal to join the conversation.

Thankfully, Jerri was an excellent cook.

She had roasted a rack of lamb and served it with a savory green sauce composed, she said in a loud whisper, of mint, thyme, marjoram, and cilantro.

She'd mashed boiled turnips and blended in chunks of a mild, orange, farm cheese from her neighbor. There was a crusty loaf of sourdough-rye with plenty of butter, and a bowl of kale and mustard greens with slivered garlic and ribbons of a frilly wild mushroom.

"We call it cockscomb," she said and giggled. "Sam and I picked gallons last month and dried the lot."

"*Clavulina cristata*," Josephine offered. "It's a crested coral fungus."

Three of the Forshees looked impressed and pressed Josephine for information.

Watching Jerri interact with her family, I wondered what my mother had been like. Whenever I'd envisioned my family, it was a nameless, faceless group of people; I didn't imagine the individuals. Was my mother warm and maternal like Jerri?

Thoughtful and serious like Josephine?

Cool and self-possessed like Earl?

"My, I shall have something of note to offer the ladies at the next farm luncheon!" said Jerri. Happy, she stood and cleared the dinner things from the table.

Josephine and I rose to help.

"Please, sit! Karl can help."

Her older son rose obediently and gathered the plates, leaving the four of us alone at the table. I'd been enjoying the evening immensely, imagining how a dinner with my family could feel, but with Jerri's exit, the warmth I'd enjoyed evaporated.

Forshee walked to the easel where the painting was drying. "Now see here. I wanted a bridge fitting with the character of the place."

He blinked, an expectant look on his face.

I waited.

Josephine snorted. "This is a farm. A tidy farm, but a farm none-theless."

"Truth, you speak true," Jerri agreed, reentering the dining room.

"Now, Artist," Forshee tried again, "this bridge doesn't fit with the character of the place."

"What did you envision, Farmer Forshee?" I asked, matching the formality of his language.

"Well now, well now." Forshee puffed, and his brow smoothed, clearly happier with the direction of the conversation. "I thought the place could use a stone bridge. Something with arches and a decorative pattern." He pointed at the painting. "This bridge, it is a fine bridge, but it is not the *right* bridge."

"You asked for a bridge fitting with the character of the place," I repeated.

"Now see here!" said Forshee, his face contorting. "You are an artist."

"Guilty," I said, my lips twitching.

"But this here... this is not an artistic bridge." When I said nothing, Forshee continued, "I could have drawn this bridge."

"If he had given you the bridge you've described, it wouldn't fit your holding," Josephine snapped. "And if you could have drawn a bridge, why didn't you?"

I could get used to her unwavering support.

Forshee cleared his throat. "But, after the bridge... the right bridge, you see... the house could have used a sprucing." He gave me a look.

Though I'd toyed with changing the painting to fit what I'd known Forshee wanted, his attempt to bully me provoked my temper again.

My pulse pounded, and I clenched my hands under the table. "I see. You intended to continue improving your property, as the bridge wouldn't have fit with the character of the place. You would have thus needed the character of the place changed to fit the new bridge."

Forshee nodded, relieved to be understood.

"What we agreed to, *Sir*, was a bridge in keeping with the character of the place. As I've delivered, I declare our business concluded." Heat coiled in my stomach, and the back of my neck prickled.

"My word," chirped Jerri, "would you look at this pie?" She set the dish down in the center of the table. It was double the size of a standard pie, the pastry shiny and brown. Jerri had adorned the crust with a swirl of leaves made from the same pastry.

"Now, this pie has a kick. I canned last year's apples in the brandy we distilled from our own hard cider." She topped each generous wedge with a thin slice of cheddar. "Had I known you were coming, I would've taken a hand at a frozen custard. At least the cheese is homemade."

Happy for the change in conversation, I admired the plate she handed me and dug in with enthusiasm. "Oh, Jerri, this pie." I shook my head. "I am overcome." The sweetened fruit melted across my tongue and contrasted with the sharp tang of the cheese, exciting my mouth with an almost painful sensation. I too would lose my jaw if I stayed here for any length of time.

The look of frustration on Forshee's face heightened my enjoyment as he watched me take pleasure in his wife's culinary skills.

Jerri beamed and handed around the rest of the plates. "I boil maple syrup dry for baking, and I trade for allspice from a community somewhere south of Orlando Depot!" She sat back, impressed with her own worldliness. "I use a pinch, just a pinch, but to the allspice I add"—she gazed around the table with wide eyes— "pansies!"

We looked blankly at her, then at each other.

I eyed Josephine's half-eaten plate, and she slid it to me.

"The flower?" Josephine asked. "Pansies *are* edible."

"Truth!" Jerri giggled. "And let me tell you—"

The feeling in the room darkened as Forshee gathered his energy to try again. I finished Josephine's pie in quick bites.

Forshee inhaled and opened his mouth.

"Mistress Jerri," I interrupted, giving her my most charming smile, "I'm afraid we're exhausted. Will you please excuse us for the evening?"

Josephine made a wan face and slow blinked.

Bless her.

"Oh, my dears, of course, of course. Let me show you the way."

After we'd said our good evenings, Jerri led us to adjoining rooms and pointed out towels and washbasins.

"We may be a simple farm, but we have a lavatory! The toilet is here," she announced proudly, "and does, of course, flush!"

I SHIVERED IN THE CHILLY DAMP. THE DAY HAD DAWNED SO misty and gray, I could barely see the outline of the barn. Josephine limped, so I ambled, though I was eager to get back onto the road and avoid another altercation with Forshee.

"How far do you think we can get today?" Josephine asked.

"We have two options: southwest to pick up Route 16, or southeast to take Route 109 to Sanford and then Route 202 to Rochester Depot."

"Which is shorter?" she asked.

"The southwest route is more direct."

"Why consider the second option?"

I shrugged. "All the map updates at the filling station came from the southeast. I don't know if the other way is passable." I juggled the food parcels Jerri had pressed into our hands, the smoky-bacon scent delicious even though I'd overindulged at breakfast.

"If we stay on the major roads, it could be easier to find tools, materials, accommodations, and supplies. The lesser-traveled roads could route us through hundreds of kilometers of empty land with no farmsteads or communities to provide resources or aid. If the road is blocked, we'd have to backtrack."

The barn was brightly lit and smelled of hay and horses.

I stepped in and raised my hand to greet Karl. "Heya."

"It's a brisk one, isn't it?" Karl said with a smile. "I'll have them tacked up in a moment."

Josephine craned her neck. "Where is he?"

"Still in the paddock," Karl said, avoiding our eyes. "I thought I'd get these fellows ready first."

I frowned. "Through there?"

Karl nodded without looking up.

Josephine left, and I stowed the food parcels in Magnesium's packsaddle before following her through the side door.

Quick hoof steps clattered in the fog.

Josephine whistled, and the animal materialized out of the gloom. He stopped out of reach, restless.

I ducked between the wooden fence boards.

He shied backward a meter, then approached with his head lowered, licking and chewing.

"He's handsome," she said.

"He seems soft enough, but unsettled. I may need to ride him for you."

Josephine stretched out her arm and stroked the horse's neck. He trembled, but didn't move away. "You're a pretty thing," she crooned.

"He's a mite skittish," Karl said from behind us.

The horse bolted, swallowed by the mists.

"Your father said you'd trained the horse." My stomach flipped; I should've insisted on inspecting the horse before painting the bridge. With her injured knee, this horse was useless to Josephine.

Karl cleared his throat.

"I said Karl broke the horse," Forshee corrected as he sauntered around the corner of the barn. "He's been on him, oh, three times."

"He's only ridden the horse three times?" I asked, incredulous. "And Sam? You said Sam had ridden him."

"Sam sat on him yesterday," Forshee replied with a nasty smile.

The bruise on the boy's eye.

My chest tightened, and I clenched my jaw, searching for the right words.

"Karl can work the jitters out in two weeks. In the meantime, we can talk about the accommodations you'll need." Forshee smirked.

"Karl, fetch the horse and bring him into the barn." Josephine turned and ducked back through the fence boards. "You," she said to Forshee, "come and show me the horse's saddle."

Forshee blinked.

"Now!" she snapped, walking into the barn.

I swallowed my chuckle as I followed them.

Forshee appeared with an old saddle. "This is the only one I can part with." Scowling, he hefted it over a stall door.

Josephine looked it over. "The tree is sturdy, and the seat and fenders are fine, but the rigging has rotted."

Forshee shrugged and leaned against the barn wall.

Karl entered, leading the frightened horse by its bridle.

I leaned forward to take the horse, but Josephine stepped in front of me and held her hand out for the reins.

"Strap the saddle onto the packsaddle," she instructed Karl, before walking the horse out of the barn.

I followed her to the barn door.

Josephine led the chestnut into the small square paddock, murmuring. I strained my ears but couldn't make out any of the words.

"About the accommodations," Forshee began.

I gritted my teeth. "You, Sir, are a scoundrel."

"Now wait a moment!"

"You traded a bridge for a saddle mount. You have your bridge, and you give us an unproven horse?"

Karl approached with Magnesium and Oxide. "Should I take their tack back off?"

Forshee grinned.

"Let's go," said Josephine.

We turned and stared.

Josephine sat astride the unsaddled horse. Nervous, he danced from side to side, but lowered his head and backed up when asked.

This damsel needed no rescuing.

Wordless, I led my horses out of the barn and into the lane. I settled on Oxide, pleased to be riding again. He danced sideways, as ready to depart as I was.

The stirrups, still set for Josephine, were too short. While I was adjusting the second stirrup, Charcoal barked.

I looked up. "Where's my dog?"

Forshee stepped forward. "We'll keep the creature here. He won't be able to keep up, anyway."

Anger coursed through me, stoking the fire which had burned in my gut since yesterday. Maybe I should reverse the sturdy and serviceable bridge I'd provided. I could deepen the gully, making it more dangerous. "Release him."

Forshee crossed his arms, his posture an illustration of defiance.

Karl dropped his eyes and studied the gravel drive.

Livid, I was about to repeat my demand when Charcoal trotted into the drive.

The boy, Sam, slid out of the barn, giving me a small wave.

In a smooth motion, Josephine spun the chestnut toward the main road and sprang away. I twitched Magnesium's lead, wheeled Oxide, and took off after her, my horses spraying gravel behind us. The wind whistled in my ears, and I grinned at Forshee's shouts of anger.

The horses clattered across the new concrete bridge, and we turned south sharply.

Glancing back to make sure Charcoal kept up, I squeezed Oxide into a smooth gait and caught up with Josephine.

She turned, a smile twisting her scarred face. "Didn't think a girl could ride, did you?" she shouted.

"Let's take the side road and skip the main route!" I shouted back. "Why?"

"I don't want to encounter another Forshee for a while."

She nodded and pushed her horse faster.

I urged Oxide into a lope, but as his nose stretched beyond Josephine's mount, her horse smoothly drew away.

Josephine's peal of laughter lightened my heart.

We jockeyed with each other, racing down the road for the better part of an hour. I shouted a whoop of victory as I finally pulled in front of Josephine. My victory was short-lived as Josephine turned the chestnut onto the side route.

Blast, the woman can ride.

CHAPTER TWELVE

" All right, Artist, spill."

"What?" My gut had been cramping for over an hour, and I'd been busy devising a reason to stop and relieve myself without Josephine present.

"Your story. At the filling station, you promised to tell me why you hadn't accepted a commission."

"Ah." Blast. How was I going to get out of this?

"And?" Josephine stopped her horse.

"They sent me to the abbey at three," I began.

"Yes, you've said."

"Quite. I—"

"Are you all right?"

I wiped the sweat from my forehead. "No, I'm not."

"Whatever is the matter?"

"Let's just say Jerri's food was too rich for my stomach."

She wrinkled her brow. "But I ate what you did."

"Sorry, Josephine." I gasped as a strong cramp hit. "I need a break."

"Would you like to make camp?" she asked.

"I, uh... I'd like you to keep riding and let me catch up when I can."

"But I can... oh." She blushed. "Yes, of course. I'll continue on."

"Thanks," I said, mortified.

She clucked to the chestnut, and they jogged around the next bend.

I was off Oxide in a flash and squatting behind a large tree a moment later.

Ugh.

This was one part of traveling I wouldn't miss when I did finally settle.

When I was sure I'd finished, I fussed with my tack, unsure how to answer Josephine. Though I'd only known her for a few days, I was loath to tell her the unvarnished truth. Chagrinned, I caught up with her before I'd decided how to handle it.

"I'm afraid we've got a problem," she said.

"Oh?" I craned my neck. The road beyond Josephine ended abruptly in a tangle of blowdowns. I stood in my saddle, expecting to see a hairpin turn up the slope.

Nothing.

"Here, let me look." I dismounted and tethered my horses. Walking to the first blowdown, I climbed onto the downed trunk to survey what lay beyond it.

"Can you see the other side?"

"No."

"Is there a way around it?"

I studied the hillside. "Maybe." If we couldn't get around this obstruction, we'd lose an entire day of progress.

"I could scout the downhill side," she offered.

I shook my head. "Your knee doesn't need the punishment. Can you watch the horses?"

She nodded, and I whistled for Charcoal.

The hill was steep, the footing loose, and I struggled to keep my balance as I lunged up the hill.

Too steep for horses.

I scrambled up to a small landing to see if the road cleared farther along.

Charcoal bounded around me with a stick in his mouth, cavorting like a puppy.

"Watch it, dog. If you knock me over, you're finding your own supper tonight."

I thought I could see where the pavement cleared and side-stepped down the slope. The loose soil slipped, and I slid along it, arms windmilling. Somehow, I stayed on my feet and reached the road's surface.

Hands on my hips, I surveyed the blockage. "We're not cutting our way through this one."

Charcoal dropped his stick at my feet and danced.

I picked it up and tossed it over the edge of the road. With a yip, he raced after it. I watched him disappear into a jungle of brush.

Could we travel on the downhill side?

Birds twittered as I picked my way down the hill, traversing the slope above the brush line.

"Matthew?"

"Here."

"You've been gone ever so long. When Charcoal returned, I got worried."

I scrambled up the last few meters and stepped onto the road. "I'm fine."

"What did you find? Can we get past this?"

"The uphill side is too loose and steep for the horses, and this tangle is so great it would take a fair amount of time to cut a way through."

"Could you use art to clear it?"

"Yes, but it would be faster to walk through the ravine."

She squinted at the slope. "I'm riding without a saddle."

"Right. Well, what about riding Oxide and letting me lead the others?"

"Yes, all right. If you're sure?"

"Or we turn back and lose a day."

Josephine sighed. "Leg up?"

We got the horses to the bottom of the ravine without difficulty and walked the dried creek bed.

This soon proved to be a mistake.

The ravine narrowed, growing brushy. Brambles entwined with the bushes clutched at my clothes, hair, and skin. The ground turned boggy, and I frequently sank to my knee in the mire. The horses struggled to move through the sucking mud, staggering sideways. I had to jump out of their way more than once. The air was warm and muggy, and flies buzzed us maddeningly.

"Tell me," Josephine blurted.

"Tell you what?" I swatted at a fly and swore as a bramble tore at the back of my hand. A fly bit my neck, and the bitter-sour flavor of bile hit the back of my tongue.

"Why you're traveling."

I sighed and swallowed several times to clear the taste from my mouth.

"At least tell me where you were planning to go before you met me."

"I was going to visit my friend Liang Zhen," I blurted. Why not?

"Who's he?"

"An artist who graduated the year before I did. He accepted a commission somewhere down south and I thought I'd look him up."

"Ack."

"Sorry, what?"

"Cobweb," she said with a look of distaste. "I broke a cobweb with my face."

I moved a branch aside for Magnesium, who lunged out of a deep spot in the mud.

"Why haven't you accepted a commission?"

The woman was relentless. I rubbed the sweat from my brow

with the back of my arm and took another step forward, losing my boot in the mud. "Blast!"

"Are you okay?" Josephine turned in the saddle. "Oh, dear." She chuckled.

"Yeah, funny, Scholar Pliny." On one foot, I bent to retrieve my boot.

The chestnut snorted and jerked his lead, pitching me forward into the mud.

I lay with the rancid smell of earthy-manure oozing around me and listened to Josephine's peals of laughter.

Using considerable effort, I turned over, staring up at Charcoal.

He sniffed my face and smiled.

I grinned and grabbed his collar, letting him pull me into a sitting position.

Josephine tried to smother her giggles.

"I'm looking for my family," I admitted. I was sure I looked ridiculous, coated in brown slime, wallowing in the muck.

"Looking for your family?" She arched her brow. "In the mud?"

I chuckled and struggled to my feet, retrieving my boot. "Yes, or news of what happened to them. It's why I haven't accepted a commission. Let's find somewhere to take a break. I'm sick of this mud sucking at me."

"Are you sure? You seem so comfortable in the filth."

I picked up a handful of mud and threatened her with it.

She squealed. "Okay! I'll ride ahead and see if I can find an island or something solid for a brief respite for your delicate feet."

"And for the rest of my delicate self. I'll keep slogging through this until you return, shall I?" I wasn't sure she'd heard, but her peals of laughter floated on the humid air.

While I rinsed off the worst of the muck, Josephine tethered the horses and retrieved one of the food parcels Jerri had packed for us.

"Why don't you know where your family is?" she asked, settling next to me.

"I received no correspondence during my years at the abbey."

"None?"

"No... and the masters either couldn't, or wouldn't, tell me anything."

"How do you know where to look?"

"I don't, but I've been getting flashes."

"Flashes? Like creative inspiration?"

"No, flashes of an image or parts of an image, like a color or a vague shape. I paint what I remember from the flash, but I'm not sure if I'm putting the shapes into the right positions."

She studied me. "How long have you been receiving the flashes?"

"A few came before I left the abbey, but more since beginning my travels."

Josephine dug through the food Jerri had packed. "It's why you refused to join a community?"

"Yes. I received offers, but I need to find my family first." Could I risk another serving of Jerri's food? Though I was hungry, I was not eager to repeat this morning's diarrhea.

"That must have gone over well."

"Mmm. My refusal to choose a community caused an uproar at the abbey, and I left on uneasy terms." Though it had been terrible to leave with their disappointment heavy on my shoulders, telling Josephine was easier than I'd expected.

"I see. Have you had other flashes or insights? Is it something you grew up doing?"

"No, this is new for me. Have you read about people having flashes?"

"No. There are mentions of visions in literature, but frankly, it's never been an area of interest." She cut a piece of quiche in half and passed me a portion. "You have so little information. What specifically are you looking for?"

I sighed, squinting at the quiche. "I'm not sure. Maybe someone who can tell me where to go once the image is more complete. The painting is personal, so please don't speak of it."

She nodded. "I won't, but if you're looking for answers, consider confiding in the people we meet."

"I will," I promised, finishing my meal.

"If you've rested, we should move again."

I groaned. "Once more into the deep."

"I think the saying is once more unto the breach."

"Just my luck I'm traveling with a scholar."

Josephine winked at me. "But soft! What light through yonder window breaks?"

"What?"

She pointed at the slope. "I think we can get back on the road right up there."

"Right. Here, let me help you up."

We made it to the top of the hill without further incident and were trading horses when Charcoal pricked his ears and growled.

"Hear that?" I asked.

We stood, silent.

"There it is again."

Josephine frowned. "What?"

"Ah. Now I will believe that there are unicorns," I said, smiling.

"The Tempest! You *are* educated."

"Artists spend their lives studying classical art," I said, smug. "Let's hope what I hear is a unicorn and not Caliban."

CHAPTER THIRTEEN

The noise was neither unicorn nor monster born, but merely the pitiful braying of a donkey. We found him not long after we reached the old road harnessed to a small wooden cart.

A dead man, presumably the donkey's former owner, sat next to the cart.

Josephine shuddered and focused on the donkey. "Oh, the poor thing! Look, he has marks on his neck."

"He's rubbed himself raw. I'll turn him loose." The barren circle of earth around the cart revealed the donkey's short reach. Freeing the animal took some effort, and as soon as I removed the harness, he scrambled to the closest patch of grass and ripped at the blades.

I pushed against the cart with my foot and inspected the man. Death had twisted his face in a rictus grimace, and he'd died with his fist clenched above his chest. "Poor old fellow. The shoulder of the road must have given way. It looks like he tried to muscle the cart up over the stump."

I tugged back the tarpaulin and surveyed the cargo. There were two heavy-looking trunks, a bedroll, an oat sack, a small hatchet, and various pots and pans. A blanket-wrapped parcel sat in the cart's corner, tucked behind a trunk.

Curious, I pulled on the blanket, exposing the top half of a beautifully carved harp. "Was your fellow a minstrel, Donkey?"

The little animal ignored me.

Josephine glanced at the cart. "What are we going to do about the man? We can't leave him like this."

If I'd been by myself, I might have left him where he sat. "I'll bury him."

"How sad. No one knows he's here."

She was right. "I'll draw a death portrait to show the next community."

"How kind of you. If it's going to take time, we should make camp."

I glanced at the sun. It was only mid-afternoon, but the days were shortening, and night would come quickly. "Good idea. A half-hour won't matter to him."

I unsaddled Oxide and let him loose to graze. Magnesium tugged on his short lead, jealous. As I loosened the girth on the pack-saddle, Magnesium lifted his front right hoof and pawed at the ground.

I swatted at his belly. "Quit."

Nonplussed, the horse switched feet and pawed with his front left.

With a heave, I pulled the packsaddle off, panniers still attached. Magnesium took a deep sigh and craned his neck to look at me.

"See?" I said, unsnapping the lead from the halter, "you get a break, too." The horse sauntered toward Josephine's, searching for the best clumps of grass along the way.

"Watch them, Charcoal."

The dog glanced at me before returning his attention to the donkey.

We set up camp, hobbling the loose horses so they could graze without wandering too far. Josephine stayed with her chestnut, who was clearly unhappy about the hobbles, jerking his front legs to the extent of the restraints with each step.

Squatting near the dead man, I sharpened my pencils and studied his face. I wanted to capture his quintessence before decay could erase his individuality. As I sketched, I imagined his face without the grotesque contortions of death. With each stroke of the pencil against paper, the lines on his face smoothed, and his expression became more peaceful and relaxed.

I lifted my chin and stretched my back.

Josephine sat on the back of the small cart, looking through the minstrel's things. She looked absorbed, so I bent back to my task.

In time, an excellent likeness emerged on the paper. The man had shaggy eyebrows and a neat mustache. Deep lines radiated from the corners of his eyes, rounding the line of his cheek, then merging with the network of lines and grooves on his neck. From the darkly tanned skin, I assumed the lines on his face resulted from years of smiling and squinting. The large-brimmed hat he'd worn had beaten down his short white hair, giving the impression it had reshaped his head.

Death portraits were a task routinely assigned to students at the abbey. I found it easier to memorialize an unknown face when I imagined the subject's life.

On my mind's canvas, I pictured him laughing with his audiences and silently watching a sunset as he traveled lonely roads. I decided he would have been a tea-drinking man with a special spot in his heart for birds.

I could picture him enjoying a pipe over a pint in pubs where he'd stroke his mustache as he wove tales with a sparkle in his eye. As I drew, I mourned his loss.

Stopping frequently to study his face, I worked methodically. It was important to me to capture the man without embellishing or changing the face in a haste to finish the task. When I finished, anyone who'd known him would recognize the portrait.

"Lucky fellow. I bet they didn't pressure you to settle. No one thought you selfish for wanting to travel, to see, or to seek."

I surveyed the old fellow and the peaceful scene.

Sunlight filtered through the bare branches, providing a soft glow to the thick carpet of leaves around us. The air was full of chirps, flutters, and song as birds flitted from branch to branch.

"May I see the sketch?"

I handed it to Josephine and studied the donkey. "Monitor Donkey for me, Charcoal. I need to bury his fellow, and I don't know what he'll think about it."

The dog searched my face, waiting for further instructions.

I smiled at him and scratched his head. "We'll eat after I finish this."

"The sketch is marvelous. I don't know how you saw this face in that one."

Warmed by her compliment, I shrugged. "Years of practice."

Death portraits always left me feeling tranquil, and I was glad we'd taken the time to perform this service for the old man.

It was a salutary reminder; life was about the journey as much as the destination.

Josephine nodded, studying the sketch.

I unbuckled the cover to the nearest pannier and rummaged through it. "Blast."

The item I needed was *never* in the first bag I searched.

In the other pannier, I found my ax and folding spade. I set to work on the grave, chopping through roots and shoveling out the loosened dirt. When I stopped to catch my breath, Charcoal inspected my work, experimentally putting a paw down to test the soil. Satisfied, he dug, spraying me with dirt.

"We're trying to deepen it, not widen the hole," I chided, "but it's slow going with this short spade." Looking at it, I shook my head.

I can *improve* things.

Digging out the small notepad I kept in my overcoat, I sketched the shape of the spade and then redrew the shaft. Looking up from my sketch, I smiled at the long-handled tool laying before me.

"This will help." The extra leverage sped up the digging, and I finished the task within the hour.

Josephine gazed at the man in the grave. "We should say a few words."

"What's appropriate?"

"Here's one of my favorite quotes from *Before* by writer Edgar Allan Poe. 'The boundaries which divide Life from Death are at best shadowy and vague. Who shall say where the one ends, and where the other begins?' Rest peacefully, old fellow."

"Remember us in your travels," I added. Sighing, I picked up the shovel and filled the grave. When finished, my arms were rubbery.

"What's his story, do you think?" asked Josephine as I stepped into the shelter.

"Who?"

She raised her chin in the donkey's direction. "Your shadow."

I looked over my shoulder at the donkey behind me.

"Ah, Donkey." I shrugged. The animal gazed at me, blinking eyes framed by thick black lashes.

"Aren't you going to give him a name?"

I scratched my beard. "He probably has one, but I don't know it."

"He seems taken with you."

"Oh, aye. After I freed him, he became my best fellow."

Charcoal gave me an accusing look.

"Second best, behind Charcoal," I amended.

Mollified, the dog lay down.

"You've named everyone else you travel with," Josephine teased.

"I've painted or sketched them."

"Oh!" Josephine giggled. "Their names are colors!"

"It's how I see the world."

Josephine was quiet. "What happens when you paint a living thing?"

"When I first make a painting or drawing, I simply paint what is."

"And then?" Josephine prodded.

I gave her a long look. "If making improvements, I begin the energy work to manifest the changes."

She finished heating our meal in silence, steam curling from the pan in rosemary-lamb wisps. I suspected she was wondering if my art could fix her scars. I ate moderately, remembering what an overindulgence of Jerri's food could do to my digestive system.

Chewing the food, I enjoyed the balance of smoky meat and herbs. Josephine had scorched the potatoes, but they were still soft enough to be edible. A quarter of an hour passed, and when I finished, I thanked Josephine for the meal and went to wash our supper things.

Charcoal accompanied me, looking over his shoulder at the donkey grazing nearby.

"Are you following me, Sir Donkey?"

The animal raised his head and studied me. He didn't retreat when I reached out to stroke his forehead. I scratched behind an ear, and the donkey's lips wiggled.

I laughed. "Let's head back, chaps."

As I approached the shelter, I had a flash, the image fleeting and incomplete. Heart thumping, I jogged to the panniers and rummaged through them.

"What are you looking for?"

"I had a flash," I muttered. Where was it? I dug through half of my equipment before I found my painting. Pulling off the linen wrapping, I tilted the canvas toward the fire.

The flash *was* a new piece of the puzzle.

"Can you paint in the dark?" asked Josephine, coming over to look at the painting.

I hesitated, fighting the urge to hide the canvas from her.

This painting was the physical manifestation of the most private part of myself; everything I owned was replaceable, except for this. The image could hold the key to my past or my future.

"No," I admitted, angling the painting toward her. "I'd get the colors or perspective wrong, but I hope I don't lose what I saw before morning."

"Tell me about it. Maybe it will help."

I looked at her. "No offense, but I don't think so. You don't know the pigments."

"Can you choose pigments, then? As a reminder for tomorrow?"

I beamed. "Now that, smart lady, is a capital idea."

CHAPTER FOURTEEN

The *tap-splat* of fat rain droplets striking the canvas tarpaulin woke me, and I pulled the covers over my shoulder, uncovering my feet.

"The bedding is too short for you," said Josephine.

I chuckled. "It is."

"Why didn't you ask for yours back? Those would fit me fine."

I sat up and stretched. "I don't know. It felt unheroic."

Josephine scoffed, and I flushed. "Have you eaten?" I asked to cover my embarrassment.

"No." She sighed. "I've been lying here in my extra-long bedding listening to the rain."

I laughed and threw my makeshift pillow at her.

"It *is* nice to not rush off, though. Did you want to paint your flash this morning?"

The shape I held in memory sharpened as I reviewed the pigments I'd laid out the night before. If I didn't capture the image, it would fade. With my whole heart, I hoped the tiny flashes would resolve into an image, providing clues to where my family was, or what had happened to them.

"Yes."

"I think you should. Perhaps the weather will clear later, too."

"You don't mind the delay?"

"Not at all. I was thinking about going through the minstrel's things to see if there's anything we should take. Other than the bedroll and the horse, I've nothing of my own."

"Right." I looked over at the pile of the minstrel's belongings we had stacked under the shelter. "There may be a few other things we want to salvage and drop off in the next community."

"I agree. The instrument looked particularly fine."

After breakfast, I set up my easel.

"I'm sorry, I don't see what it is yet," she admitted, studying the painting.

"Me neither, but I'm hopeful the flashes will resolve into a concerted whole."

I took my time dabbing different pigments onto my palette. The shades, while close to what I had seen in the flash, weren't exactly right, but I wasn't worried about getting the color precise. Pigments changed tone based on where they were in context with other hues.

At the abbey, the masters called this phenomenon 'simultaneous contrast.'

A small gray square within a larger white square appeared darker than the same gray square surrounded by a larger black square.

Lighting could also change the appearance of the color on a canvas. A painting viewed with candlelight looked different than the same painting viewed in bright sunlight.

The light through the drizzle was a pearlescent gray with blue undertones. I scooted the easel as close as I could to the edge of the shelter and dabbed paint onto the canvas.

Around midday, I took a break to check on the horses and pull together sandwiches. Josephine was working with her chestnut horse in the distance.

From my vantage, it looked as though they were dancing, leaping around each other. I watched the show for a while before returning to my painting.

When I next looked up, hours had passed.

Stretching, I set down my brush with a grimace. "Ouch."

"Hmm?"

"My hand's cramping. What are you doing?"

Josephine was sitting between neat piles. "I thought I'd sort the minstrel's belongings by things I could use, things to leave, and things to donate to the next community."

"Makes sense. What's the fourth pile for?"

"Things I couldn't decide on, or things I thought you might like."

"Such as?"

"I found sketches but didn't know if they'd interest you."

"Oh?" I rummaged through the pile, knocking it askew.

"In the leather folder," said Josephine without looking up.

I found the folio and pulled out the first sketch, chuckling. "As I imagined."

"Sorry, what?"

I held up a simple sketch of a martin. "I assumed the minstrel liked birds."

"How ever did you know?"

"I didn't, but I like to imagine things about the people I draw in death."

Josephine looked thoughtful. "There might be something in it."

I glanced through the next three sketches, but the fourth page caught my interest. "The minstrel didn't draw this."

The scene depicted a hillside tightly packed with square stone buildings. The flat roofs on the downhill buildings created terrace space for the uphill ones, leaving little room for roads. A faint outline of green suggested a park or forest at the top of the hill.

"Oh?" Josephine stood and came over to look at it. "How can you tell?"

"The man who drew this had training."

"An artist drew it?"

97

"Yes, I think so."

"It looks more... I don't know, real, maybe?"

I nodded, studying the sketch. "Yes, this drawing has perspective."

"Perspective, from the Latin word *per* meaning 'through' and *specere* meaning 'to look.' Is perspective difficult to learn?"

"Quite."

"Is it because it's a translation of a three-dimensional image onto a two-dimensional surface?"

"Almost. That's how early artists described it. Perspective is used to establish a viewpoint to best communicate a subject to an audience."

Josephine gave me a blank look.

"Let me try again. A sketch without perspective, like this one," I said, handing her the martin sketch, "provides you an image your brain easily processes."

"Okay."

I handed her the hillside scene. "This drawing invites you in to explore the space. Your mind cannot digest all the information at once. The sense of depth and space provides a world our minds interact with. We wonder what is behind this door, where that staircase goes, and who lives in this building."

"Yes, I see. Are there more pieces of art in the folder?"

I rifled through and then drew out a tiny scrap of paper. "Yes, but unless I'm mistaken, a different artist drew this."

"What is it?"

I shrugged and handed it to her. "A tree on fire?"

"Odd," she said, handing it back. "Strange subject."

I studied it again. A tree or large shrub stood at the top of a small rise, in stark contrast to the night. Its branches were lit by an inferno raging within its canopy. In and around the flames gnarled, many-fingered branches groped at the sky.

The drawing was lonely and disturbing.

I flipped through the rest of the pages but found nothing else of interest. I fed the fire and examined each sketch again. The simplest drawings focused on birds, the composer's hand hesitant, the lines unsure. I spread them around me to decipher their chronology.

"What are you doing?"

"Determining which bird the minstrel drew first."

"How can you tell?"

"When learning to sketch, people focus on the outline of their subjects."

"And when they get better?"

"They focus on light and shadow."

"What next?"

I looked at her. "This feels suspiciously like a lesson."

She shrugged. "I like to learn."

"Women aren't artists," I said, looking at the sketches again.

"I know. Still, from an abstract perspective—"

I looked up and grinned. "An art joke, Scholar Pliny?"

Josephine laughed. "I'll get supper ready. Will you look through the pile?"

Digging through the fourth pile, I found equipment like mine—an assortment of ropes, canvas tarpaulins, and a hoof rasp. "This will come in handy," I said, shaking the heavy item. "Were you able to find anything useful for yourself?"

"I think I can wear his clothes."

"Really?" I looked at Josephine's slender figure.

"He was a slight man, and it will be easier for me to ride in trousers than this skirt."

"Why are you wearing such a heavy skirt? I noticed it the day we met."

"Oh, I had a silly notion they'd take me more seriously dressed like a *Scholar*, with a capital S. I used to change between traveling clothes and my scholar costume before entering a community."

"Well, the man who absconded with your mare will hardly fit into your traveling trousseau." I had a sudden thought. "Did he get anything of value?"

"Only my favorite pens. My master gave them to me as a graduation gift."

"Well, you have your pick of mine if needed before we reach Rochester." The scent of burned rubber filled the air, and I glanced at the smoking pan Josephine was stirring.

"I found a few pencils in the minstrel's things, but I appreciate your offer. Here, the food's hot."

I took my bowl from Josephine and studied the scorched substance.

"Mutton, I think. Jerri said to soak and fry it, only we haven't any lard."

I poked at a charred lump with my finger.

It squelched.

"Thanks." I stood with my back to the fire, enjoying the heat.

"Howsyourpnt—"

My eyes widened. "Mm?"

Josephine swallowed with obvious effort and coughed. "Sorry. How's your painting coming?"

I chewed my mouthful, waiting for it to break apart.

Josephine waited.

Still chewing furiously, I pointed to my mouth and shook my head.

"Water?"

I nodded, eyes tearing.

Josephine handed me the canteen, and I tried to drink. The water mixed with the gristle, and part of the large lump slid greasily down my throat. I coughed and wiped my mouth with the back of my hand.

"It's going fine," I choked. A piece caught in my throat, and I coughed furiously.

"Better?" Josephine asked when I stopped spluttering.

I nodded and chewed, but *better* was relative.

Josephine sighed and poked at the fire. "I found dried foodstuffs and a grain, but I'm not sure if it was for him or the donkey."

I shoved the wad of meat into my cheek, the greasy-carbon flavor terrible. "This stuff doesn't chew," I said around it.

"Maybe Jerri meant for us to stew it. It's sure getting dark early, isn't it?"

Night had fallen, and the light from the fire scarcely reached beyond our shelter.

I slid the offensive gristle from my mouth and tossed it into the darkness. "I'm sorry about losing the day."

"It was a blessing to take time off. My backside hasn't ridden without a saddle in years. Have you had enough?" she asked, gesturing toward the pan.

I struggled to keep a neutral expression. "Yes, thanks."

Even Charcoal backed away when Josephine offered him the last of the mutton.

I held up my painting. "This is how far I got."

"Hmm."

"It doesn't look like much, but there's something here. I'm sure of it." I put the painting back on the easel and stepped out of the shelter to wash my hands. I kept looking back toward the painting, hoping the new blobs of pigment would resolve into a lost memory, wanting the distance to clarify the image.

No luck.

Even though we'd made no physical progress today, the day's work was satisfying.

The skies had cleared, and stars twinkled through the tangle of bare branches above me. In the distance, an owl hooted.

I shivered, missing the fire's heat.

Josephine was sitting near the fire when I returned. Without looking up, she said, "I found his records."

"Records?"

"Mmm. A journal and correspondence." She looked up suddenly. "Do you think me rude for reading his things?"

I shrugged. "It wouldn't matter to him anymore."

She sighed. "I've been pining to read. Anything. I've never been so long without a book."

I poked at the fire and examined my painting.

Charcoal lay next to me and put his chin on my foot with a groan.

Josephine looked up with a question on her face.

"What is it?"

"Are you sure you've never met him? This minstrel never visited your abbey?"

I shrugged. "No, why?"

She pointed to a passage in the diary. "Because he wrote about you. Your name is here."

CHAPTER FIFTEEN

"**W**hat? You're joking." I held out my hand for the journal.

Josephine stared at me, pressing the book to her chest. "No, I'm serious."

"Can I see it?"

She said nothing, her expression blank.

Instantly livid, my pulse hammered in my ears. What was in the journal? Why wouldn't she let me see it? My hands knotted into fists, and my stomach clenched.

I could take the journal from Josephine, leap across the fire, and snatch it from her hands. Who was she, anyway? Where would she be without my help, my generosity, my charity? What right had she to keep *my* truth from me?

Bile rose in my throat.

Josephine watched my reaction with wide eyes.

I opened my mouth to shout, but a small voice beneath my rage cried for logic.

Maybe her reluctance to share the journal was born of fear.

Fear of *me*.

A pang tore through my gut. "I'm going for a walk." Ashamed of my emotional reaction, I fled.

What just happened?

My eyes, still fire-bright, were of no use in the dark, and I stumbled, the ground lurching toward me.

I drew deep breaths of the chilly air, trying to find my equilibrium. Tripping again, I nearly fell. I stopped, trembling, hot tears welling beneath my closed eyelids.

Soft footfalls thudded behind me, and I turned, dreading Josephine's soft voice.

No words came.

Reaching into the dark, I found the donkey's long nose.

"Hello, chap," I said, my voice hoarse and throat sore.

The firelight flickered through the trees, and I turned toward the dark.

The donkey stepped closer and stood beside me, looking into the night.

I rubbed his rough coat, my fingers playing with the long hairs along his shoulder. "I'm afraid I blew it."

The donkey, warm and still, said nothing.

"All my life, people have kept things from me."

The donkey's shoulder tightened as he leaned into my scratch.

I took a step forward, and the donkey moved with me. "This was one time too many."

I took another experimental step forward, and he matched my step.

"You can see in this dark, can't you? Come on, let's go." Clicking my tongue, I stepped forward, and the donkey matched my stride. We continued for several paces before he moved to his right. I followed him, my hand resting lightly on his withers. Reaching out with my left leg, I kicked the log lying in my path.

Someone had trained the donkey to guide them through the dark.

We continued through the woods, and without fail, he helped me navigate unseen obstacles.

"Neat trick, Donkey, but can you help me find my way through an apology?"

The donkey didn't answer, and I sighed and stepped into the shelter.

"Josephine, I apologize."

Her face softened. "I didn't mean to distress you."

"I—" I stopped, not sure what to say.

She looked at me with an expression I took to be a mix of pity and kindness. I swallowed hard, afraid her sympathy would unleash the flood of emotions I was restraining.

I refused to release my feelings like a bawling child.

"Shall I tell you what the journal said?"

I nodded, my throat tightening with anxiety and anticipation. I swallowed several times.

She opened the book and cleared her throat, searching my face.

I nodded again, drawing a deep breath.

"Today, the post caught up with me. The letter regarding Matthew Sugiyama arrived, and as I read it, I feared I was already too late." She closed the book.

I waited for her to say something more. "Well?"

"That's all it says."

"Really?" Questions tumbled through my mind. I tried to grab at them, but they disappeared as soon as my mind's fingers touched them.

"Why didn't you—" I stopped, unsure of how to phrase my question. I looked at my fingers. "I'm sorry if I frightened you earlier."

Josephine stood and shook her leg. "I wasn't afraid of you. Well, maybe for a moment, from the memory of *that* man." She put her foot down and tested it, grimacing.

"Pins and needles. No, I was afraid *for* you." She limped to a pile. "I feared we wouldn't find the letter here in his things."

The letter, here.

My hands trembled as I released my fists. I drew a deep, steadying breath, thinking about the letter. The letter about Matthew Sugiyama. A letter about *me*.

"How can I help?"

"There was a bundle of papers, but I'm not sure which pile I put it in."

Crossing the shelter, I rummaged through the nearest pile. "Do you remember what it looked like?"

"No, but I had the distinct impression..."

"It's not here." I searched the next pile, my hands clumsy. Shaking a light woven blanket, a sheaf of papers tied with a leather thong slid out.

"I think I found it," I muttered. My fingers picked at the knot, trying to untangle it.

Josephine paused her search and watched me. "Do you need help?"

"Yes. No—I've got it." I tore open the sheaf.

"What is it?"

"Sheet music." I thumbed through the pages. "Only music. Are you sure you saw papers? Or was this it?"

She chewed her lip, and my heart sank.

"Papers," she said finally. "But unwrapped. They were... in something."

"Something?"

"Yes," she said. "Like a box."

"A box. I saw a box." I turned back to the first pile and pulled out a green wooden box. My fingers fumbled with the clasp.

Breathe, artist.

I closed my eyes, drawing a centering breath. When I opened them, the brass-colored latch sprang free, and I lifted the lid.

Papers. There were dozens of envelopes and scraps of loose paper.

Josephine peered into the box. "It could be any of them."

"Here," I said, handing her half before I could regret it.

Her face brightened, and she sat on her bedroll. "I'll give you the letter if I find it."

Of course she would.

I kneeled and looked through the box. The letters and loose papers didn't appear to be in any kind of order. I sorted the papers, placing the envelopes into one pile and the loose sheets into another.

The first pages included a list of what appeared to be song titles, a thank you note penned by a childish hand, and a short poem.

I glanced at Josephine. "We're looking for a letter."

"Yes, I'm sorting mine based on correspondence type."

"Good idea." I stacked the loose papers and then sorted them by appearance. Anything resembling a letter went into one pile, and everything else went into the other.

Finished, I evaluated the letter pile. It was smaller, but still substantial.

Josephine, engrossed in a letter of her own, tugged on her lip as she read.

I sighed and began scanning, my eyes flicking across squiggles that made no sense. I took a breath and willed myself to calm.

Most of the letters were invitations to visit communities and a few were personal correspondence. None of them mentioned art, an abbey, or me. After scanning dozens, my eyes ached, and I flopped backward onto my bedroll, watching the firelight flicker on the canvas above me.

"I've found something."

Josephine's voice cut into my heart.

She held up a cream-colored envelope. "The minstrel was in contact with a 'T' in these letters."

'T', like the letter sent to Victoria Oldham. It had to be the same scoundrel.

I dug through the stack of envelopes and separated the cream-colored ones.

The paper inside was smooth and heavy.

"This too, listen. 'Thanks for the report, Gabriel. Your intelligence is helping the cause. I hope we can meet in Montpelier in the spring.' That's all it says."

"Did he sign it?"

"There's a 'T', but the rest of the name is a scrawl." I looked at the envelope, but there was nothing on it other than Gabriel Halden, C/O Community of Brighton.

She cleared her throat. "This one says, 'I've heard from R. Carter, and it's much as we suspected. Send me your formal request and the next six communities you plan to attend. I'll forward the response.' Hmm, I wonder if he did?"

I tore into the next envelope. "Listen to this. 'Under no circumstances. I do not know how many revivals we have sent. I'm sorry to hear about Elijah.' Do you think Elijah is the donkey?"

"No, this creature seems fit and hale. Do you have any more?"

I opened and read the last letter aloud without scanning it first. "This says, 'Gabriel, we must stop him. Under no circumstances can he be allowed to find them...' Josephine, this is it!"

My groin tightened and armpits tingled as adrenaline flooded my body. I took a deep breath and continued.

"'... Even if it means abandoning your mission. Mishaps, misfortunes, an accident—at all costs, we must induce him to settle. Even an Avalon Society community is acceptable. This is critical; you must not let Matthew learn more.' It's signed by the same 'T'."

I stared at Josephine.

She gazed back, eyes wide.

"This is about *me*." I shook the letter. "He instructed Gabriel to stop me from traveling."

Josephine chewed on her lip. "The letter could be about anyone. You don't even know if your family is still alive."

Her lips moved, but I couldn't process the words, didn't want to hear her doubts.

My heart thudded in my chest, hope blooming, feral and wild. I wanted to race into the night, howling with excitement. "But they are still alive, Josephine. The letter confirms it. 'T' wants to stop me from finding *them* at all costs!"

CHAPTER SIXTEEN

I coughed, wincing as my head throbbed in response.

Josephine blew her nose loudly, and I groaned.

"Sorry," she muttered.

Oxide took a jarring step, and I bit back an oath, feeling sorry for myself.

A week had passed since finding the minstrel's letters, and I'd grown increasingly wary, viewing each downed tree with suspicion.

Distrust tinged all encounters with the people we met. I no longer assumed invitations for hospitality were a simple trade for my art. Anyone could be part of 'T's' plan.

"You're being ridiculous," Josephine snapped between sneezes. "We should've stopped at the last holding."

"His denials about the minstrel traveling this route rang false."

"We aren't well. We need to get out of this weather and rest."

She was right. The drizzle had lasted a week, and everything was damp. My sinuses pounded with pressure, and I hadn't been able to smell anything for days.

"I can't accept hospitality without knowing if they're part of 'T's' plan."

"How will you ever know? How can any of us know what's in another's heart?"

I didn't answer her. I didn't *have* an answer for her. She was right; it was a choice. I could view everyone with suspicion, or I could assume everyone was innately good.

But was either stance correct? Wasn't it a *good* thing to trust my intuition?

Right now, accepting so-called hospitality sent my internal alarms clanging.

Betrayed by my ability to judge the character of the people I met, my stomach churned and jaw clenched whenever I thought about the letters. Moreover, my heart was raw, bitter about my total loss of faith in the world.

Pulling my collar tighter around my neck, I listened to the horses' hoof steps squish on the mossy road. A racking cough hit me, and I gasped for breath, trying to keep the tickle in my throat from igniting another spasm.

"Matthew, we need to stop. If you refuse to turn back for hospitality, at least help me find a place to set up camp."

"We shouldn't have stopped at the filling station."

"Oh, don't start on the poor man again. I'm sure he didn't intend to infect us. Infection and disease would be an iffy strategy for 'T' to slow you."

"I wasn't starting on him." My protest sounded feeble. To be fair, the thought *had* crossed my mind.

We rode for another hour through an endless thicket of scrubby, dripping trees before Josephine spotted a clearing.

"This clearing looks perfect. We're stopping before one of us falls off their horse."

I wanted to object, but I also didn't want to be the first one to fall off. Besides, my head was swimming.

"All right," I muttered. "If *you* need a rest."

Josephine snorted and slid off her chestnut. "Let's get the canvas up right away. I'm mad to get out of this damp."

We heaved the support lines over the nearest limbs and tugged the sodden canvas up over the ropes.

"You would think this would get easier with time," I groused.

"Don't complain; we're almost done," she panted.

I unsaddled the horses and dropped the tack into a heap in the corner. Tossing Josephine her bedroll, I said, "I don't want dinner." Fully clothed, I fell onto my bedding with a groan.

"Good, because I'm not up to cooking," Josephine said sleepily from her side of the shelter. "We should get a fire going, though."

"Mmm," I agreed.

I AWOKE TO THE COLD GRAY DAWN AND CHARCOAL'S NOSE ON MY neck. I lifted my head and sat up as a spasm in my chest triggered a fit of coughing.

"Drink water," said Josephine drowsily.

"I'd heat some, but we never started a fire."

Something was missing, and I looked around. "Josephine?"

"Mmm?"

"Where are the horses?"

She lifted her head. "What?"

I staggered to my feet. "I don't see them."

"They must be here. Are they in the trees?"

I scanned the meadow, stomach knotting. "No, they're not here."

"Didn't you hobble them?" Josephine sat up.

"Didn't I?" My head whipped around as I glared at her.

And then the world died. This day couldn't get any worse.

"Charcoal. Go get them."

The dog raced into the tree line and shortly after, branches snapped and cracked, the donkey trotting reluctantly into the clearing. He turned and shook his head at the growling dog. Charcoal feinted right, and the donkey stomped his front foot.

"Where are the others?" Swaying and unsteady, Josephine walked toward me.

"Charcoal, leave it. Get the horses," I said as clearly as I could through blocked sinuses.

The dog searched my face and swung his head from side to side.

"Oxide. Magnesium. Get the horses."

Charcoal wavered before turning and trotting toward the road.

Josephine groaned. "If they made it to the road, they could've wandered quite far."

"Charcoal's a good herder. Let's make breakfast while we wait," I said, trying to convince myself as much as her.

Josephine lurched sideways, and I motioned for her to sit. "Right. Perhaps we can manage a fire this morning."

I sipped tea, but had no appetite for the lumpy porridge we made. I kept watch for Charcoal, straining my ears for the welcome *clip-clop* of hooves on the pavement and scanning the bleak, dripping trees.

Around midday, we knew we wouldn't get the horses back early enough to break camp. At this rate, we'd never reach Rochester Depot.

Life had spiraled out of control since we'd found the blasted letters.

"Perhaps it's a blessing. We need to sleep," said Josephine from her bed.

"Hard to rest in this gusting wind," I complained. I slipped off my boots and crawled into my bedroll, head pounding.

———————

"COR, ADELAIDE, HERE THEY ARE."

"What?" I lifted my head, squinting.

The bright sun cast the man in silhouette.

"This one's still kicking. How's she?"

"She has a dandy of a fever, Ara. We should get them back."

"Back to where? Where did you come from?" I croaked as I scrambled out of my bed and struggled to my feet.

"Easy lad, easy." The one called Ara stepped under the canvas and steadied me. "Your little chap showed up at our holding two days ago. He rounded up your stock and stood waiting by the gate. I left it shut, figuring you'd be by soon enough, but after the second day, my Adelaide got worried. Your little man refused food and kept the horses as close to the gate as he could."

My head swam. *Two days?* Who were these people? Could 'T' have sent them? I wasn't sure I believed the man, but Charcoal had trusted these people. Besides, did we have a choice? We were ill; if we didn't accept help, we could get worse or even die.

He held my arm to steady me while I slipped my boots on.

"Ara, I'll need you here," said Adelaide.

"Here, lad, let me help you to the wagon."

"Is Josephine okay?" My voice cracked as I clambered into the wagon.

"My Adelaide has a real knack with a fever. She'll get her sorted."

I watched, weak and helpless, as Ara carried Josephine to the wagon.

She appeared pale and still. Too still.

"Josephine." The dizziness in my head wouldn't clear. I fought to think clearly, but my thoughts scattered as soon as I reached for them.

Ara's horses stood quietly in their harnesses, and Charcoal held the donkey next to them.

"Lay back, lad. You rest."

"Our things." I hated the weakness in my voice and feeling vulnerable before these strangers.

"It's all right. We'll bring them with us."

I lay back and listened to the muffled *thud* and *thump* of our belongings being loaded onto the wagon. My hand crept toward Josephine's, and I held it as much to comfort myself as her.

The journey seemed to last forever, but when I next opened my eyes, I was staring at a plastered ceiling.

I sat up and examined the sparsely furnished room. Weak light struggled through the single cloudy pane. I was damp, my bedclothes and pajamas soaked with sweat. A glass of water stood on the side table, and I gulped it.

"Hello?" I waited, but no answer came. I crawled from the bed, pulling the quilt over my shoulders. As my hand grasped the doorknob, a horrible thought popped into my head. What if they had locked the door? Trapped me. Incarcerating me in a cell.

Gritting my teeth, I turned the knob and yanked the door.

It opened easily, its momentum knocking me backward. Dazed, I sprawled on the floor.

"Oh, my dear, are you all right?" A woman kneeled next to me, a worried look on her face.

I scraped my memory. "Adelaide?"

"You remember," she said, smiling. "I wasn't sure how much you took in; you were so ill. Here, let me help you up."

Adelaide was a small woman, but sturdy. Her hair was of indeterminate color, brown and gray like a mouse. Her eyes were sharp and her smile kind.

"If you're strong enough, come down to the kitchen. There's soup."

I nodded, ravenous.

After the simple ornamentation of my room, I found the dwelling disorienting.

They had clustered items on every horizontal surface. There were stuffed birds and small rodents, vases, and bowls of pebbles. An intricate collection of glass strung on lines cast patterns on the walls. Someone had painted the walls in a riot of hues. Tall racks of shelves filled with books, rocks, and jars of dried flowers sat everywhere, and they'd even mounted small ornaments haphazardly onto the walls.

"Is this your home?"

"We call it our treasure house," Adelaide said. "Here we are."

She sat me at a wooden table in the middle of her kitchen, fragrant with the smell of roasted chicken. At one end, a fire burned with a merry *crackle-pop*, and at the other stood an old-fashioned stove with a large simmering pot.

Adelaide spooned soup into a bright orange bowl and set it in front of me. "Here, this should suit. Let me get you a glass of water, too."

She brought a glass, then pulled out a chair and sat beside me. "Go ahead, eat as much as you can."

I nodded and sipped the broth, deep and rich with flecks of onion and carrot.

"Your friend is sleeping; her fever broke last night. I don't know what you two got up to, but you carried a nasty bug. I worked the better part of a week to get you both sorted."

I stared at her. "How long have we been here?"

"Four days."

"I'm sorry for the trouble." I set my bowl on the table.

Four days? Six, including the two days we'd waited for Charcoal to bring the horses back. Unbelievable; I hadn't realized we'd been so ill.

"We had plenty of help," said Adelaide. "The neighbors have been popping in to sit for a spell or cool you down. Changing flannels, bed baths. Everyone around here knows all about you."

My ears burned pink.

Changing flannels and bed baths!

"Ara has seen to your stock, but your little lad has been nearly inconsolable. Shall I fetch him?"

"Yes, please."

Charcoal's claws scrabbled on the wooden floor, and I barely had time to brace myself before he'd leaped into my lap.

Laughing, I tried to fend off his eager kisses. "It's all right, chap, it's okay. I'm fine."

Flooded with gratitude for Charcoal, Adelaide, and Ara, and the

116

kindness of their neighbors, I exhaled, feeling more like myself for the first time in a while.

"He is a proper little hero," said Adelaide, putting a dish of water on the floor for Charcoal. "Without him, I doubt we'd have found you."

CHAPTER SEVENTEEN

Troubled, I watched a solitary snowflake twist toward the ground. "We may not make it to Rochester Depot before the weather turns."

"Yes, I've seen several flakes too." Josephine shivered in the wool coat she'd taken from the dead minstrel. "We need to pick somewhere to overwinter."

"I know." I clucked to Oxide to pick up the pace.

Josephine had needed a full week to recover. I didn't regret the time we spent with Ara and Adelaide; they'd restored our health and my faith in the goodness of people. In return, I'd painted shelves in every room; more places to display their treasures.

However, the delay had narrowed our traveling window.

Josephine grinned and urged her chestnut into a trot.

I made a kissing sound, and Oxide broke into a slow lope. The panniers bounced on top of Magnesium's packsaddle with a *thwack-thud*.

Donkey trotted on my left.

"We're in a three-and-a-half horse race!"

We jockeyed down the road, laughing as the horses, fresh after

118

their long rest, fought for their heads. My heart lifted as we raced, thrilled by the wind on my face and the knowledge we were finally making progress toward our destination. Too late, I heard Josephine's cry of warning.

"Look out!"

Rounding a bend, I struggled to keep my seat as Oxide slid on his back legs, trying to avoid an overturned cart. Magnesium, running behind us, hit Oxide in mid-stride. I lost a stirrup as Oxide wheeled, fighting to keep on his feet. For a sickening moment, I thought we'd fall in a tangle of flailing hooves. By the time Oxide stopped, I was halfway out of the saddle, dangling sideways.

"Are you all right?" Josephine shouted.

I nodded and wrapped my arms around Oxide's lathered neck, swinging to the ground on shaking legs.

Josephine jumped down and slid her hands down the chestnut's front legs before straightening and surveying the surrounding wreckage.

Personal items lay strewn across the road. Beyond the cart I'd almost hit, a half-dozen vehicles blocked the route. People scurried to pick up their belongings, shouting at each other.

A man ran toward us, his chest heaving with exertion. "I tried," the man wheezed. "I tried to warn you." He coughed and spat.

Josephine nodded. "We tried to stop, but we were traveling too fast."

"What happened here?" I asked, checking my horses for cuts and scrapes.

The man pressed his left hand on his ribs and gestured at the chaos. "My wife and I were traveling north. We found the fracas here at the crossroads, and they sent me to warn travelers coming from your direction. People are arguing, but I don't know them."

"Peter!" a woman wailed.

His head whipped around. "And then the world died," he muttered. Jerking his head in the cry's direction, he said, "My Kileen is expecting. Please excuse me."

He hurried away, and I looked at Josephine. "I'll secure the horses. Do you want to see if he needs help?"

Josephine nodded, handed me the chestnut's reins, and hurried after Peter.

I tied the horses to a stand of slender trees. Mine were breathing hard, so I loosened their girths. Josephine's chestnut looked as though she had hardly ridden him. He shied nervously from my touch, looking in the direction Josephine had gone. The donkey and dog stood together as if unsure whether they should stay with the horses or follow Josephine.

"Charcoal, stay. Watch them."

The dog whined, but stayed put.

I stopped to help a group of men push a wooden wagon back onto its wheels before wandering through the wreckage, looking for Josephine. Before I could find her, women tending to an elderly man with blood streaming down his face hailed me. Two wailing children clung to the blonde woman.

"Sir, we need water for this man."

"Yes." I hurried to retrieve a canteen and three wax pouches from my saddlebag.

The blonde smiled with gratitude when I returned. She wetted a cloth with the water I'd brought and cleaned the man's head wound.

I squatted and held out a wax pouch for each child. With enormous eyes, they watched me. When I pantomimed sucking on a pouch, the older child snatched one and bit into it with glee. Emboldened, the younger shyly accepted the second pouch.

"I'm Molly," said one woman. "You've made their day."

"Matthew. A sweet can turn my day around, too."

"What are you two eating?" the blonde asked her children.

"A bit of honey," I said, handing her the last wax pouch. Gesturing to the old man, I asked, "What happened?"

"He got thrown from the wagon when the horses reared," the third woman said tearfully.

"Were any of you hurt?"

"We weren't in their wagon," said Molly. "We were in the trap." She pointed at a small, closed, two-wheeled carriage parked on the side of the road.

"The pony ran away," one of the little ones said.

"What?" His mother looked up. "Typical."

"What's your pony look like?"

"He's a sturdy little dun with two white socks," said Molly.

"And his tongue sticks out. Like this." Two childish faces pantomimed a horse trying to free his tongue from a restrictive bit.

Grinning, I said, "I'll see if I can find where he's gone." I approached a group of men talking in low voices. "Someone has sent me to look for a wayward pony."

One man turned. "There are horses and mules scattered throughout these woods. Harnesses broke—"

"Or were cut," another interrupted.

"What, on purpose?" I asked.

The first man nodded grimly. "We have all manner of catastrophe here."

Josephine tugged on my arm.

"There you are."

With an apologetic wave at the men, she pulled me aside. "Kileen looks like she's about to give birth here on the road. Peter is trying to calm her."

"What do you think?"

"I think she needs to rest and not move. Peter said—" She stopped and squinted at me.

I waited.

"Peter thinks someone damaged their cart... *on purpose.*"

"These men say the same." I turned back to the men. "There are two more who think someone tampered with their cart."

"Why would anyone cause such mischief?" someone asked.

No one had an answer.

I gave Josephine a sidelong look, but she shook her head in warning. Nerves jangling, I swallowed, but my suspicions stuck in my throat.

"Were you all traveling in the same direction?" Josephine asked.

The men looked at each other and shook their heads. After some discussion, we discovered there were seven distinct groups, including Josephine and myself, traveling in different directions. We had four wounded adults, most of the travelers were missing horses, and they reported a good deal of damage.

"Does anyone know where the nearest community is?"

"I have a map," I said.

"I'll get it," Josephine said, slipping away. When she returned, we spread my map and huddled around it.

"We must be about here," Peter said, pointing at a crossroads.

"Look, there's a community," said another, pointing at the map.

"Not far," someone agreed.

"Can we retrieve the loose stock?" a woman asked.

There was a consensus, and a group of volunteers agreed to round up the wandering animals. I whistled for Charcoal and joined the hunt, hoping to find the wayward dun-colored pony. Within a quarter-hour of hiking through the woods, Charcoal found the escapee.

I examined the pony and found a deep gash on his shoulder and another on his neck. "You won't be pulling a cart today, my friend."

Leaves jumped with a *crackle-swish* as I led the limping pony back to my stock. First, I unsaddled Magnesium and gently placed my packsaddle on the pony. Next, I hitched Magnesium to the trap, tying the injured pony to the back of the vehicle.

"I've never taught my horse to drive, but I can lead him for you," I offered.

The children giggled at Charcoal, who wiggled while licking their sticky faces.

The able-bodied worked together to shift belongings and cobble together harnesses. Many horses and mules remained missing, so men picked up the traces or pushed wagons from behind. I loaned Oxide to the elderly man with the head injury once I was sure he could drive his wagon without falling.

We even conscripted Donkey to pull a small cart carrying an unconscious woman. I led the donkey with one hand and Magnesium with the other.

Josephine rode ahead to warn the community of the oncoming influx of travelers.

Our group traveled slowly, and the distance which should have taken a half-hour stretched to nearly two. We arrived, hollow-eyed with exhaustion.

The community members, warned by Josephine, were ready with pots of soup, bandages, and blankets.

"You're so kind," cried Molly as a woman pushed a bowl of steaming soup into her hands.

"Do not neglect to show hospitality to strangers, for thereby some have entertained angels unawares," a man's voice boomed.

The chatter ceased, and I turned toward the voice.

A strange tension rose and, beside me, Josephine went still.

The man walking through the crowd was wearing long dark robes, and he stopped to greet the community members and travelers. The people he greeted smiled back, though no one spoke.

He stopped in front of the kettle emitting parsley-sage steam, and in the same booming voice, he said, "Give me a full meal of that red soup, for I am overcome with need for food."

The smiling woman manning the kettle offered him a bowl.

He took an appreciative sniff and said, "Well, what are you all waiting for?"

The chatter resumed, and I lost sight of the man as a crowd enveloped him.

"Can we leave as soon as we've eaten?" asked Josephine.

My eyebrows rose. "I'm eager to continue, but we wouldn't get far before needing to set up camp. Surely, we can stay the night?"

When Josephine spoke, her voice was low. "One night."

Questions tumbled through my mind, but the men from the

crossroads invited me to join their circle, forestalling further conversation with Josephine. Joining them, I drank the vegetable-based broth, savory with turnips and coriander seeds. The soup warmed me and lifted my spirits.

I stood opposite the robed man, studying him as I finished my meal. He was of medium height and heavyset, with light hair, more gray than blond, combed neatly to one side. He was beardless, and his rounded pink face appeared smooth and unlined.

"Stay the night," he said. "Our small community could use visitors, and any who would like to stay longer are welcome. We relish company, and we learn much from everyone who passes through." He held up his hands at the chorus of gratitude.

"Are you the administrator?" asked a man.

"We have no administrator, but Preacher Goodwin runs our community," clarified someone. "He's a great one for organizing, guiding, and helping us find our way."

"You are most kind." Goodwin smiled. "Jessica, the soup was miraculous."

She blushed and collected our bowls.

"Please, stay as long as you wish," Goodwin continued. "Be it for a night, a week, the winter, or a lifetime, New Bethel welcomes you." He smiled, bowing before leaving.

"What a gracious man," said Peter.

I nodded.

"Are you staying?"

"One night. How's Kileen?"

Peter frowned. "Shaken and afraid of giving birth on the road. She wants to stay."

I nodded sympathetically. "After today, many will overwinter here."

"Tyrone is a leathersmith and has offered to fix our harnesses and riggings. Did you need yours mended? I noticed your lady was riding without her saddle."

"My lady? Oh, Josephine." I shook my head. "No, her saddle

needs more than a day's work, and we're eager to travel south before the weather turns."

Peter clapped my shoulder. "Well met, Matthew. If I don't see you before you go, farewell and remember us in your travels."

"Well met, Peter. I wish the best to you and yours."

By the time I'd settled the horses for the night, Josephine had retired into the women's tent.

I joined the men standing around the bonfire. Warming my hands, I listened to their conversation. Most were staying long enough to have their leather repaired and replace lost provisions.

"Lucky there was a community so near," a man said.

People murmured in agreement. The conversation returned to the circumstances of the day as they tried to sort out the order of arrival at the crossroads.

Josephine and I had been the last to arrive, and the old man whose wagon had overturned had been the first, but we couldn't sort out a logical timeline for the rest. Everything had happened at once.

A shiver ran up my back, and though I tried to remain engaged with the conversation, I couldn't help but wonder if the chaos had something to do with 'T'.

CHAPTER EIGHTEEN

Morning dawned bright and breathtakingly cold. I shivered and rubbed my hands together. They made a rasping sound, my skin dry and brittle. Our constant traveling was taking a toll on our bodies.

Josephine was brushing the horses at the far end of the field when I emerged from the men's tent.

My hands were stiff as I blew on them. "The sun has stopped delivering heat for the year."

With the snows fast approaching, our traveling options were dwindling by the day. The quicker we got back on the road, the better.

Josephine nodded. "The chill woke me too. Let's leave soon."

I studied her. Though she spoke calmly, her body language was hurried and agitated. "What's worrying you?"

She glanced at me, and her eyes flicked past me toward New Bethel. She returned to brushing Magnesium, whose lips quivered when she hit an itchy spot.

The horses exhaled great plumes of white into the frosty air.

"I'd feel better speaking after we're on the road," she said.

A coil of unease wound through my gut. Silent, I picked up a brush and worked to remove yesterday's sweat from Oxide's red coat. Josephine picked dried mud and stones from their hooves while I saddled them. I was attaching the second pannier to Magnesium's saddle when a *cling-clang* rang across the meadow.

"Was that a bell?"

Josephine shrugged and released the donkey's hind foot. After ensuring the horses were secure, we rejoined the others.

My frozen hands trembled as I accepted a mug of steaming tea. Joining the breakfast line, my stomach rumbled.

Jessica was manning the large kettle again, dishing out oatmeal with sizeable chunks of apple, dried blueberries, and chopped hazelnuts. She topped each bowl with a pat of butter and a drizzle of maple syrup, its scent hanging sweetly in the air.

By the time it was our turn, my hands were almost warm. I accepted my bowl with pleasure and gave my most winning smile to Jessica. After a pause, she winked and gave me a second drizzle of syrup.

Josephine scoffed. "You like your sweets."

"Are you planning to leave today?" Jessica asked, filling Josephine's bowl.

"Yes, we're in a hurry to reach Rochester Depot," I said.

Jessica bit her lip. "Then I'm sorry to ask."

"Ask what?" I blew on my spoon. The oatmeal was nutty and sticky with syrup, the butter melting into rivulets of gold.

"The woman you brought on the donkey cart hasn't woken up."

"How sad. No one at the crossroads knew her." Josephine lowered her bowl. "What did you want to ask?"

Jessica sighed and wiped her forehead with the back of her hand. "We don't have a healer here, and our limited nursing skills didn't do her much good last night. You're the only ones leaving, so I hoped you'd take her to a healer."

No healer? All communities have a healer.

"Is there one nearby?" Josephine asked.

Jessica shook her head. "I don't know. I've only been here for a few months. Funny"—she looked off into the distance—"our team spooked, and a harness broke, so we ended up here for help, too. Strange world. Will you take her?"

Josephine and I looked at each other. I knew what she was thinking; transporting the woman would significantly slow us.

Reluctant, I nodded. "But, we're leaving soon."

Jessica wiped her hands. "Kathy, take over for me?"

A slender woman slipped behind the kettle and took the ladle from Jessica.

Jessica said, "Bring the donkey, and I'll get Jasper to find the cart and harness you used yesterday. We'll meet you at the red building."

We wolfed our meal and bid farewell to the other travelers. A shivering lad harnessed the donkey while Jessica organized the loading of the unconscious woman. The woman didn't stir as they set her in the cart, securing her stretcher. Jessica placed a hamper of food next to the woman and tucked a quilt over the top of her.

"Farewell, Matthew and Josephine. Peace be with you. Try not to jostle her, and remember us in your travels."

Josephine hugged her. "Farewell, Jessica. Thank you for your hospitality."

"And the syrup," I added.

Jessica blushed and watched us leave, her smile wistful.

WE RODE SLOWLY, LETTING THE DONKEY PICK HIS OWN WAY over the rutted road.

The woman lay still, never uttering a word.

As the distance between ourselves and New Bethel grew, Josephine brightened.

I noticed the change. "Was someone in New Bethel unkind?" I pointed to the left side of my face.

Her hand fluttered to cover her scars, but she shook her head. "No, they seemed pleasant."

"I was uncomfortable around Goodwin."

"Me too."

"You reacted to his words. Did they have significance?"

"Yes. Did minstrels visit your abbey?"

Surprised by the change in subject, I nodded and swiveled to check the donkey hadn't fallen behind. "Many times."

Charcoal trotted next to the donkey, supervising the little animal.

"Do you recall hearing the story of Lot and the destruction of the City of Sodom?"

"City?" I asked, confused. "As in *Before*? Before the world died?"

"Yes, there's a fable about a pious man who lived in a great, wicked city. Two strangers arrived, and he offered them food and shelter and protected them from the others. The strangers saved the lives of the man, his wife, and his two daughters before raining blindness, death, and destruction upon the city."

"Cheerful tale. What does it have to do with Goodwin?"

Josephine gave me a quick look. "The fable is from a book called Genesis."

I waited.

"Genesis is the first tale in an anthology commonly referred to as the Bible."

"The Bible... As in the religious text from *Before*?"

Josephine nodded. "Goodwin quoted from it. Twice."

"How do you know?"

"Scholars read all the major religious texts from *Before*."

"Could Goodwin be a scholar?"

"Perhaps, though, the women called him a minstrel. But to quote from a religious text, and to pick *that* story..."

"What of it?"

"The City of Sodom was destroyed about four thousand years before the world died. Many religious people living *Before* believed the Bible to be truth and thought the world had returned to the same biblical state of sin."

"Sin?"

"Immoral acts breaking divine law. Vices, indecent sexual behaviors, homosexuality."

"They had laws prohibiting whom they could love?"

She shrugged. "Loosely."

"So, the people *Before* were acting wickedly, like the people of Sodom."

"Religious extremists thought so."

"How was the City of Sodom destroyed?"

"According to the fable, God's wrath rained fire and brimstone and destroyed them."

"Brimstone?"

Josephine nodded. "I'm not sure how to explain it. It was part of the torturous afterlife the wicked endured for eternity."

"The world died because of God's wrath?"

Josephine snorted. "Perhaps some thought so."

"Politics, Money, Power, Religion, and Greed. These are the things we never again need," I sang tunelessly.

"Quite."

"The verse bothered you."

"The quoting of a religious verse should disquiet any of us. I'm glad we've left New Bethel."

"Josephine, we establish communities with a minimum of an administrator and a healer, right?"

Josephine nodded absently.

"New Bethel had neither, making it what?"

She gave me a sharp look. "I don't know. Where's the next community?"

"Wakefield should be a day's ride. Maybe two days at this pace."

She glanced at the woman in the cart. "Can we hurry?"

"I don't know. The jostling may worsen if we speed up."

The hours and kilometers crept by, and Josephine seemed occupied with little to say. I silently named the colors of the trees and rocks we passed and thought about 'T' to distract myself from the grim truth.

If we didn't find a healer, the woman was going to die.

When we stopped for the night, I tried to spoon broth into the woman's mouth. We slept with the unconscious woman between us to keep her warm.

In the morning, the woman's color had faded.

Again, she drank none of the reheated broth. The day slipped past, and we stopped for a second night, meeting no one. The world felt vast and empty; even the birds had left, leaving no sounds other than the groaning cart tires, hoof steps, and squeaking leather. The departure of the birds meant the real cold was coming.

Our time was running out.

In the morning, we tried unsuccessfully to get liquid into the woman again. A sheen of ice glistened on the cracked pavement, further slowing our progress.

Grim-faced, we rode on through kilometers of empty forest, acutely aware of the hours passing.

CHAPTER NINETEEN

"**B**last," Josephine muttered. "Matthew, Magnesium is off."

"Whoa, easy." I stopped Oxide and twisted in my saddle to look at my packhorse.

The donkey's cart creaked to a stop.

"Magnesium may have thrown a shoe on his hind left."

Brilliant.

I dismounted and stretched, trying to ignore the twinges and aches.

Magnesium's foot was bare, and he stomped it when I let go of the leg.

I patted the horse. "Blast and double blast, you're right."

Josephine slid from the chestnut. "Ooh, it's been too long since we took a break." She rubbed her tailbone. "I need to get his saddle repaired before my spine rubs a hole in his."

"I guess I'm walking. Oxide can carry the packsaddle. Think we can put my saddle in the cart? How's she doing?"

Josephine leaned over the prone woman. "I don't think traveling is helping. How long has it been since we tried giving her some water?"

"I don't know. Breakfast, maybe? Here." I dug the canteen out of my saddlebag. Working quickly, I transferred the packsaddle to Oxide. Josephine's saddle was on top of the panniers, so I lugged Oxide's saddle to the cart.

The two-wheeled cart had three sides and a plank bottom. They'd laid the woman's stretcher in the middle of the narrow bed, with the hamper tucked on one side. I considered laying the saddle astride the cart's sidewall, but didn't want a swinging stirrup to bang against the outside of the cart or the woman. The donkey was too narrow to carry the heavy saddle.

"Let's put it on Fox," Josephine suggested.

"Fox?"

She stroked the chestnut's neck. "Charming, cunning, and cute. And he's the same rusty, red color."

"Burnt Sienna."

"I prefer Fox, and so does he. Don't you, sweet thing?"

The horse nuzzled her.

My brow furrowed. "Do you think he'll take a saddle?"

"Take the saddlebags off, and I'll get it done. He must learn to carry one, sometime."

I stowed the saddlebags in the cart and carried the saddle to Josephine.

She encouraged the horse to walk in quick circles around her. "I'll need a few hours," she said without taking her eyes off the horse.

I wanted to urge haste, but didn't think she'd appreciate the reminder.

While Josephine worked with her horse, I pulled our things from the panniers to take stock of our remaining supplies. Based on the map, I estimated we were still more than a week north of Rochester Depot and would not get far until we could find a blacksmith to re-shoe Magnesium.

Unless the snows held off, we would not make it to the depot.

When I looked up, Josephine was tightening the chestnut's girth. I held my breath, waiting for the horse to blow up, jump, or buck.

"Karl *did* saddle him," I called when nothing happened.

The horse splayed his legs and craned his neck to look at the saddle.

"No, I don't think so."

"But he didn't fight you."

"I prefer to work in partnership with a horse, not conflict." Josephine rubbed the chestnut's neck. "We're ready to go."

We led our horses on foot to let Fox get used to the weight and heft of the saddle.

Though I expected the horse to spook or startle as we walked, he remained serene.

"How did you learn to train horses?"

"I read books about equine training and behavior during my apprenticeship. There was a technique called 'gentling' practiced before the world died."

"The people from *Before* used horses? Why?"

She laughed. "The horse has always been significant to man."

"But they traveled in autocrafts and aircrafts."

"I think they maintained their connection with horses because of the relationship."

"Relationships are about an exchange of energy. Did the people from *Before* know?"

"In the days *Before*, people didn't understand how energy worked or flowed, but they instinctively understood they could transfer and alter it. They maintained simple relationships with pets and horses because they could easily strengthen those bonds, making them feel good. Sadly, they didn't learn to do the same for each other."

I sighed. "I'll never understand them."

"Have you met anyone you took an instant dislike to?"

"Yes. More since I started traveling."

"When you're traveling, it's easy to dismiss troublesome people because you'll never interact with them again."

"Right."

"What if you'd settled in Hamilton?"

I'd told her the full story about meeting Victoria Oldham in Hamilton while she was recuperating at Ara and Adelaide's holding. "I'd have spent more time with Victoria and made it my priority to understand her."

"Right. Eventually, your energies would have synced, and you'd have enjoyed spending time together."

"It worked at the abbey when there was friction."

"The people of *Before* lived estranged from each other. Instead of forming community with their neighbors, they often maintained relationships with people who lived far away."

"How backward. Who would you turn to if you needed help?"

"They relied on themselves, family, or paid for help. It made them a private, closed-off, and isolated people. Although they lived in great cities, they had difficulty with empathy and did not know how to relate to one another. I smell smoke."

Startled, I raised my eyes and scanned the treetops. "Right." I glanced at her. "Let's not mention who we are."

"Agreed. Our primary concern is finding a healer."

We met no one at the first two holdings we passed. At the third, a man working in the roadside ditch greeted us.

Josephine introduced us and asked for the nearest healer.

Seeing the unconscious woman, he put his left hand to his mouth and whistled. "I'll send my daughter Corinne ahead to warn Marvin," he said.

A girl of about fifteen approached at a trot. "Father?"

"Corinne, this is Matthew and Josephine. Saddle Mack, find Marvin, and let him know someone is transporting an injured woman to him."

She nodded and hurried down the drive.

"Thank you, Stowe. Marvin is the healer?" asked Josephine.

"Yes, in Wakefield."

"How far?" I asked.

"Not far. Maybe three-quarters of an hour."

I nodded and lifted my hand. "We best be on our way. Well met and farewell."

Stowe raised his hand. "Farewell, and remember us in your travels."

We'd passed the next bend when we heard the clatter of hooves behind us. Moving to the left, we let Corinne pass by in a full gallop. Roughly a half-hour passed before the *clackety-clack* of hoofbeats thundered toward us. I shouted a *heya*, and the hoofbeats slowed.

Rounding the bend at a moderate pace, Corinne slowed her horse and trotted toward us. "Whoa, Mack," she said, patting the sweaty horse. "Sorry, it took a while to find Marvin. He was birthing a baby."

"How far are we from Wakefield?"

"Minutes. The road bends, so you don't see it until you cross the bridge."

"Can you ride back with us?" Josephine asked.

"Yes, I'll show you right to Marvin."

I glanced at the donkey's cart. "Are you an apprentice in Wakefield?"

The girl shook her head. "I'm going to the next community over."

"What profession have you chosen?" asked Josephine.

"Administrator. There are two apprentices in Wakefield, but Sally, the administrator in Brookfield, has only one, and she'll graduate soon."

Josephine nodded. "Are you sorry to move so far?"

"Yes, but I'm excited to live in a community."

We rounded another bend, reaching the bridge.

Wakefield was a small collection of squat houses on a wide oxbow along the banks of a narrow river. Despite the moving water, the air smelled dank and fetid.

The community members, alerted by Corinne's earlier visit, were standing in groups clustered on the green. A small boy sitting on the bridge let out a whoop when he saw us.

"They're here, they're here!" he shouted, running toward the others.

By the time we pulled onto the green, the healer was present. He directed the men to pull the stretcher from the cart and lower the woman to the ground.

We introduced ourselves and watched as Marvin kneeled beside her, prying one eye open at a time. He checked the woman's pulse at the wrist, then pinched and prodded her hands and feet. He stroked her hair and hovered his hands above various sections of her body as if feeling for heat, his expression grim.

I recognized his expression.

Sure enough, Marvin sat back on his heels, sighing. "I can't help her. She's dehydrated and unresponsive."

I stifled a groan.

"Can't you do anything at all?" asked Josephine. "We've been traveling for days."

"Was she in this state the whole time?"

We nodded in unison.

Marvin tilted his head. "I could push fluids for the dehydration, but you still must take her to Brookfield."

"Brookfield has healers?"

"Yes, two, with apprentices. I'm on my own here," he said, his tone apologetic.

"How far is Brookfield?" I asked.

"An hour west," said a woman.

"Can we send a messenger to alert them?" Josephine asked.

A small man with long white hair stepped forward. "I can go, but I'll need a horse." After a brief discussion, they procured a horse, and the volunteer raced away.

"Should we give her fluids?" Josephine asked, her brow furrowed.

Marvin shook his head. "I don't think an hour will matter. What she needs is bed rest."

"Is there a blacksmith in Brookfield?" I asked.

"Yes, they're much larger than we are."

"We should make a start then."

Josephine nodded in agreement.

"Will you take messages to Brookfield for us?" a young man asked Josephine.

"Yes, but can you fetch them quickly?"

"I have them here," he replied with a shy smile, holding up a bundle of notes. "We often trade with Brookfield."

Josephine accepted the missives and tucked them next to the hamper.

What if the next healer couldn't help, either? Would we keep moving her until, what? She died?

I wished fervently we hadn't agreed to transport her. I'd barely figured out what to do with my own life and was now responsible for three. The weight of it pulled on my shoulders. I straightened quickly, hoping no one had noticed.

Now, I was almost sorry we hadn't mentioned my profession. I'd have readily traded my skills to transfer the responsibility for the woman to someone else.

They reloaded the woman's stretcher, and we pulled back onto the road. The community members shouted messages of luck and farewell at our departure. The small boy who had acted as sentry skipped along beside us, peppering the air with excited chatter until his mother called him back.

"Farewell," he cried, waving until we were out of sight. "Farewell!"

CHAPTER TWENTY

We arrived in Brookfield a quarter-hour earlier than expected, which made the journey feel short. A light snow had started, the flakes swirling through the air as the wind gusted.

Brookfield stood on a small rise overlooking a large lake. The green at its center was well-maintained, with small sheep pens on the north side and buildings on the west, south, and east. A wide, plank boardwalk separated the green from two-story buildings with steep, slate-covered roofs.

Beyond the buildings was a second green, descending toward a boardwalk connecting the lakeside buildings to a pier. Small boats bobbed on the lake, tied to a network of floating docks.

The healer's dwelling was on the southeast corner of the green, closest to the road. As in Wakefield, the Brookfield community members were waiting for us. The healer was a slim woman with long red hair, her coloring reminding me of Earl's, but the healer's energy was different—focused and intense.

"Nora Standish. Welcome to Brookfield." She conducted a brief examination, muttering while she worked. "What did Kwan say?"

"She was unresponsive, dehydrated, and he couldn't help."

"The poor man is covering too vast an area," said Nora. "Well, we can at least try to keep her comfortable."

"Comfortable? She won't recover?"

Nora shook her head. "Doubtful. I saw little during the reflex tests, and her pupils are unresponsive. How was she injured?"

All the work and worry, only to learn the woman wouldn't recover. I'd hoped she'd awaken, maybe even providing answers to what had happened at the crossroads.

"We don't know," said Josephine. "Distressed travelers found her."

"What kind of distress?" Nora asked, her eyes sharp. "Pathogenic?"

I shook my head. "Mechanical. Spooked stock and failed harnesses and riggings."

Nora stared at me. "All at the same time?"

"Yes." A shiver ran down my spine, and I blinked away a snowflake stuck to my eyelash.

"Strange. Let's move her inside before the weather gets worse," she said. "Brian, Kami, can you put her in the sunroom?"

A woman and a young man lifted the stretcher and climbed the steps onto a covered porch. A girl held the door open and followed them inside.

Nora turned back to us. "We'll work to keep her comfortable. I've seen many cases like this where the person lingered for weeks before slipping away. My wife, Kami, is also a healer, and we have two apprentices, so nursing a patient isn't the burden for us it would be for Marvin Kwan."

She turned and scanned the crowd. "Sally, a minute?"

A short, smiling woman approached. "Well met, Travelers. I'm Sally Park."

"The administrator?" Josephine asked.

"Well, yes." Sally peered through the glasses perched at the end of her nose. "Have we met?"

"No, but Corinne Viken assisted us in finding Marvin Kwan."

"Ah, yes," Sally said. "Corinne will be a significant addition to Brookfield. She's scheduled to come early next week and will celebrate Year's End with us. What are your plans?" she asked.

Josephine and I looked at each other.

I shrugged. "Before the accident, we were on our way to Rochester Depot."

Nora looked thoughtful. "How long ago?"

"Three days," I said, frowning as the snow thickened.

"Thank you. Please excuse me; I'll go help settle in..." She paused and arched her eyebrow in question.

My lip twitched. "We don't know her name. No one knew who she was."

"So," said Sally, "on good roads, Rochester Depot is a two- to-four day journey from here."

"We need a blacksmith first," I said.

"And a leathersmith, if you have one," Josephine added.

"You'll be here for a few days at least." Sally nodded, satisfied. "What are your professions?"

Josephine laughed. "You're very direct. I'm a scholar."

"Artist," I admitted.

"My, what illustrious guests," Sally said, grinning. "I have an empty single dwelling if you're... attached?"

Josephine's face flamed.

"We're not," I answered quickly. Too quickly. "But I'm happy to share if she is," I added feebly, avoiding Josephine's eyes. My skin prickled, but Josephine nodded, her face relaxed.

"You're welcome to use it while you're here," Sally said with a sharp nod. "If you decide to overwinter here, we welcome you for the season."

"Thank you."

Sally beamed. "Let me show you the dwelling. You can hitch your stock here on the railing."

As we tethered the horses, Sally continued, "We have livery

space at the blacksmith's workshop, and our leathersmith's shop is located in the darker blue building next to the yellow house. Your dwelling is on the lakeside. An engineer and her husband occupied it before they moved west. Here we are."

We stopped in front of a white, two-story building.

"It's plain, but I expect you could spruce it if you stay," she said, a speculative look on her face. "We have youngsters here who could use a winter of formal teaching," she added to Josephine. "There hasn't been a resident scholar in these parts for, oh, maybe five years or more?"

Josephine shivered as we entered the building. "It's colder in here than outside."

Sally nodded. "We don't heat the unoccupied dwellings. We turn off the plumbing, so it matters little if the temperature drops unexpectedly."

She rubbed her arms and stamped her feet. "There are two rooms on this level and a third bedroom upstairs. I've always liked this great room. The engineer turned it into her workshop, and her little ones were constantly inventing small things with the scraps and odds and ends she salvaged."

"Is there much salvage at Rochester Depot?" I asked, interested.

"Yes, and Ruth, the engineer, was a wizard with untangling the things she needed from the leftovers of *Before*. She'd even salvaged in Manhattan Depot," Sally said proudly. "She set up a system of generators too, so we have power for two hours every evening in the winter."

"We had evening power at the abbey, but I haven't seen it since."

"Where did you study?"

"In Maine, at Popham."

"Are you an Arcadian?"

I shook my head. "No, they sent me to the abbey very young."

"If this is suitable, I'll show you to the blacksmith's workshop."

We followed Sally outside.

The donkey and dog were standing morosely on the boardwalk,

waiting for us to reappear. When I stepped outside, the donkey heaved a bray of relief, his harness jangling.

"Please treat the dwelling as your own, and the dog is welcome. This fellow..." Sally squinted at the donkey.

"Will be fine in livery," I said.

Sally flashed a relieved smile and led us over the green. The grass was quickly turning white, and the air smelled of snow and smoke.

"Here we are. Canning? Canning, I have custom for you."

From within the shadows, a man's voice called, "Come on in, Sally."

"Actually, I'll leave them here for you," Sally called back. "I have arrangements to make." She turned back to us. "We often spend our evenings in the pub. Can I offer you supper there tonight? I'm sure our community members want introductions."

We nodded, and she hurried across the green, waving her hand above her head, whistling a merry tune.

"She's always whirling about. You get used to it."

A tall woman stepped out of the gloom, wearing a thick leather apron. She had a square face and light brown hair swept back into a ponytail. She was wearing a sleeveless red and brown plaid shirt, revealing heavily muscled arms.

"I'm Genevie Canning."

"Matthew Sugiyama."

"Josephine Pliny."

"Well met, Matthew and Josephine," Genevie said, wiping her hands on a grimy towel.

A tall man joined Genevie, wearing a matching scorched apron. He had a bald head, a goatee beard, and wore a black shirt with short-ened sleeves showing similarly muscled arms. He stood next to Genevie and crossed his arms, frowning.

"This is my husband, Whistler," she said, jerking her chin in his direction.

"Well met, Whistler," I said. "I need a blacksmith. My horse threw a shoe yesterday."

Whistler looked at me without speaking.

Josephine nudged my ribs. "I think Genevie is the blacksmith."

I blinked at Genevie, fighting the urge to further embarrass myself by babbling an apology. Heat crept up my neck.

Genevie winked at Josephine. "My husband is the baker." She turned to the frowning man. "Thanks for your help in shifting the scrap. I can handle the rest if you need to get back."

The man nodded once, curtly. Still frowning, he gave me a warning look and stalked across the green.

"Chatty fellow," I muttered.

"He usually is," agreed Genevie. "Can scarcely get a word in."

She ran her hands down Magnesium's forelegs, asking him to lift each. She then moved to his hind end and looked at his feet, taking longer with his left. "Packhorse?" she asked, inspecting the foot.

"How did you know?"

She released the foot and stood, patting Magnesium on the hip. "He wears his fronts more than his hinds. Horses naturally transfer their weight to the front feet unless corrected by a rider." She looked at me. "He has a quarter crack developing on his front right. How long are you planning to stay?"

I shrugged.

"Sally offered us a dwelling for the winter," said Josephine.

Genevie smiled and studied us. "Then you're not healers or administrators. We're full up there."

"Mmm," I agreed.

"Not a minstrel, either," continued Genevie.

"Why not?" asked Josephine.

Genevie ticked her fingers. "One, he's too pretty. Two, too reserved; a minstrel would have had a flock of community members flitting around them already." She turned to Josephine and examined her. "You're a scholar, and he's an artist. Am I right?"

"Yes!" gasped Josephine. "But how?"

"You hide your face, but your scars are old. It suggests you wouldn't have chosen a profession requiring you to be at the center of a crowd, so no minstrel or administrator. Similarly, you don't strike me as a craftsman interacting daily with community members. Sally wouldn't have invited you to stay if you were a healer, as we have two masters and two more in training. You don't walk with the swagger of an engineer, and you're traveling, so not a farmer. For a woman, it leaves a scholar."

Josephine blushed. "And him?"

Genevie looked at him. "Not a minstrel, administrator, farmer, or healer, for the reasons I've already said. Thus, artist."

"Why not a craftsman or engineer?" I challenged.

"Too pretty," Genevie said with a flat look.

We gaped at her.

"And also, there are paint smudges on your pannier bags."

I roared with laughter, and Josephine joined in. We howled, bellies heaving with the effort to breathe.

"Well met, Genevie," I gasped, trying to catch my breath.

The blacksmith chuckled, eyes flashing merrily as we attempted to compose ourselves. "Are you staying for the winter?"

Josephine and I looked at each other for a long moment, then nodded.

I waited for the panicked, trapped feeling to arise, but it never came. Instead, a strange calm fell around my shoulders, soft and comforting. The relief illustrated how much I'd worried about where to spend the winter.

Genevie beamed. "Well then, we'll talk turkey later. Let's get these fellows settled in," she said, motioning toward the horses. "I must insist on knowing their names; I refuse to play the hostess to strangers."

Josephine laughed. "This is Fox," she said, patting the chestnut. "He's green but a great friend already."

Genevie nodded. "Well, Fox, let's give you the center stall there." She pointed, and Josephine led her horse to the stall. "There's hay in the corner," Genevie called. "Give Fox a meal."

Genevie turned back. "Who's this handsome fellow?" she asked, stroking Magnesium's neck.

"This is Magnesium."

"Like the metal?"

My eyebrows rose. "How did you know—"

"Blacksmith," Genevie interrupted, pointing at her own chest. "Metals are kind of my thing."

I laughed. "Yes, but he's named for the pigment. Magnesium Green."

"Green? He looks blue to me."

My eyes crinkled at the corners, and I struggled not to smirk. "To create a color matching his coat, I'd use a combination of Payne's Gray and Magnesium Green."

"Ah. And the name Payne could have portended misfortune," said Genevie, with a twinkle in her eye.

Josephine, who had rejoined us, laughed. "Are you sure you aren't a scholar?"

Genevie winked at her. "The day is short; who knows what comes next? And what about this brute? What color are you?"

"Pigment," I corrected automatically. "He's Oxide, for Light Oxide Red."

"Okay, you can put Rusty here next to Fox, and Grass Stains can be at the end, next to the hay. A proper rainbow we're boarding at livery today."

Chuckling, I took my horses to their stalls to unsaddle.

"You can leave your tack here if you like," Genevie called.

A twinge of doubt ran through me as I inspected Magnesium's packsaddle. I'd hidden my sword in the spine. With Genevie's sharp eyes, would it remain hidden if I left my tack here?

"Thanks, Genevie, but I'll carry the tack to the dwelling. It needs a good cleaning, anyway."

Problem solved.

Upon seeing me over the stall wall, the donkey stepped forward for inspection.

"Ho ho! Who have we here?"

"Donkey," we chorused in unison.

"What? Are pigments reserved for only the noblest of creatures?" the blacksmith cried in a mocking voice.

"I haven't painted him yet," I called from the stall. "I won't know what to call him until I do."

Genevie snorted. "You are," she cocked her head to the side, considering, "a delightful shade of brownishgreyishyellowishblack. But it's a mouthful." She frowned.

"Brownishgreyishyellowishblack would be hard to call in warning," agreed Josephine.

"Or when needing to scold the chap."

"Or when explaining who got lost."

"Or who's for dinner."

At the last statement, the donkey raised his muzzle and gave Genevie a reproving look.

"I meant who's coming for dinner," she amended, looking guilty. "Don't donkeys have a sense of humor?" she mock-whispered to Josephine.

"It's never funny to think about being consumed," Josephine responded seriously.

The women stared at each other, and Josephine's lip twitched. The donkey chose the moment to draw in a squeaking and shuddering breath, braying loudly. The women lost it, laughing and sputtering, doubled over in mirth.

The donkey followed me to an empty stall with an air of injured pride I well understood.

CHAPTER TWENTY-ONE

Entering the pub with Genevie and Josephine was astonishing. They'd packed the room, but for once, I wasn't on display. Their warm smiles and greetings immediately made me feel at home, welcomed and accepted.

"Sally must have made the rounds!" Genevie shouted over the din. "I'm going to find Whistler."

"All right!" I yelled in response. Too late, I realized the noise within the room had died. "Dinner time?" I asked with a self-deprecating smile, bowing to the keeper behind the bar.

Someone laughed, and the chatter resumed. The people closest to the door crowded forward for introductions.

"I'm Aloysia Kevorkov, cheesemaker," said a short, blonde woman.

"Teja Hilty, toymaker. Well met!"

"Metallo Lefevre, carpenter. We're so pleased you're visiting."

"Well met, Artist Sugiyama and Scholar Pliny. Wilmer Meachum, glassmaker."

"Chimham Padgett, farmer. Well met!"

"Opaline DiNitto. I apprentice with Metallo."

We waded into the room, smiling, nodding, and introducing ourselves. I'd never lived in a community and wasn't sure how easily they'd accepted us as members. Winter would feel very long if I couldn't figure out how to sync energy with so many strangers.

"Oh good, there you are," said Sally. "We've turned on the heat in your dwelling, and the beds are being aired. We had little to get the larder stocked, so come back here for breakfast. How did you find Genevie?"

"We love her," said Josephine.

"She's a treasure, and Whistler's baking? Heaven. Is your stock squared away?"

"Yes, thanks," I said.

Sally tapped her chin. "You needed another introduction."

"The leathersmith," Josephine said.

"Utter worm hogger," Sally muttered. "Oh!" she exclaimed, seeing our surprised expressions. "I have a bad habit of, erm..."

"Colorful language?" Whistler suggested.

Sally laughed and slapped the large man. "It's one way to put it." Glancing around, she lowered her voice. "I haven't yet synced with Horam, our leathersmith."

"It takes time," said Josephine sympathetically.

"Yes, and I've only been at it for, oh, three years, I suppose," said Sally.   •

"You're busy," Whistler offered generously.

"Especially when Horam is around," Sally agreed. "Oh, pulsating wank sample, here he comes. Hullo, Horam. Well, must dash!"

I stifled a bark of laughter as she disappeared into the crowd. "She's a delight."

Whistler nodded, eyes crinkling.

"Sally?" Horam sniffed. "She's competent, I suppose." He looked at the three of us. "I'm Horam Minter, craftsman leathersmith."

I inclined my head toward him. "Matthew Sugiyama, artist. This is Josephine Pliny, scholar."

Horam gave a perfunctory nod in Josephine's direction. "Well met, well met. Are you overwintering?"

"Yes, Sally's offered us the vacant dwelling," I said, raising an eyebrow at Josephine.

"Wonderful! The community could use a few things." Horam nodded. "Come and see me if you need anything. I'm in the dark blue building." He paused and added unnecessarily, "You can ask anyone."

"Josephine needs her saddle mended," I said. "We'll visit you tomorrow."

"Wonderful!" He gave me a long look. "And who...?"

"We each have services to offer."

"Wonderful!" Horam boomed again. "I have many ideas. I was thinking—"

"Why don't I escort you to supper?" Whistler asked Josephine, providing his arm.

"Wonderful!" she said, mimicking Horam.

Whistler's eyes crinkled, and he drew her away.

"I have ideas," said Horam, not noticing Josephine's departure. "Surely, we'll come to a mutually beneficial agreement."

"Indubitably," I said, hoping to catch someone's, anyone's, eye.

"In what medium do you work?"

"Oils, primarily."

Nora and Kami entered the pub.

"Wonderful, wonderful! Oils are simply delightful."

"Have you seen much art?"

"No, ah, but then who has? Though one hears about limitations posed by sculptors."

I didn't know what he meant. "Please excuse me. I need to ask Nora about the woman we brought."

Horam nodded and continued as though I hadn't spoken. "Now, I've heard watercolors can be nice. Very nice."

I excused myself and slipped away, not sure Horam noticed. I shook my head and smiled, making my way toward the healers standing at the bar.

"Well met, Nora," I said.

She smiled in greeting. "No change in the patient."

"Yes, I was afraid so." I leaned forward and admitted, "I needed an escape."

"Oh?" She looked behind me. "You've met our *wonderful* leathersmith."

"Yes, and I'll get to spend a great deal of time with him tomorrow."

"Then stick with us tonight." She patted my arm. "Kami, Matthew Sugiyama."

Kami bowed. "Well met. Sugiyama... Cedar Mountain?"

"Yes! I rarely meet other people of Japanese heritage."

"My grandfather was an artist as well."

"Oh?" I asked, surprised. "Where was he trained?"

"He grew up in an abbey in Virginia, but if you believe the family legend, he traveled to Japan after his education."

"Fascinating. They didn't press him to join a community at graduation?"

"Yes, and the way my father tells the story, they branded my grandfather a selfish graduate. We don't know if the traveling tale is true, but he spoke Japanese when his siblings and my great-grandparents couldn't. He taught me some vocabulary."

"I've never heard of anyone crossing the ocean in my lifetime."

"Me neither," said Nora. "At least not one who crossed and returned."

"In what medium did your grandfather work?"

"A type of Chinese watercolor he called ink and wash. Sometimes, he drew calligraphy, to ease communication between persons—"

"Or groups," Nora interjected.

Kami nodded. "Or groups." She rubbed the back of her head.

"There are a few pieces of his artwork in our dwelling if you'd like to see them."

"Yes," Nora agreed. "Do come. We'd be pleased to have you. Josephine, too."

"Delightful, thank you."

A hand landed heavily on my shoulder. "Hullo, Genevie."

She inclined her head. "Matthew. Nora, Kami. Have you had supper yet?"

We shook our heads.

"Follow me; the line is short." She turned and deftly wove through the crowd.

"The pub always serves some kind of soup or stew," said Kami from behind me as we followed the women. "I don't know if they even have anything other than bowls here."

I smiled, turning my head. "How often do you eat here?"

"What?"

"How often do you eat here?" I tried again, louder.

"Watch it, Artist," warned Genevie.

I turned my head back and stopped quickly, rocking up onto my toes. "Oh, pardon, Ms.—"

"Teja. Teja Hilty. We met earlier, but there was such a crowd of us. I'm the toymaker."

I nodded in recognition. "Yes, thank you. And thanks for the warning," I said to Genevie. "I would have smashed right into Teja."

"I don't think she'd have minded," chuckled Genevie.

"Oh!" Teja blushed and shook her head. "Filter, Genevie. Filter."

"Genevie has no filter," said Kami, grinning. She slid her arm around Nora's waist.

"Genevie used to win all the local debate competitions," Nora confided. "Nobody could match her quick wit."

"She has competition now," said Whistler, joining us. "This one could fight head-to-head with my wife."

Josephine smiled and raised her hand far above her head. "Not without a ladder."

"Well, with words then," Whistler amended. "Josephine knows her baked goods, too." He gave her an admiring smile.

"Whistler took me on a tour of his bakery," Josephine shared. "We sampled the breads and decided on this pepper loaf."

"Oh, good," said Nora. "We were about to get supper."

Teja took the loaf from Whistler and smelled it. "You bake a gorgeous loaf, Canning. This will go well with Paxton's stew."

"Is Paxton the keeper?" I asked.

"Brewer," said Kami. "We all take turns as keeper as part of our community labor hours."

"What are the labor requirements in Brookfield?" Josephine asked. "We forgot to ask."

"Ten hours a week, or fifty a month if you need to skip a week," said Teja, slicing the bread.

Nora passed out bowls. "Labor here is seasonal, though I suppose it's true for most communities." She filled the first bowl and handed it to Josephine, exchanging it for an empty one. "Year-round labor hours include milking, minding the children, building, and general maintenance." She handed the next bowl to Nora. "And being keeper here."

"Salvage runs," Kami offered. "Road and boardwalk maintenance." She gestured for me to take the next bowl.

"What's the seasonal work?" I tasted the stew, rich with beef marrow and onion. The bread was tangy, with a sponge-like texture and a kick of spice.

"We have an orchard to harvest in the fall," said Whistler, "and the community garden in the summer."

"There's canning too," said Nora, blowing on a spoonful of stew.

"Right, vegetables in the fall and fish in the spring," said Teja, handing around slices of bread.

"Oh, jockey butler and wrinkled old sock licker!"

I almost sprayed a mouthful of stew. I coughed and chuckled, wiping my mouth with the back of my hand. By the time we departed, my expletive vocabulary would have expanded beyond my wildest dreams.

"What, Sally?" asked Teja.

"I already ate, but I would have waited if I'd known Whistler was bringing a loaf of his pepper bread." She frowned at him. "It's my favorite."

Whistler paused with the spoon halfway to his mouth. "I already put a loaf on your counter."

"Do you want a slice, Sally?" Teja asked.

Sally peered at the toymaker through her spectacles. "Puke nut, why not?"

"Hey, Sally, you kiss your mother with that mouth?" asked Genevie.

"No, but I kissed *your* mother after she taught me how to swear," replied Sally tartly. She turned to Josephine. "Find me tomorrow, and I'll work you into the labor schedule." Taking a bite of the bread, she moaned. "Best loaf yet, Whistler."

He grinned. "You say it every time."

"Because you keep getting better... with practice." Sally winked at Nora.

The eight of us chatted well into the night, the conversation ranging from personal histories and amusing anecdotes to questions about why we were traveling. I kept my answers vague and let Josephine talk about the community she planned to join when she finished her errand for her mentor. Long after the lamps had been lit and most of the other community members had departed, Nora pointed at Josephine.

Josephine was swaying, her eyes closed. As I watched, her chin dropped toward her chest, and she slumped toward me.

I put my arm around her and smiled at my new friends. "Time to go. We've had a long day."

Sally patted my shoulder. "We're so pleased you're here. Don't forget, breakfast tomorrow. I believe Metallo is keeper."

"He makes a great omelet," said Genevie. "Maybe we should come for breakfast, too."

Whistler smiled at his wife as she tucked her arm through his.

"Sure, if you rise before noon." He turned toward me. "I'm up early and will bring over pastry around seven."

I nodded. "Looking forward to it. Thank you all for the welcome. I'll see you tomorrow."

Snow crunched beneath our feet as we walked to the dwelling. I was glad we weren't sleeping out-of-doors tonight. Charcoal's face popped into the window as we climbed the steps onto the porch.

"So happy we're home," Josephine murmured sleepily.

Home.

Could it be as easy as picking a place with people you liked and making a life for yourself? Could I live with never finding my birth family? Never finding out where I'd come from and why they'd abandoned me into the abbey system?

Could I be happy here?

CHAPTER TWENTY-TWO

"**B**last and double blast!" I dropped the hammer and sucked on my thumb. If we didn't finish the roof tonight, we'd start up here first thing in the morning during the coldest part of the day.

Opaline's grinning face popped over the crest of the roof where she'd been laying shingles. "You're not supposed to hold on to the nail after its point has bitten into the wood," she reminded me, brushing snow from her shoulders.

"Yes, Opaline. *Thank you*, Opaline." I looked at my thumb and winced. "Likely to lose the thumbnail."

"I don't think Metallo will let you off the hook for a boo-boo."

"Maybe Metallo should be up here in the wind, and I should smooth plaster inside," I said, cross. The endless rows of crooked shingles mocked my efforts. I looked around for the offending implement. "Have you seen my hammer?"

"It slid off the roof."

"Oh, triple blast!"

"You have a tool belt," she reminded me.

I gave her a flat stare, but she returned my look, unimpressed.

"Teenagers," I muttered, climbing down the ladder.

"I heard you!" she called.

"Don't you have shingling to do?" I asked pointedly.

Her face popped over the roof's edge. "Nope, I finished my side. I'm going to supervise *you*."

I stepped off the ladder and bent to pick up the hammer, brushing the snow from the handle. Spotting me through the window, Metallo stopped sanding and turned his palms up in question. I gave him a reassuring smile and climbed the ladder.

Opaline was sitting on the edge of the roof, one leg dangling into space and the other crossed over the first. "Your line is sliding again. Metallo will notice and make you start over."

"I'll fix it after I'm done," I growled.

Her eyes brightened. "With art?"

I nodded and returned to the shingle I'd been attempting to set. The nail had bent, so I used the claw of the hammer to pull it straight.

"It will bend again if you try to use it."

I sighed. "Pull it?"

"Yup. But put it in your pouch. If you toss it, we'll have to dig it out of the snow later. We save the scrap."

I nodded. "Must keep Genevie busy, hammering out all the bends."

Opaline giggled. "She melts them and pours new ones!"

I winked at the girl.

"Why are you helping with the building?" she asked.

"I promised Horam I'd help with his daughter's new dwelling."

"I don't think this is what he had in mind when he traded with you."

"Me neither. He turned a lovely shade of violet when he realized I'd be helping the construction crew instead of painting her a house."

"I wouldn't say you're *helping* with the construction..."

I pantomimed throwing my hammer at her.

"Why didn't you just paint the house? Wouldn't it be easier?"

I smiled and placed the shingle in place, tapping the nail before cautiously letting it go.

"Whale on it. One blow, straight in. Don't hit the shingle, or you'll shatter the slate."

I raised the hammer.

"Move your hand to the end of the handle. Put the hammer on the nail to judge the distance, then raise and strike without taking your eyes off the nail."

I followed her directions and struck the blow. "Yes!"

This construction project offered the first labor hours I'd ever performed. While the tasks weren't hard, the physical exertion was more than I'd expected.

Still, it was fun to learn new skills, and the project had given me a chance to develop relationships with Metallo and Opaline.

"Nice job, artist! You only have three hundred more to go."

I grinned triumphantly. "Never underestimate the talents of an artist, young lady. Watch this!" I swung the hammer at the next nail and drove it successfully.

"You've got it. So, why didn't you paint the house?"

My eyes crinkled, and I thought about how to explain it to her as I set the next shingle. "When Metallo readies to build a dwelling, does he mill the wood immediately?"

"Of course not. First, he looks at the site, then drafts what he plans to build."

"On one sheet of paper?"

"No. There are endless pages in a plan. Sheets for the foundation, the framing, the roof pitches, the details, the door, lots more. He's going to let me design the next one," she added. Pride shone in her eyes.

"Why does he use so many pages?"

Opaline looked puzzled. "Because a dwelling is more complicated than what you could put on a page." Her eyes brightened. "If you painted a house, would you only paint what's visible?"

I drove another nail and tested the shingle. "Yes, partly. It's one thing to improve a structure, or landscape, or—"

"Crooked roof?"

"Crooked roof." I pretended to scowl. "But if I painted a new three-dimensional structure, I'd essentially paint a facade attached to nothing. It would fall over."

"What about painting it from the top, as if you were in the sky looking down?"

I considered it. "With a roof or without?"

"With."

"I suppose then what you may end up with is a roof, laying on the ground."

"Oh! Because you couldn't see the walls from straight up!"

I grinned at her. "You're sharper than these nails."

She rolled her eyes. "Okay, then without a roof."

"Would you like it with a first story or a second?"

She nodded. "Right, and those wouldn't be sitting on a foundation." She brightened. "But you could paint a foundation!"

I nodded, and she beamed.

"You and Metallo had already finished the foundation, or I would have offered."

"Oh. Dang, a foundation is a lot of work." She picked at her fingernail. "So, no way to create a three-dimensional structure with art?"

"There is. If you're talking about something like a dwelling, a sculptor would be more useful than a painter."

"What if there's only a painter?"

"Well..." I attached three shingles. "It would be a matter of finding out what the parts of the house were. For instance, I could paint a foundation and then paint the first wall, anchored to the foundation and braced."

"Like we build!"

"Yes. Then, after the painting dried, I could paint the second wall, removing one brace. I'd repeat the process, but unlike carpenters, I couldn't finish the outside and then work indoors."

"Why not?"

"How would I paint the plumbing lines if something already covered the walls?" I asked. "And how about the interior walls? Doorways?"

Opaline sighed. "You could mess it up a hundred ways."

"Yes. It's faster to build things by hand." I caught the scent of roasting pork on the wind, and my stomach growled. People were walking toward the pub; Chimham must be the keeper tonight. I could almost taste the pork and the fatty, crispy skin.

"You can improve things once the structure exists."

"Yes."

We smiled at each other.

"Opaline? Matthew? Let's call it a day. It's cold out here," called Metallo.

"Now he notices?" I whispered to Opaline. "We told him it was cold at teatime."

She smiled and stepped onto the ladder. "He's probably at a stopping point and decided we were *all* done. But I'm sure he'll allow you to keep roofing. Oh, Metallo," she called in a sing-song voice.

"Don't you dare, you little—"

"Yeah?" Metallo stood at the bottom of the ladder, looking up.

"Can you steady the ladder? It's shaking, and our hands are cold," she asked sweetly, giving me a pert wink.

I grinned back and shoved the hammer through the loop on my tool belt. "Nice."

"Horam dropped off the mended saddle for Fox today." Josephine pulled a ceramic dish from the oven and set it on the stove to cool. She dampened the firebox and sliced the loaf of bread Whistler had left.

"We finished the roof on his daughter's house," I said, washing my hands in the sink.

The wind gusted, hurling icy pellets at the windows, making a *tink-tink* against the glass.

"Metallo finished the plaster, so we only have the floor left to install."

Charcoal leaned against the cabinets, looking mournful as I glanced at the smoking dish.

Josephine poked the dark brown kernels with a wooden spoon. "It's a barley casserole. Chimham said it was impossible to ruin."

"What's in it?" I asked, retrieving three bowls from the shelf.

"Barley, chicken, some of those wild mushrooms Corinne gathered, chicken stock... Wait, did I forget the stock?"

"Maybe it's supposed to be crunchy?"

Josephine scrutinized the dish. "Should I add water and let it sit for a few minutes?"

"Sure. Did we get butter today?"

"I didn't check the box."

I opened the kitchen door and lifted the lid on the wooden dairy box. "Butter and eggs," I called.

"Well, we won't starve," Josephine said, adding water to the casserole. Steam billowed from the dish, and she coughed, stepping back. "This is my last night of cooking for the week, so you're on for tomorrow."

I groaned. "Maybe Paxton can teach me to make a stew."

Josephine grinned. "Because the last three times he tried to teach you worked so well? You're a worse cook than I."

"That's enough from you," I said with mock severity. I set three bowls of soupy casserole on the table.

Charcoal jumped into his chair and sniffed his bowl.

"Besides, we always eat his stew for at least three days."

"Best three days of the week," Josephine agreed. She chewed a mouthful of the casserole. "It's edible if you don't bite down too hard."

Chuckling, I eyed the dog, who tentatively licked liquid from his bowl.

"Now that I have a saddle, I'll work with Fox. With luck, he'll be ready to ride in about a week."

I tried a spoonful from my bowl. The casserole was horrible, the burned-bone flavor coating my tongue. I rolled it in my mouth, trying to figure out how to spit it out without Josephine noticing.

"For what?" I mumbled.

Josephine tilted her head. "Rochester Depot? Are we still taking a trip to get supplies? I still need to search for records."

"I guess I forgot." I wiped my mouth, hoping Josephine hadn't seen me spit the casserole into my hand. "I've been so busy with the house construction. Never done labor hours before."

It bothered me I had forgotten about our planned foray to Rochester Depot. Though we no longer planned to overwinter in the depot, I needed art supplies to pay for my stay in Brookfield. I hadn't expected to find myself happy in a domestic situation, but liked Brookfield. I enjoyed the people and the routine of community life.

Josephine set her spoon down. "Have you changed your mind about traveling?"

I tore the spongy bread into small pieces and said nothing.

Josephine waited.

"No," I admitted. "I love it here, Josephine, but not enough to forget why I started my travels."

My words hung heavily in the air and mingled with the bitter stench of the burned casserole.

I loved it here. I hadn't known it until I'd said it out loud, but I felt closer to the people of Brookfield than I had to the students and masters with whom I'd lived for years at Popham Abbey. Although nothing would prevent me from leaving Brookfield in the spring, I would enjoy every moment of the time I had with them until then.

Sighing, I rubbed my jaw. Finding answers to who I was and where I had come from had to be my priority.

CHAPTER TWENTY-THREE

"Bless Sally for thinking ahead," murmured Josephine over her steaming mug of soup.

"I would've had enough supplies to last through the winter if Sally hadn't been so determined to squeeze every drop of pigment from my brushes," I groused.

"We'll be back soon, and you can continue to grace Brookfield with your illustrious illustrations," she said.

I snorted.

The deep drifts and bad roads had caused the normally two-day trip to Rochester Depot to stretch to three. I looked at the spires and tall shapes on the horizon. Despite loving life in Brookfield, I was excited to reach the depot. You never knew who you'd meet in one. There was always the possibility of a casual conversation leading me toward the answers I was seeking.

"We should be there in three hours, barring complications," I said, sitting on the snow. The cold numbed my backside and was creeping up my back, tightening the muscles. "Soup for breakfast is new."

Charcoal whined.

"Sorry, here's yours," I said, nestling a bowl in the snow.

The dog slurped his meal.

"Sorry, I didn't check the bag before dumping it in the boiling water. I suppose we'll have porridge for dinner one of these nights. How are the stores doing?"

I grinned. "We have meals for another eight days, plus the donation for the librarians. But, if it took three days to get here, we should plan for four to get back in case we have more weather."

"We've been lucky so far."

Nodding, I took a tentative sip of the soup. "Still hot," I said, making a face.

"We'll only have four days in the depot, instead of six."

"Right. Is it enough time?"

"Depends on whether the records are in a central location, or if they're scattered around. *If* they've maintained records at all."

I nodded and tested my soup again. The heat stung my tongue, but I relished the bright flavors of carrot, garlic, and sun-dried tomatoes. "Hopefully, Rochester Depot has a librarian who can help. The soup's cool enough to eat now."

"I'm excited. I've never been to a depot. Have you visited many?"

It was nice to know more about something than Josephine did. "A fair number. At the first one I visited, I learned in the years after the world died, fights for control stemmed from a misguided fear of scarcity."

The bits of rehydrated vegetables had slid from view, so I swirled my mug. "When the survivors realized there was no point in fighting over the mountains of supplies leftover from *Before*, their priorities shifted. The lives of the few people still present became more valuable than possessions. As subsequent generations were born and died, librarians prioritized saving data and knowledge not yet lost. Wouldn't it suggest Rochester had preserved their records?"

Josephine frowned. "I hope so. My master said they typically store records in the most structurally sound buildings."

The soup warmed my core. "In the depots I've visited, they store supplies and equipment in the warehouse. Warehouses contain everything from small hand tools for obscure tasks, to the indestructible snack foods of *Before*, to materials such as art supplies."

"The world *Before* was truly a land of plenty. Were the depots well organized?"

"Mmm. The administrators living in the depots were interesting. They're referred to as librarians, and they curate and ensure the supplies are safe from the weather."

Josephine finished the last of her soup and investigated her mug. "Do you think we can convince anyone to provide us with dried meals when we get back?"

I laughed. "We're eating better now than we did at the dwelling. Even Charcoal thinks so."

The dog wagged his stub.

The rest of the trip passed quickly. As we neared the outskirts of the depot, other roads joined the one we were following, widening into a vast, flat surface.

I shook my head. "How many people must these roads have provided passage to? What a marvel."

"There are countless mentions in the literature of blockages, or 'gridlock,' on roads such as these," Josephine said. "People of *Before* determined their quality of life by how much traffic they encountered daily."

"Traffic?"

"A generic term they used to describe the congestion of their transport systems."

"Why was congestion a bad thing? I meet the most interesting people while queuing."

"Good question. Maybe because they rode in individual autocrafts. Perhaps they weren't able to communicate between the vehicles."

"If I'd been an administrator back then, I would have asked engineers to build autocrafts to carry many people together."

"They did, using trains and streetcars to move people in and around the cities. And long autocrafts, too. But many preferred individual transportation."

"How strange they didn't all choose to travel together. They must have missed out on many stories and songs."

She grinned. "If it were easy to understand the people of *Before*, we wouldn't need scholars."

I laughed. "You're right. Look, there's the sign for the warehouse."

We moved to the right edge of the road and followed a curved, sloping ramp that disgorged us onto a long, straight path. Josephine shivered as we turned into it.

The tall structures along the path created a dense shade. Some were skeletal, providing little information, and others looked as if they had just been built, their mirrored glass windows intact after being abandoned for hundreds of years. The air felt dead and smelled of glass, snow, and metal. Our hoof steps crunched on the snow, deafening in the silent depot.

"Every time I'm in a depot, I'm surprised by how many people it would have taken to support such a large community," I said, breaking the silence.

"The sheer number of people living within this depot's footprint is staggering," Josephine agreed.

"How would an administrator, or team of administrators, coordinate the schedules of so many individuals? The scheduling of labor hours would have been a monumental effort."

"The people of *Before* paid for services," Josephine reminded me. "They didn't perform labor for their communities."

"Politics, Money, Power, Religion, and Greed," I muttered. "I always forget about money."

Following the warehouse signs, we turned at the next intersection. Here, the road was wider, and the buildings had shorter frontages. Large spires and towers stretched above us, but sat farther back from the street's edge, allowing more light to reach us.

"This is better," remarked Josephine.

We continued for a half-kilometer before I stopped Oxide. "Look." I pointed at a warehouse sign hanging over a tunnel entrance.

"An underground warehouse?" asked Josephine. "Is there such a thing?"

"I've never heard of one," I said. "Should I go in alone? You could wait here with the horses."

Josephine looked at the tunnel opening. Fox, picking up on her hesitation, shifted his weight.

"Yes, thanks. I'll wait here."

Accompanied by Charcoal, I walked to the tunnel's entrance.

"Heya!" I called. Hearing no reply, I turned, shrugged at Josephine, and stepped into the gloom. A few meters in, I stopped to let my eyes adjust to the dim light. The tunnel curved down and out of sight. The meager light neither strengthened nor dimmed as we descended, but the air grew noticeably warmer, and I loosened the top buttons on my overcoat.

"Heya!" I called again. Should I go back and get Josephine?

Charcoal barked frantically, and a heartbeat later, the ground shook.

CHAPTER TWENTY-FOUR

"Heya!" a deep voice shouted.

Charcoal continued to bark, and I hissed for him to quiet. "Heya!" I called back.

Walking forward, we rounded the last bend and stopped. A giant of a man strode toward us.

Beside me, Charcoal tensed.

The man stopped several meters away and raised his hand. "Well met, Traveler," he said, his voice full of gravel. He was broad through the shoulder and towered over me. He had thick hair the same color as his full russet beard, and his hooded eyes were intelligent.

"Well met. I'm Matthew Sugiyama."

"Ben Hensly," the man replied.

"Is this the way to the warehouse?"

Ben nodded, his eyes watchful.

"Are you a librarian?"

"No," he said.

I waited.

"Engineer," he said eventually.

"Artist," I replied.

His brows raised.

"Is a librarian available?"

The man nodded and turned to lead me farther down the tunnel.

I hesitated. "Is there somewhere inside to leave stock?"

Ben looked puzzled, but inclined his head.

"I'm traveling with someone," I said. "They're waiting up top with the horses. I should go get them."

Ben nodded once and leaned against the wall, saying nothing.

"I'll be right back." I wanted to ask him to wait, but his silence unnerved me. People were usually excited to meet an artist, and I didn't know what to say to someone so underwhelmed.

As I stepped out of the tunnel into the afternoon light, I sucked my breath in, shocked at the brightness of the day and the bite of the cold. After the mineral smell of the tunnel, the air outside smelled of rust and ice.

Josephine looked anxious.

"This is the warehouse entrance," I confirmed.

"Did you speak with a librarian?"

"No, but I met an engineer who is waiting for us. I hope. The tunnels are a maze." I took Oxide's reins from Josephine and walked toward the entrance.

"We can take the horses in?"

"They have stalls inside. Come on."

Josephine hesitated.

"They light the tunnel," I said to encourage her. "And it's much warmer inside. I'll take Fox for you."

Josephine nodded with a doubtful expression. "What was the engineer like?" she asked as we stepped into the tunnel.

"Succinct, and I don't think he liked me much." Ben's cold welcome bothered me. Maybe it had nothing to do with me; perhaps he disliked all strangers.

We descended the spiraling ramp side by side. The *clip-clop* of the horses' hooves bounced off the tunnel's walls. As we walked, I hunched my shoulders; the weight of the earth above us oppressive. However, the warmth was welcome.

To my relief, the engineer was waiting where I had left him. I opened my mouth to make the introductions, but he beat me to it.

"Ben Hensly, engineer, temporarily billeted at Rochester Depot. Well met, Lady." He beamed at Josephine.

He wasn't morose or stranger averse after all; he just hadn't liked me. Had I done something wrong? People warmed to me quickly, even when they didn't know I was an artist.

"Well met, Ben. Josephine Pliny, scholar." She presented the fair half of her face, letting her hair fall over her scars.

"May I escort you, Josephine?"

She nodded, smiling.

I followed with the horses, like an afterthought.

The tunnel leveled and stretched as far as I could see. It had smooth walls partially covered with tile, and adequate lighting from a series of glowing orangish bulbs. The ground was free of debris, and I hoped the horses wouldn't defecate.

The ground beneath our feet rumbled.

Alarmed, Charcoal barked, and the horses planted their feet, snorting.

Ben turned and waited.

"What was that?" whispered Josephine, looking fearful.

Ben's eyes crinkled at the corners. "Train."

"Train?" My surprise turned the question into a bark.

Ben nodded again. "Ready?"

When neither of us answered, he strode away. Josephine quickened her step to catch up.

My brain buzzed. *Train.*

"You've built a working train?" Josephine asked.

Ben nodded. "To connect the principal parts of the depot."

"How is it powered? Does it run on rails?"

Ben smiled at Josephine. "We salvaged all the generators we

could find and built a massive set of alternators in the middle of the depot."

I urged Oxide into a faster walk so I could listen.

"I'm afraid I don't know how alternators work," she confessed.

"At their heart, alternators are straightforward mechanical things; we place an iron core in the center of a coil of iron, wound around like a spring. This is the heart of the electromagnet. We add a copper ring around the iron heart. When the copper spins, it creates an electromagnetic field—what we call electricity."

"If it's easy, why don't more communities build alternators?" asked Josephine. "Everyone could have power."

Ben chuckled. "It would seem so, but there are two obstacles. First, you must generate spin. Second, you need to store the energy."

"How are you creating spin here?" I asked.

"They built Rochester Depot around geothermal vents. We're capturing the heat to turn the copper coil."

Josephine looked delighted. "Like a candle spinner?"

"A what?" I asked.

"You can put a pinwheel above a candle, and it will spin on its own, as long as the candle burns."

"Yes, a convection pinwheel," said Ben. "Our generators use the same principle."

"How are you storing the power you generate?" she asked.

"We're not storing the energy so much as we're deploying it to work for us. We've created electromagnets in the track above which the train floats."

"Like the maglev trains from *Before*?" Josephine asked. "Fascinating."

"Yes, we're using the same theory. However, we have only one power source, so we can only send the trains out from a central location."

"How do you get them back?"

Ben grinned. "That's what I'm working on. My idea is to have each train pull the other. We only have two lines, so it should work."

"I hope we haven't taken you from your work," said Josephine.

Ben shook his head.

"Can we ride it?" I asked. "We were speaking of trains and autocrafts on our way here."

Ben nodded. "We'll go there next. First, we'll stable your horses here."

We'd arrived at a crossroads in the tunnels. Ahead of us, the tunnel ended about a hundred meters past the intersection. They had outfitted the tunnel stub with stalls, each approximately four meters square, made from tubular steel bars. A concrete channel a meter high ran along the tunnel wall to the rear of each stall and provided fresh water. Stocky ponies occupying two of the stalls nickered in greeting.

A short stack of hay bales sat in the far corner, out of the reach of the stable occupants. Next to the hay sat a series of scuffed wooden saddle racks. Saddles sat on three of the seven racks.

Charcoal investigated the bales of hay before hopping up and laying down to supervise us.

I looked at the third saddle. It was large, with an ornate design on the seat. There was no sign of another horse in the stable, and I wondered who the saddle belonged to.

Josephine surveyed the stable and nodded with satisfaction. Working quickly, we unsaddled and bedded our horses.

I carried our saddles to the open racks, eying the large saddle. "Whose saddle is that?"

"Mine," said Ben.

"Is your horse stabled here?" I asked, looking at the stocky ponies doubtfully. Neither looked large enough to carry a man of Ben's size.

"No," said Ben.

I waited, but the engineer volunteered nothing else. Flustered, I let the matter drop.

"Ready!" Josephine exclaimed, patting Fox and smiling brightly.

I bet Ben would have told *her* why he had a saddle but no horse. Glowering at Ben's back, I followed them.

Charcoal jumped down from the hay and trotted next to me with a mulish expression matching my own.

My HEART POUNDED AS THE TRAIN HURTLED THROUGH THE tunnel. Josephine, eyes closed, clutched a metal bar. Ben put a hand on her shoulder to steady her as the train lurched to a stop.

She opened her eyes with a wince and said, "I'm fine, but need to get off and catch my breath."

Ben nodded and gestured toward the open door.

I drew a deep breath to steady myself and followed them off the train while Charcoal belly crawled next to me.

How fortunate the people from *Before* had been in the technologies they had available to them. The ride had been wild and exciting, but no one else appeared as affected as I was, so I kept my thoughts to myself.

Ben didn't need another reason to dislike me.

The doors slid shut, and the train glided away.

Puzzled, I turned to Ben. "This train is silent and doesn't rumble like the one we heard earlier."

Ben said nothing.

I tried again. "Why did we hear rumbling if they make no sound?"

"The trains glide, frictionless, in one direction, but to get them back, we drag them against the magnetic field."

"The noise is truly appalling. What's the solution?"

Ben rolled his shoulders. "We need to reverse the magnetic field."

"Ah, why you need copper," Josephine said.

"You catch on quickly. Here comes a librarian," said Ben.

The man walking toward us was in his mid-fifties, with a stoop and the pale skin of a person who spent most of their time indoors. He wore his gray hair braided tightly against his scalp in narrow rows. Each braid reached his mid-back, and tiny bells hung from several.

I raised my hand in greeting. "Well met, Librarian. I'm Matthew Sugiyama."

"Josephine Pliny."

"Well met, well met! My name is Mercer Dolby. I'm an administrator here at Rochester Depot. Engineer Hensly, the train is a marvel. I traveled in minutes what used to take a half-hour."

"Thank you, Librarian."

Mercer turned to us. "How can I direct you?"

"I'm looking for records," Josephine said. "Primarily records about equity and social justice, but also cultural festivities."

The librarian mulled over her request. "There are two places you should check. We've stored printed media in the Blue House, but research and personal journals are at the Annex. Unfortunately, the two locations are about as far from each other as they could be."

"I suppose I'll look at the printed media first. How do I get to the Blue House?"

The ground trembled under my feet. I peered down the dark expanse but saw nothing.

"You'll take Train One to the last stop," Mercer replied. "From there, go up the staircase and take a left at the first tunnel. We've clearly marked the entrance to the Blue House."

"Is there anyone there?"

"This time of day? No, probably not. Some past librarian cataloged much of the media though, and you'll find an index of where you can expect certain lines of knowledge."

Now, I could feel and hear the rumbling. From the dark came a team of stocky draft-like horses hitched to the train. As they passed, we covered our ears.

"How do the horses stand it?" Josephine shouted.

Mercer shook his head, unable to understand.

The train rounded the bend, and the sound faded.

I blinked several times. "How did you convince the horses to pull something so noisy?"

"I built them earplugs," Ben said with a sheepish smile. "They also wear a soft material on their shoes to reduce vibration."

"How long until the train comes back?" Josephine asked.

Ben rubbed his jaw. "Five minutes to run to the end, then fifteen to pull it back. It should be here in several minutes."

Josephine nodded.

Mercer turned to me. "What are you here for?"

I tugged on Charcoal's ear. "Art supplies."

"Ah, an artist! Well met." The librarian's eyes gleamed. "How long are you planning to stay?"

"Four days," said Josephine.

Disappointment flashed across Ben's face.

"Well, we can offer accommodation," said Mercer, bells ringing as he nodded. "We have a communal living quarter nearer the geothermal vent and plenty of space."

"Delightful," I said, hoping I didn't sound sarcastic. I wasn't sure how comfortable I was with living and sleeping underground.

At least *Mercer* was friendly.

"Good. I believe we have art supplies, but I'm afraid the difficulty will be in retrieving them."

"How so?"

"Our main supply warehouse is a large, partially subterranean structure. Most of our goods are retrievable via a network of platforms and catwalks built over the years. They kept the more specialized supplies much higher up. At one time, they were accessible by stairs. The stairs have long since fallen, and because we had few inquiries for the supplies stored at the Crown, no one has bothered to repair or replace them."

I nodded, thoughtful. If I couldn't reach the supplies, I'd have trouble traveling in the spring. Maybe I could repair the stairs. "How long ago did they fall?"

Mercer cleared his throat. "About a hundred years before I was born."

"Ah."

"I'll come," rumbled Ben. "I've studied various types of lifts. Maybe I can help."

"Thank you." Was he warming to me?

"Here comes the train," said Josephine.

I squeezed her shoulder. "Are you feeling well enough to get back on?"

She nodded. "Yes. I was queasy at first, but I'm better."

The train glided to a stop in front of us, and the doors slid open. We stepped in and took hold of the metal bars. From somewhere came a hollow *boom*.

The librarian shrugged. "Sometimes the horses kick."

"The horses are riding the train?" Josephine asked with a delighted laugh.

"Yes." Mercer smiled. "How else could they pull the train back?"

"May I ride with them?"

"Please, be my guest. The driver for this line today is Kort Niva."

Josephine looked around for an exit. "How do I reach the front?"

"We'll get off at the next stop, and I'll hold the door so you can move to the front car," Ben offered.

Josephine thanked him with a quick smile.

I watched the tunnel walls flash by and wondered how it would have been to travel on a train full of people. When the doors opened, Ben stood in the doorway to prevent them from closing. Josephine gave him a small wave and hurried to the first car. She waved again before stepping into it.

Charcoal whined as Josephine disappeared, and I scratched his head, wishing she'd stayed with us.

"I'll spread the word about your arrival and organize bunks for you. See you at supper!" The librarian disappeared up the left staircase.

Ben watched the train slide away and stood staring in the train's direction after it was out of view.

"Ben?" I asked.

"Mmm." He continued to gaze down the track.

"So... what now?"

Ben walked to the staircase on the right without checking to see if I'd followed.

Charcoal and I trailed after the big man.

What had I'd gotten myself into? And why had Ben volunteered to help me reach the supplies I needed?

CHAPTER TWENTY-FIVE

Ben led us into a long room with a rounded ceiling. There were four pairs of tables spanning the length of the room, a stack of plates and glasses sitting at the end of each. Ben grabbed a plate and waited for me to follow suit before choosing a seat.

I sat across from him so I could watch what was going on.

Charcoal jumped onto the bench and leaned against me.

Ben studied us. "Lunch."

I nodded. I was hungry and in no hurry to get to the art supplies. Besides, this would give me a chance to get to know Ben better.

People filtered into the room in ones and twos. I watched them with interest, and several waved at Ben. They spread out across all four tables instead of clustering together in the custom of communal dining rooms. None came to our table for an introduction.

"Is this normal here?" I asked in a low voice.

Ben looked at me. "Normal?"

"Sitting so far apart."

Ben looked around and shrugged. "At lunch, I guess we do spread out."

"Is there any reason?"

Ben shook his head. "No, but it's often like this at depots."

"Matthew Sugiyama?"

My forehead wrinkled as I turned. "Yes?"

A plump woman with no pigment in her hair, skin, or eyes smiled at me. "I'm Mabel, from Crumstock."

I nodded. "Well met, Mabel."

She furrowed her colorless eyebrows and glanced at her companion. He was younger than me and wore a tailored overcoat of dark blue velvet.

He cleared his throat. "I'm Logan, also from Crumstock. *Crumstock*," he repeated.

I nodded again and scratched Charcoal's chest as he leaned against me.

"Crumstock, of the Avalon Society," said Mabel. The pitch of her voice had risen.

"Avalon Society," I repeated. "Sorry, I'm not familiar with it. Is it near?" I'd heard or seen the term somewhere, but I couldn't place why it seemed familiar.

Mabel and Logan flushed simultaneously, but it was more noticeable on her because of her extreme paleness. I looked at Ben, who had leaned back and crossed his arms.

"The Avalon Society," said Mabel in a clipped tone, "is a network of premier communities."

Logan put his hand on Mabel's arm. "Matthew, the Avalon Society is a tightly knit group of private communities. We strive to provide the very best to our residents."

He had the habit of enunciating hard consonants, his t's, and p's distracting. He leaned forward and waited.

I scrambled for something to say. "Sounds nice."

Logan beamed. "It is. We select community members through an application process, meaning we have the best craftsmen, healers, and such. Our scholars are well-traveled and highly informed."

"Well-traveled?"

"Yes, our scholars travel between the Avalon Society communities to share information and ideas. Our artists—"

"You have artists?"

"Yes, of course. We only invite the top student of each abbey, as you well know."

"Do I?"

"We invited you," said Mabel in a flat voice.

Another community invitation.

Why didn't anyone understand I had no intentions of joining a community? If Logan kept talking, I'd risk alienating Ben, and I needed his help to reach the art supplies.

"I'm sorry, I don't recall one." I dragged my fingertips on the underside of the table, feeling the rough and splintered wood. No one ever sanded the underside of a table.

Logan pursed his lips. "Ah, no wonder you didn't respond."

"I meant no disrespect. There were many invitations. I don't remember a Crum... Cromstick, did you say?"

"Crumstock," said Mabel, her nostrils flaring. She had turned a deep purple.

How would I paint a person with her coloring?

Beside me, Charcoal tensed.

"Mabel, could you find out when they're serving lunch?" asked Logan.

She nodded curtly and left.

"I'm sorry about Mabel," said Logan. "She takes great pride in being a resident of Crumstock. May I sit?"

"Please." I hoped Ben didn't mind the interruption.

Logan sat, nodded once at Ben, and turned back to me. "I don't think the invitation would have mentioned Crumstock. We have many communities. While all are wonderful, some have more advantages. I dare say they invited you to one of those."

"Your premier society has a hierarchy within its own communities?"

Logan laughed and spread his hands, palms up. "All of our

communities shine. Some, because of sense and situation, sparkle. I invite you to visit us. We'd love to show you what we're all about, and we're confident you'll join us after seeing what we offer."

"I'm overwintering in Brookfield."

"Right, Brookfield. You could stop in Newfane on the way back, near what used to be the community of Union. Less than a half-hour out of your way."

"I'll consider it and confer with my traveling companion."

"Companion? I wasn't aware you were traveling with anyone."

"Aware? Why, have you been watching me?" I stiffened. Had 'T' had sent him to distract me? Gabriel's letter flashed onto my mind's canvas.

The *letter* had mentioned the Avalon Society.

"Beg your pardon, poor choice of words," said Logan. "The librarian didn't mention you were part of a party."

"Yes, I'm traveling with a scholar." I waited for Logan to ask about Josephine, but he didn't. Although I'd grown up accustomed to the privilege and respect people gave artists, I hated elitism in all forms.

A lady with a blue apron carried a large tray into the room.

"I'll think about it, Logan. Lunch is here."

Logan nodded, his face expectant.

Why wouldn't he leave? I cleared my throat. "If you'll excuse us, we're going to eat, and then we have work to do."

"Yes, of course." Logan jumped up and bowed. "We'll be here for the next few days if you'd like to continue our conversation. If not, please consider stopping in Newfane. Their resident scholar, Alma Sanu, is impressive."

"Thank you." I watched Logan intercept Mabel, who'd followed the woman delivering lunch. They left without looking at us.

After they'd left, I shook my head and rolled my eyes at Ben. "His self-importance. Insufferable."

"Strike one," said Ben.

"I'm sorry they interrupted us."

"Strike two."

I grinned. "Are you going to pitch me something?"

Ben smiled back. "Lunch." He thanked the woman who'd brought a steaming bowl of pasta and a basket of bread.

I inhaled, my mouth watering, the scent of tomato and basil in the middle of winter intoxicating. I hoped I'd offend no one if I made a plate for Charcoal.

Ben passed me the bowl of pasta. "Dig in. It may not sparkle, but the food is good."

DULL AND DROWSY FROM LUNCH, I GAZED AT THE SOARING ceiling. "The Crown is up there?"

"And then the world died," Ben swore.

I nodded my head in agreement. The warehouse was cavernous—I estimated it to be over eighty meters long, thirty meters wide, and almost forty meters tall. The curved ceiling's ornamentation ran the length of the room. Massive granite columns supported the walls, and a long gallery ran above the columns.

The Crown.

If we couldn't figure out a way to reach the Crown, I wouldn't have enough art supplies in the spring to travel.

From our vantage on the second-story balcony, the many free-standing platforms appeared as if they'd sprouted at random, creating a giant maze. Swinging catwalks and ladders built between different levels of the platforms compounded the haphazard organization. Each platform level featured several rows of double-sided shelves.

A single central aisle on each platform provided access to the items stored on the shelves. The warehouse was dimly lit by grimy windows near the curve of the ceiling, and someone had strung a series of yellowish lights between the granite columns and platforms.

A pony-pulled cart rumbled down the far wall, and people moved through the network of walkways. A woman in a swirling red cloak raised her hand in our direction.

I waved back, feeling tiny. "This is incredible. I didn't know a warehouse could be this large."

Ben nodded. "Eudokia told me it's the largest warehouse left in New England, north of Manhattan Depot."

"Eudokia?"

"Another administrator."

My gaze wandered back up toward the Crown. "How many administrators are here?"

"I've met twelve, but I've only been here for three weeks."

"Are you salvaging for your community?"

Ben shrugged. "I'm between communities."

Curious.

If I knew him better, I would ask what it meant, but I didn't want to discuss my situation, so I let it drop. "What do you suggest?"

Ben gave me a speculative look. "How are you with heights?"

"Fine, I think. I recently piloted a flier built by an engineer."

"A flier, really? You should be fine."

"What are you thinking?"

"I've studied lifts and have one in mind."

"Is it technology from *Before*?"

"Yes, though the technology was obsolete long before the world died. The design for a dumbwaiter is from the Victorian era. Ironic."

"Dumbwaiter? Not a measure of your estimation... I hope."

Ben looked at me.

Charcoal swiveled his head back and forth between us.

Feeling awkward and ridiculous, I shifted my feet. "So..." I began.

Ben's broad smile split his face. "You're okay, Artist."

Intense relief flooded me as our energies synced. There was nothing better than clicking with someone—perhaps the reason I enjoyed meeting new people. Each new acquaintance was a potential confidant, helpmate, and friend.

Ben and I would remain in harmony now; no more awkwardness,

no more wondering about what he thought of me. "Back at you, Engineer."

Working together, we drew up plans for what Ben wanted to build. With surprising efficiency, an administrator named Bernard helped us find all but one component.

"I'm sorry, I don't think I've seen spare lumber in a long while," said Bernard. She wore a necklace festooned with tiny bells, like those I'd noticed attached to Administrator Dolby's braids.

"Do you have any cast-off lumber? Of any size?"

She frowned and chewed her lower lip. "There's a broken pallet in the hallway," she said, brightening.

"Perfect."

She led us to the refuse pile. "This is usually what we set aside to burn."

"It's useless," said Ben, eyeing the broken pallet.

"Let's carry it back anyway," I said, winking at the librarian.

She blushed and returned my smile. "Anything else?"

"We have what we need," Ben rumbled.

She nodded and wandered away.

Ben watched her go. "Do you always have this effect on women?"

I lifted the pallet. "Effect?"

Ben jerked his chin at the retreating librarian.

"Honestly, I've had so little interaction with women, I don't even know what's normal."

"No women?"

I shook my head. "All men at an abbey. Well, men and boys. Sometimes a woman would bring supplies of some sort, but she'd only interact with the Headmaster." After a moment, I shared, "We did occasionally have female models."

Ben raised his eyebrow in question.

"Some were nude," I admitted, my neck flushing, "but nude or clothed, they were inanimate. They held a pose and didn't move for an hour. During breaks, they didn't speak with us. A pity. Some were... attractive."

Ben snorted. "What about Josephine?"

I knit my eyebrows. "What about her?"

"Are you two...?" Ben raised his brow again.

"Together? No, not as a couple, though we live together."

Ben nodded, a satisfied smile on his face. "I'll need an hour to assemble this. Our next task is to figure out how to climb up to attach the lift."

"Where will we attach it?"

Ben pointed. "There, adjoining the arch. We'll need an anchor in the ceiling."

"Right, I understand."

Circuitously, I explored the cavernous room before returning to the pile of supplies we'd gathered. Retrieving charcoal from my saddlebags, I sketched the broken pallet. Using my art, I repaired the pallet, enlarging it into a solid platform.

When finished, I flipped the page and wandered back to the balcony to consider the easiest way to reach the crown. Ideas toyed on the edges of my imagination, but nothing solidified. I shook my head to clear it and sketched the warehouse. Task done, I gazed at the ceiling.

For me, a rope would suffice. However, we might need help to install the dumbwaiter, and a rope wouldn't be a practical way for multiple people to reach the ceiling.

I drummed my fingers along the left side of my jaw. The librarian said they wanted to control access to the crown, so a staircase wouldn't work. I paced on the balcony, studying the wall. A ladder? The thought of climbing a forty-meter ladder made me cringe.

Distracted, I watched a spider climb over the railing and continue up the wall. It marched methodically, shifting its center-of-gravity back and forth laterally as it climbed.

If only man could scale things as easily as a spider, think of the places we could go.

My smile dropped as Ben bellowed, "Artist!"

CHAPTER TWENTY-SIX

My pulse leaping, I scrambled to gather my scattered things and hurried down the stairs.

Ben was standing by the heap of supplies when I arrived. Speechless, he pointed at the wooden platform I'd improved.

"What?"

"This was a broken pallet," Ben accused.

"Right."

"Now it's a solid platform."

As if to prove Ben's point, Charcoal climbed onto the planks and sat down.

"Didn't we need it? Oh! Haven't you worked with an artist before? I'm an artist, and I improve things," I said, pantomiming sketching.

Ben blinked at me.

Move on, Artist.

"I've had an idea to reach the Crown. When I was a boy, we had an hour of free time after lunch, before afternoon classes started."

Ben waited, expressionless. I was rambling.

"The abbey where I studied, Popham, sits at the sea's edge off the

186

coast of Maine. For fun, we decided to climb the exterior wall. Each boy tried, in turn, to climb higher. A boy a couple of years younger than me was the first to make it to the roof's edge. Once he did, several of us ran up his line, and after we understood how to climb, we had competitions to get to the roof's edge and back down the quickest."

Ben had a strange look on his face, so I finished my thought in a rush. "We could climb the wall to reach the ceiling."

"What stone was the abbey made from?"

"Granite."

"This is marble."

"Yes?"

"It's smooth."

"Ah. Yes, but I alter it." I pulled out my sketch pad and flipped to the drawing I'd made of the wall. "I watched a spider crawl up a wall," I said as I sketched, "and realized two things. One, spiders don't climb straight up. They move upward with a slight lateral movement, shifting back and forth as they climb."

Ben gasped.

"Two, spiders use a safety rope. If they lose their footing, they swing gracefully from a web line they've attached." Finishing the improvement on the wall, I added small rings at two-meter intervals. "Like this."

Ben looked at the wall, his eyes narrowed.

The marble wall was no longer smooth. Irregular chunks jutted from the surface as though built by a poor stonemason. Ben backed up, bumping into the nearest supply platform.

I'd drawn the jutting stones in a zigzag shape up the wall, with discrete iron rings placed on the left side of the zigzag.

Ben stroked the wall thoughtfully and then turned. "Have we met?"

I shook my head.

"Have you heard of me?" Ben asked.

"No, why?"

Ben ignored my question and asked, "Do you know how to tie a bowline knot?"

Confounded, I shook my head for the third time.

Ben turned and sorted through the items we'd gathered for the lift. He stood, holding a three-meter length of rope. "Learn this knot before we climb." Ben handed me a rope, then held his piece of rope at shoulder length. He quickly tied a knot, and I mimicked his motions.

"Again."

I shook my knot apart, trying to remember what Ben had shown me. When I tried to dress the knot, the whole thing pulled apart.

"A knot like this, and no art supplies needed," Ben said.

Stung, I fought the urge to throw the rope at his smug face.

"Again."

After I'd mastered the knot, Ben transferred my rope to an anchored point on the storage platform and handed me a handkerchief to use as a blindfold. Arguing was fruitless, so I tied the blindfold.

"Tie the knot, now."

Without sight, the knot was difficult. I fumbled through the motions and lifted the blindfold to check my work. The rope was a mess, the knot clearly not the same neat bowline I'd been tying. It took three tries before I had a passable knot and another four before I could tie the knot without thinking.

Pulling off the blindfold, I tossed the handkerchief at Ben. "I own this knot."

Ben nodded and pushed away from the wall he'd been leaning against. "Can you add an anchor point to your drawing?"

"Yes."

Ben turned his blueprint over and roughly sketched what he was looking for. "We'll be connecting the webbing to this point and suspending the large pulley from the webbing. The anchor must look like this, and we'll bolt it to the ceiling with these long iron arms."

"All right, I understand. Something like this?" I drew the anchor Ben had described onto a fresh sheet of paper.

Ben examined it. "Yes, but this arm needs bracing with a bracket here."

I changed my sketch and turned the pad back to Ben for review.

"Very good."

I flipped back to the sketch I'd made of the wall. "Here?" I asked, pointing to a place on the sketched ceiling.

"Farther up."

I flipped back to the anchor diagram Ben had drawn and tore the sheet out of the pad. I closed my eyes to visualize the improvement, then drew. Ben stepped backward and craned his neck to watch the progress on the ceiling. People clapped when I'd finished; we'd attracted a crowd who gaped at us.

With a small smile, I snapped the sketchbook shut. In time, I'd learned to tie Ben's knot, but he'd never match my art skills.

Ben handed me a coil of rope. "Put this over your shoulder."

"Won't I need it to tie in?"

He shook his head. "You'll use this one for climbing. The coiled rope is for pulling up equipment once you reach the Crown. Here, you need a harness. Don't worry; I've knotted many." Seeing the skepticism on my face, he grinned. "Haven't you worked with an engineer before?"

I swallowed. "Climb?"

Ben waited.

I turned and faced the wall.

"Oh, do be careful!" called a worried female voice.

I turned. "I shall endeavor to do so, Administrator Bernard."

"Tamara. Tamara Bernard."

"Tamara."

With a deep breath, I reached for the first handhold.

Charcoal whined.

Climbing quickly, I reached the first ring and tied a bowline. I continued up and tied into the next two rings before pausing. I glanced down, stomach churning.

"Climb, Artist," Ben called.

I took two deep breaths and continued. The edges of the marble were sharp and scraped my fingers as I worked my way up the wall. The ninth ring was almost within grasp when my brain calculated my progress. Nine rings had to be nearly halfway, which meant eighteen meters off the ground. My left hand slipped, and I gasped.

Eighteen meters.

Without meaning to, I looked down, and the room tilted. Dizzy, I clung to the wall, breathing in shallow gasps.

"Artist, are you napping?" Ben called from below.

Way below; I was too high. Why did I think I could do this? Nausea rose, and I swallowed with difficulty.

"I think I'm stuck," I shouted, my voice high and frightened.

"Are you at the ring?"

"Yes, but I'm stuck!"

"Anchor yourself!" Ben shouted in a calm voice.

"I'm trying!" Panic rising, I could barely feel my fingers.

Charcoal barked with increased urgency.

"Close your eyes and breathe. Keep them closed and anchor yourself."

I trembled. Out of desperation, I closed my eyes and took four deep breaths. The spinning slowed and subsided. With my eyes still closed, I settled my weight on my feet, searching for the ring with my left hand. Once I found it, I drew the rope through the ring and tied it off. Opening my eyes, I was grateful to see the bowline knot tidy and well-ordered.

Thank you, Ben, for the blindfold.

I pushed upward on trembling legs. Climbing the rest of the wall, I reached the ledge and dragged myself over the railing, landing in a grateful heap on the floor. I popped back over the edge. "Nothing to it!" I shouted to my audience, though my legs were shaking.

Charcoal spun in a circle and yelped several times in a high-pitched tone.

Ben turned to the crowd. My breathing returned to normal as I watched him gesture to the people and pat my anxious dog. He turned to the wall and stretched a few times. With surprising speed, Ben climbed the wall, anchoring at every other ring. When he reached the top, I helped pull him onto the Crown.

"You're barely out of breath."

"I've climbed," Ben admitted. "I'm known for it, which is why I thought we'd met."

"Why didn't you go first?" I asked, narrowing my eyes.

Ben winked. "You needed confidence."

Despite myself, I laughed. "If you'd made it look easy, I might have found it impossible," I admitted. "What's next?"

"We haul gear," Ben replied.

Joining the ropes we'd carried, Ben anchored it to the top-most iron ring.

"Coming down!" Ben bellowed in warning.

The tiny figures on the ground moved out of the way as Ben tossed the rope. After the rope settled, they moved forward to secure the items Ben had requested. Working together, we hauled up the materials, wrestling the large wheel and two pulleys onto the ledge. Ben sent the rope back down and pulled up the next load on his own, webbing straps with iron rings attached.

"Webbing?"

"Webbing is stronger than most rope," Ben answered. He sent the rope down a last time and stood at the Crown's edge, looking at the anchor attached to the ceiling two meters away.

"How are we going to reach it?" I asked, glancing at the people far below.

"Options," said Ben.

"You want me to give you options?"

"Option one," Ben continued, as if I hadn't spoken, "we string a line to the anchor and rig a harness."

I shivered. "Option two?"

"We build a catwalk for access."

"Option three?"

"I toss you out there, and you grab it."

"What?"

"Option four," Ben continued, "I climb."

I cocked my head and looked at the curve of the ceiling. "Option five is to capture, train, and ride a dragon?"

"Option three it is," Ben deadpanned. "Unless you can draw me a trained dragon."

After talking it through, we combined options one and four. With surprising ease, we strung a line, attached a harness, and after showing me how to belay him, Ben swung out over the edge of the Crown with serene confidence. He attached the large wheel, then hooked the smaller pulleys to the anchor. Next, we hauled up the steel cable and strung it around the wheel and pulleys.

With practiced grace, Ben rappelled down the wall to organize the attachment of the lift to the cable.

After he reached the ground, I explored the supplies stored in the Crown. A thick layer of yellowed dust smelling of musty books covered everything.

At some point, Librarians had grouped similar objects, but no one had organized or cataloged the items. There were innumerable piles of boxes and cartons with hastily scribbled labels. Each heap seemed to correspond with a single item type.

Camera.

Pneumatic lines.

Electric Kitchen Appliances.

Telephones.

Computer Parts.

Art Supplies.

"Ah, here you are," I said, smiling.

"You've gone peculiar. The air must be thin up here."

I jumped and whirled, knocking over a box. A cloud of dust

OIL AND DUST

erupted, causing me to sneeze in quick repetition. Ben stood to the side of the aisle, leaning against a box labeled 'Wireless Mice' and watching me gasp.

I rubbed my nose. "Blast it, a man your size should make more noise when you move!"

"Should I ask to borrow bells?"

"Is it why the librarians wear the tiny ringers?"

Ben nodded. "Come. The lift is here, and I want to show you how it works. Also, this passenger refused to stay behind."

Ben stepped aside, and Charcoal smiled widely, looking pleased.

CHAPTER TWENTY-SEVEN

"What a triumph," I said, eager to convey the wonder of the lift to Josephine. What we'd accomplished was marvelous; who knew the limits of an artist-engineer team?

In the crowded dining room, Charcoal leaned against my leg under the table. This time, there were no empty seats, which meant neither Mabel nor Logan had corralled me for another Avalon Society pitch. With luck, I'd avoid them for the duration of our stay.

Josephine's eyes were warm. "You found what you needed?"

"Yes, I found boxes of art supplies. Tomorrow, I'll dig through the cartons and bins."

"I'll help," offered Tamara. "How many people can the lift carry?"

"As many as you can fit onto the platform," Ben assured her. "Plus, the wee chap," he said, pointing under the table.

"Is it difficult to pull up and down?" Josephine asked, pushing her plate away.

"Not at all," I said. I tore a sizeable chunk of the sourdough rye with my teeth, the bread chewy and nutty. "Threwealfort—"

"What?"

"If I may?" Ben asked.

I nodded, chewing.

Ben turned to Josephine and Tamara. "You turn a single large wheel to go up or down."

"What keeps the wheel from spinning and dropping the lift?" Tamara asked. "I don't know if I'm strong enough to hold it still."

"It's built with a load brake," said Ben. "Unless you turn the wheel, the lift won't move."

"I'd like to see it," said Josephine. "May I join you?"

"Yes. Are you coming?" I asked Ben. After syncing, working together had been fun, and I was eager to learn more about him. His energy reminded me of Popham.

"I'd like to, but I'm behind on my work," Ben said, grimacing. "Can we sup again tomorrow?"

"I'd welcome your company." I looked at Josephine, who nodded.

"What are you working on, Ben?" asked Tamara, nibbling on a giant drumstick.

"Salvaging copper wire. If I can't find enough, I won't be able to finish the train project and fulfill my promise to get the trains running."

"Did Administrator Rutter direct you to the old switching station?" asked Tamara.

Ben swiped the back of his head with his palm. "I don't believe so. He told me to check the Wu towers next—the three green-glass buildings near the park."

Tamara nodded. "I haven't explored the complex, so I don't know how much scavenging they have done. Mercer told me... Oh, there he is. Administrator Dolby?"

The older man turned and beamed when he saw who'd called him. "Administrator Bernard, I see you're taking care of our guests. How was dinner?"

"Very good, thank you, Administrator," said Josephine.

"Mercer, please," he chided. "How did your search in the Blue House go?"

"Slow," Josephine admitted. "I'm going back tomorrow."

"Perhaps I could find a free librarian," he said thoughtfully. "Would you welcome the company?"

"Yes, thanks."

"Good, good. How about you, Artist Sugiyama? Were you able to reach the Crown?"

"Yes, and Administrator Bernard has offered to help catalog the supplies tomorrow," I reported, wiping the turkey grease from my hands. "Terrific dinner."

"Wonderful! I've never been to the Crown myself. I suspect we have you to thank, Engineer Hensly?"

Ben ducked his head.

"With help from Artist Sugiyama," Tamara said, casting a smile toward me. "Administrator Dolby, Ben is salvaging copper wire. Do you think a switching station could be useful?"

Mercer tapped his jaw. "There are seven switching stations in Rochester Depot. The nearest is by the east tunnel."

Ben nodded.

"The one where the concrete fell last spring?" asked Tamara.

Mercer smiled. "Yes, the old parking structure. We salvaged much of the smaller pieces for foundation stones, but many were far too large for us to shift. You're welcome to use any of the copper you can extract."

Ben rubbed his head. "I'll look tomorrow. Thank you."

Mercer smiled and clapped his hands. "Now, I'd like to ask for a favor. We would appreciate a story at the fire tonight."

I smiled, about to decline when Ben said, "Delighted."

"You'll join us?" Tamara asked.

Josephine and I looked at each other with surprise.

Taciturn Ben, a storyteller?

"Wouldn't miss it for anything," I said, beaming.

"AND WHEN BEN MADE THE YOWLING MOOSE CRIES?" JOSEPHINE giggled. "I thought I'd never catch my breath!"

Nodding, I wiped my eyes. "I wouldn't have imagined a reticent man could tell tales in so many voices." Still chuckling, I gestured. "This way."

Tamara popped out from behind a stack of cartons. "Hullo! I think I've found what you're looking for!" She disappeared back behind the stack.

"Matthew"—Josephine drew on my arm—"take care. She's besotted."

"Tamara? With me?"

Josephine shook her head in mock exasperation. "You don't know the havoc your smiles can wreak." She patted my arm. "The view from here is incredible, but I must get back to the ground soon."

"Let me tell Tamara, so she doesn't feel stranded."

Josephine was resting her elbows on the railing and looking over the edge when I brought Tamara back.

"Oh, I'm sorry. I didn't mean to disturb your work," Josephine said to the librarian.

Tamara shook her head. "No, it's fine. The librarians met this morning, and we agreed no one stays in the Crown when the lift lowers."

Josephine tilted her head. "Makes sense."

I helped the women step into the lift. "Since we're all going down, perhaps we should wait for lunch before coming back up."

Tamara, turning the lift wheel, nodded. "They serve lunch around one, so we'll have an hour."

While Tamara wound us down, I assessed the warehouse. From this height, I could tell the platforms took up more space than they should. Maybe I could offer to rearrange them. Moving the platforms would be like moving gigantic chessmen on a board—an interesting artistic exercise. I hadn't worked on a subject so large, but theoretically, I could reshape anything I could paint or draw.

Not that I needed more work.

The librarians had given me a long list of projects they wanted me to consider in exchange for our room, board, and art supplies.

Crouching to scratch Charcoal's head, Josephine asked, "Is the switching station on the same line as the Blue House? If so, maybe I'll visit Ben before returning to my search. Can the kitchen provide a traveling meal?"

"Yes, if you don't mind missing the hot food. They always have cold meals prepared."

"It's a plan," I said. "First, the kitchens for a traveling meal for Josephine, then the train to visit Ben." It would give me a chance to see if Ben wanted to collaborate on the projects the librarians had suggested.

In the kitchens, we found prepared traveling lunches, including meals set aside for Ben's party. The kitchen staff gratefully crated the food when I offered to deliver it.

Stepping onto the train, I marveled at how quickly I'd become used to the convenience.

"Hullo, Ben," Josephine called when we reached the stop. "We've brought the lunch parcels."

Smiling men accepted their meals with thanks. The air smelled of ice and rust, and I realized I hadn't been outside since we'd arrived. Turning my collar up, I shivered. The clouds hung heavy and malevolent above us, and I wondered if a storm was coming. We were due to leave in two days.

"We should have come back for the hot meal," said Ben, gloomy.

"Not going well?" I asked. "No copper?"

"There's plenty of copper, but it's under a lot of rubble."

"Can't you strip out what's over there?" asked Josephine, pointing at two short, many-armed towers. Wires hung from them like weeping vines.

"The longer the strand, the better," Ben explained. "Each strand we splice decreases the efficiency of the wire."

Josephine nodded. "What rubble do you need to move?" She pushed a piece of concrete the size of a loaf of bread with her foot.

Charcoal investigated the chunk of material, suspicious.

Ben pointed behind us. "That's what we're trying to move."

We turned in unison.

"Oh," said Tamara.

It was an impossible task. The parking structure must have been over three levels tall before it had crumbled. Instead of falling and shattering, the structure had settled onto the switching station's metal skeleton. The top two decks, largely intact, rose from the ground at a forty-five-degree angle. Someone had chained a rusty bicycle frame to the steel cabling on the edges of the structure.

Fracture lines ran through the concrete where the structure's decks had encountered the switching station towers, giving the impression of a giant jigsaw puzzle, recently completed.

"We tried levering fractured pieces out, but the weight of the rest of the structure has them pinned."

"Is there anything left to try?" Tamara asked.

"Someone suggested setting charges with explosives on the far side of the structure on the theory the structure would settle back over its own foundation."

"Explosives?" Josephine asked. "Are there any left from *Before*?"

"Not that I'm aware of," Ben replied. "We've been testing other options, but we may need to abandon this site, which will require us to haul materials a longer distance." He nodded at the traveling meal Josephine held. "Are you eating with us?"

She smiled and shook her head. "I'm afraid I have my own shifting and digging to do at the Blue House. Speaking of, I should get at it."

The task in front of Ben was huge, which meant little to no chance to work with him on the projects the librarians had suggested. Sighing, I kicked a chunk of paving, and Charcoal's nails clicked on the pavement as he followed the rolling material. I'd been looking forward to collaborating with him.

"We should head back, too," I said to Tamara as my stomach rumbled. "We'll walk you back, Josephine."

Ben nodded, his face disappointed. "See you at dinner."

"I'll save you a seat," said Josephine.

Ben's eyes brightened.

"Looking forward to another of your tales," I called as I followed the women toward the station.

THE NEXT TWO DAYS DISAPPEARED IN A FLASH. WE breakfasted together each morning, and I spent the days working on improvements requested by the librarians. In the afternoons, I worked to reorganize the warehouse's storage platforms. After the evening meal, we lingered and listen to Ben's stories. Some were side-ripping funny, some were mournful and tragic, and some were disquieting or downright frightening.

Too soon, we reached our last evening in Rochester Depot.

"Are you sure you can't stay?" asked Eudokia again. "I've heard the weather may turn."

Josephine laughed. "It's been wonderful, but we must go before you charm us into staying forever."

I grinned in agreement. "I've enjoyed myself."

That I'd again found myself happy in a communal setting wasn't lost on me. Between my experiences in Brookfield and here, I'd learned I enjoyed community life.

Tamara blushed. "You have done marvelous work for us. We're in your debt."

Mercer nodded. "You've more than earned your keep. Please tell the people in Brookfield they have credit here should they need salvage or supplies."

Josephine stifled a yawn.

Ben stood. "I'll walk you to the bunks."

She nodded and smiled. "Eight tomorrow?" she asked me from across the table.

"Yes, meet you at the stables." She waved, and I watched them leave.

Charcoal leaned against my leg, and I reached down to scratch his head. "I haven't picked up the last set of supplies yet. Did you have time to finish cataloging the pigments?"

Tamara passed me her ledger. "Yes, this is everything I found."

I perused the list and nodded. "Are they laid out in the cabinets?"

"Yes, the ones you painted for us. Note what you take so I can revise the inventory."

"I'll go collect them. Shall I leave the ledger on the platform?"

"Yes, fine. I'm starting the next section tomorrow."

"Thank you again, Librarian Bernard," I said with a small bow.

She turned pinker and smiled back. "Farewell, Artist Sugiyama. Remember us in your travels."

Cranking the dumbwaiter to the Crown, I examined the changes I'd made to the warehouse. The platforms stood in a tidy grid with catwalks between them, making the storage and retrieval of supplies as easy as pushing a cart between sections.

Using Ben's dumbwaiter as a model, we'd painted similar lifts at each end of the platform network. There was now also space for the pony carts to haul materials between any of the platforms, instead of only along the far wall.

Charcoal lay down to wait while I gathered art supplies.

I replenished my pigments and tested two new brushes for flexibility.

An idea that had been teasing the edges of my mind during dinner solidified, and I pulled out a blank canvas, stretched, framed, and ready for paint.

"If this works," I said to the dog as I climbed onto the lift, "we'll soon have all three bedrooms filled in Brookfield."

CHAPTER TWENTY-EIGHT

Leaving Rochester Depot soon proved to have been a mistake.

After hours of gritting my teeth, my jaw ached. When I tried to relax, my teeth chattered so fiercely, the vibration drove me mad. My eyes little more than slits, I'd been leaning into the wind and breaking trail through the drifting snow for hours. With visibility at a meter or less, the only way I'd kept us on the road was to slide my foot under the snow along the edge of the paved surface. My thighs burned, and my back screamed as the wind shrieked and howled.

Oxide followed, with his forehead pressed into my back. At first, I'd tried to push him off, and he'd obey only until I turned around, then he used me as a human shield to protect his ears and eyes from the stinging snow. I gave up; I didn't have the energy to keep the horse off my back.

"Josephine?" I shouted into the wind. "Josephine!"

There was no response.

Fear balled in my gut. I whistled for Charcoal, comforted by the answering bark.

Stopping, I shouted Josephine's name again. Hearing nothing, I pivoted.

Oxide snorted as a blast of wind and ice hit his head. I patted his neck in apology and asked the horse to stand. I worked my way down his side, fumbling for the rope tied to the saddle horn. When the snow started, Josephine had suggested tying Fox to Oxide's saddle to prevent losing track of each other. I was glad I'd listened to her; the weight at the other end of the rope was reassuring. I planted my feet and pulled hand-over-hand on the rope until Fox's head appeared out of the swirling white.

"Josephine!" I shouted again.

"Here! Can you hear me?" she shouted back.

The relief flooding through me was temporary, replaced by the anxiety I'd been pushing away all afternoon. I maneuvered closer so I could see her.

Josephine sat hunched on Fox's back, wrapped in a heavy woolen blanket caked with snow and ice.

"Are you okay?"

"Yes!" The blanket shifted, and I saw her face. "We need to find shelter!"

"I know, but we'll never get a tarpaulin up in this wind. Can you remember any structures on the way to Rochester Depot?"

She shook her head, and fresh cracks appeared in the crusted snow on the blanket's surface. "I don't remember seeing much on the way. Are we close to the damaged bridge?"

I groaned. I'd forgotten about the bridge. How far had we traveled since leaving Rochester Depot? We'd set out early two days ago, hoping to arrive in Brookfield today. We'd made good time at first and even camped early yesterday when the first lazy flakes fell.

"I've lost track of time and distance," I shouted, "but I don't think we'll reach Brookfield today."

"It's likely around noon. My stomach's been griping for hours. We're not traveling over three kilometers an hour."

"Yes, no faster." I closed my eyes, picturing the map I'd updated before leaving Rochester Depot. "We must be near Union since we haven't reached the bridge. Do you remember anything about Union?"

"No. There weren't any buildings on the route we traveled."

I shivered. "I need to keep moving or I'll freeze. If memory serves, Union was some way off the primary route, so we must find the side road." I turned and worked my way back to the front. Oxide was standing with his nose nearly to the ground, ears folded tightly against his head. I gave a couple of gentle tugs on the lead, and he lifted his head with a weary sigh.

We continued picking our way through the swirling nightmare. I stumbled frequently, my feet catching on invisible obstacles under the snow. The day darkened too rapidly, increasing my worry.

Lost in misery, I plodded into the unceasing gale.

Distant barking broke through my haze, and I lifted my head, shifting my weight too fast. Adrenaline shot through me as I tripped and pitched forward, barely catching myself.

We'd reached the edge of a crossroads.

With effort, I corrected our course, turning west.

Charcoal appeared through the gloom, whining.

"I'm looking for a camp!" I shouted.

He turned and shuffled through the snow with his nose down.

I continued forward, scraping my foot against the edge of the hard surface. This road felt narrower and less maintained. The edges of the pavement had broken and buckled, making the edges treacherous. I switched Oxide's lead to my left hand to keep the horse closer to the center of the road as I continued to plow through the snow at the frayed edge.

We inched along in the deepening gloom. We needed to find shelter. If not... My mind wouldn't let me finish the thought.

As I shifted my weight to ease the burning ache in my left hip, Oxide stopped, jerking me backward.

Dazed, I lay in the snow. I needed a brief break.

A short rest and then I'd stand.

A WRACKING COUGH WOKE ME, AND I GRUMBLED, TRYING TO pull the shroud of unconsciousness back over me. I moved, seeking the softness of sleep.

The cold was bitter and so startling that sleep instantly became impossible. I opened my mouth to utter an oath, clamping it shut as the chattering of my teeth unnerved me.

My shivers turned violent, and I tried to sit.

"Blast!" I swore as my head collided with something hard.

I collapsed, and the icy world spun.

"Matthew, lie still." Josephine's voice shuddered from the dark.

Ignoring her warning, I groped around me. My hands slid over rough wood above my head, splinters tearing at them.

To my left was a strange object, hard, cold, and wet. To my right was a vibrating ball.

"And then the world died," I cried. "What's happening?"

"Be still, let me explain."

"Has someone buried me?" I moaned.

Icy fingers groped my face.

Terror seized me, and I wheezed in alarm.

The icy hand slapped me. Hard.

"Matthew!" Josephine's voice was sharp. "You're safe; I haven't buried you. We're in a building, and I dragged a wooden crate over us."

"Us? What do you mean us?"

"You're pounding on my foot," she snapped.

The anger in Josephine's voice quieted my confusion.

"Beg pardon," I whispered. "Blast!"

"What?"

"I bit my tongue."

"No wonder; our teeth are chattering hard enough to shatter them. Try clenching your jaw before you speak. Lie still. I'm tired."

The dense, spiky, fur-covered ball shuddered beside me.

"Charcoal?" I breathed into the dark.

The ball unwound, and the dog's breath warmed my hand.

With sudden clarity, I understood Josephine had wedged us beneath a wooden structure, and we were slowly freezing to death.

"Josephine," I said, remembering to grit my teeth.

Silence.

"Josephine!" I shook her foot.

"What?" came her voice, sleepy in the dark.

"We need to get warm."

"Mmm."

"Josephine! We need to get warm!"

"So says you," she murmured.

I shook her again.

"Let go, you brute!" Her voice was shrill.

"Good, you're awake. We need to warm up."

"How?" she asked, her voice drowsy. "Everything we have is wet."

"I'm going to push this crate up." I took a deep breath and shoved at the wood over my head before she could argue. Though the air under the crate had been frigid, the deep cold that washed over us was painful and frightening. It settled in my bones and smelled of ice and stone.

"Matthew!" Josephine yelped.

Without the crate, the darkness lightened. I reached down and hauled her to her feet.

"We need to build a fire. Where is the packsaddle?"

"We didn't bring it." Her voice quivered.

I shook my head to clear it. "Right. Where are our saddlebags?"

"On the horses. I thought they would be warmer if I left their saddles on." Her voice shook as she shivered.

I rubbed my numb hand briskly up and down her back. "Where are the horses?"

Josephine said nothing, and my heart sank.

Had she left them to die in the blizzard?

"B-b-behind you," she stuttered.

I squinted in the gloom. My arms outstretched, I took one step, then another.

Oxide nickered.

"There you are."

The horses stood side by side, head to tail, pressed tightly together. I patted Oxide's flank and dug into the nearest saddlebag. Rummaging through it in the dark, I had a moment of terror.

What if I've lost the flint?

My fingers closed around the small canvas sack. Heart lifting, I pulled it from the saddlebag and turned, rubbing my hands together vigorously.

"Josephine?"

"Here," she said.

"Were you able to see much when you brought us here? Can you describe the room?"

"It's long and narrow. I dragged you as far from the door as I could to keep us out of the wind."

I nodded, picturing the scene. "Go on. You're doing well."

After a pause, she continued. "There are high windows along this side, none on the other. The glass was missing from at least three. A wall separates the room about halfway back, but there are openings on both sides, so it's more like an interrupted space than two separated rooms."

I crept to the left with my arms outstretched. "Concrete walls?"

"The modular b-block they used *Before*."

"Any holes in the roof?"

"I don't remember. It worried me the roof could collapse under the snow, but we needed to get out of the wind. The ceilings are high," she added.

"How high?"

"I couldn't see them."

"We can chance a fire in here then. I have tinder. Where did you find the crate?"

"Under the eaves, near the front door. I remember other lumber too."

"I'll go scavenge. Come on, Charcoal."

The room got progressively colder, and the scream of the wind louder, as I moved toward the open doorway. Stepping outside, I searched for the pile of refuse Josephine had seen. Cautious, I patted the snow. With numb hands, I could easily cut myself on something sharp.

"There's too much snow to ask you to look for a stick," I muttered as the storm battered us.

Charcoal whined, pressing close to me for warmth.

My hand brushed something hard. Tugging, the crust of snow broke.

I pulled harder, and the object slipped free.

Unprepared for the sudden movement, I smashed my lip with the back of my hand.

"Blast!" The nauseating coppery tang of blood slid across my tongue as I sucked on my injured lip. "Here," I growled, handing the dog a milled plank. "Go give it to Josephine."

The dog shivered but didn't move.

I shrugged and pulled another plank loose from the drift. When I'd accrued six pieces of rough-hewn lumber, I tucked as many as I could under my left arm and dragged the longest back into the dark building.

"Josephine?" I called.

There was no response.

CHAPTER TWENTY-NINE

"Josephine," I called. My pulse raced, and a different chill ran down my spine. "Josephine. Josephine! Josephine!"

"H-h-here," her voice whispered from the dark.

"I found wood."

"B-b-build it in the c-c-crate."

"What? Why?"

"You can m-m-move the fire if n-needed."

My hands numb, I dragged the crate to the partial wall in the center of the room and stacked the wood I had gathered into a cradle shape. Shaking, I filled the center of the cradle with twists of bark fibers from the canvas sack. The flint made a *snick* as I struck it experimentally, hissing at the bright sparks.

"Mm-mm-magnesium," Josephine whispered.

Confused, I asked, "My horse? We didn't bring him."

"On the f-f-flint."

"Oh." I fingered the backing on the flint. She was right; it was magnesium.

With my knife, I scraped the blade against the back of the flint. I

209

couldn't see the magnesium flakes but heard them drop onto the wooden crate.

With luck, they were landing on the fibers in the center of the cradle.

When I thought I had enough, I sheathed the knife and turned the flint.

"I'm going to strike," I warned. Closing my eyes in a silent plea, I struck at the flint with the iron.

Nothing.

Striking again, I squinted as sparks flew from the flint, but they winked out before they landed. Swearing, I kneeled before striking the flint again. Bright sparks fell to the side of the tinder. I adjusted my hands and scraped the iron on the flint a half-dozen times.

Sparks rained, and several landed on the magnesium shavings. They flared a bright yellow-white and quickly caught the bark twists, but just as quickly, the small flames winked out.

"Here," said Josephine, handing me a flat disk and crowding closer. "B-beeswax."

I nodded and shaved off a few flakes of the wax, letting them fall near the bark. Again, I laboriously shaved magnesium, trying to pile it in the center of the remaining tinder.

"Is that enough?" Josephine asked, her voice shuddering.

"I'm afraid," I answered, continuing to shave magnesium.

Charcoal moaned, and though a tear spilled from my eye, I couldn't feel it track down my frozen face.

Please. Please.

I struck the flint.

No sparks.

Setting the flint and steel down, I rubbed my hands until they stung, desperate to regain feeling. I set my hand down to pick up the flint, but it wasn't where I'd left it.

Panicked, I groped in the dark.

"What? What's wrong?"

I said nothing, pawing for the flint.

"Matthew? I can hear your breathing! What's wrong?"

Grasping the tools, I shuddered. "Nothing. I'm striking the flint again."

This time, the sparks fell and ignited the magnesium. Translucent flakes of beeswax shivered before melting. Flames licked the puddled wax and crawled along the surface of the bark twists.

Breathless, I added slivers of kindling with shaking fingers. As the slivers caught, I laid thin sticks across the growing fire.

"H-here," said Josephine, handing me small pieces of crumbled wax. "I chew-chewed them off," she admitted when I looked at them.

Painstakingly, I placed the wax crumbs in a pile near the flames. Nothing happened, then the wax glistened before suddenly melting, releasing the scent of honey. Flames danced across the surface of the puddle, licking at the wooden crate beneath.

When it caught, Josephine cheered.

Charcoal squirmed between us, crowding as close to the fire as he could.

After feeling returned to my fingers and toes, my stomach clawed at me.

Josephine elected to cook while I tended the fire and fed the horses. We worked in harmony, occasionally catching the other's eye in the flickering firelight, and smiling. We were safe. As a team, we'd handled our crisis, emerging victorious.

"Do you mind if your bedroll smells like a horse?" I asked, unsaddling the horses.

"No, but they were frozen solid."

I unrolled the first and watched as a shard of ice fell off the far edge. "They've defrosted but need to dry."

With a murmur of apology, I tossed the first over Oxide's broad back. The horse jumped and snorted before returning to his meal. Gingerly, I put the second bedroll over Fox, who didn't seem to notice.

"I don't know how much they'll dry," I admitted, returning to the fire.

"They'll work better than a wooden crate," said Josephine, beaming. "Here."

The soup tasted heavenly, sweet and savory with carrots and barley. Best of all, it was warm. We ate in cheerful silence, listening to the *sizzle-pop* of the fire. By the time I'd finished my meal, I'd stopped shivering. Afterward, Josephine heated snow, and we sipped hot water and watched the fire flicker.

"We should have stayed at the depot," I said.

"I could have used another week," she agreed, shifting, stretching, and rubbing her back.

"Come, lean on me."

She scooted closer and settled against me with a sigh, warm and comforting against my chest.

Charcoal stood, turned several circles, and dropped, grumbling, onto her lap.

Josephine rested her head on my shoulder, and the tightness in my chest eased.

"Matthew," she said, caressing the dog's head, "can I ask a question?"

"Of course."

"Why have you never offered to..." She stopped.

"What?"

"Well, you've never offered to fix my face."

My brows knit. "Why would I?"

"My scars."

It hadn't occurred to me. "Your scars are part of you and tell your story."

"They make me different, and people treat me so. Perhaps with an improvement..."

"If you want me to paint your portrait without scars, I'll do it. But, Josephine," I said, pressing my cheek against her head, "it won't be an improvement. You're beautiful and memorable. Without the scars, you'll still be beautiful."

She craned her neck to look at me, a strange look on her face.

A tear spilled from her eye.

Wiping the tear, I kissed her forehead. Over the past months, I'd developed feelings for her, but brotherly, not romantic. In truth, I'd said nothing because I didn't want her to stop looking at me with admiration; I liked the view of myself I saw reflected in her eyes. Now, the question in her eyes disturbed me, and I pulled back.

"I'm going to flip the bedrolls," she said, scrambling to her feet.

Charcoal groaned and tottered to my side.

I patted the dog and watched her walk away. Had she seen what I'd been thinking? My skin prickled and itched as if it didn't fit. I rubbed at my wrist—a self-soothing habit I'd developed during childhood.

Charcoal sagged against me and slid down until his head was on my outstretched leg. He grumbled and fell asleep again.

I smiled at the dog and leaned my head against the wall. My eyes followed the sparks and smoke toward the ceiling, resting on an engraved design in the lintel above the open doorways. I took another sip of my water.

Tepid.

Pushing the complaining dog away, I stood and added boiling water to my mug.

"What are you looking at?" Josephine asked.

"There's a sword engraved on the lintels."

Josephine joined me. "*Excellentiam super omnia*. It's Latin."

"Meaning what?"

"Excellence above all... but I don't know what it means."

"Could it be an Arthurian reference?" I asked, adding a plank to the fire.

"Arthurian? Why?"

"This could be an Avalon Society building. If so, we're at the edge of Newfane."

CHAPTER THIRTY

I groaned without opening my eyes. My body ached, and my mouth tasted of ash. I cracked an eyelid, expecting to see a tarpaulin flapping above me, not a soot-darkened wooden ceiling. Confused, I glanced around the room, pausing at the sword etchings above the lintel.

The nightmare came crashing back.

The blizzard, the dark, the bone-crushing cold.

"Mmm," groaned Josephine.

I stood and laid my bedroll over her. Hoping to find the wink of embers, I kicked at the remnants of the fire. It was cold and dead, and we'd burned everything I'd pulled from the crusted snow.

Josephine's eyes opened.

"We can't start another fire. I'll see if I can find someone."

Josephine sat up. "Someone?"

"Newfane, remember? We could use a meal before we make the last push to Brookfield."

She rubbed her eyes. "Right. Let's all go; I don't want to be separated. What's it look like outside?"

214

Charcoal's nails clicked as he led me to the open doorway. The snow had piled in soft drifts and sparkled in the sunlight.

"It's not snowing anymore. Let's pack up."

We led the horses through the drifts, testing the ground. The snow was knee-deep, but light and fluffy.

Josephine laughed as Charcoal burrowed through the snow, snorting. "It's fine to ride in. Leg up?"

After I helped Josephine, I clambered onto Oxide.

He pinned his ears and turned his head toward me, his expression aggrieved.

"Sorry, boy. I'm not moving well today." Once astride, I looked at the building in which we'd sheltered. "It's under construction."

"Right. We owe Newfane an apology for the mess we made."

We rode for a half-hour before Charcoal pricked his ears and barked.

"What do you smell, chap? Bacon, I hope."

An answering bark from somewhere ahead lifted my spirits, and I urged Oxide into a faster walk. Rounding the next bend, a man waded through the snow toward us. Behind him, blocking the road, was an ornate iron gate.

"Heya!" he called.

"Heya! Is this Newfane?"

"So it is." The man said nothing, waiting.

"*Excellentiam super omnia*," said Josephine from behind me.

The man smiled. "*Etiam.* I'm Barker, the resident metalsmith."

"Is this your work?" I asked, gesturing at the gorgeous gate.

"So it is. Who are you here to see?"

I rubbed my jaw, trying to remember the name Logan had mentioned. "Your scholar, Elma Soona."

"Alma Sanu? She's not here."

"Mabel and Logan asked me to visit."

The man brightened. "Ah, from Crumstock. Good people."

"So..."

The man looked at me, then shook his finger. "You're Matthew Sugiyama."

I leaned back. "Yes."

"Why didn't you say so? Please, come in, come in." He unlatched the gate and swung it backward; it opened without a sound.

Josephine and I looked at each other and shrugged.

Barker closed the gate after us. "The center of the community is ahead."

Although I couldn't see the landscape under the blanket of snow, I had the distinct impression we were riding up a formal drive. They had evenly spaced the trees on either side, and by the shape of the snow, they were likely under-planted with shrubbery.

Josephine sighed. "Pretty."

"Very," I agreed.

We arrived at the edge of the snow-covered green and stopped the horses to admire the picture. Similar trees surrounded the space, and I had the impression there was a pond in the center. The buildings around the green were handsome in style and color.

A slim woman wearing a dark blue cloak waved to us. "Heya, Matthew."

I sighed. Barker must have signaled ahead somehow. Were artists so rare?

"Heya. This is my friend, Josephine."

"I'm Elaina, a healer. Can I offer you a hot meal?"

"Well met, Elaina. We'd welcome a meal." Dismounting, we handed the horses to a young man who appeared at Elaina's side.

She escorted us into the community. "We'll go to our inn for a meal, and I can give you a tour afterward if you'd like."

"Newfane is exquisite," said Josephine.

"Especially in the snow," Elaina agreed. "Newfane only became a part of the Avalon Society ten years ago, so we're not as well situated as most."

"According to whom?" I asked.

"Most of the Avalon Society members who have passed

216

through have been quick to find Newfane 'charming', which I believe means rustic and unfinished," she said with a small laugh.

"What would a..." My mind went blank.

"A more developed community offer?" Elaina asked, finishing my question.

I nodded.

"Our communities typically have an administrative building, a library, a school, and a meeting hall where guild members can gather."

"How wonderful," Josephine said.

"Yes. Here we are," said Elaina, pausing at a handsome door with wrought-iron detailing. "After you," she said, pushing it open.

I stepped inside and whistled. I was used to pubs and inns being friendly but dim places, full of scarred wooden furniture. While this room had plenty of wooden furniture, there was nothing rough or shabby about it.

Sunlight sparkled through a long wall of windows and glass-paned doors opening onto a patio overlooking the central green. The ornately carved furniture was heavily polished and gleamed in the light.

They'd laid the floor with red bricks in a charming herringbone pattern. Tall iron planters gracefully sported ferns and ornamental vines, the latter tumbling cheerfully down the sides.

A stone fireplace at the far end of the room warmed the space and perfumed the air with a spicy fragrance. A long, gleaming bar sat opposite the wall of windows.

I stepped up to the bar and stared.

A great number of paintings hung on the wall behind the bar.

"Matthew?" called Elaina softly.

I held up a hand to let her know I'd heard her and continued to inspect the nearest painting, an oil depicting a handsome autumnal scene full of russets, golds, and oranges.

"Who painted this?" I asked.

"One of our newest Avalon Society members," a deep voice answered.

I nodded. "Liang Zhen."

"Zhen? Weren't you traveling to visit him?" asked Josephine in a low voice.

I nodded.

"Yes, Liang Zhen," said the man approaching. "You trained at Popham Abbey?"

"Yes, I finished the term after Liang." I tilted my head, studying the composition. "He painted this purely for decoration."

The man standing beside me beamed. "Yes, art for the sake of *art*. Here at the Avalon Society, we provide our community members the time and space to create and perfect, for the pleasure of honing their craft. Won't you join us?" He gestured toward the table where Elaina stood.

"I'm Ricardo Vicente, the community's healer," he said.

"Oh?" I asked, glancing at Elaina.

"I'm also a healer, but focused on the emotional health of our members," she said.

I blinked and pulled out a chair for Josephine.

We nodded at the other guests who had joined us at the table. They murmured greetings and gave brief introductions. Although normally good with names, I forgot each as soon as the next person spoke. Healer Elaina, Healer Ricardo, administrator, craftsman, minstrel.

The cream of the community.

I couldn't help but compare their stilted manner with the warm reception we'd received from Brookfield.

A young man served plates of quiche and green salad to each of us, and I wanted to swoon at the heady smell of the quiche; ham, butter, and cheese. He set a basket of freshly baked rolls in the middle of the table.

"Is Liang here?" I asked, reaching for a roll.

"No," said Elaina with regret. "He stayed with us for a winter before traveling to one of our larger communities."

"He's in Florida," said the minstrel, a large woman with fair skin and deep-set eyes crackling with energy.

I nodded, tearing the roll into small pieces.

Charcoal crowded close and nosed me for a bite.

I fed him pieces under the table. What would the baker think of feeding his 'craft' to a dog?

"Now," said Ricardo, "we're here to talk about you and your plans."

"My plans?" I asked. I glanced at Josephine, who was sipping tea.

"Yes," said the administrator, a thin and intense man with an interesting ochre skin tone. "You haven't chosen a community to settle in."

My head pounded. I didn't want to have this conversation, now or ever, yet here it was *again*. Appetite gone, I pushed a forkful of quiche around my plate and didn't answer.

"It would delight the Avalon Society to welcome you," Ricardo pressed. "Our communities would be honored by your consideration."

"What about my friends?" I asked. "Can they join, too?"

"The application process is lengthy," said the craftsman vaguely. She stopped as the administrator shot her a glance.

"As you've seen, the Avalon Society can offer amenities difficult to come by," Elaina paused and said delicately, "in other communities."

"What about Josephine?" I asked bluntly. "She's sitting right here."

The administrator gave me a pained smile. "Unfortunately, we only have permission to invite you," he said, nodding at Josephine.

Josephine looked unconcerned as she accepted another piece of quiche from the young man serving us. "This is delicious. Did you make it?"

"Yes, I'm the chef here at the inn. I'm pleased you like it."

I looked at my glass of water. The light from the windows caught in the facets of the heavy base, sending shards of rainbow-colored light skipping around the room. I took a sip.

Charcoal lifted his head from my thigh, watching me.

The sides of my tongue curled in response to the water, and I eagerly finished the glass. Lowering it, I looked at Elaina.

She had long, silky, dark hair curling around her like a shadow. Her dark eyes conveyed warmth and concern, and her skin was several shades darker than Bowman's, with a tint appearing more blue than Bowman's warm brown tones.

Why didn't I trust her? "I'd like water for my dog."

Elaina flinched, frowning. Glancing around the table, her brow smoothed. "I'll see to it."

Strangely, her conciliatory reaction to my rudeness was soothing. A heady sense of power flooded me, and my appetite returned. "When is the scholar returning?"

My question surprised everyone.

"Likely not until spring," said the minstrel tentatively. "Why?"

"I've heard she's well-traveled." I tasted the quiche, and it melted on my tongue, rich and savory, bursting with smokey ham.

"She is," nodded Ricardo. "She'll return as soon as she can. Traveling in the winter here..." He shook his head.

"So we found," Josephine agreed. "We took shelter last night in one of your buildings, out by the crossroad."

"One of our buildings?" Ricardo looked around the table.

"The piggery," said the administrator softly.

I choked on my quiche and smiled at Josephine. So much for the mess we'd left.

Charcoal lapped his water noisily, and several of the people at the table frowned at my dog. I put a sizeable chunk of quiche on my bread plate and placed it in front of him with a *clink*.

He wolfed down the eggs and smiled, his tail stub wiggling.

Finishing my breakfast, I pushed my chair back. "Thank you for your hospitality. I'll check back in a few months, or you can send word to me in Brookfield."

"On the matter of picking a community?" asked Ricardo.

"I'm not interested in deciding now. Thank you for the meal. Could someone point us toward the livery?"

"But this is the Avalon Society," cried the craftsman with astonishment. "And we have invited you to join."

"Yes, and I've declined to consider it at this time. Our horses?"

"But we represent the best of the best," the craftsman pushed, undeterred. "The very best, do you see? And we *want* you."

I drew myself up to my full height. "And I decline to consider your offer today."

So what if they thought me rude?

Their arrogance nettled. Although they wanted me, I didn't want them. If they valued me, they should value my friends too.

"Where are our horses?" I asked again, not bothering to keep the edge from my voice.

Ricardo followed us out onto the porch. "The Avalon Society has much to offer. Perhaps you can verify our claims with your friend Liang."

"I'll write to him when the roads clear. On the surface, Newfane *is* picturesque."

Ricardo stiffened at my implication.

As if to prove my point, Charcoal lifted his leg and urinated on the side of a planter, leaving a splash of vibrant yellow on the pristine snow.

It was perhaps the most beautiful thing I'd ever seen.

CHAPTER THIRTY-ONE

"Beautifully scripted, Usha," Josephine said to her pupil.

Usha beamed. "My dad said if I improve enough, I can write a new sign for the workshop."

"Impressive." Josephine turned to the next table.

I enjoyed watching Josephine teach. We had lessons from scholars at the abbey, but their style was to push information at us. Josephine worked to build a relationship with each of her pupils. Moreover, she listened to them.

"Very good, Misha. Nicely done, Fedora." The red-headed twins grinned at her with identical gap-toothed smiles.

"Miss Josephine!" A small hand shot up.

She walked over to the boy. "How can I help you, Nyke?"

"I don't remember how to do an uppercase F," he said, his brow wrinkled.

As she bent to show him, a snow flurry outside the window caught my attention.

In the three weeks since the icy night spent outside Newfane, I'd felt more at home here than ever before.

Returning to Brookfield had been joyous.

Even Charcoal had celebrated, racing around the green with the other dogs and jumping into snowdrifts, barking happily.

The only sad note was the news the woman we'd brought to Brookfield had died without waking.

"Miss Josephine!" Nyke shouted.

Josephine jumped, and the children giggled.

"Sorry, Nyke, go ahead."

"I've been telling and telling you," said the little boy in an aggrieved tone.

"You're right; I let my mind wander. I'm sorry, please continue."

The boy glared, but nodded. "I'm having trouble—"

My eyes widened as I glimpsed a friend through the window.

My plan worked.

"Josephine!" I blurted, interrupting the boy.

"Yes?" she asked, flushing.

"Miss Josephine!" Nyke reddened. "Miss Josephine, my Fs!"

"I'm sorry Master Padgett, how rude of me." I bowed low in apology.

"I forgot my F, and I'm writing a sign, too!" the little boy shouted.

"Yes, I see. Please excuse me, children. I have news to share with your teacher, but I should have waited my turn." I turned to Josephine. "Scholar Pliny, please forgive my interruption. I'll return at three when school lets out."

Josephine looked puzzled, but played along. "Thank you, Artist Sugiyama. I'll see you at three."

I bowed and exited the pub. Once outside, I made a face through the window, and the children giggled.

When Josephine excused the children at ten to three, Charcoal and I sauntered into the pub.

"What was that about, earlier?" She tidied up the lettering boards and moved the tables and chairs back to their usual arrangement.

The door opened, and the wind blew in snow and the scent of wood smoke.

Chimham, heavily bundled, wrestled the door shut. "Hullo,

Josephine. I passed Nyke on the way, and he barely had time to greet me. Is everything alright?"

Josephine nodded. "Yes, he's working on a surprise for you. Are you keeper here today?"

Chimham nodded cheerfully. "Yes, I'm on duty this week, and I'm roasting a pig for the Year's End feast."

"A whole pig? Are we celebrating something? Is it your birthday?"

"My birthdays are both in June. I suppose I like to celebrate... anything. Anything at all," she said, winking at me.

The door opened again, and Rodas the butcher walked in with a pig slung over his shoulder. "Where do you want it, Mitéra?" he asked, walking into the kitchen.

Charcoal followed him, nose in the air.

"Mitéra?" I asked, following Rodas.

"It means mother in Greek," said Chimham, pointing to the long steel-covered prep table. "There is fine, thank you. Rodas is my oldest. I thought I should let you know so you can stop looking scandalized."

Rodas bent and kissed her cheek, then left with a wave to Josephine and a nod for me.

I envied their closeness, their easy camaraderie. Would my mother and I have had a strong relationship? An arrow of pain sang through me, and Charcoal leaned against my leg.

Josephine laughed. "I thought it was only you, Jorma, and Nyke. Is Jorma a Greek name, too?"

Chimham shook her head, dark curls bouncing. "No, Jorma has a Swedish background. We met when we were nine and my family moved here. Our families farmed next to each other."

"You grew up wanting to be farmers?" I asked.

"You bet. Although, combining the holdings has made me question my decision. Especially after Rodas pursued butchering instead of farming."

The door opened again, and we peeked into the pub. A tall,

bearded man ducked under the door frame, and Josephine turned away.

I waited, holding my breath.

Her head snapped back. "Ben? Ben Hensly?"

Laughing, Ben strode into the room, picked her up by the waist, and swung her in a circle before enveloping her in a hug.

My grin split my face. "This was my announcement."

"Whatever... I mean how... I mean..." She slapped Ben on the chest and finally asked, "What are you doing *here*?"

"He invited me," Ben said.

Josephine looked at me. "You? How? *When?*"

"Blame me later," I said, clapping Ben's shoulder. "Ben, this is Chimham. She farms the holding on the north side of the community. Chimham, this is Ben Hensly, the engineer we met in Rochester Depot."

"And?" Josephine demanded. "How are you here? Oh, and put me down, please."

Ben chuckled and released her. "It's a bit of a tale," he warned.

"Another to add to your collection," I said, clapping him on the shoulder.

"Come into the kitchen so I can hear the story," said Chimham. "I need to start supper."

We followed her, perching on stools at the steel prep table. Charcoal sat next to Ben's stool, looking as pleased as me.

"I'll choose my words with care," said Ben, eying the pig.

"Chimham is a pussycat. Don't worry about the pig." I swiveled to watch Chimham quarter the hog.

"Go on," Josephine prodded.

"Well"—Ben took a deep breath—"Matthew invited me on the back of a painting. The end." He grinned.

Josephine waited, looking puzzled.

Ben yawned with mock exhaustion. "What's for dinner?"

"Lamb stifado, if I can get some help," Chimham replied. She hauled a large basket of tiny onions to the edge of the table. "Peel these."

Ben lifted the basket onto the prep table.

I took an onion and squinted at it. "Is there a trick to this?"

Ben shrugged. "The skins slip if you blanch them. May we?"

Chimham smiled and nodded. "The pots are over there, and we keep a kettle of water simmering."

"Don't you need lamb for lamb stifado?" asked Josephine, eying the pig.

"This pig is for the Year's End feast," Chimham reminded her.

Josephine turned back to Ben. "I want the entire story. With details."

Ben and I exchanged glances and burst out laughing. "I told you she wouldn't like your 'bit of a tale,'" I said.

"I owe you the first egg of the New Year," he agreed.

"Peel onions," ordered Chimham.

"I'll blanch, and you can slip the skins," Ben said to us.

I didn't know what he meant.

He sighed. "Here, watch."

He put two large handfuls of onions into the simmering water. After a moment, he scooped them out with a long-handled sieve and dropped them into a bowl of cold water. "You pinch this end, where the roots are, and the onion pops out."

We nodded.

Ben slid the next batch of onions into the scalding water. "The morning you left, I took my crew to the switching station to reclaim what copper wire we could reach without shifting the concrete. I planned to solder the longer lengths together," he explained, dumping blanched onions into the cool water.

"The water gets warm, so don't burn yourselves," he warned. "When we arrived at the switching station, we found three giant wooden spools wound with copper wire. The parking structure lay flat, sectioned into half-meter chunks."

"What?" asked Josephine, surprised. "How did—"

Ben held his hand up to interrupt her, and she stopped. "A bright red box sat on one spool like a present. Inside was a painting matching the scene." He shook his head and gave me an admiring look. "I didn't know you could paint such a large change."

I inclined my head. Successfully moving the storage platforms had given me the confidence to tackle the parking structure.

"How did you find us?" Josephine asked.

"There was an invitation, with directions, on the back of the painting."

"You planned this!" she accused me, laughing.

"Mmm. But I didn't know if Ben would accept." I peeled part of the onion I'd been working on, and it almost slithered out of my grasp. None of them popped out like Ben's had.

"How long can you stay? Did you finish your work in Rochester? When do you move into your new community?"

Ben's eyes darkened. "They rescinded their offer." He shrugged. "There are plenty of communities like Newfane. I've had other offers but have made no decisions." He shook his head. "Here's the last of the onions. No, the wire allowed us to finish the project. The trains move easily in either direction now, fulfilling the obligations I had in Rochester. Since I finished earlier than expected, I came here to convey my thanks in person."

I set my onion down. "Newfane? You had an invitation from the Avalon Society? Why didn't you say anything when Logan and Mabel approached me in Rochester?"

"I didn't want to sway your decision," he said.

A horrible thought occurred to me. "Did they rescind because of me?"

Ben shrugged. "I don't know. Perhaps your refusal changed things."

"You can stay in Brookfield!" Josephine's smile faded. "Is there an empty dwelling?"

Ben shook his head.

If we couldn't find a place for Ben, he might not stay. "How would you feel about moving into the upstairs bedroom?" I asked Josephine.

"Oh, marvelous! Yes, stay with us. I'll move my things upstairs straight away." She stood up. "If you can do without me?"

Ben eyed the tiny pile of onions she had peeled. "I think I can manage."

"Oh, Matthew, your—"

I nodded, understanding immediately. I'd been using the upstairs room as a makeshift studio, and my mystery painting stood on an easel next to the window. "Right, I'll come and help shift things. If you can do without me as well?"

"Go," said Chimham with a wink. "I'll put your friend to work and keep him busy until the rest of the community arrives to take a peek at him."

I grinned and slipped off my stool. "Have at him."

As Charcoal and I followed Josephine out of the kitchen, Chimham said, "Thank you for getting them out of here. Those two are hopeless in the kitchen."

CHAPTER THIRTY-TWO

Welcoming Ben into our dwelling had been easy. "We're eating better too," I said.

"What?" asked Josephine.

"Oh, sorry. I didn't mean to say it out loud."

Josephine stretched. "Why are we eating better?"

"Because Ben is cooking."

Charcoal grumbled and flipped over on his mat.

Josephine laughed. "Remember the last meal he let us cook?"

I grinned, the memory now a story Ben loved to tell. "Our welcome breakfast didn't go well."

"I didn't know I shouldn't *bake* the sweet rolls Whistler provided."

"I didn't know one doesn't fry bacon in oil."

Josephine laughed. "And neither of us knew scrambled eggs should never be brown."

I snickered and picked up the cold sheet pan. "No," I said, imitating Ben.

Josephine picked up the cold frying pan. "No," she said, shaking it at me.

"We are horrible cooks, Josephine."

"Without the pub, we would've starved." She smiled in agreement. "We ate there at least four nights a week because one of us—"

"Or both of us—"

"—ruined the meal."

I set the sheet pan down. "Genevie loves him. Actually, I think he gets on with everyone here."

Josephine nodded. "He's a good listener. Are you going to tell him about your painting?"

I shrugged. "I don't know."

"Do you know where to travel next?"

"No. I was hoping to talk to the scholar at Newfane first. I've had a few flashes since we've been back from Rochester Depot, but nothing I recognize."

Josephine chewed her lip. "We told Sally we'd stay for the winter. It's not Year's End yet, but..."

"I know, she'll want an update soon. How about you? Do you know where you're going next?"

"No," she said shortly, setting the pan down on the stove with a *clang*.

"No, what?" rumbled Ben, coming through the kitchen door with an armload of firewood. He set it next to the stove and looked at us. "No, what? And were you touching my pans?"

"No to the pans, and no, I don't know what my plans are at winter's end," Josephine said in a small voice.

"How about you, Ben?" I asked.

"I figured I'd tag along with you both," said Ben, kneeling and loading the firewood into the stove.

Charcoal supervised and got his ears rubbed by Ben in reward.

I blinked. "Oh! I hadn't realized—"

"What? That we'd travel together at winter's end?" Ben looked at me. "Why not? Do you know where you're going?"

We shook our heads.

"Me neither. We may as well travel into the unknown together."

"Traveling together is a terrific idea," I blurted, the idea of returning to my solitary journey suddenly unthinkable.

Ben latched the stove's door. "Josephine?"

Her cheeks pinked. "Yes, of course."

"Good." Ben nodded. "We're having roasted duck with sauteed greens, mashed turnips, and an apple pie for dinner tonight."

My mouth watered. "Really?"

Ben nodded. "I invited Genevie and Whistler. I thought it would be fun to get a small party together tonight. Did you know the people of *Before* celebrated the eve of the new year more than Year's End itself? You can help."

"It's true. They had huge global celebrations on the eve of each New Year," said Josephine.

A global celebration? How would that even work?

We worked in comfortable silence, Ben dressing the ducks while I peeled turnips and Josephine washed the greens.

Charcoal sat at the table, watching intently.

"How do we make a pie?" asked Josephine.

Ben salted the ducks. "Whistler's bringing the pie."

I smiled. Whistler's pies were spectacular. Glancing at my friends, I made my decision. If we were going to travel together, it was time to trust them with my complete story.

"Ben, I have a destination. A place to go, I mean."

Ben nodded.

"But I don't know where it is."

"Go on."

"Well"—I looked at Josephine, who nodded encouragingly—"I have a painting I've been working on."

"I'll get it," she offered.

"Yes, thanks. With the easel."

She returned with the painting and easel and stood them against the wall opposite the stove.

Ben put the ducks in the oven and turned, leaning against the

231

stove with his arms crossed. He studied the painting, then looked at me.

"I'm not sure how to begin," I admitted, waving a half-peeled turnip, the spicy scent peppering my words. "I guess maybe from the beginning?"

They nodded.

"I was sent—"

"We're obviously just in time," said Genevie, striding into the kitchen, followed by a flurry of snowflakes, Whistler, and Sally. "Go on, you were sent? To? From? A parcel? A package? A wife?"

"I brought *pie*," said Whistler, as if to apologize for his wife's interruption. "Sweets always go well with a tale."

Genevie snorted. "Fine, then I brought Sally. She's sweet, too."

"Thank you, dear, but compare me with baked goods again, and I'll write to your mother about the trout-faced hag she raised." Sally shook the snow from her hat and turned to Josephine. "Excuse my mouth. I'm off duty."

Josephine laughed. "Hullo, Sally. I see we have a full house tonight. Should we expect anyone else for supper?" she asked Ben, brow arched.

He grinned and shook his head.

Genevie straddled one of the kitchen table chairs. "Go on. I want to hear the story."

I flushed. "I wasn't expecting..."

"What, an audience? Get over yourself. You tell yours, then I'll tell you the story of Whistler having his tail removed."

Whistler chuckled. "You just did, wife. I'm with her, Matthew; I barely know anything about your history. Go ahead."

Helpless, I looked at Josephine, but she didn't notice, taking the pies from Whistler.

"Spill," ordered Genevie.

Maybe they should know too; they might have some ideas of where or how I should look for clues about my family. "Okay, Okay. But I warn you, this isn't an entertaining story like one of Ben's."

"Well, tell it once, and then Ben can tell it forevermore, but better," Genevie teased. "Besides, we have what, an hour before dinner?"

Ben looked at the clock on the wall and nodded.

"I'll take over," said Sally, appearing at my elbow. I handed her the turnip, and Genevie kicked out a chair.

"All right." I settled into the chair and raked my fingers through my hair. I stared at the painting. "Some of you have heard pieces of this before. They sent me to Popham Abbey on the coast as a small child. They told me I'd traveled most of a year before arriving. All of us lads had individual rooms, dressed similarly, and enjoyed communal meals in the dining hall, but as I aged, I noticed they gave some of us more than the others."

Josephine tilted her head. "More? More what?"

I frowned, considering her question. "Well, I had a room on the ocean side, like the masters, instead of facing the courtyard. After my tenth birthday, they assigned me a single room while the other boys typically shared."

"Luck of the draw?" asked Sally, wiping her hands. "Sometimes, I assign a larger dwelling to a newcomer because it's what's vacant, not because they're any more important than the next." She took a seat next to Genevie and patted the chair next to her for Josephine.

"True," I admitted. "There were other things, though. Private lessons with masters, better quality brushes, finer smocks, the best positions in the room, more in-depth assessment of my needs."

"Did you ask the masters about it?"

I nodded at Josephine. "At first, I felt guilty. I never had to worry about using too much pigment, or clay, or bronze. Even if I shared with others, they gave me more without reproach or caution. When I asked my mentor about it, he said they had provided for me."

"You know nothing about your family? Still?" Genevie shook her head. "How terrible. They never visited or wrote? You don't even know if you have family living?"

I shook my head. "No, nothing. I hoped at graduation I'd be told something, anything. Who my parents were, why no one ever visited, who'd left me at the abbey. Maybe even if someone was coming to take me home." I shook my head again. "Nothing."

"Correspondence has become difficult," Whistler said. "I remember my mother writing to friends when I was young, but over time, the letters stopped arriving. She never knew why."

The kernel of hope I kept deep inside burned brighter. "Maybe they didn't know I wasn't receiving their messages."

Josephine nodded. "The scholar I apprenticed with, Edward Dossett, mentioned the same thing. There used to be a regular correspondence between scholars, and you could ask, by mail, for records."

She shook her head. "Perhaps traveling has slowed, and there are fewer people willing to carry messages than there used to be. Now, we scholars each conduct our own research, unless you know someone who's going to a depot and will look for records for you. Speaking of, I have the research I collected for Edward. Since we don't know where..." She stopped and looked at the table.

"Where you're going next," said Sally, finishing Josephine's sentence. "It's no secret you're leaving at winter's end. Though—of course—we're hoping you'll change your minds."

Whistler and Genevie nodded in agreement.

Sally stood and walked to the stove. "Oh blast, these have already started boiling." She reached her hand for the pot and grasped the handle before Whistler shouted a warning.

"Bum-banging brawny packer!" she screeched, dropping the pan onto the stove.

JAMI PARKINSON

CHAPTER THIRTY-THREE

B en sprang forward and swept Sally toward the sink.

"Dipping rag rider—that hurts!" she yowled when the water hit her palm. "Colder!"

"No," said Ben, gripping her wrist.

"He's right, Sally," called Whistler from the table. "Cool but not cold or the scar will pucker."

"Sodding turd bandit, I know," she hissed through clenched teeth, "but it hurts."

"Swear away," said Genevie. "I'm delighted to learn synonyms for the word 'ouch.'"

"Go dance on a pin, you bucket bender."

"Maybe you should continue, Matthew," said Whistler, trying to hide his smile.

"No, wait. I want to hear." Sally snatched her hand from Ben and glared balefully. He moved aside, and she stalked back to her place at the table. "Go on," she snapped.

I stalled, debating if I should tell them about the infrequent and random flashes I'd received. Maybe they'd have some insight into what I was seeing or why. "Before I graduated, I had a series of... well,

I call them flashes." I looked at Josephine for support. "Maybe they're memories, or visions, or perhaps something I dreamed."

"What do you see?" asked Genevie.

"Shapes." I shrugged. "Just shapes or colors. Maybe small pieces of a larger whole." I pointed at the canvas standing next to the wall behind them. "I've titled it '*Home*'."

We studied the painting.

"Does anyone see something in the squiggles?" Genevie asked. Whistler made a move to hush her, but she continued, "I've seen images of art from *Before* when people splattered colors on any old surface or painted a red square and a yellow swish. Is this that?"

"I think you mean *abstract* art. No, I think this is a picture of my family home."

"The home you have no memory of?" asked Sally.

I squirmed. Sally was right; it sounded farfetched when said out loud. "Yes. After graduation, I started traveling, hoping to see or find something familiar, maybe to speak with someone who could point me in the right direction. It's how I ended up here."

"You could make Brookfield your home," Whistler said after a long pause. "I'd welcome you as permanent community members."

"Thank you, Whistler. Truly." Whistler's words warmed me, and my eyes stung.

I blinked several times and scanned their faces. "Please understand, I need to know where I come from. Why they sent me away, and why no one wrote or came to see me as the other parents did. I need to know..." Shamefaced, I looked around the room. "I sound selfish, don't I?"

It hadn't mattered to me before, but it mattered now, in front of *these* people.

No one spoke, and I fidgeted, wishing I'd kept quiet. I'd expected them to be more encouraging, excited by the possibilities lurking in the flashes. Instead, the room was flat and stale, perfumed by the greasy scent of roasting duck.

I glanced around the table, but only Whistler held my gaze, his eyes warm and full of compassion. Sally scowled at her palm, and Genevie stared at the ceiling.

Charcoal scratched at his neck, his leg thumping against the wooden floor.

Ben's voice, slow and thoughtful, cut through the tension. "I'll help you find your home."

"Me too," said Josephine less than a heartbeat later.

Genevie frowned. "How will you start?"

Good question.

I sucked in air. "I planned to speak to the resident scholar in Newfane about the painting, but she's gone until spring."

Genevie glanced at the painting. "I'm not sure anyone would recognize those blobs of color yet. Maybe when there's something more solid to chew on?"

"Or a distinguishing feature," agreed Whistler.

"We could ask Edward when we reach Warwick," Josephine said. "Maybe he'd have ideas too."

Sally poked at her scalded palm and hissed. "If you want to leave early, you must skirt Lake Winnipesaukee, go west through New London, or south through—"

Josephine and I shook our heads.

"We had a terrifying experience on the southern road," Josephine reminded her.

"I'd rather not revisit the journey, either," I added. "Besides, the bridge north of Union is out."

Ben nodded. "Crossing the river during winter when it was narrow and sluggish was hard enough. I'd not want to attempt it at spring thaw. New London then, and south to Warwick."

Sally scowled at her palm.

"What's the route like?" Ben asked me. "I haven't seen a map for a while."

Am I supposed to have memorized all the routes in New England?

I shrugged. "I only copied the routes east of Rochester Depot."

Ben drummed his fingers on the table. "We'll head west to New

London and decide the best route for Warwick from there. There may even be a filling station open early for the season."

Everyone nodded in agreement, but instead of relief, resentment flashed through me. Shouldn't Ben have asked what I wanted to do?

"Then where?" Sally asked Ben.

He shrugged. "Depends on yon painting. Perhaps our artist can put a few more shapes on it, something recognizable."

Sally waved her scalded hand. "It's possible? Can you put more effort into your painting?"

My eyes tightened. "I don't know how much control I have. The flashes come when they come."

"Have you tried?" asked Whistler. "Have you focused on the image?"

"No," I admitted, crossing my arms. "When I get a flash, I add what I'm shown."

"Reactively," said Genevie, nodding.

"Yes." Licking my lips, I raised my palms. "How could I possibly invite flashes? I don't know where they come from."

Whistler tilted his chair onto its back legs. "During my apprenticeship, I learned the rough proportions of flour, water, yeast, and salt for bread. And sugar, butter, eggs, and flour for cakes. But all of my creations—"

"Pepper bread!" Sally interrupted.

Whistler's eyes crinkled. "—such as my beloved pepper bread, came about when I had the time, materials, and desire to create something new."

"Go on," I said.

"I get the ingredients I have, and I sit with them, imagining eating something different. My hands select ingredients, and I add, measure, and mix them. In the end, I've created something new. I document my process and create it again and again, testing, making minor adjustments, and trying out each iteration with anyone who will be a taster."

He smiled as Genevie patted her belly.

"I keep refining until I know I'm finished."

"I do something similar," said Genevie. "Unlike Whistler, I often know what I want to create, but not how to get there. I start by looking at my scrap. You can combine different metals to create new materials with advanced properties," she explained.

"I can further refine the final product by adding metals that will make it easier to melt, or make the final product hard, sharp, or malleable, and so on. All blacksmiths learn about alloys while apprenticing, but because there are infinite possibilities of what you could create..." She broke off with a self-conscious smile, shrugging.

Josephine studied me. "What do you think about setting aside time to... well, create, I guess? Not to paint something you see or make an improvement, but to see what happens if you give your creativity time to play?"

"I've never painted without a goal, and I've never painted to create." I paused and watched Ben cross the kitchen.

Liang's painting in Newfane popped onto my mind's canvas. "I've never painted for myself."

They were trying to be helpful, but was it possible to will the flashes on command? My armpits prickled.

"We have a path forward," Ben said. He bent and peered into the oven. "Dinner's ready. Who's hungry?"

My stomach tied knots throughout dinner. I laughed and joked with the others while being crushed by dread. What if nothing happened when I tried to will the flashes? What if I had nothing to show when it was time to leave?

Traveling with Ben and Josephine had seemed a lark when Ben had offered; three friends embarking on an adventure. Had accepting been a mistake?

Perhaps I hadn't been entirely honest with them about my motivations.

Truthfully, I had held no expectation I'd find my family soon. My quest had been largely theoretical, an ambitious and romantic journey where I'd have an excuse to explore and meet people without tying myself to any single place. However, after learning 'T' was trying to prevent me from finding my family, my need for answers had strengthened. But what if it took years? Or what if I found nothing?

I tried to calm myself with a second helping of pie. Maybe I was spinning about something that wouldn't happen. Perhaps I'd finish my painting, or someone at Warwick would recognize it, or me, or at least point me to someone who could. Maybe the scholar from Newfane would arrive before we set out.

Whistler's voice cut through my thoughts. "Matthew, are you all right?"

I looked up, startled. Everyone was looking at me. "What?"

"Are you okay?" asked Genevie, glancing at my wrist.

The skin on my wrist, raw and bruised, stung. "Oh, fine. I had an itch," I lied.

The masters had described my tendency to rub my wrist when I was nervous as a character flaw.

An artist should be above such mundane, corporeal feelings.

The moment forgotten, my friends returned to their conversation about the Year's End celebration.

I dropped my hands beneath the table and almost immediately, my right hand clamped once more around my left wrist. Genevie stared at me, so I grabbed my water glass with my right hand and tucked my left under my thigh.

Gulping the water, I tried not to drown in anxiety.

CHAPTER THIRTY-FOUR

The pub's door opened with a burst of snow and the spicy scent of freshly cut evergreens.

"Happy Year's End!" we shouted in unison.

All evening, community members had streamed into the party.

This was my first proper adult Year's End party, and though fun, in the moments I had to myself, I couldn't shake my melancholy.

Smiling, laughing people who'd become dear filled the room. After a lifetime of feeling alone, I was part of a community. Leaving Brookfield would be painful.

Charcoal shoved his wet nose into my hand.

Enough was enough; now was the time to enjoy the company of these people... while I could.

Pushing away bittersweet thoughts, I grinned at Genevie, who'd slid through the crowd toward me. "What's wrong with Sally? I gave her a Year's End kiss, and she told me... well, I won't repeat it, but I set her down."

"What like this?" Genevie asked. She picked Josephine up into a giant hug, planting a kiss on her scarred cheek before setting her down.

Josephine blushed, but smiled at the taller woman. "Happy Year's End, Genevie."

"Put me down, you llama wanker!"

We turned and laughed as Sally struggled in Whistler's embrace. He set the small woman down and winked at his wife.

Ruffled, Sally put her hands on her hips and glared at us. "They have tossed me around like a child's top for the last quarter-hour. Really." She smoothed her sweater with her hands. "It's not dignified to carry an administrator like a Year's End parcel."

"No one thinks less of you, Sally," said Whistler. "Besides, having a pocket-sized administrator is handy. We can pick you up, point you in a different direction, and off you go."

Genevie shouted in laughter as Sally turned and stamped away. Through the crowd's noise, we heard her squeal of displeasure and laughed again.

"Happy Year's End, Josephine," I said, kissing her smooth cheek.

"And to you, Matthew."

"Where's mine, you handsome thing?" asked Genevie.

When I bent forward to kiss her, Genevie tugged my coat collar toward her, pulling me off balance and drawing me into a deep embrace. My ale sloshed over my hand as she kissed me, her lips warm and full against mine.

"Wow!" she shouted, releasing me. "Happy Year's End!"

The surrounding people whistled and cheered, and Charcoal capered around, barking.

Horrified and delighted, I flashed Whistler a small smile of apology and shook spilled ale from my hand. Should I confess his wife had given me my first kiss?

Giddy, I grinned at my friends.

Whistler pulled his wife into an imitation of the embrace she'd given me. She came up from the kiss, flushed and breathless, smiling into her husband's eyes. People cheered again, and he bowed before escorting his wife away.

Ben kissed Josephine's cheek. "Happy Year's End, Josephine."

"Happy Year's End, Ben." They smiled at each other.

"How long has this been happening?" asked a voice in my ear.

I turned. "Happy Year's End, Nora. Kami."

Kami nodded at Josephine, who was chatting with Ben, animated and expressive. "He's very taken with her."

I watched my friends. "How do you know?"

Nora laughed and patted my shoulder. "You're not emotionally observant, are you?"

"Emotionally observant?"

Kami nodded. "If you're like my grandfather, you observe the physical world around you in terms of color, shape, shadow, and pattern."

I stroked my beard. "Yes?"

"As healers, we watch for behavioral changes in people. When someone's behavior changes, there's always a reason."

"Like what?"

"Usually, there's a stimulus of some sort, internal or external."

"What's an external stimulus?"

Kami shrugged. "A bear. Hunger. Storms."

"Okay, sure. Internal?"

"Internal stimuli could be physical or mental. Mental could include a conscious effort to change, such as cutting sweets from your diet."

Nora cocked her head. "Physical could be an oncoming illness, tumor, chemical imbalance, or a rash."

I shoved my left hand in my pocket, hoping they hadn't noticed the raw skin on my wrist.

"We observe patterns of behavior because even a slight change could mark a symptom of illness," said Kami.

"Is Ben ill?" I asked.

Nora and Kami exchanged a smile.

"Not ill," Nora said, "but perhaps..." She looked at Kami.

"In love," Kami supplied.

The words struck me with physical force, and I swallowed as

though the air in the room had disappeared. "Ben... *in love* with Josephine? He barely knows her."

"Do you have feelings for her?" Nora asked, her brow furrowed.

Did I? Josephine was dear to me. As dear as a sister. I was protective of her; she'd become my family. *My family.* My heart swelled.

I was no longer alone.

Even if we traveled separate paths, she'd remain with me. If needed, I'd drop everything to help her, and she'd reciprocate.

"I care for her, but *in* love?" My voice trailed off, and I shrugged, sipping of my ale, the bitter-clean flavor washing over my tongue. "What do I know about love?"

Kami patted me on the shoulder. "What do any of us know, my brother?"

THE SUN SHONE WITH NO REGARD FOR MY ACHING HEAD.

I'd drunk too much ale at last night's party and couldn't imagine why Sally had asked us to visit her so early. She was up to something, and I hoped she wouldn't try to talk us into staying in Brookfield. "Did the note say anything about why she wanted to meet?"

"Would you like to read it again?" asked Josephine.

I flinched and tossed a stick for Charcoal. Though her words were mild, I'd clearly irritated Josephine. "Sorry, no. I should apologize anyway."

"For what?"

"I picked her up last night," I admitted, watching Charcoal root through the snowdrift for the stick.

"Me too," agreed Ben.

Josephine scoffed. "You think Sally wants to meet because you picked her up at a party?"

"And called her a pocket-sized administrator," I added. "Well, Whistler said it, but I agreed."

Josephine shook her head. "You should give Sally more credit. We women are more than our physical form."

"Not for an artist," I muttered.

Josephine gave me a sharp look.

"I respect women!" I protested.

Charcoal ran past me and banged into the back of my knee with his stick. I scowled at him.

"Don't worry your pretty little head about it," said Josephine, knocking on Sally's red door. "But try to be on your best behavior."

Sally opened the door with a bright smile. "Come in, you're just in time."

Josephine shot a warning look at us.

I looked at Ben, who wagged his finger at me and followed Josephine.

Charcoal brushed past me and scampered into the house.

"I thought we could have tea while we chat," Sally said, ushering us into the kitchen.

Relieved we weren't in trouble, I took off my overcoat and hung it from a hook next to the door. My stomach clawed at my spine at the scent of the mint tea. I'd risen too late to catch breakfast at the pub.

Ben pulled out a chair for Josephine, and she smiled at him warmly. Since Nora and Kami had clued me in, I'd been observing them. It was fascinating to watch them through this new lens.

"Sit," Sally said, picking up the teapot. "Now, I need to get the business of your dwelling sorted out. But first, milk or honey? Here you go, love. I wanted to talk to you about something important." She passed the last cup to Ben.

"Honey? Milk? Well, it's on the table, help yourselves." She picked up her own cup and leaned back in her chair, blowing on the hot drink. "Now, every... oh sucking barnacles, the treats!"

She jumped up and bustled around the kitchen, putting pastries and cookies on a large square plate. "Help yourselves. Where was I?"

"Every," I said, selecting a jam tart as I settled onto my chair.

"That's all you've said." The tart was sticky with apricot jam. Chewy chunks of the sun-bright fruit clung to the flaky pastry.

Charcoal sat under the table between my knees, watching for dropped crumbs.

Sally laughed. "I had too many ciders last night. Right." She leaned forward, looking at each of us. "Every community is different, but each benefits from the skills of its members. You three have valuable, rare skills."

We exchanged guilty looks.

Josephine fidgeted with her cup, turning it around and around with her slender fingers.

Sally was right. By deciding to help me look for my family, neither Ben nor Josephine would contribute their skills to a community. My anxiety rose, and my wrist stung. I sat on my left hand to prevent further injury.

Sally's eyes flicked between our faces. "I'm not trying to talk you into staying, though you'd be welcome if you wanted to."

Avoiding her eyes, I leaned forward and played with Charcoal's silky ears.

"I understand you need to go, but I'd like you to consider finding a community to settle in. You'll improve and enrich the lives of any community you join. And it may improve your lives in return." She nodded with satisfaction. "There, my plea to you. Find a community to call your own and settle as soon as you can."

Ben patted her hand. "Thank you."

I looked at Charcoal. "I want a home, a permanent home, someday. My time here in Brookfield has convinced me of it, and I dread leaving, but I must find where I came from."

Sally nodded. "Yes. I'd find it difficult to settle if I were missing a piece of myself. Maybe that's why people change communities when they lose a partner. But when you can"—she gave me a look—"settle."

"I will. I promise," I said.

"Also," she added, "settle if you find yourself without further clues to follow. We only get one shot at life."

Reaching for a cookie, I fought to keep from rolling my eyes.

"Sally, you said we needed to sort out the dwelling?" asked Josephine.

"Yes. Not to be indelicate, but when are you leaving?"

I laughed. "After your pretty speech, we've worn out our welcome?"

Sally peered over her spectacles at me. "Young man, the world spins on with or without you."

My smile turned sheepish, and my neck flushed.

"Folks are clamoring to be a part of our fine community. People," she continued with a stern look, "who will not call me a pocket-sized administrator."

Wincing, I leaned forward to apologize.

Sally held up her hand to forestall me and winked at Josephine.

Ben and I sat back and grinned.

Safe.

I shoved the cookie into my mouth.

"We have a rough timeframe, but if we need to leave sooner, we can," said Josephine.

"I've had a letter from a couple looking to settle. A farmer and engineer who are coming in April."

"We were planning to leave in the first weeks of March," said Ben. "There won't be any risk of overlap."

My heart squeezed. March was merely eight weeks away.

"Fine," said Sally. "I'll write and let them know we expect them. Rodas is traveling east and can carry the message."

"Where's he going?" I asked.

"He wants to study salt-curing preservation with a butcher in Falmouth, near the coast. My, Brookfield will feel empty this spring."

"Who else is leaving?" Josephine asked, picking up a cookie and nibbling at the edges.

"Oh, Corinne is going home to pack for a few weeks. More tea? Rodas is traveling to Falmouth, and you three are leaving. Bridget has finished her apprenticeship and is sending out feelers. Oh, and the Cannings."

"Genevie and Whistler are leaving?" I leaned forward in my chair.

"Not permanently," said Sally. "Thank goodness. Genevie wants to go to Portland Depot to look for metal scrap, and Whistler yearns to see the sea, says he. They were planning to go in early summer, but because Rodas is visiting Falmouth, they thought they'd travel together. They'll leave the week after you, in mid-March."

"Change," said Ben.

"Yes," Sally sighed. "Change is the one thing we can always count on. Change and death. Oh, blast the rest, *I* will miss you. More tea?"

CHAPTER THIRTY-FIVE

The mid-morning light shone weakly as I tightened the packsaddle straps. The day had come, and it was time to get back on the road. As excited as I was to continue my journey, I'd been dreading today. The lump in my throat had been steadily growing as I'd said my goodbyes at breakfast.

If I'd known leaving would be so painful, would I have overwintered here? No, as painful as leaving was, I cherished the memories I'd created and the relationships I'd made.

"Oh brownishgreyishyellowishblack, I'll miss you," said Genevie to the donkey as she adjusted his harness. "The children will, too. He's become a great favorite with the little ones." She raised an eyebrow. "Sure you don't want to leave him?"

"We need him," Ben called from outside the livery.

"Now *him*"—Genevie jerked her chin in Ben's direction—"no one will mind seeing the tail end of."

"Ben?" asked Josephine, brow wrinkled.

"Ben? No, Ben is lovely. But his ass isn't!"

"Mule!" Ben shouted back.

249

"You're the mule for wanting to ride an ass." Genevie walked to the open doorway and leaned against it, arms crossed.

I grinned at Josephine from across Magnesium's packsaddle. "Watch this," I mouthed.

She nodded.

"Genevie, we could leave Donkey with you if Ben would leave half this kitchen behind," I called.

"Leave it. I don't care if you eat!" Ben shouted.

Josephine snickered. "I have room if you need it."

I shook my head. "If these panniers look empty, Ben will find something else to bring."

"An omelet pan."

"A waffle iron."

"A zester."

"I can hear you," Ben growled. We jumped and turned, swallowing our giggles.

Ben shook his head in disgust. "How did either of you ever make it on your own?"

"Impeccable manners?" Josephine asked.

"My dashing smile?" I said, matching her innocent tone of voice.

Genevie snorted and half-punched Ben on the shoulder. "Mind your father, chickens."

"Yes, Ma!" we chorused.

Ben shook his head and stalked out, muttering, our hoots and jeers following him across the green.

Sobering, Genevie leaned against Oxide. "I'll miss you."

I looked at her and smiled sadly. "Come here, old girl."

Genevie walked to me, and I put an arm around her shoulder. She beckoned to Josephine, who joined us.

"I'll miss you too, truly," said Josephine, wiping her eyes on her forearm. "Oh blast, I promised myself I wouldn't cry today."

"Good luck," said Genevie. "Sally assembled the community to say farewell."

We turned and looked across the green where the people of Brookfield had swallowed Ben from sight.

I sighed. "I never know what to say."

Genevie bumped my shoulder with her head. "Later gator."

"After a while, crocodile," I replied.

"Don't let the ants in your pants make you dance," Josephine added.

I laughed, but it tasted hollow.

Josephine shrugged. "It's what we said when we were little."

"I like it," I said. I gave each woman an extra squeeze. "Let's go rescue Ben."

We walked the horses across the green and hitched them near Ben's giant mule.

"I'll miss you," said Corinne with tears in her eyes. Josephine gave the girl a hug, murmuring soothing sounds.

Horam Minter gave me a powerful hug. "You're all right, Artist."

"Take care of our girl," Metallo said, joining us. "Brookfield won't be the same without you."

A pack of sobbing girls enveloped me the moment the men left.

How am I getting out of this?

I caught Josephine's eye, and she grinned, coming to my rescue.

"Excuse me, Fedora, Misha, Opaline. Can I borrow him?" The girls tearfully nodded, and Josephine smiled in thanks, giving each girl a farewell hug.

"Thanks," I whispered. "I didn't know what to say to them."

"Matthew, people keep asking me to take care of their girl."

"Me too." I rubbed my jaw. "I thought they were talking about you."

She shook her head. "Why would they ask *me* to take care of their girl?"

"Maybe Ben knows something?"

"There he is. Ben?"

Ben turned, his eyebrows wiggling. "We need to get going," he

251

said in a low voice, "or we'll be camping at the edge of Brookfield tonight."

I folded my arms. "People keep asking us to take care of their girl. Who are they talking about?"

"Sally," Ben said, walking to the hitching rail and untying his mule.

"Sally?" Josephine mouthed at me.

We made a last check of our girths.

"How do we get out of here gracefully?" I asked, giving Josephine a leg up.

The community members drifted in our direction, many wet-eyed.

"By getting on your blasted horse and riding away." Sally sat on top of a chubby, dapple-gray pony.

"You *are* joining us," said Josephine, her voice surprised. "We didn't—"

"Talk later," Ben interrupted. "We'll have time."

I tied the donkey's lead to a small rope loop hanging from Magnesium's packsaddle.

Sally watched from her pony. "What's it for?"

I secured the loop. "I tie the donkey to this circle of rope, which is weaker than the donkey's lead. If needed, this rope breaks. Standard for a pack string."

Sally cocked her head to the side. "But then the donkey is loose."

"Right. We usually do this with larger horses, so if a horse in the string loses his feet and falls off a ledge, he won't pull the horses he's tied to with him."

"Fall off a ledge? That happens? Horses fall?" Sally asked, her face blanching.

Josephine bit her lip. "Sally, have you ridden much?"

"No," said the older woman shortly. "I've never traveled, and there was no need to learn. Why, are you saying I'm too old to learn?"

"Never," I assured her in what I hoped was a gallant tone, "but we may need to take it easy for the first couple of days until you get used to it."

"Used to what? I sit on this horse and get off when we arrive."

Josephine's lips twitched. "Well, none of us are in peak riding shape, so we'll take it easy, anyway."

"Ready?" Ben asked from the front. "Matthew, ride sweep?"

I waved my hand in acknowledgment.

"Sweep? What's he sweeping?" asked Sally.

"Come, ride next to me, Sally, and I'll explain," said Josephine.

Ben's mule strode away, and Josephine followed with Sally to her right.

The saddle leather was foreign and hard beneath me as I settled myself. Out of saddle shape, I was in for a rough few days. Twitching the rope to alert Magnesium we were leaving, I swallowed several times.

People shouted well wishes and waved.

Charcoal whined, watching the rest of our party turn onto the road.

A lump grew in my throat as I scanned Brookfield, memorizing the scene and the faces. I'd come back. As soon as I found my answers, I'd return to visit. This wasn't goodbye, this was farewell, for now.

Still, it hurt to leave what had become my home.

A warm wind scented with the hint of buds and spring flowers blew across us, and Charcoal whined again.

"I know, boy," I murmured to the dog. "Time to go." Clucking my tongue, I waved one last time before following my friends.

AS SOON AS BROOKFIELD WAS OUT OF SIGHT, I SQUEEZED OXIDE forward to ride abreast with the women. Already heavy with guilt about Ben and Josephine accompanying me, I needed to understand why Sally had left Brookfield.

"All right, Sally, spill."

Sally shrugged. "What?"

"After your speech about finding a community—"

"Matthew," Josephine warned. "I think what he's asking, badly mind you, is why you've changed your mind about traveling."

My lips flattened, and I shifted on the hard seat. "Yes, what she said."

"I stand by what I said," Sally said, raising her chin. "Can't it be because I'm so bad at farewells, I tagged along?"

"No," said Josephine. "What's going on?"

Sally sighed. "After we had tea at my house, I thought about change. I've always welcomed, or at least accepted, change around me. But I've never allowed myself to experience it."

The pony listed to the side, and Sally straightened in her saddle. "I made choices; choices like not getting married, having children, or traveling when I was younger. Do you know I've never been farther from Brookfield than Wakefield?"

Josephine and I exchanged glances.

Sally shook her head and cleared her throat. "Even that was a day trip; I didn't spend the night. If I ever want to experience change, I need to leave Brookfield. This felt like the right time."

I twitched Magnesium's rope to warn him back. "Why didn't you go east with Rodas and the Cannings?"

"They're visiting colleagues by invitation, and I didn't want to be a fourth wheel. Since you aren't expected or invited anywhere, what difference does another person make?"

"Truth," said Josephine.

"I also realized I've never worked to improve myself," Sally continued. "I have you to thank, young lady."

Josephine's eyebrows rose. "Me? Why?"

"You seek and search, encouraging others to strive for knowledge too."

I watched Charcoal investigate the brush on the side of the road and listened to the *thud-suck* of the horses walking through the mud. "She *is* a scholar."

Sally scoffed. "Yes, but I'm talking about self-improvement. I'm an administrator, and I think a skillful administrator for Brookfield."

We murmured in agreement.

"But could I have been a *better* administrator? Maybe there are newer or smoother ways of keeping a community running."

Josephine nodded. "You're on a journey of self-discovery."

"Quite."

"A journey *of* change," I said. "The journey *to* change."

The road narrowed, and I let Oxide fall back. Though the trees above us were bare, the branches sported the faintest hint of green— more evidence of the changing season. Birds flitted between branches, chirping and singing.

The air smelled of mud and manure and possibility.

My journey was one of change, too. By searching for an understanding of who I came from, I might better understand who I was, or maybe even who I could be. But what about my friends? Their reasons for joining me on this journey were unclear. Their motivations sounded murky; there had to be more to them than wanting to help me. Even Sally saying this was a journey of self-discovery seemed thin.

"Matthew."

Sally had dropped back to ride beside me. Josephine was chatting with Ben in the front.

"Sorry, I missed what you said."

Sally smirked. "Yes, you were preoccupied. Too bad. The joke I told would've knocked you off your horse."

"What joke?"

"Sorry, I meant it to be told once and as it has, it is no more."

I grinned; she was teasing me. "I'm glad you've joined us."

Suddenly serious, she said, "Me too." She patted her pony's neck. "There was another reason I came."

Here it was. "What?"

"You."

"Me? What about me?"

"From the moment I met you, I've known our futures were tied."

Our futures were tied?

"I felt nothing." But my words weren't true. Something had drawn me to Sally, Ben, and Josephine. Our meetings may have been accidental, but the connections between us were visceral. Maybe what I'd taken as affinity was something more, something deeper.

Sally shook her head. "I didn't expect you to. You're not exactly known for your sensitivity to the emotional states of others."

"I don't mean to be insensitive."

"Insensitive isn't the right word. You're not unkind, but you're... unobservant of emotional truths."

"Unobservant. Funny, it's the second time I've been told this. My epitaph should read The Unobservant Artist."

Sally laughed. "If I'm around for your funeral, I'll make sure it's worked into the eulogy." She shifted in her saddle.

"Do you need a break? See, I notice things."

"Noticing an old lady has aches and pains is one thing. Announcing what you've noticed to the world is another."

"Blast. That's it again, isn't it? Not being aware of how you'd feel about it."

Sally was right. My youth had been so focused on improving my skills as an artist, I'd never entertained the idea of improving my skills with people.

My solo journey hadn't required more than civility, but now, traveling with friends, I needed to work on myself and consider how my thoughts and actions would impact them.

It was no longer all about me.

"Quite. However, I'd welcome lunch."

"Got it." Standing in my stirrups, I winked at her and shouted, "Hey, Ben! The uninvited, out-of-shape old lady wants a break!"

"Brain-boiled crap head," said Sally, smiling and stretching her neck.

CHAPTER THIRTY-SIX

The late afternoon sun warmed my back as I considered the progress I'd made on *Home*. In the days since we'd left Brookfield, we'd developed a rhythm allowing us to make progress toward New London while providing me time to work on the painting. The day we'd left Brookfield, I'd thought Ben crazy to call for a stop so early...

IT WASN'T EVEN MIDAFTERNOON WHEN MY FRIENDS HAD CALLED for a stop to set up camp for the night. Astonished, I'd protested the early stop. My companions had listened, but by the glances they shared, I could tell they'd discussed the issue.

"What?" I asked.

"We need you to work on your painting," Sally explained.

"We're stopping early, so you have useful light," Josephine added.

"Even though it'll take longer to get to Warwick?"

"Yes," said Ben. "We'll need to know where to go next."

Defeated, I dismounted, admitting, "The extra time I spent in Brookfield was helping."

"Did you get more... what was it you called them, *flashings?*" asked Sally, handing her reins to Ben.

"Flashes. No, not yet."

"What were you able to do?" Josephine asked.

"Expand the existing shapes."

Blank faces stared at me.

"When I look at something, I see shapes, color, light, shadow, and gradient."

I'd lost them.

"Let me try another way. If I hold my fingers like this, I'm making a frame, like around a painting."

They nodded.

"Now, looking through this frame, what do you see?" I held my fingers up in two L shapes, and they peered through them.

"I see sky and trees," said Josephine.

"Try harder," I said. "Sally?"

"Blue sky and dark trees. There are pieces of blue through a frazzled branch there. How'd I do?"

"Better," I said. "Ben?"

"The sky is dark blue in the upper left corner and fades to a whiter blue next to the tree. The tree is a triangle shape here, and more like a cylinder here. It's dark green at the base, but a brighter green there where it's illuminated by the sunlight."

"Very good." I turned to the others. "What Ben described is closer to what I would expect an artist to see."

"What's the right answer?" asked Josephine.

I grinned, ever the student. "There's no *right* answer."

Sally held her own fingers up and squinted through them. "What do you see?"

I stooped to look through her frame. "Here's a French ultramarine rhomboid. Here's a sickle shape in Prussian green. This shape is square, and starts as sepia, transitioning to terre verte, with a raw sienna line at the edge."

Josephine frowned. "How would you describe the scene if you didn't know the proper name of the colors?"

"Deep blue, gray-blue, dark blue-green. My point is not the name of the pigment, but how I see what's in the frame."

Charcoal stretched out on a patch of snow and sighed.

Ben nodded. "You don't see trees and sky."

"Yes."

Ben turned to Josephine and explained, "When I look at a machine, I see angles, levers, gears, sprockets, bearings. Sally sees a tractor."

Josephine's eyes widened. "You view the world in terms of the components you used to recreate it. Interesting."

"Mmm. Add depth, perspective, shadow, contrast, and yes, you're loosely correct."

"When I look at Ben's face, I see a roundish head covered in fur," said Sally slowly, "and you see—"

"The shape the shadow creates between his brow and his ear. The plane of his forehead. The symmetry of the ovals of his nostrils."

Ben ran his palm over his nose and down the rest of his face. "Where does it leave your painting?"

"Right. When an image flashes, it draws my eyes to the bright or dominant shape. I try to memorize its placement, color, perspective, and outline."

They nodded.

"What I've been doing between the flashes is trying to remember what framed the dominant shape."

"Framed?"

I cocked my head to the side, considering how to explain it. "When I held up my hands like this, I created a frame for you to look through, to cut the whole into a smaller piece, easier to view."

"Yes." Sally held up her own fingers in a frame again.

"Now, imagine my arms are creating the shape." I positioned my arms in a circle, encompassing my head and the space beyond my right shoulder. "What's within this frame?"

"Branches," Josephine said. "I mean, a circle of dark green bisected with a dark brown line. And your head."

I laughed. "Now what's framing my frame?"

Sally walked up and poked at my side. "Your frame touches your torso here. But also dark green cylinders, some unnamable shape here in bluish-white, and—I suppose—the round shape of your shoulder. Oh, I see."

I dropped my arms. "Very good. Before we talked, when I got a flash, I focused on the dominant shape and spent my time recording it. Now, I've filled in more of the image."

"Can we see *Home*?" asked Josephine, reaching down to scratch Charcoal's head.

I retrieved the canvas from my saddlebag, setting it against a rocky ledge at the side of the road.

When I'd first shown them the painting before Year's End, the canvas had been primarily white with unconnected shapes of various hues. Now, little white remained on it.

"There's a horizon," said Josephine with surprise.

Sally squinted. "Still doesn't look like much."

At the time, it hadn't...

I CHUCKLED AND SHOOK MY HEAD AT THE MEMORY. NOW, AFTER almost two weeks of traveling, the painting was more complete than it had been on our first day on the road.

A vague outline had emerged on the far horizon, and I suspected it would resolve into a distant mountain range. The shape of the near horizon was too regular to be a natural phenomenon and could be the ruins of a depot. The murky gray-green expanse between the two horizons was puzzling.

Mention of my name sharpened my focus. I looked up, finding my allotted art time had passed. The sun had sunk below the tree-tops, lighting the new buds with a shimmery golden light. Though insects still buzzed near me in a cacophonous symphony, the bird calls had slowed as they'd begun settling for the night.

My friends huddled together, talking in low voices, and my internal alarms rang. "What's wrong?"

Charcoal crowded me as my friends broke apart with guilty expressions.

"Josephine? Sally? What's going on?"

The women shook their heads.

"Ben?"

Ben studied me before speaking. "Supplies are low."

I cocked my head. "Since when? We've been eating well."

Silence.

"Haven't we been eating well?"

"Matthew," said Josephine.

I looked hard at the faces of my friends. They were visibly thinner, with hollows at their eyes and cheeks. This wasn't unexpected. We all lost weight while traveling because, despite Sally's assertion, riding was physically demanding.

I rubbed my jaw. "Why haven't we been eating more?"

Charcoal leaned against my leg and whined uneasily.

My friends exchanged glances but said nothing.

Cold tendrils of fear crept through my veins, and I stamped back and forth in front of the fire to warm up. "Why haven't you said anything?"

Ben held up his hand. "Sit, please."

"I don't want to sit. I want to know what's going on!"

"Oh, dipstick plonker, sit down!" Sally bellowed.

I stopped mid-stride and blinked.

"Sit, Matthew," Josephine said, pointing at a log near the edge of the fire.

My jaw clenched, and I drew my coat around me to sit. I glared at them. "Well?"

"We ran low on supplies two weeks ago," Sally began.

"What? Why didn't you tell me?"

"Can I continue?" Sally snapped. "At first, we thought we'd find a farm or community to trade with."

"Why didn't you stop anywhere?"

Josephine lifted her chin. "We *have*. We've stopped at every holding we've encountered. No one has anything to spare. The people we've passed were in worse shape than us."

"What? Why?"

"Early spring is always lean," said Sally.

"Why don't you know this?" asked Josephine.

I shrugged. "There wasn't scarcity at the abbey. Sometimes, we ate more fish than flesh, and we'd have pies and puddings made from canned fruit in the winter, but we weren't ever hungry. There was always plenty."

My friends exchanged glances.

"Not in our experience," said Josephine. "Early spring is always a lean time of year."

My eyes flicked to Ben, who nodded. "This spring, people have little to share—much less than we expected."

My chest tightened, and I stood and strode around the fire, circling my friends, rubbing my wrist behind my back. "Why? What's changed?"

Josephine shrugged. "We've heard tales about revivals."

I paused in mid-step. "Revivals?"

Ben cleared his throat. "We think they're a type of traveling minstrel show. They typically hold minstrel shows at a community green or a holding with enough space to accommodate a crowd."

I nodded. "Minstrels visited us several times a year at the abbey. People came from all over to attend the shows."

"Several times a year?" asked Josephine, eyes wide. "You've led a charmed life."

Her harsh tone was uncharacteristic, and her words stung. "Why?"

Sally's eyes glittered. "Minstrels are as rare as artists, Matthew. Most of us will have only seen a minstrel show a handful of times, over an entire lifetime."

I flushed. "I didn't know. Sorry."

"The revivals were popular," Ben continued. "The people often stayed to watch the show multiple times."

"Now, in my experience, minstrels are typically solitary," said Sally.

The minstrel we'd buried flashed onto my mind's canvas, and I nodded.

Sally continued, "They may travel with a companion or two, but what made these shows different is large groups accompanied the minstrels, often thirty or more. The hosts would, as is customary, provide supplies, meals, and lodging for everyone."

"As New Bethel did," I said, looking at Josephine.

She nodded. "Yes, but at the end of these shows, these *revivals*, the minstrels collected supplies from the show attendees."

"What?"

Ben nodded. "They followed the folks who had attended back to their holdings and pressured them to give what they had."

"Or, most times, more than they could afford to give," said Josephine with an uncharacteristic bite to her voice.

"Like—" I stopped and looked at my friends.

"Like payment," said Sally, finishing my thought. "Yes, what we thought, too. Not only was the large group fed and housed by their hosts, but they also extracted more from the show's attendees."

"Where is this revival group?" I asked, shoving the butt end of a branch back into the fire.

Sparks streamed toward the sky, and I blinked, my eyes tearing as the bitter smoke scoured my face.

"That's what's strange," said Josephine. "This seems to have happened with two distinct groups."

"Two minstrels?" I asked. My stomach clenched, a shiver tracking down my spine. "But you said minstrels were rare."

Sally nodded. "Quite. As far as we could tell, there are two traveling revivals, one moving northeast, and one heading northwest."

"We missed them both by skirting the lake," said Ben.

Josephine snapped a small stick and tossed it into the fire. "Which brings us back to our present situation."

"Running out of food," I said. If we couldn't resupply, we'd be forced to pull off the road and work with a community until we could replenish our stores.

The occasional hiss of damp wood tempered the *pop-crackle* of the fire.

My hands tightened. "This explains nothing."

Charcoal scanned my face, nuzzling my hands.

Sally sighed. "Glistering arse sock, Matthew, we've thoroughly explained the situation. You know what we know."

I clenched my jaw, trying to keep my temper in check. "I do not know," I began quietly, "why you didn't tell me any of this until today."

Josephine flushed and looked away, and Sally and Ben looked at each other.

"It was my call," said Ben evenly.

"We all agreed to protect you," corrected Sally.

"I am not a child!" Inwardly, I cringed. Like a child, I was shouting at my friends. The logical voice inside my head murmured my behavior wasn't helpful.

My eyes narrowed. "You should have told me."

Now I sounded petulant. A man-child throwing a tantrum.

"Look here, young man," said Sally, "we were trying to help you, and you're being beastly."

I flapped my arms, accidentally biting the inside of my cheek. "Blast."

Josephine stalked away in silence.

"Pirate chesticle!" Sally sighed. "We should have told you."

"Perhaps." Tasting blood, I deflated, my temper exhausted and remorse rising as Josephine disappeared into the woods. "But done is done."

"Done is done," Ben repeated.

CHAPTER THIRTY-SEVEN

Ben was stirring a bubbling pot when I returned to the fire with Josephine in tow. With night falling, I'd gotten worried and gone to find her.

Saying nothing, Ben handed me a steaming bowl.

I studied my meal—a meager barley soup with tiny flecks of floating vegetables and small chunks of meat. "This is what we've been eating." I lowered my nose towards the bowl, but it had no aroma.

Charcoal sniffed his own bowl and looked at me sadly.

If we couldn't fix our food situation, we wouldn't make it to New London, let alone find clues about my family.

This wouldn't have happened if we'd stayed in Brookfield. My friends were hungry because they were trying to help *me*. Why hadn't they wavered when I'd insisted we travel in early spring? They must have known it would be tougher to stay provisioned, even if the revivalists hadn't stripped the larders bare.

Josephine handed her empty bowl to Ben. "Sometimes, we've snared a squirrel, or Ben's caught a bird to add to the soup."

"What about the horses?" I asked. "This is the feed we brought for them, isn't it?"

Ben nodded. "Because we've stopped so early, they've had extra time to forage."

"Donkey is superb at finding patches of new grass. The horses have learned to follow him around," said Josephine, her voice cheerful.

I nodded and sipped the soup. It had less flavor than scent. "Since I know about our food situation, can I help?"

"Can you paint a loaf of Whistler's pepper bread?" Sally asked.

I shook my head. "Sadly, it's outside of my abilities."

"What can you paint?" asked Ben. "What are the rules?"

"Well, I can paint improvements to things, but unless I can see the whole object at once, it has to be a solid object. I must work within the season, so I can't paint a tree flowering in fall if it's a spring-flowering specimen. Creating something from nothing can take years to complete and isn't practical. Last, everything I paint has to observe and follow the natural order of things."

"No flying cows," said Sally.

"No flying cows," I agreed. "And with compounds"—I shrugged —"I could improve an ugly loaf of bread to be a beautiful loaf, but the resulting bread would taste the same as the original."

"What about changing something we have into something new?" asked Sally.

"Well, take the cooking pot. If needed, I could repair the pot or create a new one using it as a starting point. But the new pot won't do things this pot cannot."

"Like what?"

"Heating more slowly or becoming nonstick."

Josephine nodded. "Anything else?"

I hesitated. "There is one thing, but we never to mention it."

"Go on," urged Sally. "We're family."

Warmth bloomed throughout my core. *Family.* My throat tightened painfully, and I took a breath to clear it. "This is for your ears only," I warned.

They nodded, leaning forward.

"I don't erase," I said.

Josephine opened her mouth to say something, but I held up my hand to forestall her question.

"I *can* erase, but I don't. Improvements are a reordering of energy. Erasing is different and involves the destruction of energy, the destruction of matter. This violates the ethos of the artist. They train us to improve, not erase. Understood?"

They nodded.

"Then of erasing, we shall not speak again," I said firmly. The firelight danced across their faces, throwing strange shadows onto the nearest trees.

Ben cleared his throat. "All right, we know the rules. Suggestions?"

"A few edibles are available in early spring, but they'll be picked clean. Can you do something?" asked Josephine.

"Give me an example."

"Well, squirrels or birds gather the hazelnuts before we can. If we found a hazelnut tree, could you put nuts back onto it?"

"Yes."

Sally brightened. "We could also find partridge berry shrubs and oaks for acorns."

Ben rubbed the back of his head. "I saw boar tracks yesterday. If I find a promising gully, could you paint a corral trap?"

I nodded, taking another sip of soup. "A fish trap could be helpful, too."

"Our salt satchel is almost empty," said Sally. "Could you refill it if there is some left?"

"Yes."

The women exchanged smiles.

"Should we take a few days off to forage?" I asked.

Ben considered my question. "We're still a week from New London."

"Our supplies won't last a week," said Josephine.

"I'd welcome a roast pig," said Sally. "Have you seen any signs here?"

Ben shook his head. "Nothing today."

Josephine sighed. "So, we can continue forward and hope we find more tracks, or turn around and lose two days of travel."

"Plus, the time to hunt and forage," I added.

"Will the map show us anything?" Sally asked.

Nodding, Ben said, "Good idea."

"Sure, I'll get it." I returned with the map, spreading it on the ground. "We're here," I said, pointing to a location.

"Yes, here's the lake we passed earlier," Josephine agreed. "The map doesn't show any nearby holdings."

I tapped the map. "Look, the road switchbacks here, suggesting elevation."

Ben studied our route. "Topography would explain why there are no holdings. Might be a good place to scout for tracks."

"There's a small pond or tarn at the top," said Sally. "If it holds fish, we should camp there."

Ben rubbed his jaw. "I agree. Who's in favor of continuing forward tomorrow?"

We raised our hands.

"Me too," said Ben almost cheerfully. "All right, we'll leave tomorrow and try for this pond."

Charcoal growled, his hackles rising.

I pivoted. Josephine gasped as a man stepped out from behind a large stump.

He was tall and thin, his narrow face gaunt and eyes hooded. He wore trousers a size too small, exposing his ankles over broken leather boots. In the firelight, his coat looked odd—threadbare, frayed at the cuffs, and with a frilly ruffled collar which may have been a deep purple when new. He wore a hat with ear coverings neither fastened

269

up nor hanging down, but flared at the sides as if intending to flap away. The man held a branch almost as thick as his bony wrist.

"Now see here," Sally said in a thin voice.

The fire popped, and I flinched.

The man glowered balefully and tightened his grip on the branch.

"None of that," growled Ben from behind the stranger.

I hadn't seen or heard Ben slip behind the man, but he grabbed the man's arm, wresting the branch away.

The man's shoulders slumped.

"Who are you?" asked Josephine. "Why are you spying on us?"

Sullen, the man stared at us.

Ben threw the confiscated branch into the fire and stirred the soup. He filled one of the empty bowls, handing it to the man without a word.

The stranger stared at the bowl for a long moment and then drew it to his mouth with shaking hands. When he lowered the bowl, his face was streaked with tears.

"Tyrell. Tyrell Fruchtman," he croaked.

"Tyrell," said Sally, her voice sharp. "I'd say well met, but we aren't."

Tyrell stared at the ground and flushed.

"Nevertheless," Sally continued, "I think we deserve answers. Why were you lurking in the trees?"

"What were you planning to do with the branch?" added Josephine, moving next to me. "Hit us? Take by force what we've offered freely?"

I put an arm around her and drew her close for support and comfort. She leaned against me, warm and trembling. Ben tossed a surprised glance in Josephine's direction but said nothing.

Tyrell sighed, shoulders drooping. "I don't know," he admitted. "I've been hungry for so long."

"Are you alone?" I asked. Josephine stiffened, and I tightened my arm around her.

Tyrell rubbed his jaw and shook his head. "My wife and children are waiting a kilometer back. The smell of the food..." He broke off and stared at the fire. "The little one cried, and we were afraid you'd hear him."

My guilt ignited as I looked at my half-finished bowl of soup. It had gone cold, and I'd planned to give it to Charcoal.

Had Tyrell heard me complain about the simple meal while his family starved?

"Go," said Ben evenly, taking the half-finished bowl from Tyrell's hands.

"Sir—" Tyrell pleaded.

"Go," said Ben again. "Bring them here. We have little, but we'll share what we have."

Tyrell wiped his eyes and hurried from our camp. We watched until he was out of sight.

"Josephine," said Ben in a warning tone.

"Yes?"

"We have enough to share."

"And?"

"You were unkind."

Josephine glared at Ben and stalked off into the tree line.

Sally sighed. "I'll go after her this time. We need more firewood anyway."

Ben nodded and picked up the spade to shovel more of the coals into the pit.

I glowered at him. Ben supposedly cared for Josephine. Why was he treating her so harshly?

"What?" Ben asked without looking up.

"Someone attacked Josephine."

Ben looked at me, his eyes dark. "Today?"

I shook my head. "No, before we arrived in Brookfield. It's how I met her; I surprised her attacker."

Ben cocked his head and waited.

"The man was trying to—" I stopped, unwilling to say the words.

Ben studied my face. "So she gets to behave unkindly?"

Why was he being so obtuse? "Tyrell scared her."

"He startled all of us."

"But she—"

"Matthew, she's not alone anymore. Neither are you nor I. We are stronger together."

The truth of Ben's words sank into my core.

"Yes," I whispered.

"We need to trust each other, and we need to guard against allowing our combined strength and security to make us feel superior towards others."

"Superior? That's too strong."

"If we'd met Tyrell after replenishing our stores, would we have been so unwelcoming? Or would we have offered what we had?"

Chastened, I sat and put my arm around Charcoal. "I take your point."

"So do I." Josephine stood beside the fire, holding an armload of branches.

Sally carried a similar stack and stepped past Josephine, dropping hers at the edge of the flames. "Should we invite them to travel with us?"

Ben shrugged. "A decision for us to make together."

Josephine frowned. "Can we postpone our decision until after we hear their story? The world feels ever less secure."

"Seems prudent," said Sally. "Ben? Matthew?"

We looked at each other.

"Aye," said Ben. "But we listen to the story with open ears and open hearts. Agreed?"

THE STATE OF TYRELL'S FAMILY HORRIFIED ME. FOR THE FIRST time, I truly understood how privileged my upbringing had been. I'd never witnessed true deprivation before. Where Tyrell looked like an unstuffed scarecrow, his wife and children were emaciated to the point of barely being able to walk.

The children's faces were angular, hollowed in places, their skulls in sharp relief. There was no flesh on them; where children should be all roundness and pink, these were gray, sallow, and bony.

Josephine and Sally dashed forward to help the children, while Tyrell helped his sagging wife to a seat near the fire.

Upon seeing their condition, Ben watered down the soup and ladled bowls of broth without solids for the three new arrivals. When they proved they could keep the broth down, Ben filled the bowls, this time with small chunks of meat included.

The children, Moira and Conlin, fell asleep without finishing their second helpings, and Tyrell quickly finished their half-eaten portions.

Mute, I watched my friends help the Fruchtman family.

I didn't know how to help and was afraid of saying the wrong thing. My stomach growled loudly, and embarrassment washed through me, though no one noticed.

Piling wood onto the fire, I built it until flames leaped at the sky.

While the children slept, Tyrell and Kennedy Fruchtman shared their story. They were farmers and had worked a holding together. When a revival came to the area in early fall, they attended the show. Becoming friendly with the revival members, they invited the group to their holding for a visit.

The revivalists had spent the visit regaling the Fruchtman's with tales espousing the romance of the road and invited them to join the next revival meeting. They offered to help with the harvest for a portion of the reaping. The Fruchtmans, relieved to have the extra help, agreed.

The harvest had gone well, and the Fruchtman's enjoyed the next revival.

Upon arriving home, they found strangers occupying their holding. There was no trace of the revival members who'd stayed to tend it for them.

The strangers had built new livestock sheds, plowed the recently harvested wheat fields, and steadfastly refused to leave. The Fruchtmans consulted the local administrator, who was astonished to see them.

"The revivalists told the administrator we'd abandoned our holding to join the revival," Tyrell admitted. "The administrator had reassigned our home."

"That was the end of it?" Josephine asked, aghast, brushing back the older boy's hair.

Kennedy nodded. "Three generations of my family had farmed the holding, and we lost it."

The fire popped, and sparks landed on my knee. Cursing, I stood and brushed my leg.

What could I do to help? I didn't have words of comfort or wisdom; nothing I did or said could change the past.

I added wood to the fire, and the cloud of green wood smoke raked my throat until I coughed.

Josephine frowned at Kennedy. "It seems unfair. Sally, why would an administrator give their holding away?"

Sally shifted the sleeping child to her other shoulder. "An administrator's priority is to keep a community running. Communities rely on the surrounding farms to provide food. What else was he to do?"

"Still," said Josephine, looking doubtfully at Kennedy, "it seems cruel."

Kennedy's smile was small as she moved away from the fire. "It was our fault. The community was kind enough to assign us a dwelling for the winter."

"Why did you leave?" I asked, poking at the radiant coals and squinting at the intense heat.

"I thought we might find an abandoned holding," sighed Tyrell, dragging his seat farther from the flames. "Winters are hard, and people abandon holdings to move into communities."

"What will you do if you can't find a new farm?" asked Josephine. She glanced at the fire and shook her head at me.

Tyrell shrugged. "We'll try to find a community who needs or wants an additional farm nearby."

Sally looked at Tyrell. "You'll need a community with enough resources to support your family until you establish the holding."

Tyrell sighed. "Yes. Our best option is to find an established holding. We're good farmers."

Sally glared at me as I attempted to wrestle a log onto the fire. "Matthew, stop. It's already too much."

She faced the Fruchtmans. "Travel with us until you find a new holding."

She looked at us with a steely gaze. "It's that, or we leave them here to starve."

CHAPTER THIRTY-EIGHT

"Hullo!" I shouted happily. "We bear a boar!"

The sun had barely risen over the treetops, and though the morning was bitingly cold, I didn't feel the chill. Mists rose over the tarn, and concentric circles rippled on the surface. Sally was right; there were fish here.

The grazing horses nickered and whinnied in greeting, and the laden donkey brayed in response. I smiled at the little animal and looked at the dead pig. It would solve our major problem; even with the Fruchtmans, this was enough meat to feed us for days. Although it had taken an entire day to reach this campsite, moving our party here had been the right choice.

Charcoal streaked across the camp, dancing with excitement and yipping like a coyote.

"Sow," Ben corrected. "We have a fair bit of work ahead of us," he warned.

I didn't care what it took; I could already taste the pork.

Ben scratched his beard. "I have one serious question before we start."

"What?" asked Josephine.

"Roasted or stewed pork for dinner tonight?" Ben asked, smiling.

Startled, I gaped at my friend. When had his smiles become so rare that each was notable? He must have borne a great deal of anxiety about our dwindling food stores. Guilt clawed at me, and despite their excited chatter, a chill of dread snaked through me.

When Ben had said we were stronger together, I'd accepted the truth of his words. But would my friends have needed strength if they hadn't accompanied me?

Again, my thoughts turned to 'T'.

Josephine knew I had an unknown adversary, but I hadn't mentioned it to Ben or Sally. Why hadn't I said something during those first days on the road? It would have been easy for Sally or Ben to turn back then. But we'd been on the road for weeks now, and if I told them today, I wasn't sure either could return to Brookfield.

The presence of the Fruchtmans made telling my friends the whole truth even more difficult. With luck, we'd find a holding for them soon.

As soon as the opportunity presented itself, I'd share everything I knew with Ben and Sally.

Sally rubbed her hands together briskly. "Let's plan our day."

After a quick discussion to designate tasks, we turned to the work at hand. While Ben and Tyrell butchered the sow, I dug a shallow pit next to the fire. Josephine gathered firewood, and Sally and the children hunted for boughs in the length Ben had specified.

Josephine and I took the donkey and went to cut and fetch the boughs Sally found as Kennedy built up the fire and set a pot with water to heat near it.

Tyrell carried over the pile of fat he had trimmed from the meat and put it in the simmering pot to render the lard. He collapsed next to his wife, looking exhausted.

Ben and I built a square frame to stretch the pig over and a triangular-shaped structure on which the frame would rest, which we set over the pit.

"Look, it's a pig-canvas on an easel."

Josephine chuckled, shoveling glowing coals from the fire into the pit and rebuilding the flames.

Before midday, the pig was roasting over the bed of coals.

Ben and I flipped the frame front to back and top to bottom twice an hour or sooner, when the *sizzle-pop* of roasting flesh grew distracting.

Lunch was a thick stew of organ meat, pig blood, ramps Josephine had collected, cracklings from the lard Sally was rendering, and ground acorn meal.

Each bite decadent, my senses swooned at the earthy scent and flavors. After lunch, we sat dazed and sated around the fire.

"I feel like I'm being watched," said Josephine lazily. "But I'm too full to care."

Sally sighed. "Yes, I felt eyes too."

Ben straightened, scanning the tree line. "Have you seen anything?" he asked me.

I sprawled against a log, my arm flung over my eyes, uncomfortable but too lazy to move. Before my eyes drifted shut again, I noticed Charcoal.

All day, he'd guarded the roasting pig, but now stared at the path to camp, his body rigid.

Uneasy, I sat up, pointing at the dog.

Ben quietly stood. "Keep talking," he said in a low voice.

Josephine, her dark eyes following Ben as he stooped to shovel more of the coals into the pit, asked brightly, "Sally, who did you apprentice with?"

With a resigned expression, Sally replied, "I was afraid you'd ask."

Curious. "Why afraid?"

Sally made a face. "My teacher was my nephew."

"Your nephew?" asked Josephine.

Sally nodded as she watched Tyrell toss the remaining firewood into the flames. "My father was the youngest of three. His elder sister

278

was twenty years older and had a child immediately after marrying. My father was almost fifty when I was born."

I scratched my beard. "Your nephew and father were the same age?"

"Yes, roughly."

"I'll get more firewood," said Ben. He walked to the tree line opposite from the direction Charcoal faced, disappearing into the woods.

"Was it strange to apprentice with family?" I asked, thankful Ben was scouting for the invisible eyes. It amazed me the large man could move without noise.

Sally shrugged. "I have nothing to compare it with. I grew up in my nephew's household, so it made it a simple transition to go from being a fosterling to an apprentice."

"Why?" asked Tyrell curiously.

"He married my aunt."

I barked a laugh and poked the coals. "They married your nephew to your aunt? Small community. Tiny."

"Listen, you dingleberry sniffer, it wasn't like that," Sally snapped. "My aunt was my mother's half-sister and unrelated. Well, by blood."

"Where were your mother and father?" asked Kennedy.

Sally narrowed her eyes.

"Come on, Sally," I cajoled. "I want to hear the rest."

"Dead."

"Mmm," I replied, lips twitching. "How did they die?"

"Oh!" said Josephine. "Matthew, you shouldn't—"

"It's fine." Sally sighed. "He's obviously heard the story."

Josephine looked puzzled.

"They drowned," I said.

"That's not funny," Josephine warned, her brows knitting.

My lips twitched again, but I said nothing.

"Oh, all right," Sally sighed. "They drowned because they were drunk and went skinny dipping."

Josephine gasped.

"In December."

Josephine pressed her lips together, trying not to smile.

"The worst part," said Sally, "was someone found them in, well..."

"A passionate embrace?" I offered.

"Frozen solid," Sally agreed. "Stupid fools."

"How old were you?"

"Eight months. My nephew and aunt took me in and changed my name to Park."

"What name were you born with?"

"Sally Winters," she said, shaking her head in exasperation. "Can you even imagine?"

My belly shook with silent laughter, and I struggled to hold a neutral expression. Josephine's face reddened, and tears leaked from Kennedy's eyes.

A hissing wheeze exploded behind me. We turned en masse and saw Ben doubled over, holding his stomach with tears streaming down his face.

Watching Ben dissolve, I chortled.

Josephine lost it and laughed so hard she honked, sending us into fits of hysteria.

"Ben, did you find anything?" Sally gasped between laughs.

"No," he squealed, and we all laughed again.

When our mirth slowed, Sally got up, shaking like a dog. "Enough silliness. It's time to get back to work."

"Uh oh, the administrator rises." With a groan, I heaved myself to my feet. "Time to paint."

Sally grinned at me. "Correct. Let's get to fishing."

"Here's another fat trout," said Sally. "This trap was just the thing."

I gritted my teeth, trying to saw along a trout's spine without pulverizing the flesh or nicking the bone. The fish was cold and slippery, shivering in my grip like it was still alive.

We'd never preserve enough fish in time if I didn't improve my filleting skills. "It's harder to clean fish than butcher a hog."

"Sow," said Sally and Josephine in unison.

"The fish will travel better than the pork if we salt it," said Tyrell.

"I've filleted and salted eight today," said Sally. "Do you think we'll want more?"

Josephine sighed and looked at the fish in front of me. "Yes, we'll need a good supply." She wrinkled her nose. "Salted fish sounds terrible."

Sally nodded. "I'm leaching the last batch of acorns. If we can grind them, we can make a thickening flour and have a proper chowder."

"Maybe Ben packed something. Are we eating the partridge berries tonight?"

"We could make pemmican," said Kennedy. "We'd have more than fish to travel with then."

"Pemmican?" Josephine frowned. "I've heard the name before, but I don't remember where."

Sally slit another trout open. "It's something my grandfather used to make every fall to see us through spring. Another way to preserve meat."

"Mine too," said Kennedy. "I remember packing it for long trips every summer."

My fish slithered out of my grasp, landing in front of Josephine. "How did he make it?"

"When we butchered in the fall, we'd render the lard, and he'd cut thin strips of pork to smoke. I think he ground the dried meat. We'd pack the ground meat, fat, and dried berries into a square dish. Once it solidified, it kept for months."

Josephine handed the fish back. "Do you remember how much of each thing went into it?"

"Even parts. One to one to one."

Josephine nodded. "Maybe we should dry these berries."

Sally examined our camp, her expression doubtful. "We dried our berries in the sun or in the oven overnight."

Josephine squinted at the sky. "It's been bright today, but I don't think we'll see the sun. At least it is not drizzling."

"Could you put the berries on a tray near the fire?" I asked. The pemmican seemed unappetizing, but finding and transporting food for eight was going to be a problem. The more we could do now, the better. If we didn't gather enough, we'd stop again, and who knew if we'd find as productive a campsite. Traveling was becoming complicated.

"Let's try," said Sally. "Matthew, can you ask Ben if he brought anything to grind the pork?"

"And find out how much longer the sow will take!" called Josephine.

I found Ben dragging a short tree, roots still attached. "Did you knock it over yourself?"

"No, I suspect there's a bear nearby."

"A bear? Great. Exactly what we need."

"It's interested in the pork. Probably the eyes we felt watching us earlier."

"Speaking of, they asked me to ask you when the pig is ready."

"They?"

"Okay, me too. Lunch was great, but I can't stop thinking about dinner. The smell is maddening."

Ben laughed. "I've been thinking the same. Here, help me drag this back." Stepping into the clearing, Ben looked at the sky. "She's been roasting at least eight hours."

"At least." A root snagged my overcoat. "Blast, this thing is getting me dirty."

Ben grinned. "You've smeared your face with mud and blood."

"What?"

"Yeah, since we brought the sow back to camp this morning."

If Headmaster Sinclair could see me now.

I swiped at my cheek with my free hand. "Thanks for letting me know."

"Ladies," Ben said, dropping his end of the trunk near the fire. "Let's eat."

Sally squealed and dropped her fillet into the salt sack.

As Ben and I lifted the pig from the coals, fat dripped onto the hot coals with a *splat-sizzle*, sending the heavenly smell of roasting pork straight up my nose.

We heaved the frame onto the makeshift table, where it landed with an impressive *thud*.

Ben cut into one cheek and smiled. "Here," he said, passing out slivers of meat.

The meat was tender with crispy edges. I closed my eyes and slowly chewed, letting the salt-fat flavor coat my tongue.

Charcoal, drooling, nudged my hand.

"Oh"—Sally sighed—"this might be the best thing I have ever eaten."

Ben nodded, sectioning out the ribs. "Give me a second, and I'll have enough for us all."

Josephine handed out bowls, and we crowded around the pig with radiant smiles. Sally handed the first two bowls to the children.

Moira, sitting on her mother's lap, gnawed on a rib happily. Conlin tore at the meat and tossed the bone he'd picked clean to Charcoal. He held his bowl up, face greasy and eyes glazed.

Ben looked at Tyrell, who shrugged and nodded. Ben set another rib on the boy's bowl and wordless, Conlin shuffled back to his place next to his mother.

Kennedy smiled with her eyes while biting into her own rib.

Trying to marshal my patience as the women took their turns, I maneuvered the root ball of the tree into the blaze. When I accepted the bowl Ben handed me, my hands shook with anticipation. Sinking my teeth into the meat, my eyes rolled backward.

This bite, this moment, this group of people... I'd never been happier.

Chewing slowly, I looked at my friends. Whatever came, I'd do my best to protect and provide for them.

CHAPTER THIRTY-NINE

I scowled at the heavy clouds threatening rain. "It's been nearly a week, and we're still two days from New London."

Josephine looked behind us. "Shh, the Fruchtmans will hear you. You're hungry; it's past time for lunch."

We'd waited four days for the Fruchtmans to be strong enough to travel, using the time to salt fish, dry pork, and make Sally's grandfather's pemmican. Even with the delay, the Fruchtmans were not strong enough to travel on foot, so we put them on our horses, which meant I was once again walking.

Tyrell had protested, declaring himself well enough to walk, but he agreed to ride when he realized he was slowing us.

Sally had offered to contribute her pony, but we'd convinced her to ride ahead to scout.

The going had been rough; the roads were in terrible shape, potholed and muddy, covered by fallen trees, and in some places, flooded. Sally's scouting forays had helped us find alternative roads when needed.

"Matthew! Josephine!" Sally came into view, bouncing on the back of her pony, arms and legs flapping.

"Blast," Josephine muttered. "It's never good news when she comes bolting back."

"Hullo, Sally. What have you found?"

Breathlessly, she shook her head. "The bridge is out a kilometer ahead."

Ben stopped next to Josephine. "Is the river fordable?"

Sally shrugged. "It's high. There's a lot of debris."

"Perfect," Ben muttered. He sighed and looked at me. "Map?"

I nodded and glanced at Oxide.

Kennedy shifted the sleeping weight of Moira and nudged the horse toward me.

I pulled the map out of the saddlebags and unfolded it. The ground was too damp to lay the map down, so I tossed it over the top of Magnesium's packsaddle.

Tyrell, riding Ben's mule, nudged the animal forward, craning his neck to see the map. "Where are we?"

I traced the route we had followed with my finger. "We camped here last night, and this is probably the river ahead."

Josephine sighed. "We've traveled all day and covered such a short distance." She looked at Sally. "How bad is the bridge? Is it something Matthew could fix?"

Sally cocked her head. "The far side looked fine, but the road's buckled on this side. It's missing the whole middle."

Ben traced a road. "This is our alternate route if we can't cross the river."

"So far?" Tyrell shook his head and sighed. "It's beyond where we camped last night."

"Is there a place to camp at the end of the road, Sally?" asked Ben.

She rocked her head back and forth. "I suppose. It's not like we'd be blocking anyone if we set up smack in the middle of the road."

Ben nodded and raised his eyebrows at us. "Well?"

"Let's go check it out." The idea of backtracking and adding two more days of walking was unappealing.

Within a quarter-hour, we arrived at the end of the road. The roar of the unseen river unsettled the horses.

"Let's tie the horses here," said Josephine.

With help, the Fruchtmans dismounted.

"I'll stay with the children," said Kennedy as Conlin kicked a stone and rubbed his backside.

As Sally reported, the pavement had buckled and twisted at the edge. Cautiously, I moved to the shoulder of the road to get a better look, not trusting the pavement to support my weight.

When Sally had first told us of the bridge, I'd wondered if someone had sabotaged it to deter me.

What a daft, arrogant idea.

The bridge had crossed a wide river channel and fallen long ago. The near and middle sections were missing, but the far side looked solid.

After observing the damage, I wasn't sure if I was relieved or disappointed. My eyes swept over the ruined bridge as I considered how I'd fix it.

Ben joined me and pointed at the far bank, a hundred meters upriver from the bridge. "They ford the river there when the water isn't so high."

Logs and other debris littered the roiling water. A cracking sound, like a tree splitting in a storm, occasionally punctured the roar of the mud-brown water. Its fetid scent made the idea of crossing it even less appealing.

I shuddered. "It's not safe to cross."

Josephine, standing on the other side of the road, shouted something inaudible, pointing at the bridge supports.

We craned our necks but saw nothing.

Josephine beckoned, and we scrambled across the broken pavement to join her, Sally, and Tyrell.

"There's a rope between supports!" Josephine shouted as we neared.

"We can hear you now," I said.

Josephine flushed and pointed.

She was right; someone had strung a rope from support to support. "What is it?"

Ben examined the structure. "Footbridge."

"Footbridge? *That*?" asked Sally.

Tyrell nodded. "Yes, I see it. You can make out the steps before it passes beneath the tree."

Sally shuddered. "There's no way I'm crossing it. On foot *or* on My Darling."

Josephine grinned. "Best pony name ever."

"What do you think?" Ben asked me.

I rubbed the back of my head. My hair was getting long; maybe there'd be a barber in New London. "I could paint a new bridge, using the far side as a model, but are the supports solid enough?"

We heard a thin cry, and half-turned, looking at Kennedy and Moira. Tyrell shrugged and turned back to the river.

Ben studied the water. "See how the debris has stacked between those two supports?"

Josephine nodded. "It looks like a platform."

"The river has squeezed it together, like a raft. The force of the water must be immense, but the supports look unaffected. See how they're all in a perfect alignment? If they'd weakened, I'd expect them to be askew."

The faint wail came again, and Tyrell sighed. "I'll go help Kennedy."

"Are we going to camp here?" asked Sally.

Ben looked at me. "Your call. We can't cross the water, and the stock will never make it across the footbridge, so it's a new bridge or we backtrack."

This would be a big job, but I was confident in my skill. "I'll improve the bridge, but it'll take time."

Again, the faint cry floated over the roar of the river.

Sally and I looked back at the Fruchtmans. Tyrell was squatting and talking to Moira, who was spinning around him, arms wide.

"Odd," Sally muttered. She turned back to the river and gasped. "Is... is that a *child*?"

"Where?"

Our eyes scanned the bridge, bridge supports, and swirling brown water.

"There!" said Sally, pointing. "No, not—"

"Oh!" gasped Josephine. "There, on the footbridge."

"Blast, blast, blast," swore Ben.

Shaking my head, I scanned the expanse. In the middle of the bridge clung a small child, her screams terrified. My heart hammered in my chest.

The thin, keening cry floated again, and I couldn't bear it.

Ben and I scrambled down the steep slope, rocketing over large boulders and chunks of broken asphalt.

Up close, the footbridge looked impossibly flimsy and fragile. What I had assumed was rope was differing lengths of steel cable, clamped together at odd intervals. The cables were of different thicknesses, and they had doubled or trebled the thinner strands.

They'd pieced together the footing with scraps of sheet metal, lengths of iron scaffolding, and unevenly milled lumber, with the occasional branch lashed to cover a hole. Large gaps showed between treads.

Ben shook the nearest cable.

The footbridge sighed and twanged, and the child shrieked again.

"Will it handle our weight?" I shouted.

Ben shrugged, grimacing.

The child screamed, waving an arm and kicking her foot.

"We don't have time to improve the bridge!" I shouted. "We need to act *now*."

Ben studied the supports as if trying to gauge the likelihood of reinforcing the footbridge.

Desperate, I bounded onto the bridge without waiting for Ben's decision. Running lightly, I leaped from one step to the next, hoping each would hold long enough to support my weight. The frayed metal fibers repeatedly punctured and lacerated my fingertips as they skimmed the waist-high cables. The footbridge sighed and twanged, each alarming sound audible above the roar of the brown water rushing beneath.

When I reached the girl, I bent down in a fluid motion to pick her up. She clung like a limpet to the footbridge, one arm and leg hooked around a tread. Again, I tried to wrest her up, but she screamed louder, refusing to let go.

I shouted, "I need you to let go. We need to get off this bridge!"

She slapped my hand and pointed down.

I peered between the treads at the debris and swirling brown water. I shook my head, and she pointed again. This time, I leaned over the edge of the footbridge and looked directly down onto the mass of debris trapped below.

The body of a woman lay on a log below us.

And then the world died.

"She's alive?" I shouted.

The girl nodded, her face tear-streaked.

"I'll get help!" I yelled. "I'll come back for her!"

The girl looked at me. The bridge wobbled and twanged, and I gasped, hooking my elbow over the cable railing.

"I *promise*. I'll come back and try to help, okay?"

The girl nodded.

"Let go, and I'll carry you."

Slowly, she reached her arms toward me, one leg still curled around the railing's support.

The bridge shook.

For a heart-stopping moment, I pictured us tumbling into the raging waters, and bile flooded my mouth. Pushing the thought away, I hoisted the girl and settled her over one hip. She clung to me, furnace-warm. I picked my way back to the shore, where Ben was waiting with the others.

I handed the child to Josephine.

"Matthew, your hands," Sally gasped.

They were red and seeping blood. I stared at them.

Ben reached out his hand to help me off the footbridge, but I shook my head.

"There's a woman back there."

"Where?" asked Ben, scanning the footbridge.

"On the logs."

Josephine paled and tightened her arms around the child she was holding. "What?"

"I promised I'd try."

"What do you need?" asked Sally, snapping into administrator mode.

"Rope?"

"I'll come," said Ben. "We'll need a length of canvas too, Sally."

Josephine blanched. "You can't climb onto the debris; it could give way at any minute!"

I clenched my fists, testing my hands. "No time to waste. Take the girl to Kennedy?"

Sobbing, Josephine turned, picking her way across the rubble as she cradled the child.

Sally's mouth tightened. "We'll go for supplies. Be careful."

I flexed my hands. "Secure Charcoal too. I don't want him following me."

Making our way back to the center of the river, the footbridge creaked and groaned.

"She's there!" I shouted.

Ben tried to look over the edge, but the footbridge tilted and sighed ominously. I threw myself to the other side to balance Ben's weight.

"You'll need a harness," Ben shouted. "I'll belay you."

"What about a rope ladder?"

Ben shook his head. "The logs are unstable. Your weight could shift them, and you'd go under."

"How do we bring her up?"

"If she's alive?" Ben shouted back. "We'll try a canvas sling. If she's not..."

I nodded, stomach queasy, wishing I hadn't made the promise to the girl. This was stupid. For all we knew, the woman was dead.

The footbridge bounced, and we glanced at the shore. Tyrell picked his way toward us, coils of rope over his shoulder. Sally waited on the shore. She waved and, without thinking, I waved back. Seeing my wave, Tyrell paused and turned to look behind him.

"No!" Ben and I shouted in unison as Tyrell's foot slipped.

For a heartbeat, Tyrell appeared frozen, looking at the water through the gap his foot had stepped through. With a frantic lunge, he pitched forward and caught the handrail, arresting his fall.

I let out a strangled cry, and Ben grabbed the back of my shirt before I could move to help.

With glacial speed, Tyrell picked himself up and continued. When he reached us, his face had a greasy sheen. Ben clapped him on the shoulder and took the rope, fashioning a harness for me, like the one we had used to climb to the Crown.

"Hook this end through the ring!" he shouted, pointing at an iron loop two meters above his head. I nodded and took the end of the rope. With my hands flat against the rough concrete of the bridge support, I stepped into the cradle of Ben's hands and lunged for the ring. The pitted, rough metal scraped my injured hands. Though flakes of rust fell when I grasped it, it seemed sturdy enough, and I threaded the rope's end through the ring, tying it securely.

"Done!" I shouted, lowering myself back down the rope.

My bloodied hands burned.

"I'll send you down on this rope!" yelled Ben, leaning closer. "Try not to touch the logs and lay flat in the harness while we lower you."

I nodded.

"Check if she's alive. If she is, get a rope under her."

"Where?"

"Back of the knees, armpits. If she's unconscious, she'll sag in the middle, but if we can get her up a half-meter, slide the canvas under her."

"Let's do it!" I shouted before I could lose my nerve. I climbed over the railing, light-headed and heart hammering.

"Give the rope a sharp tug when you're ready!" Ben shouted as they lowered me toward the roiling brown water.

CHAPTER FORTY

Decimeters at a time, I slid closer to the woman and the rushing water. When low enough, I shouted, arresting my descent.

From this height, the mass of debris was unstable, heaving up and down within the eddy as the strong currents fought the natural buoyancy of the logs. Strangely, the noise from the river had diminished, though the mineral smell of the water had increased. In the relative quiet, I frantically checked the woman for a pulse, leaving bloody fingerprints on her cool, clammy skin.

I couldn't find a pulse, but she seemed marginally warm to my icy fingers. Even if she was dead, I couldn't leave her. I'd made a promise.

With trembling hands, I wrapped the second rope behind the back of her knees and slipped it under her arms. I tugged on the rope and waited with my hand under the small of her back. Ben and Tyrell hoisted her body into the air. Unfolding the canvas, I slipped it beneath her.

My motion had introduced a slow spin to my rope, so I touched a stub on a nearby log to steady myself.

The log bucked under my hand before disappearing, and the mass of floating debris undulated and rotated.

Mouth dry, my hands shook as I slipped the rope underneath the canvas and secured it around her torso in a makeshift hammock. The log she was lying on shifted, and I snatched her limp arm to keep it from being pinned, folding it across her chest.

The debris mass groaned.

Panicked, I tugged on the rope, signaling Ben even though I hadn't fully secured her legs. Her body rose toward the footbridge.

She'd lifted almost a meter when a loud crack startled me. The debris shuddered, and a log at the edge of the swirling mass sucked down, out of sight. I yelped as the log surfaced next to me, above my eye line.

I must get out of here.

Ben and Tyrell, intent on pulling the prone woman to the footbridge, were unaware of how precarious my position had become. As the debris broke apart, I swung my body into an upright position, keeping my legs out of the way. On arms of rubber, I climbed the rope toward the bridge, hands shrieking with pain. Sweat burned my eyes, and I tried to wipe my forehead on my straining biceps as I climbed.

I hauled myself onto the fragmented decking of the footbridge in time to see Ben hoisting the rescued woman over his shoulder. Tyrell reached down to help me up, but lost his balance and pitched forward, landing across me with a grunt.

Exhausted, we lay on the swaying bridge, waiting for it to stop shaking.

Tyrell rolled from me and crawled toward the shore. Spent, I retrieved the ropes, glancing below. The debris mass had dispersed, leaving only swirling brown water beneath the footbridge.

We'd rescued her just in time.

My legs quaking, I stumbled off the footbridge. "Is she alive?" I nearly fell and staggered back to my feet. "Alive?"

"Hurry. Catch him before he falls into the water!"

I stumbled again and again as my friends helped me climb the steep bank.

"Alive?" I croaked as we reached the top. Nauseous, I shivered violently.

"Rest, my friend," said Ben's voice from a great distance.

LANGUIDLY, I SWAM TOWARD THE LIGHT. THE WATER WAS deliciously warm, and it tempted me to stay where I was floating. I wallowed, luxuriating in the sense of peace and serenity.

"I don't know. We'll ask when he wakes," a woman's voice said, rousing me.

"Is he still sleeping?" asked another voice.

"No," I croaked, reluctant to release my dream. "I'm awake. Have I been sleeping long?"

"Did she say anything?" asked Sally.

I shook my head to clear it. "Who?"

Sally frowned. "Did she say anything? The little girl."

"Little girl?" Nothing made sense.

"Did he hit his head?"

"Matthew." Something in the tone of Ben's voice brought reality rushing back.

I sat up and looked around, blinking. "Sorry, what?"

Sally sighed. "We have a little girl who hasn't said a word and an unconscious woman. We were hoping you could tell us something about them."

The world whirled around me as I tried to stand. "I'm sorry; I'm having trouble focusing."

"You've been asleep for hours and missed lunch," said Josephine.

"Am I the only one who slept?"

Sally ticked her fingers. "Ben, Tyrell, you, the unconscious woman you dragged out of the river, Moira, and Kennedy."

"Perhaps we've been pushing too hard," Ben admitted. "I've never been one to nap. Now..." He looked at us.

"Now," Josephine repeated.

"Let's walk," said Sally.

I followed them on jelly-like legs until we were out of earshot of the others. My hands were stiff beneath bandages I didn't remember receiving.

"Now what?" Sally asked.

Scowling, I studied my bandaged hands. "What are we talking about?"

Josephine sighed. "*Concentrate*. We have Tyrell and Kennedy plus their two kids, an unconscious woman, and a mute girl. What are we going to do with all of them?"

I pawed the back of my head, shrugging. "Suggestions?"

"Make camp and reevaluate tomorrow," said Sally promptly. "We need to figure out shelters and food while Matthew paints. Maybe the woman will wake soon."

"And if she doesn't?" Josephine asked, raising an eyebrow. "We *are* still trying to reach Warwick, aren't we?"

"What are you proposing?" I asked wearily. "To leave them some dried fish and ride on as soon as I can paint a bridge?"

"That's not fair," Josephine snapped. "We're trying to help you."

I flushed. "You implied I'm slowing our progress on *purpose*."

I looked at Ben for support, but he met my gaze impassively.

"Well, maybe if you stopped trying to rescue everyone, we could get somewhere," Josephine responded hotly.

"Begging your pardon, Miss Pliny," I said as coils of heat rose through me. "If I could remind you how *we* met?"

Josephine stalked away.

Exasperated, I turned to the others. "Can you believe her?" I slapped my bandaged mitts together.

Sally squinted at her shoes, and Ben said nothing.

"Really?" I shouted. "That's all the support I'm going to get?"

"Don't ask us to take sides," said Ben.

Sally held up her hands. "Regardless of who's right or wrong, we have six people who need our help. I'd like to know what we're doing."

Ben nodded. "We need a plan."

"Fine," I said, my eyes tight. "*I'll* go paint a bridge. *You* figure out the rest."

Charcoal followed me, his eyes anxious.

My horses were still standing saddled where we'd tethered them and nickered with relief as I approached. Fuming, I pulled their saddles off, trying to dig out my art supplies, but the bandages made my hands useless. Growling, I unwound the bandages and left them where they fell. I chewed my lip as I stalked to the end of the road to set up my easel.

As soon as I got the paper clipped to the easel, a light rain began.

"Brilliant."

I walked back and retrieved a tarp and ropes to construct a temporary shelter.

No one said anything or offered to help.

Stomping back to my easel, my temper grew, and I fueled it with memories of how I'd helped each of them. How dare they judge me for helping others?

With savage movements, I hauled on the rope, tightening the tarpaulin overhead until it was taut and shed rain.

My hands hurt.

The paper on my easel was now too wet to use, prompting yet another trip to my packsaddle for fresh paper. I tore the sodden paper from the easel, clipped in the new piece, and scowled at the river and ruined bridge.

The paper lay ready, dry, sheltered, clipped in place, and blank.

I mixed pigments but couldn't get the colors right. The swirling brown water changed shades between glances from my palette to the scene in front of me. The bridge supports glimmered wetly one moment and glistened with slime the next. I paced, frustrated by the rapidly shifting light, the color density of the pigments at my disposal, and the lack of support from my friends.

The paper, devoid of pigment, mocked me.

"What's it for?" a small voice asked.

I turned, expecting to see Moira Fruchtman. Instead, the girl I'd rescued stood outside the shelter.

"Come underneath," I said. "It's raining," I added, not knowing what else to say.

The girl stepped under the tarpaulin and stood next to Charcoal, looking from me to the empty paper.

"I'm... I'm—" I raked my fingers through my hair, wincing as the cuts on my hands snagged.

I'm fixing the bridge? I'm trying to capture light? I'm making the path easier for my ungrateful friends?

"I'm Matthew," I said feebly, bending to meet her eyes. "What's your name?"

The grave girl studied me. We could have been related. Though her face had a child's roundness, we shared similar high, wide cheekbones, upturned monolid eyes, thin lips, and fair complexions.

No response.

I straightened. "I'm having trouble mixing the right colors for the bridge."

"Do you have to paint it with the right colors?"

Frowning, I considered her question. "Not if I sketch in charcoal. With a sketch, I work to capture the scene, not the light." I dug into my pack for a pencil. "Thank you, that was helpful."

I examined the scene before sketching the outlines.

The girl moved closer, watching.

I waited for her to speak, to ask the questions everyone asked. When she didn't, I stopped and turned, expecting to see she had wandered away.

She waited for me to continue.

Shrugging, I returned to my work.

I was working on capturing the shadows cast across the turbid water when the girl walked to the other side of me, so she could watch what I was doing and look at the scene I was sketching. Again, I expected her to ask me something, but the child remained silent.

"I don't mind if you talk while I draw."

Silence.

"When I was at the abbey learning how to sketch, the masters would often tell stories. I learned how to listen to the stories while drawing."

"I like stories."

"Me too. Ben, the big guy, is a terrific storyteller. Maybe he'll tell one tonight. What stories do you like?" I sketched, waiting for her to answer. When none came, I stopped and turned to look at her. She stood in the same place, this time holding a small stick.

Charcoal watched the girl with interest.

I returned to my work but kept my head tilted so I could monitor her in my periphery. While shading the edge of the far bank, I watched her move her stick, copying my movements. With short, exaggerated strokes, I sketched the vegetation in the foreground. Again, she mimicked me, but when I turned toward her, she lowered her arm, impassive.

"My name is Matthew," I said again.

No answer.

I sighed and continued sketching.

Strange girl.

I worked on the scene, aware the others were setting up camp. I expected someone to come to fetch us, but they gave us a wide berth.

Fine. Whatever.

I took my time sketching the river. "I've always enjoyed drawing water. The ways it moves and flows."

"I like how it shimmers up above."

Pausing, I thought about her statement. "I once lay on my back and tried to draw the flickering of water on the ceiling of the sea cave."

"Did it look right?"

"No." I sketched again. "Over and over, I returned to it. I tried pencil, acrylic, watercolor, oils. Those are all different mediums, different ways of creating art."

I squinted at the drawing, comparing it to the scene.

The girl stepped closer and pointed at the second bridge support.

I examined the drawing, looked at the bridge support, and laughed. "You're right, how silly of me." I added the texture of the concrete to the surface and looked at the child.

She nodded in approval.

I continued, focusing on the detail of the existing bridge deck. "I thought my problem was with capturing water, so I drew water. Luckily, the abbey stood at the edge of the ocean."

"What's an abbey?"

"It's where they train artists. You get sent to one as a small boy, and you live there and learn how to draw, paint, and sculpt from master artists. I was younger than you when they sent me to live there."

"How old are you?"

"Old. How old are you?"

No response.

"Who's the lady we rescued?"

Silence.

Shrugging, I continued, "I painted the millpond nearby. I painted the ocean—the waves hitting the pebbles, the birds landing on the water, and the fish underneath it. I painted a creek tumbling over a big rock."

Wiping the charcoal with the side of my finger, I smeared it. "I painted a lighthouse and won an award. Once I'd mastered painting water, I went back to the cave to try again." I shook my head.

"No good?"

"No good," I agreed. I finished the bridge decking, but skipped the railing. "Done."

She pointed to where the railing should be. "Not here."

"Right you are. Good eye." I sketched the railing. "I'm finished for tonight, and I'm hungry."

"I'm hungry, too."

"Let's go see what Ben has cooked."

Together, we walked back to camp.

Sally looked up as we approached. "How did it go?"

"I've lost the light for today. I want to look at it tomorrow with fresh eyes."

She nodded. "Are you hungry, honey?"

The child slid closer to me.

"She is," I confirmed.

Sally smiled. "My name is Sally."

The girl met her eyes but said nothing.

I shrugged. "Is dinner ready?"

"I don't know what Ben is cooking, but it sure smells good. Why don't you go over there and sit down?" said Sally to the girl, pointing toward the fire.

The girl slouched to a log near the fire and dropped onto it.

Charcoal sniffed her face, stub wiggling, and the child giggled.

"Did she say anything to you?" Sally asked in a low voice.

"She asked questions."

"So, she can talk." Sally nodded. "Did you get her name? Or the name of the woman?"

I shook my head. "She didn't answer when I asked." I looked around. "Where's Josephine?"

Sally narrowed her eyes. "You leave her alone."

I raised my hands, but Sally shook her finger at me. "Let's not argue amongst ourselves. We have enough to deal with."

I sighed. "You're right."

"Apologize when you see her," said Sally.

"For wha—"

Sally narrowed her eyes.

"I'll see if Ben needs help," I muttered.

I approached Ben, flexing my stiff hands and sniffing the pork-scented air.

Charcoal joined me, nose twitching.

"I've lost the light for today. The girl talked but didn't tell me her name. What can I do here?"

"Firewood," said Ben.

I waited, but Ben said nothing else.

"My new friend likes stories," I said, trying to engage him.

Nothing.

Shrugging, I turned away. "Come on, Charcoal. Apology. Firewood. Fine. Whatever."

CHAPTER FORTY-ONE

Unsettled by dreams of muddy water and staggering scarecrows, I woke early. The disturbing images receded when I opened my eyes, but the uneasy feeling didn't abate. The camp was quiet, and I lay still, trying to remember what in my dreams had troubled me.

Charcoal nudged my hand, and I stroked the dog's neck.

Kennedy's poultices had done their work, and my hands were less swollen.

With the addition of so many, we'd divided the camp into male and female sleeping areas. Ben, Tyrell, Conlin, and I were under one shelter, and the women were under the shelter nearest the fire. Based on the snorts and sighs around me, I was the only one awake.

My arms protested yesterday's exertion as I rose and dressed quietly.

A misty rain pattered as Charcoal and I walked to the end of the road. The donkey stood beneath the tarpaulin shelter and raised his nose to greet me. Obscured by the animal, I didn't see the girl standing beside the donkey until I reached them.

Charcoal, stub wiggling, sat at the girl's feet and smiled at her.

"Good morning. Sleep well?" I asked, not expecting an answer.

Pulling the previous day's sketch from my portfolio, I handed the folder to the girl. She opened it, paging through the sketches and paintings.

"Today, I'm sketching the new bridge using the remaining part as a model."

She watched me select charcoal pencils. "Are they different?"

I nodded. "Each has a different density. There are two main kinds of pencils we artists use for sketching. One is graphite, and the other is charcoal. I enjoy working with charcoal."

"How are they made?"

"Very good question." I pulled a new charcoal pencil from my pack. "They make these pencils from hollowed-out wood. Here, where it's black, is a hole they fill with charcoal or graphite. Charcoal comes from scorched materials, usually wood. Different woods make different charcoals."

At the mentions of his name, the dog scampered around us, eyes wild and tongue lolling.

"I can pull a stick out of the fire and draw?" she asked, playing with Charcoal's ears.

"I suppose. If you burn the wood, it becomes ash. But if you bury a hard stick in the glowing coals, it drives out the water and turns black. You could use it, but your hand would turn black too. A pencil maker grinds the charcoal, adds a binder, and compresses it into the hollowed wood."

"What's a binder?"

"Mmm, I suppose it's a compound used to combine things."

"Like glue?"

"Well... could I make a ball from a handful of sand?"

The girl shook her head.

"What if I got it wet?"

"The sand would clump but fall apart when it dried. You could add clay or mud or... oh. A binder?"

"Yes. Many binders are clay-based. More binder results in a

305

harder pencil and a finer line. For a thick, dark line, you want more charcoal and less binder. These three pencils have different amounts of binder, so they produce different line thicknesses and different colors, from a light gray to dark black."

"Oh. Which one does the new bridge need?"

"I sketch with a medium-weight pencil. For fine detail, I use a hard pencil, then add contrast and shading with a soft one."

She nodded and stepped back.

I scrutinized the sketch, appraising it for errors or omissions.

If the sketch wasn't good enough to move forward, I'd start over and redraw the bridge. For my best work, I needed mental clarity, so yesterday's argument could've affected my mind's sight. My eyes flicked from the scene to my drawing to assess my work, but the drawing was good—anchored, balanced, and complete.

Satisfied, I closed my eyes to sharpen my mental vision of the finished bridge.

Once focused, I sketched using rapid strokes. A deep cracking noise rose over the river sounds, and birds erupted from the surrounding trees in a cloud of alarm.

Beside me, the girl observed my work but remained silent.

When finished, I set my pencils down and stretched, my neck popping and cracking. The girl stood at the edge of the old road, one hand resting lightly on Charcoal.

I checked the drawing one last time before joining them.

"Let's try it out," I said, holding my hand out to her.

She took it and stepped onto the new pavement without hesitation. We ambled to the bridge's midpoint, where she dropped my hand and grabbed the railing to peer over the side. Mouth dry, I followed her, ready to catch the back of her coat if she leaned out too far.

"Look," she said, pointing.

I leaned over the railing and peered down at the footbridge. "Not a good bridge." The brown water rushing beneath it made me dizzy, and I gulped as I swayed, the air tasting of rain.

"Scary," she agreed.

Faint cheering floated over the river's noise, and we grinned at each other. We'd gained an audience. Sally waved, and I waved back, releasing the cold metal railing.

"Let's take our bow," I said, making a deep, formal bow.

The girl copied me, and Charcoal stretched next to her.

"My friends usually tell me their names," I said, walking toward our camp. "I hope we're friends."

"We are. I'm Akiko."

"Well met, Akiko."

"How d'you do that?" Conlin asked, hands on hips and eyes narrowed as he squinted at the bridge. His sister peeked around him.

Akiko and I looked at each other.

"Art," I said. The scent of porridge and wood smoke floated toward us. "Is breakfast ready?"

Conlin held his ground. "Are you a wizard?"

Smiling, I shook my head. "No, just an artist. May we pass?"

Akiko ignored the boy and stepped around him. Conlin flinched as she passed but said nothing, giving me a sideways glance as he stepped out of my way.

"The lady woke up," he reported, falling in step with me.

"Wonderful news. What's her name?"

Conlin shrugged, uninterested. He ran back toward camp, and his sister trotted after him.

Reaching my friends, I stiffened, yesterday's tensions fresh in my memory. The care I'd taken with the bridge was partly in apology for my part in yesterday's fight.

Would it be enough?

"Well done," said Sally.

The tightness in my chest loosened.

Josephine smiled but said nothing. It was a start and was all I needed. I reached for her shoulder and gave it a small squeeze. Her face softened, and my heart lifted.

The new woman stepped out from behind Ben.

"Hullo," I said, catching my breath.

She had large, dark, expressive eyes which smiled when she did. Masses of dark, tight ringlets framed her symmetrical, oval face. She smiled again, genuine and warm, and time slowed.

"Hullo, Artist. Well met."

"Matthew," I said, my heart thundering. "Matthew, please."

She looked down and smiled. "Very well met, Matthew. I'm Cara."

When she looked up and smiled at me from beneath her lashes, I was lost.

"I HOPE NEW LONDON HAS A BAKER. A GOOD BAKER," SAID Sally.

"I want to sleep in a proper bed," said Josephine. "Ben, what about you?"

"Boots."

"What?"

Ben stuck out a foot and wiggled an exposed toe. "Boots," he repeated.

Cara laughed, and I grinned at her.

Though no one asked, what I wanted most was to whittle our party back down to a manageable number.

"Ben, if you hadn't spun tales last night, I'd wonder if you could speak in full sentences," Cara teased.

Ben winked at Cara. "We should reach New London this afternoon. What are you looking forward to?"

Cara sighed. "Hot water. I need a bath."

Hoping no one had noticed my flush, I concentrated on Ben's exposed toe to keep visions of Cara in a steaming tub off my mind's canvas.

"Mmm," agreed Josephine. "A hot bath and an actual bed."

"A hot bath and a change of clothes," Cara corrected, looking at her grimy coat and trousers. "I've enjoyed sleeping under the stars," she said, throwing a smile at me, "but I need clean clothes. If—"

"I'll help," I blurted. "We'll exchange artwork for a trousseau."

She smiled and stroked my arm, sending shivers down my body.

"Thank you. I'll need a few simple things to hold me until I can settle."

"Settle?"

"Yes, I need a home. Any home. A place to plant roots; I'm not built for the road."

"Maybe because you can't remember your past?"

"Mmm. Or maybe I'm not meant to travel. Wouldn't you like a snug little house? Waking up each day with a loved one?"

Cara stumbled, and I extended my arm. She entwined hers, and my heart fluttered as we strolled together.

Too soon, Ben called for a stop. We'd arrived at an open meadow, and the horses pawed to be let loose.

Cara smiled as she released my arm. "I'm on lunch duty with Sally. See you."

Though tempted to follow and volunteer my labor, I knew Sally would tease me if I offered.

Cara passed Kennedy with a nod, turning to wave at me again.

Kennedy grimaced as Moira squirmed in her lap.

"Here, let me help," I said, reaching for the girl.

Murmuring her thanks, she handed me her daughter. The child squealed and ran toward her brother the moment her feet hit the road.

"I'm sorry we're monopolizing your horses," said Kennedy, dismounting.

Josephine shook her head and patted Fox's neck. "No, you needed to rebuild your strength. How are you feeling?"

"Better. I still tire too easily, but I'm feeling more myself than in a long time," said Kennedy. "It's a blessing we haven't found a holding yet. Farming is hard work."

"Is it rewarding?" I asked.

"Most of the time. Opening a jar of your own tomatoes in the middle of winter provides a taste of summer sunshine when the world is bleak and cold. It makes the effort worth it."

Josephine looked around to make sure we were alone. "Kennedy, can I ask a question?" she said in a low voice.

"Certainly. What about?"

"The revival."

Kennedy flinched. "What of it?" she asked, looking at me.

Josephine followed Kennedy's gaze. "Would you mind giving us a moment?"

I glanced from her to Kennedy. Though I wanted to hear the conversation, I said, "Of course."

"Thank you," Josephine called as I walked away.

My friends bustled about, completing their tasks. Somehow, I'd lost touch with the daily workings of our party.

"Lonely in a crowd," I said, watching them.

Charcoal pressed his nose into my palm.

Feeling as useful as lipstick on a mule, I leaned against a sun-warmed boulder and tossed a stick for Charcoal. He bounded through the tall grass, flushing a grouse whose wings drummed a hurried *thwap-thwap-thwap*.

Even with the repaired bridge, it had taken nearly four days to get here.

Our party had grown from four travelers on four horses to ten travelers, three of them children.

The weaker members of our party took turns riding the four saddle animals, leaving five or six of us walking, slowing our pace. Finding campsites large enough to accommodate all of us and transporting the stores required to feed ten added pressure, but the delays no longer bothered me.

Cara fascinated me, and I used the time to get to know her, content to leave the logistics to Sally and Ben.

Cara still remembered nothing from before she had woken in our camp.

"Retrograde amnesia," Sally had diagnosed.

When we'd crossed the new bridge, Cara shuddered while observing the footbridge. "I'm afraid of water. I don't think I would've tried to cross it." She'd wrinkled her nose.

The urge to kiss her nose, to kiss *her*, had only grown since then.

Charcoal disappeared into the tall grass with the stick, leaving me with nothing to do. I whistled, but he didn't reappear.

How had Akiko and Cara ended up at the bridge?

Akiko had said nothing when questioned. Though she'd volunteered snippets of conversation to Sally, Ben, or me, she withdrew if Josephine or Cara joined us. She gave all the Fruchtmans a wide berth and didn't join the games of Conlin and Moira, preferring to spend her free time with Charcoal and the donkey.

At first, we'd tried to press Akiko for information, but when she'd steadfastly refused to answer, everyone had given up, leaving decisions about the child to me.

Akiko accepted that they'd charged me with her wellbeing and was obedient on the rare occasion I asked her to complete a task or chore.

Ben and I had scoured both sides of the river but found no traveling supplies or evidence of a camp—no clues on how Cara had ended up in the river or Akiko on the footbridge.

Though Cara couldn't remember her history, she knew if she preferred porridge or toast, roses or daffodils, and blue or green.

Each piece of information she shared shone like a treasure.

I scanned the meadow again, looking for my dog. White moths fluttered around the milk-thistle flowers. Finding nothing, I tilted my face to the sun, basking in its warmth.

Like the others, I was ready for a respite from the endless, cracked pavement. I wanted a bath and a meal made of something other than dried pork or fish. If I never smelled chowder again, it would be too soon. My eyes flicked open, and I sniffed the air, groaning at the fishy aroma.

Truthfully, I wanted a holding for the Fruchtmans and to find

Akiko's parents so we could leave them behind. Warwick was still weeks away *if* we resumed our previous pace.

Most of all, I wanted answers.

Who was Cara? Where had Akiko come from? How had they ended up at a broken bridge in the middle of nowhere?

And one more answer, one nagging worry I hadn't been able to shake: could 'T' have sent them?

CHAPTER FORTY-TWO

"**M**atthew, a moment?"

I searched Josephine's face and saw worry. My heart twinged as I remembered the days of easy companionship with Josephine when syncing had been effortless. If we couldn't reestablish our relationship, the struggles of travel could erode our party.

"Of course. Please sit."

Josephine fidgeted. "Privately?"

Cara stiffened, but patted my hand. "Go. We'll continue our conversation later when you're free."

Handing her my empty bowl, I gave Cara a quick smile. "Lunch was delicious," I lied, the taste of salted fish heavy in my mouth.

Walking from camp, eyes followed us. "Ben thinks we'll reach New London today by mid-afternoon."

Josephine nodded. "Yes, he said. Let's see if there's a view."

We headed toward a metal tower, skirting the verdant meadow. The air was heavy, scented by grass and wildflowers.

When we were out of eyesight and earshot of the others, I turned to her. "I think we're clear. What is it?"

Josephine looked relieved. "First, I want to apologize. I hate the distance growing between us."

My heart flooded, and I smiled at her. "The gap is closed."

She brushed her hair back. "I wasn't sure you understood when I asked..."

Taking her hands in mine, I focused on her eyes. "My dearest friend, my sister, I know you well enough to know when you're worried about something. Spill."

She nodded and bumped her forehead against my chest. "Remember the man in New Bethel?"

I searched my memory. "Preacher..."

"Goodwin."

"Right, Preacher Goodwin. What of him?"

Josephine glanced behind us. "Let's keep moving."

The view at the edge of the meadow was expansive. Dark clouds threatening rain obscured the sun, casting the valley in shadow. Bird nests festooned the rusty iron tower above us. Their occupants flitted busily, scolding and chattering.

Josephine leaned against the tower and picked at the flakes of rust. "Kennedy told me they called the minstrel she watched Preacher Richards."

"How strange. Preacher isn't a common name."

She shook her head. "I think it's a title."

"Oh?" My eyebrows raised. "Like scholar?"

"Well..." Josephine pulled on her lip. "In the days before the world died, Preacher was an honorific used by speakers who were passing on the word of God."

"Who?"

"God."

"As in religion?" Anxiety snaked through me, and my breath quickened.

"Yes. Preachers were usually of the Christian faith."

"And you think Preacher Goodwin and Preacher Richards are

spreading messages of religion? Surely not." I shook my head. "Not today. We've learned. We've grown past the need for such things and know how dangerous religion is."

Josephine knit her brows and didn't speak.

"It must be a coincidence. What else did Kennedy say?"

"Preacher Richards *propositioned* her."

I snorted. "What does Tyrell think of him now?"

"He doesn't know. You mustn't tell him, Matthew, I promised to keep her secret."

"Right, I won't repeat it. What else?"

"Nothing concrete. Only..."

I nudged her. "What?"

"She suspected they'd set her and Tyrell up."

"Set up to what?"

"Lose their farm."

"What? Why?"

Josephine shrugged. "I don't know, and Kennedy didn't either, but she felt they designed her misfortune."

Josephine didn't look well. Her skin was slack and her eyes tired.

"You're worried."

She sighed. "I don't know. Even if I'm right, what could we do?"

"Should we tell the others?" Maybe it was time to bring Sally and Ben up to speed. I still hadn't told them about 'T'.

Josephine tugged her lip again, eyes unfocused. "Maybe. No, not yet. Let's wait until we learn more."

"Agreed." I scanned the sky. "Let's head back. Ben will want to leave soon."

Josephine stiffened. "We're being watched."

The hairs on my neck rose. "Who's there?"

Charcoal snapped at a fly, unconcerned.

I scanned the trees, and my gut relaxed. "I see you."

Akiko stepped out from behind a trunk.

"What if she heard us?" whispered Josephine.

I beckoned for the child. "Good day, young miss. May I escort you fine ladies back to camp?"

The girl looked at me but didn't answer.

"We were speaking in confidence," Josephine scolded.

Akiko ignored her. "Preacher Talbot isn't a good man."

"Talbot? Who's that?" asked Josephine, her voice sharp.

Silence.

Josephine elbowed me.

I squatted and looked at Akiko. "We were discussing Preacher Goodwin and Preacher Richards."

"I don't know them."

"You've met a different man named Preacher Talbot, and you think he's not a good man," I summarized.

"Sort of."

"Ask her where she met him," Josephine said.

"I can hear you."

"Akiko doesn't answer questions," I said.

"Oh!" said Josephine. "I never put it together. How foolish. I didn't like the preacher I met either."

"I didn't meet Preacher Talbot, but I heard stories. I don't like people who say one thing with their words and a different thing with their face," said Akiko.

"Understandable." Josephine touched her scar self-consciously. "I hope my scars don't frighten you."

"Why would I be afraid of your scars?" the girl asked.

"Well... I mean, we haven't..." Josephine looked at me.

"She thinks you don't like her because of her scars," I said.

Akiko looked at Josephine with an expression that could have been pity. "I don't talk when I have nothing to say."

Josephine's cheeks flushed. She straightened and stood awkwardly.

I cleared my throat. "Let's head back. I'd like to hear why you think Preacher Talbot is a bad man, but only in private with the three of us."

"Yes," said the child. "But I'd tell Ben, too. Only Ben," she added, taking my hand. Her hand burned against mine, tiny and fragile.

"The four of us," I agreed. "As soon as we're alone."

CHAPTER FORTY-THREE

"Here we are," Sally announced as we stopped at the crest of the hill overlooking the community of New London. Fragmented sunbeams broke through the dark clouds, casting random spotlights on the community.

"It's bigger than I thought," said Josephine.

"Bigger than Brookfield," Sally agreed.

Ben and I exchanged a glance.

"What is it?" asked Cara, catching our look.

"It's still," I said. Nerves jumping, I scanned the community.

"What do you mean?" asked Josephine.

"There's no one walking around," said Ben.

"No smoke coming from the buildings," I added. The air was clear, with no hint of smoke from morning fires. If they'd abandoned New London, not only would it force us to keep traveling at our sluggish pace, but I wouldn't find the answers I wanted.

Sally shrugged. "There must be an explanation. They'll be at an afternoon event or community meeting. You'll see; come along." She clicked at her pony and started down the hill.

I followed Sally, alarms trumpeting.

When we reached the green, Sally stood in her stirrups and looked around. "Strange," she muttered.

"Sally?" asked Josephine.

"They should have seen us coming down the hill. News of travelers spreads like a cold."

"That looks like a pub," said Ben. "I'll check it out. Matthew and Cara, go look in the livery. Josephine and Sally, knock on a few doors. We'll meet back here in ten minutes."

Akiko frowned. "Where do I look?"

"Can you check behind those buildings? Maybe they are having a picnic. Take someone."

"I'll go," Cara volunteered, holding out her hand.

"I'll take Matthew and Charcoal," said the child.

Cara flushed.

I flashed Cara a sympathetic smile. "Terrific."

"Should we wait for the Fruchtmans?" asked Josephine.

"They're twenty minutes behind us," I said. "We'll be back by then."

The group nodded, and we headed in different directions. Akiko and I found horses in paddocks behind the smithy, but no signs of people.

Screams of terror shattered the calm.

Charcoal, Akiko, and I sprinted back to the green.

Sally burst into view, and Akiko gasped. Sally, face white, rushed across the green toward us with arms outstretched and hands like claws. Her eyes were wild, and her mouth gaped as she screamed.

Ben slammed open the door of the pub and raced toward us.

Sally's pony wheeled and bolted. Magnesium and the donkey, ears pinned, followed.

"Charcoal, go get them!"

The dog streaked after the fleeing stock.

Akiko clung to my leg, and I nearly fell as I caught Sally in a bear hug.

Sally struggled and continued to shriek, her eyes rolling.

Her expression was terrifying.

Ben reached us and pulled Sally from me. He held her tightly, looking her over. "Are you hurt? What is it? What's happened?"

She shook and continued to screech.

Akiko, trembling, wrapped her arms vice-like around my waist and buried her face in my hip.

Josephine and Cara reappeared, sprinting toward us.

Ben wrapped Sally in a tight hug and held on, arms bulging as she struggled. When she gasped, he loosened his grip but continued to hold her. Her body shuddered with sobs, and he rocked her back and forth.

Frozen, we stared at her. Shards of ice raked my mind, and my mouth filled with bile.

"What's happened?" Ben asked again.

Sally drew a ragged breath and nodded.

Ben loosened his grasp, and she took a step backward, still clutching his shirt.

"I found them," she sputtered, expelling air with a *whoosh-hiss*.

"Who?"

"The people. People of New London. But they're not..." She searched our faces. "They're *not* people."

"How are the people not people?" asked Josephine in a thin voice.

Ben ignored Josephine and kept his focus on Sally. "Start at the beginning. Did you find the administrator's house?"

Trembling, Sally nodded.

"You found the people of New London?" I asked. Dread pooled in my gut, icy sweat dripping down my spine as I tightened my arm around Akiko.

"Where?" asked Ben.

Sally panted, unable to catch her breath, so Ben audibly sucked in air at a slow pace, exhaling as slowly. She nodded and copied him.

When Josephine frowned at me, I realized I'd joined their breathing exercise.

"Tell us," Ben said.

Sally nodded, pressing the heel of her hand against her forehead. "I looked for a—a ledger or community diary in the administrator's dwelling and found nothing. Instead, I found..."

"Go on," said Josephine, stroking her back.

Sally's lips trembled. "I found *them*."

"The records?"

"The people," she whispered.

Cara gasped and swayed. "Where?" she whispered.

Sally's eyes filled with tears. "Cellar."

"And then the world died," breathed Josephine. "Ben, I found religious pamphlets. I think a revival came through here."

"A revival?" asked Cara in a high-pitched voice. "Why would revivalists murder a community? No"—she juddered her head—"I don't believe it."

Murder? My mind reeled.

Sally, still shaking, moaned.

It made me shudder. "Sally?"

"Brookfield," she gasped. "What if they reach Brookfield?"

There was suddenly no air. "Brookfield?"

"Sally, they're fine," said Josephine with a panicked expression.

Sally wailed again.

"Matthew!" said Josephine, wild-eyed. "Can you do anything?"

"Me? I... like what?" My mind raced, but all I could envision was a blank canvas.

"I don't know!" Josephine shouted. "Something! Something to keep Brookfield safe."

"But... yes." Pulling my notebook out of my pocket, I sketched Brookfield from memory. I didn't know what could keep them safe, but the first step was to draw the community.

"Stay here and help Matthew," Ben instructed Sally and Akiko. "Josephine, Cara, come with me. Which dwelling, Sally?"

She pointed at a blue building with yellow trim and sank to the grass, shaking. Akiko released my leg and kneeled beside Sally.

Sally reached for Akiko's hand and held it, patting it lightly. "Hurry, Matthew."

Dredging through my memories, I sank to one knee, balancing my notebook as I sketched.

A rough impression of Brookfield appeared on the page. Was it correct, or correct enough? What would happen if I had it wrong? Could I even effect a change from so far away?

I'd never tried to use my art on a subject I couldn't see.

My hands were cold and clumsy when I stopped drawing.

"Let me see." Sally reached out a hand for my notebook.

My pulse pounded in my ears as I fought the urge to slap her hand away and run.

"Matthew?" asked Akiko in a small voice.

My anger evaporated. "Sally, I don't know if it's right."

She nodded, her eyes filled with tears. "Let me see."

She and Akiko studied the sketch.

"It's right. You've got it right." Sally held the notebook out for me.

I hesitated before taking it.

Now what?

Sally's voice caught. "How will you—help them?"

"A wall," I answered. Until I said it out loud, I hadn't known how to protect Brookfield, but now it seemed an obvious choice.

Using rapid strokes, I drew the outline of a wall around the perimeter of the community. Unsure how to treat the lakeside, I continued the wall along the edge of the shore. I closed my eyes, the wall solidifying in my mind.

Seven meters high, a meter wide, constructed of smooth stone. I left no openings.

I transferred my mental image to the paper.

Were my fingers tingling in the usual way? I couldn't tell.

Dizzy, I finished the sketch. "Here." I shoved the notebook at Sally.

She looked at it without expression. "Do you think it worked?"

"I don't know," I admitted. "I've tried nothing like this."

Sally nodded and clutched the drawing to her chest. "We must go back. Now."

Must we?

I'd drawn a wall, though I didn't know if it had worked. What else could I do?

If we turned back, it might be months before I reached Warwick. Months more before I could resume my search for the answers I needed.

If the others wanted to turn back, should I continue by myself?

Faces of the friends we'd left behind flashed in my mind, and my nausea rose.

"I can't go on without knowing," said Sally, her tears welling. "Without knowing if—"

She was right. I couldn't abandon my friends in Brookfield. Rising, I helped her up.

Akiko pointed at the hill. "The Fruchtmans are here."

I snapped my sketchbook shut. "Will you go tell Ben and the others? Stay outside; don't go in the building."

She nodded and trotted toward the administrator's house.

Former administrator's house.

Nerves jangling, I scanned Ben, Cara, and Josephine's faces when they returned, searching for answers.

No one would meet my gaze.

This time, Josephine wrapped her arms around Sally, and together, we waited as the Fruchtmans rode across the green.

"We stopped at the last two holdings," said Tyrell, handing Moira to Cara before dismounting, "but there was no one there."

He helped Conlin down from Ben's mule. "I can't understand it. The holdings look fine, but there's no sign they've begun the work for spring planting."

"The dwellings were furnished," said Kennedy, "but we didn't find food." Her cheeks pinked as she added, "We wouldn't take anything without permission."

"What's happened?" asked Tyrell, searching our faces. He pulled Kennedy closer to him.

"The community of New London is dead," said Josephine in a tight voice. "We found their bodies stacked in the cellars of two buildings."

"Dead?" asked Kennedy.

Tyrell blinked, mouth open.

"We need to return to Brookfield," I said.

Silence hung heavy on the air, then Josephine nodded.

Ben looked from me to Sally. "You're right. We'll redistribute what we have, but we'll need more horses."

Kennedy's eyes welled, and Tyrell bit his lip. Looking at his children, he nodded once. "We'll help you repack, but my family and I are going to stay."

What? "Here?"

Tyrell jerked his chin. "At one of the abandoned holdings."

Kennedy nodded. "We can farm either. With luck, settlers will repopulate New London. How can we help? We can't leave the dead in cellars..."

"No," said Ben, looking at the abandoned buildings.

"We should burn them," said Cara.

Her words clanged in my ears, and I swayed.

Ben nodded. "Yes, we could light both buildings without threatening the rest of the structures."

My gut churned, but Josephine nodded. "I agree."

"How long?" asked Sally. "I want to leave as soon as possible."

Swallowing my nausea, I studied her and Akiko. They didn't need to be here for this. "Why don't you two ride out? We'll finish here and leave right after."

"Akiko will need a horse," said Josephine.

"I want to ride with Matthew."

I kneeled before the girl. "We'll be riding fast, and it would be better for you to have your own horse."

"Can I ride Donkey?"

"No, I'm not sure he'll keep up with us on his little legs."

"But I don't want to be left here," she said, her voice plaintive.

My heart went out to her, and I pulled her into a hug, her body hot against mine. "You won't. We found horses behind the livery, remember?"

I looked over her head. "Josephine, can you pick her out a horse?"

"Yes. I've seen her ride and know what she can handle." Josephine faced Sally and Akiko. "What if I joined you?"

"Is there a horse for me, too?" Cara asked. "I don't want to stay here either. Not by myself."

My heart lightened; I'd been dreading Cara's decision. It was too soon to say goodbye, but I hadn't known how to ask her to join us.

"There were at least six in the paddocks. Enough for you, too," I said to Kennedy and Tyrell.

They nodded.

"It's settled," said Ben. "Kennedy and Sally, can you organize the supplies? We must travel light, and I want to make sure your family has enough until your holding can support you. Matthew and Tyrell, we'll need a fuel source to start the fires. We'll stay until we're sure the fire won't spread."

Kennedy shook her head and raised her chin. "Tyrell and I will watch the community after you set the flames. Thank you for saving my family, and remember us in your travels."

CHAPTER FORTY-FOUR

After Ben and I caught up to the women the first night, we continued our rapid pace. Each day, we rode fast, starting at dawn and breaking our journey at dusk. By the time the women rode in, we had camp set up and dinner ready.

Not that anyone had an appetite.

Exhausted and hollow-eyed, we'd taken to speaking in terse one-word sentences. Some nights, we fell asleep without eating, and Ben reheated our supper for breakfast.

If I never had leftover stew for breakfast again, it would be too soon.

The frenetic pace was soothing. It had taken six weeks to reach New London, which meant we now faced long days in the saddle. As we rode, my mind spun what-if scenarios, and I worried my improvements hadn't worked or that I'd done too little, too late.

Sally assured us Brookfield was fine, but her muffled sobs woke me on more than one night.

Cara and I had only brief moments together, but when we did, she asked endless and exhausting questions. Too depleted to ease her ever-increasing insecurities, I withdrew.

"Will there be space for me?" she asked one night.

"Space?"

"In Brookfield. Will they welcome me? You already have ties there."

Pulling her into my arms, I closed my eyes, burying my nose in her curls. "I welcome you. I will make room for you."

She clung to me, and I wished we were on a different journey. A journey with hope in our thoughts instead of dread in our hearts...

"I hope they haven't run into trouble," said Ben, snapping me back into the present.

"Sorry, what? I was kilometers away." I finished tying the line we used to tether the horses. We couldn't risk a delay, so we tethered the horses and only let one graze at a time.

"The women," Ben repeated.

"They should've arrived," I agreed. "Should we wait or ride back?"

"Exactly," said Ben. He yawned.

I yawned too. "You don't seem worried."

"I've little worry left to spare."

I didn't either; I was spent. We'd lived in a perpetual state of anxiety, and it had been weeks since I'd experienced peace.

"We should..." I stopped, unsure of what we should do.

"Mmm," Ben agreed, lying on his bedroll with a groan, "we should."

I sat on my bedroll, then lay back, wanting to sink into the earth. "We should," I repeated as the fire crackled and popped.

Ben snored, and I smiled, but as tired as I was, sleep was far off.

I pictured Brookfield ensconced within its new wall and rotated the image, looking for a flaw in my design.

Surely, they were safe. No one could breach my fortifications.

"I'm glad you had the sense to stay put and not come flying to our rescue."

My eyes popped open at Josephine's voice. "I'm not sleeping."

Ben snored loudly, and I grinned. "What took you so long?"

"Akiko's horse threw a shoe. We had to put her on My Darling with Sally. Cara is ponying the mare, and I rode ahead to make sure you didn't worry."

"Supper's ready if you're hungry. Why didn't you reset the shoe?"

"You had the rasp and the nails."

Of course I did.

"I'll check the horses in the morning before we leave."

Josephine nodded and dropped to her bedroll. "I've thought of nothing other than lying prone for hours."

"Better yours than my thoughts."

She rolled to her side and propped her head on her hand. "How much longer do you think we have?"

"I don't know. Three days? It's hard to judge. We weren't moving fast when we left Brookfield, and our pace slowed further when we met the Fruchtmans. And then Cara and Akiko."

Josephine rolled onto her back with a sigh. "I don't suppose you've had any time to work on your painting."

I laughed bitterly, and Ben's snoring ceased.

"Hi, Ben," said Josephine without moving.

"Ah, Josephine. I wasn't sleeping."

We giggled.

Ben cleared his throat. "Supper?"

Josephine yawned. "I'll wait for the others."

"Where are—"

"Talk to him," Josephine interrupted. "Will someone unsaddle my horse?"

I grinned at the tarpaulin overhead. "Will you scribe me a letter in trade?"

"No, but I'll have Sally share some choice words with you."

"I'll do it," said Ben, standing. He stretched and rotated his trunk.

"Ben, I was about to get up," I said lazily.

"Mental whale rider," said Josephine, mimicking Sally. "Get it done. Duel about it after if you like."

Ben wheezed, and I chuckled. "I've missed this. I've missed us."

Josephine turned her head and smiled at me, her eyes warm. "We're here whenever you're ready to come up for air."

"What?" I sat up.

"Matthew and Cara, sittin' in a tree," sang Ben in falsetto.

"Now hold on," I protested.

"K-i-s-s-i-n-g," they chorused.

I flushed. "I'm going to get water for the horses. They'll need a drink."

My friends were right; Cara besotted me. Even before our race to Brookfield, I hadn't considered working on my painting since we'd met.

Cara was unlike anyone I had encountered. Though warm and caring with me, I'd caught flashes of irritation and impatience in the way she interacted with the others. She admired beautiful things and was the first to notice a sunset or rainbow, but she tossed the wild-flowers I brought her without a touch of sentimentality. She had a musical voice but lacked a lyrical nature.

The contradictions drove me crazy, and I wanted to spend all my time with her, trying to unlock the puzzle.

I couldn't understand why the others weren't drawn to her. All the people I cared for in the world were here together, but the divide between them was palpable. Whenever the subject came up, I tried to be patient with the teasing, hoping it would smooth the tension.

Bucket swinging, I walked through the brush to the stream. Moonlight filtered through the trees, and I made it to the water without tripping.

A branch cracked near me, and I froze at the soft breath and ripping sound.

Long ears flicked, silhouetted in the moonlight.

"Is it you, Donkey?"

Another snap as the donkey stepped closer.

"Splendid fellow. Not sure how you keep up, but I'm glad you're traveling with us." I rubbed his neck, and his lips wobbled.

Ben and Josephine's laughter floated above the gurgle of the water.

"Wish I knew what the old minstrel called you."

Thinking about the minstrel immediately brought the letters to mind, and the mysterious 'T.' I still didn't know who he was or why he'd want to slow me.

Could the destruction of New London have been his doing?

The donkey pulled away to graze, and I shivered.

How could anyone orchestrate something so terrible? Ben had counted thirty-nine bodies, including women and children, in the cellars of the two dwellings. I shook my head, but the memory of the bodies stacked like firewood wouldn't clear. When we flooded the basements with oil to set the pyres, I'd been violently ill.

If 'T' *had* orchestrated the deaths, did it have anything to do with the religious pamphlets Josephine had discovered? Would people kill to defend religious beliefs?

Unthinkable.

There was no sense in causing death. Life was for creation, not destruction.

Maybe the deaths were from natural causes. Ben hadn't found visible wounds on the bodies he examined, but perhaps a sickness had swept through the community.

Adrenaline shot through me, and my heart thudded.

If it *was* a sickness, could we have caught it? Infected, we could spread it to Brookfield.

I felt fine, and no one else had complained of illness. Our pace was exhausting, but our resulting weariness natural.

I picked up the bucket and took a step nearer the stream. The bank beneath my foot crumbled, and my left foot splashed into the creek, ankle-deep.

Wonderful.

Charcoal waded around me, investigating the water.

I filled the bucket and heaved myself onto the bank. One foot wet, one dry, I walked back through the brush toward camp. As I emerged onto the road's edge, I froze.

Even if the people of New London *had* died of an illness, someone had hidden the bodies in the cellars instead of organizing a proper burial. I shuddered, skin crawling as I thought through the implications. I'd talk to Ben tomorrow after the women left camp.

No point in terrifying everyone.

"Stop daydreaming, you long-titted worm pincher! Come help this child down. Me too."

I laughed and set the bucket down. "Good evening, Sally. Nice of you to join us."

I lifted Akiko down and held My Darling for Sally. The girl leaned sleepily against me.

I flashed a smile at Cara and gripped Sally's shoulder to steady her as she dismounted.

"Waffle handler," she groused. "Is there water? I need to wash up."

I pointed in the stream's direction. "The donkey's down there, so don't be frightened if you hear snapping branches."

"Come, girl, let's get this road grime off of us before we eat."

I tied My Darling to the line and had barely pulled his saddle off before the pony dropped to the ground and rolled.

"Blast it, you little sausage," I growled, dodging the flailing hooves. I reached up and snagged his lead, untying him.

"My Darling likes to roll when he's unsaddled," called Sally from the dark.

"Thanks for the warning," I said through gritted teeth.

When the pony finished rolling, he clambered to his feet and shook vigorously, like a dog emerging from the water. A shower of dust, horsehair, and pine needles hit me, coating my clothes. I sneezed repeatedly.

"You're a mess, big man."

I cracked an eye and grinned at Cara. "Want a hug?"

"Uh, no." Her eyes danced.

I lurched forward, arms outstretched. "Oh, come on, embrace me."

She squealed and dropped the horse leads, laughing as she backed away. "No!" she called over her shoulder, walking to the shelter.

"Embrace me!"

Akiko's mare gave me a shove, rubbing her forehead on my back.

"Knock me down, girl, and we'll be eating horse stew instead of fish."

She bobbed her head in agreement.

I tethered them and finished carrying the tack to the shelter.

Ben's mule watched me with interest and stamped his foot in warning as Charcoal approached him.

"Leave it," I said automatically.

"You leave it. Looks like you need a bath," said Sally, returning from the stream. "The water's fine."

"No, it's cold," Akiko argued.

"I agree. I tested it with my left boot earlier," I said, holding my wet foot up for inspection.

Akiko giggled and kicked at my boot.

"Well, go douse the rest of yourself," said Sally.

I swiftly kissed her cheek, and she patted mine softly before turning her head toward the fire.

"Ben, if I have to endure another fish stew, I will roll a dead tramp over you while you sleep. Where's supper?"

CHAPTER FORTY-FIVE

The taste of ashes grew stronger. We jolted down the road after Ben in a ground-covering, bone-jarring trot. I didn't remember this stretch of unending road, but snow had covered everything when we'd left Brookfield. If we didn't reach it soon, I was afraid my heart would seize from anxiety.

Ben's mule suddenly slid on its haunches, and Ben raised his fist in a warning.

Grateful for the break, I slowed Oxide. "What is it?"

Ben shook his head, saying nothing.

Magnesium bumped into Oxide, who whipped his head around, ears pinned.

Ben hissed for me to be quiet, and I settled my horses.

We waited.

My pulse thundered in my ears, and my chest was tight and airless as I tried to quiet my breathing. My nerves magnified every sound—the shuffle of a hoof, the jingle of a bit, the sigh of a horse—amplified. The urge to shout welled, and I bit the inside of my cheek for distraction.

Thundering hooves broke the relative quiet of the morning.

Alarmed, we moved toward the side of the road.

The clatter of hoofbeats grew louder.

"Steady," said Ben in a low voice. "We may not be well met."

My mind flashed to the sword hidden in Magnesium's packsaddle, but there wasn't time to retrieve it. "We've no way to defend ourselves."

"Let's hope we don't need to. Here we go."

I sat as tall and imposing as I could.

Four horses burst into sight and headed straight for us.

"Ho!" shouted Ben.

My heart leaped. "We know them!"

Scarce meters from where we stood, Genevie and Whistler slid their horses to a stop. Genevie was both laughing and crying as she flew into my arms, solid and warm, smelling of salt and smoke.

"What are you doing here?" I asked, peeling her from me and holding her at arm's length.

Genevie's face crumpled, and she wept. I stared at Whistler, whose face was white with exhaustion and strain.

Ben shook Whistler's arm. "What's happened?"

"B-B-Brookfield. Some—Something's wrong." Genevie took a step back and looked around. "Sally? Josephine?"

"They're behind us; they'll catch up. How far are we from Brookfield?"

"An hour, maybe two," said Whistler. He bent and dry heaved.

My gorge rose, and I swallowed repeatedly to clear it. Fear clawed at my heart.

The look on Genevie's face stoked the rising terror I'd fought to suppress.

"Here, water," said Ben, handing Whistler a canteen.

Whistler shook his head, taking a deep breath before standing. "We thought we might find you in Warwick."

"We didn't know what else to do," said Genevie. She drew in a shuddering breath. "Why are you riding this way?"

My stomach clenched.

"We needed to check on Brookfield," said Ben.

Whistler looked from Ben to me. "You built the wall."

It worked. My wall had appeared.

Hope fluttered in my chest, and I wanted nothing more than to race the rest of the way to see it for myself.

A tear tracked down Whistler's cheek. "You knew something happened. An artist thing?"

"No." How could I answer his question? "I need to go. If you keep riding that way, you'll find Sally and the others."

"What others? I'm coming with you," said Genevie, vaulting onto her horse.

Nodding, Whistler remounted.

Ben stood by his mule and looked at me. "Do we need to warn them? Prepare them?"

Love welled for the man. He put everyone else's needs before his own. "They suspect. Alarming them won't help."

Ben nodded and rubbed his jaw. "Let's go."

THE MIDDAY SUN WAS HIGH IN THE SKY, AND THE AIR SMELLED and tasted of soot and ash.

Ben gasped when he saw the stone wall. "It worked."

Vaulting off my horse, I yanked out my sketchbook.

Genevie bit her lip. "There's no way in. We looked, we tried to see—"

Flipping to the correct page, I rotated the sketch, searching for where to add an entryway. With a deep breath, I changed the wall near Nora and Kami's dwelling.

"Come on," I said, snapping the book shut. We ran to the other side of the community, our horses trotting behind us. As we neared the entryway, Oxide balked. I tugged, but he lowered his head and refused to budge.

Genevie sprinted past me, her horses loose.

335

She bellowed, and I dropped Oxide's lead, racing to the entryway.

Brookfield was gone.

Rubble, ashes, and a scorched wagon were all that were left at the healers' dwelling, wisps of smoke rising from the blackened, twisted beams.

Turning sideways, I vomited, gagging again and again at the taste of char. I couldn't process the destruction in front of me.

So much waste.

It would take an age to rebuild Brookfield. Desperate, I pulled my artist's objectivity over my heart.

Shadows and planes, not soot and ashes.

Genevie kneeled, chin on her chest. Whistler strode past me with tears streaming down his face. He stopped next to his wife and slowly turned in a full circle.

Charcoal pressed tightly to my leg and whined.

Where was Ben? "I'm going to—" I stopped, my voice hoarse. The Cannings hadn't heard me, so I left the ruined community.

Outside the wall, the air tasted cleaner, and I gulped a great lungful as I scanned the grassy hillside. Near the crest, Ben was making camp at the edge of the wood.

We trudged up the hill, away from Brookfield.

Spring daisies were in full bloom, and insects buzzed industrially as we climbed. Their normality soothed me.

"Ben?"

"I'm making camp."

"Yes." I waited. "Why?"

"The women will need a place to go... to be." He stopped, pulling the rope around the trunk of the tree, head bowed.

"Ben?" I took a step closer and tentatively put my hand on his shoulder.

He nodded at me, jaw trembling. He'd been weeping, the muscles in his jaw jumping. Closing his eyes, he tilted his head toward the sun. "There's nothing I could do there. Nothing. Here"—

he shrugged at our equipment—"we'll need a camp for tonight. There's nowhere left to..."

"Sleep," I said, finishing his sentence. "I'll help."

Working quietly, we set up the shelters.

"I'll put together a meal," he said without looking at me.

"Good idea. I'll round up the stock."

Sending Charcoal to fetch the Cannings' horses, I caught Magnesium, who grazed nearby. Ben had removed his panniers, but I pulled off the rest of the packsaddle and turned him loose again. I set the packsaddle within reach of my bedroll.

Frequently checking the road, I avoided looking at the wall. After the women arrived, we'd need to organize a trip to Wakefield for news and supplies.

Oxide's reins had tangled around his foot, and he trembled as I approached.

"You're all right, chap. Come on." Leading the horse to the campsite, I hitched him to a tree.

He flinched when I pulled his saddle off, near panic.

I found a brush and stroked his sweaty coat, feeling the muscles ripple under my hands.

Slowly, he relaxed, his lower lip drooping.

"That's better," I crooned.

One of the Cannings' horses snorted, and Oxide's head flew up, eyes wide with alarm. It was no use, and I released him.

He whirled and bolted, bucking as he crossed the field. Reaching Magnesium, he lowered his head to graze.

Charcoal brought the Cannings' horses and held them in a tight huddle. The leader, a dominant mare, tossed her head with displeasure.

"Good boy."

The dog grinned at me and spun toward the road. The donkey stood at the edge of the hillside.

"Must mean the women will arrive soon. Go get him. Bring him here."

337

Although I was dreading their reactions, I was glad they'd arrived. At least we'd be together again.

Unsaddling the horses, I staggered under the weight of their panniers. "What in the world are you guys hauling?"

The mare snorted at me and pawed, but we didn't need a spooked herd milling about. "You're stuck here until the others arrive."

The mare swished her tail.

Charcoal brought the donkey and Ben's mule. "Clever chap."

Neither the mule nor donkey was flighty; they wouldn't cause any trouble when the women arrived.

Ben had already unsaddled his mule, and the donkey had carried nothing since we'd left New London. "Charcoal, release."

The dog sat, head swiveling as he monitored the livestock in the field.

"Go on, you can graze," I said, making a shooing motion. The donkey stepped forward and pressed his head into my stomach. After a minute, the mule stepped forward, too. I stroked their long ears and watched my horses graze.

"Here they come," Ben called.

Cara was in the lead, the others not yet in sight.

"Come on," said Ben, patting his mule on the neck.

"This will be terrible."

He nodded. "Watch Sally."

We reached the road and waited for them to ride to us.

"It's bad, isn't it?" asked Sally from astride My Darling.

Taking the pony, I nodded.

Sally sighed and dismounted, rubbing her tail bone. "I knew it would be."

Akiko slipped off her horse. "Where should I take her?"

Ben pointed at the hillside. "We've set camp up there."

"Camp? We're not staying in Brookfield?" asked Josephine sharply.

I couldn't meet her eyes.

Cara dismounted. "I'll help unsaddle."

"Thanks."

Sally's pony and Fox snorted as I led them up the hill, followed by Akiko and Cara. I didn't want to see what came next.

Shrieks and wails tore through the air.

"Matthew?" asked Cara, her voice panicked.

I stopped walking, my head bowed. "There was a fire. Only soot and ashes left."

"I thought the smoke smelled too strong."

"All of it's gone?" asked Akiko.

I nodded and turned, looking at the wall. It hid the rubble, and I wasn't sure we could have seen anything, even if the buildings were still standing.

"All of it," Cara repeated. "The entire community burned?" She dropped her horse's rein and sprinted down the hill.

"Cara!"

"Take the saddles off here," said Akiko, removing the girth from her horse.

I pulled the saddles off and left them lying in a heap before trotting down the hill to the entryway. Cara and the others would need my support.

Josephine was weeping, huddled on the ground in the entryway.

My throat tightened. "Where's Sally?"

Ben beckoned.

I walked toward him, looking for Cara.

Ben stepped past me, nudging a stick with his foot. "Don't step on that."

His voice struck an odd tone.

"What?"

"It's a bone."

I shuddered, looking around. The inside of the wall was black with soot, and near its base lay several heaps. On unsteady legs, I walked to the nearest.

A skull gaped at me, blackened, missing its jaw.

An eerie keening filled the air before Ben encircled me with his arms. It stopped when I took a breath. It had been coming from me.

"Matthew." Ben's voice was urgent. "Breathe. This isn't your fault."

I gasped for air as my eyes skimmed the wall; a half-dozen more heaps lay at its base near us. My vision dimmed as comprehension brightened.

"Breathe, just breathe."

Brookfield had burned, and I'd trapped the people inside the inferno with my wall.

CHAPTER FORTY-SIX

Walking through the misty morning, I surveyed for a suitable site. The cemetery needed a tranquil location with a lovely view and enough room for... everyone. A lump stabbed my throat. Grief and despair had battled and raged in my heart until I was numb, but at odd moments like this, pain sliced through me, leaving me gasping and raw.

Charcoal investigated a rotten stump as I paused on the slope we'd been climbing and turned to look at Brookfield.

I'd walked farther from the wall than planned. From here, the wall fluttered at the lake edge, the water sparkling and blue.

Motion to my left caught my attention, and I stopped to scan the slope.

Charcoal also paused, gazing in the same direction.

Nothing moved.

The dog lifted his nose and sniffed. With a glance at me, he trotted toward the invisible.

Shrugging, I followed the dog.

Charcoal disappeared, and I whistled. He reappeared at the top of a slight rise, then turned and disappeared again.

Cresting the hill, I found him sitting with Akiko. She perched on a rock, knees bent, arms around her shins. Seeing me, she stood and stretched.

"Hullo, Akiko. It's early, isn't it?"

The girl shrugged. "This will be the graveyard."

She was right. "Yes, it's perfect."

Akiko grinned—a rare sight. She ticked her fingers. "Not too far, big enough, won't spoil the water, peaceful."

I recoiled, knowing what she meant. "Not too far and won't spoil the water?"

"Bodies are heavy and rot fast."

"Here, I thought you were only ten years old. My mistake."

She nodded. "I'm eight."

A jolt went through me. Only eight. Even younger than I'd thought. "You knew I'd come here."

She tilted her head and narrowed her eyes. "Aren't you going to draw the graves?"

"Yes."

Akiko sat down on the rock and poked her finger at Charcoal's open mouth. The dog snapped his muzzle shut and turned his nose. She waited until he opened his mouth to pant again, repeating her provocation.

Charcoal gave her, then me, a pained look. With a grumble, he slid down the side of the rock and lay at its base.

"I'll set up to draw the site where I can see the entire area."

Akiko nodded and pointed. "Up there."

"I could set up here instead."

"No."

"I'd need a good reason to choose a different spot," I teased. The banter felt good, a welcome change from the sorrow I carried.

Akiko sighed. "The sun will climb that way. If you set up there, you'll have the sun at your back, and you can see the wall. If you set up here, you'll have the sun in your eyes, and you won't anchor your drawing. Right?"

342

I stared at the girl. Everything she said was correct. I would've chosen the same spot if I hadn't been teasing her.

Clearing my throat, I walked to the spot Akiko had picked. "I'll get started. If I have this ready before breakfast, I can concentrate on the portraits afterward."

"I want to help."

Digging into my pack for the paper, I asked, "Sketch or oils?"

"Sketch, because you don't know how many graves to draw."

"And?"

"You can add more graves to a sketch without waiting for paint to dry."

"Exactly right." Her perception was astounding.

I sketched the hillside, the rock Akiko lounged across, and the wall in the distance. We'd left the wall in place, though I'd changed it some, opening a second arched entrance on the water side. Genevie had gone to Wakefield to craft decorative iron gates for each of the entryways.

"Why?" I'd asked before she left. "I can add what you want in my sketch."

"Because I loved them too," she'd answered, red-eyed.

Whistler had stayed to help us move the bodies.

I stopped sketching and thought about the day we'd found Brookfield...

After my breakdown, my friends had helped me to our campsite and collected the discernible remains for burial. Whistler had shifted the rubble from Genevie's cellar door to retrieve shovels, and they'd found the bodies of the people of Brookfield in the cellar. "Stacked, exactly like what we found in New London," Ben told me.

In my grief and despair, I hadn't understood what Ben was saying.

"They didn't burn."

My mind swirled. "Then who—"

"We think it was the people who set the fires," said Sally. "Your wall trapped them after they started the flames."

343

After they started the flames.

The knowledge eased my guilt little. I'd caused destruction; my art had hastened death.

"Why didn't they burn?" I asked sometime later, thinking of the bodies they'd found. "We set fire to the dwellings in New London in funerary."

"My workshop floor was slate," Genevie answered. "Sparks." She pantomimed hammering metal...

"Matthew, draw," said Akiko, bringing my focus back to my present task.

Nodding, I sketched. Other than the scratching of my pencil and the songs of the early spring birds, the morning was quiet.

As the sun rose, the faint scent of cloves perfumed the air from the wild phlox in the meadow.

The sensation of the pencil in my hand, the scratching sounds, the work *itself* soothed me, providing a measure of peace.

"Do you have another sketching book?" Akiko asked, breaking my trance.

"Yeah," I said without pausing. "Why?"

"I want to help with the portraits."

"Uh-huh." I continued sketching.

"I want to draw portraits," she repeated.

"Girls can't draw," I said, shading the rock. My eyes shot up. "You want to draw?"

She nodded once.

I leaned back and rotated my head, stretching my neck. They only sent boys to the abbeys to learn art; there were no women artists. Encouraging her was preposterous.

Akiko sat with a stillness belying her age.

Why can't women be artists?

I'd never considered it, never thought to ask the question. Was she even capable?

"You're doing it again."

My eyes focused. "What?"

She rubbed her left wrist with her right hand.

I looked at my wrist. I'd fallen into my old habit, and the past two days had taken their toll. The pain in my wrist was bright and clean and helped me feel... something.

"Describe this." I pointed at the rock.

"It's a rock. There's a rectangle of lighter gray on top and triangles of dark blue on the side. The shadow stretches out in a straight line and curves back toward us. There are little lines of yellow on the front. I think it's moss. There is a dip there at the back, but it's not the right shape to lean against." She looked at me. "I tried earlier."

Turning, I pointed at the tree. "Describe it."

Akiko described the tree with notes about shape, shadow, and color.

"Did you talk with Josephine about how I look at the world?"

She shook her head.

"Ben? Sally?"

"No. Why?"

I retrieved my small sketch pad and selected a medium hardness pencil. I handed them to the girl. "Sketch the rock."

She nodded and sat on the ground. Crossing her legs, she rested the pad on one knee and started drawing.

I went back to my work and finished the preliminary sketch. I'd begun opening graves when Akiko brought me her sketch pad.

I took it, expecting to see a childish scribble, but her drawing was good.

Very good.

"Here," I pointed, "you've missed the shading. There are shadows here, but not here. The rock also has texture you haven't drawn. Can you fix it?"

She nodded, scurried back to her spot, and sketched, tongue protruding from the corner of her mouth.

Pride and fear wrestled as I watched her. I wanted to trumpet how extraordinary this girl was *and* keep her potential secret and safe.

"Akiko?"

She looked up.

"This is our secret, right?"

She beamed and bent her head back to her task.

After breakfast, the grim work began. My friends carried the bodies from the cellar and tagged each person with a scrap of paper to establish the order of burial. Ben and Whistler transported the bodies to the graveyard where I drew the death portraits. Akiko kept track of the finished drawings and recorded the location of each burial.

As needed, I altered the cemetery sketch to keep families together.

After the first hour of watching me draw, Akiko asked, "Can I try?"

"Can I redraw the portrait if I think it's necessary?"

She nodded.

"Very well. Why don't you take the child while I draw his mother?"

"Why?"

"Children are easier to draw than adults."

She nodded. "Because of age."

I blinked. "Right. The skin and muscle tone are even with young people. Wrinkles, scars, blemishes, sagging skin, inconsistent skin tone, and textures increase the difficulty."

I clipped a sheet of heavy paper to a portable drafting board as she studied the dead child. He was chubby with red curls and couldn't have been over two.

He looked like Teja.

"Akiko, are you sure?"

Mouth firm, she settled the board on her knee. Her pencil hovered over the paper before sketching with rapid, light strokes.

We worked without speaking. The creaking wagon announced the next load as I finished Teja's portrait. I groaned as I stood to greet Ben and Whistler.

"Hullo, Matthew. Another family and a bachelor," said Whistler.

346

"Okay. Put the family at the start of this row, and the man can go there, next to the tree. Oh... it's Horam." I closed my eyes.

Poor Horam.

Ben jerked his chin at Akiko. "What's she doing?"

"Drawing a portrait. Well, attempting to draw a portrait. We'll see how it turns out."

The men looked at me with identical expressions of surprise.

"Artists are men," said Whistler.

"Yes, but why? I never thought to ask."

"Why indeed?" said Ben. "Is she capable?"

I shrugged. "I don't know."

"Why are you letting her try?" asked Whistler.

"She asked; she wanted to help."

"She's seen too much for someone so young," said Ben.

"I found out she's only eight," I admitted. I glanced at Akiko and lowered my voice. "How's Sally?"

Ben shook his head. "In full administrator mode, but Josephine can't stop crying."

"What about Cara?"

"I haven't seen her."

Cara had pulled away from me last night when I tried to talk to her. Like Sally, I'd dragged the mantle of work over me, and I suspected Cara had taken my distance personally.

I envied Josephine's ability to cry; any release would be a relief. "Let's get back to it. Are there many more?"

"Around eleven," said Whistler. "Two more loads."

Ben nodded. "We'll all come up with the last load to help bury those whose portraits you've finished."

With a few corrections, I accepted Akiko's portrait and assigned her another. When the wagon arrived with the last sets of remains, my friends gathered in the oak's shade to wait for me to finish.

"Last one," I said, blowing the charcoal dust from my drawing. I handed it to Akiko, who noted the location in her log, tucking it into the stack.

"Done!" she called.

They drifted down the hill for the farewell ceremony I'd been dreading.

Josephine's sobs triggered me, and I blinked rapidly, eyes stinging. My sorrow evaporated when Charcoal's aggressive barking flooded me with adrenaline, and five strangers emerged from the woods.

CHAPTER FORTY-SEVEN

"Charcoal, quiet." The dog stopped barking but continued to growl. He'd never shown hostility before.

I shouldn't trust these people.

"What do you think?" asked Whistler in a low voice.

Ben flanked my other side. "They've been watching us."

I shivered. Had they seen Akiko drawing? Maybe, but from a distance. They couldn't know if the girl was sketching or practicing her letters. I drew strength from the men next to me, grateful the strangers had waited until we were together before approaching. I studied their body language. "They want something."

Cara put her hand on my arm. She stood behind me with an anxious look on her face. Akiko was next to her, peeking at the strangers from between us. Sally and Josephine had moved forward, clustered tightly behind Cara and Akiko.

As a unit, we watched the people approach. They stopped five meters away. Respectful, but still too close.

Charcoal continued to rumble next to me.

"Heya, Travelers," said the front man. "Well met!"

349

Considering we were standing in a freshly dug graveyard with unburied bodies around us, it was a strange statement.

When we didn't respond, he amended, "Perhaps not so well considering the circumstances, but I'm pleased to meet you." He was tall and thin with sharp eyes.

One of his companions, short with a substantial paunch, stepped forward. "Have you been here long?"

"You know we haven't, or you wouldn't have hailed us as travelers. How long have you been here?" asked Ben.

"A few days," said the tall man evasively.

"Why didn't you meet us when we arrived?" asked Sally.

"We didn't expect anyone..." the short man said. His tall companion elbowed him.

"There's only the five of us," whined a red-haired woman. "We weren't sure if we were safe. There used to be more."

The tall man's eyes flickered over my friends, and he pursed his lips.

Cara's hand tightened on my arm.

"What are your plans? Are you staying here?" the tall man asked.

"Leaving tomorrow," I answered. They seemed focused on Ben and me, and none of them looked at Akiko.

I drew a deep breath, the air scented by the freshly turned soil and the faint sweetness of decay.

"We are too," said the man with a paunch. With a quick look at the tall man, he added, "Heading south."

"Good travels," said Ben.

The red-haired woman brightened. "We could go together, for safety."

There was an awkward silence when no one responded.

"Do you have horses?" I asked, unnerved by the silence. I already knew the answer; if they had horses, ours would've called to them. My pulse drummed in my head, and I tried to swallow, my tongue thick and bitter.

"There are plenty of horses here," said the tall man.

"These animals are accounted for," said Whistler.

"There are more than you need to ride," said the woman. "There's only eight of you."

"The stock is accounted for," said Whistler flatly. "What are your professions?"

The tall man's eyes flickered, but he said nothing.

"I dare say we've earned the right to keep our horses for ourselves," said Sally, stepping forward. "After all"—she waved her hand at the graveyard—"we've done the work. We would've appreciated your labor hours, and we might have been more inclined to share with you had you offered. As it is, we shall leave with what we arrived with, and so should you. You are, however, welcome to set up your camp near ours. For safety."

The tall man opened his mouth but shut it again. He inclined his head. "Thank you, Administrator...?"

"Park."

"Park," he repeated, nodding. "I'm Joshua. This is my brother Benjamin, that's Carol, Rita, and the quiet fellow is Tobe."

"We need to finish burying these people," said Josephine softly.

We waited for an offer of help.

Instead, Joshua nodded and said, "Very well. We'll move our camp and see you later."

"Are you cooking a dinner?" asked Carol.

"Yes, so please arrive after we've finished if you want to visit. Goodbye," replied Josephine, her voice now hard and sharp.

Joshua and his companions walked back in the direction they had come.

"We have enough to share," murmured Ben.

"Yes, but they could have offered to help," snapped Josephine. "This isn't like it was with the Fruchtmans, Ben. If they don't want to help us, we should feel no obligation to help them. It's not how the world works."

"You were kind and helped me," said Cara.

"You needed our aid," said Sally. "Those folks seem to have

351

enough, but instead of offering to share or help," she said nodding at Josephine, "they only wanted to take."

"We share in the labor and the bounty if we are able. It's who we are." Josephine's expression was fierce, challenging us to object.

I nodded, and she relaxed.

"They reminded me of—" Sally stopped and looked at Josephine.

"What?" prodded Josephine.

"The people Kennedy spoke of. The attitude of these people reminded me of Kennedy's description of the revivalists and their entitled expectations."

Cara scowled. "You're assuming too much."

Not wanting to antagonize Cara, I hesitated before saying, "I thought so too, Sally."

Cara rolled her eyes and stalked toward our camp.

Chastising myself for allowing Akiko to draw in public, I looked at Ben. "We should take care."

Ben nodded, a grim look on his face. "Yes. Let's set up a watch tonight, and if they don't travel south tomorrow, we'll reassess."

SHATTERED AFTER A RESTLESS NIGHT WITH JOSHUA AND HIS band nearby, we arrived in Wakefield in poor spirits.

Cara had been waspish with me and snide to everyone. Sally had withdrawn, and Josephine frequently dissolved into tears. Ben and Whistler each wore a mantle of deep sadness, lines of sorrow carved into their faces. Even Akiko was quieter than usual and had a bruised look in her eyes.

Genevie had told the people of Wakefield little about what had happened in Brookfield. They pressed for news and details, sickening me.

Weeks passed, and though I was drowning, I couldn't talk to anyone about it.

I couldn't sleep; when I nodded off, nightmares jolted me awake.

I'd ridden to Newfane, but they hadn't heard from their scholar, so I'd returned to Wakefield in despair. If I couldn't speak with the scholar, I couldn't resume my search.

My appetite had gone, and I didn't understand how the others could laugh at Ben's stories or how he could summon the energy to tell them.

Even Akiko had deserted me, roaming the woods with the sketch pad I'd lent her, practicing her drawing away from watchful eyes. Although I'd warned her not to draw with people around, I hadn't meant me, and she'd been so difficult to find, I'd given up.

No one noticed I'd slid into a dark place.

My clothes hung from me, and I wandered around Wakefield, listless and unfocused.

As my friends returned to normal, my anger grew.

I despised the people of Wakefield for being happy and carefree, as if nothing had happened to a community with whom they'd shared ties. As if it couldn't happen to them, too. Their general complacence irritated me.

I needed to leave.

"Stay a while longer," Josephine had cajoled. "An age has passed since we've spoken."

I ignored her entreaty. "It's a two-hour ride to Newfane. Watch Akiko for me."

Ben had nodded and clapped me on the shoulder. "Send word when the scholar returns if you stay there."

My face impassive, I'd nodded, but inside, I'd been seething. They didn't care. No one asked after me, or how long I wanted to stay in Wakefield.

The search for my family seemed postponed indefinitely.

As I was leaving, a woman hailed me with a shy smile. "Thank you, Artist."

"For what?"

"Rescuing me. I was in the accident near New Bethel last fall.

353

We arrived here three weeks ago, and your friends have been so kind." She smiled, waiting for my reply.

The expected responses came readily. They schooled artists in civility and manners, but I didn't want to be civil. I wanted to belittle her, to cheapen her words, to shock her with a Sally-style tirade.

I toyed with saying I would have traded her, traded all of them, for Brookfield's safety. It would wipe the smile from her face, but the consequences weren't worth it.

Curtly, I kicked Oxide forward, choosing to say nothing. I thought I heard someone else call me, but I rode on, pretending not to hear.

The day was sullen with a raw wind and dirty gray clouds threatening rain.

The weather suited my mood perfectly.

For the first time in months, I was alone, and it was glorious. Though the relief of being by myself was palpable and visceral, it did nothing to improve my mood or memories.

Reaching the crossroads, I sat for a long time. I could go south toward Newfane. There, I could study the art in the inn or perhaps even paint. But I'd endure more arguments about why I should join them.

If I turned back to Wakefield, I'd have to explain my abrupt departure.

There was nothing north except New Bethel.

I'd heard talk of another Avalon Society community to the east. Chester? Could I intercept the scholar on her way home? If successful, I could restart my search for answers. My friends could stay and rot in Wakefield.

"I could go to Chester," I said out loud.

The wind sighed.

I chose freedom, turning east toward Chester. Away from Newfane, away from Brookfield. Newfane would think I was in Wakefield. Wakefield would assume I'd stayed in Newfane.

My deception pleased me.

Josephine would keep Akiko safe. Safer than with me and my growing rage.

Without the responsibility of guiding a packhorse, I was free to ride without paying attention to what I was doing. Oxide jogged on without complaint, and stoic Charcoal kept pace.

I passed ancient structures whose metal skeletons reached and grasped for a world long dead. If only I could have lived *Before*, when things were less complicated.

A herd of elk browsed peacefully along the roadside as we rounded a bend. I scowled at them and sent Charcoal to chase them away. After they disappeared into the woods, Charcoal resumed his place at the side of the horse, and we swept on.

The wind picked up, and I gritted my teeth and turned up my collar.

The chill was uncomfortable, though nowhere near as brutal as the night Josephine and I had taken shelter from the blizzard. We'd been so close in the days before Ben arrived.

If I was honest, it wasn't Ben who broke our closeness. The trouble had started after I'd met Cara.

Cara with her silky skin and laughing eyes. Cara who could crash my day when she frowned. Who made my pulse race when she lifted her eyebrow.

What had changed? Why had she grown distant?

Oxide slowed and swerved toward a small creek next to the road. Sweat lathered the horse.

"Sorry," I muttered, patting his slick neck while he drank. The day had slipped into the night without my notice. We needed to find somewhere to sleep.

Guiding the horse back onto the road, I kept our pace at a moderate walk to let him cool down.

Cara, my mind whispered, but I resolutely shoved her image away.

"Leave me alone, Cara."

Charcoal looked at me, but I had nothing else to say.

The road climbed steadily, one side dropping away steeply, and a spiny shrub covered the other, leaving nowhere to camp. Each time we appeared to crest the hill, I'd find we'd climbed another false summit. The road bent and climbed again and again.

Twilight deepened into darkness, and hours passed before Charcoal huffed and Oxide lengthened his stride.

Lights twinkled through the trees.

"We're somewhere, I guess."

Rounding the bend, we arrived at a brightly lit filling station. "We're in luck, boys. No camping tonight."

I stopped Oxide under the awning and a chubby boy with freckles sauntered out of the station.

"I'm looking for a meal and a bed."

The boy nodded and jerked his thumb toward the door. "Take your horse?"

"Yes." I unbuckled my saddlebags and slung them over my shoulder. "We've traveled far."

The boy nodded. "I'll give him extra grain with his hay."

I pushed the door open and shivered as humid air enveloped me.

The station was lively and packed with people. In the corner, a young woman strummed a guitar and crooned a tuneless song.

I pushed my way through the crowd and nodded at the keeper behind a short bar. "Meal and a bed?"

The keeper nodded. "Profession?"

"Artist. Is there a map to update?"

The keeper searched my face. "Yes, but it can wait until tomorrow. Most of these folks won't clear out until near midnight. The map would be payment enough but, if you're agreeable, I'd rather talk to you about my son."

"Done. Why is the station so full? I don't remember passing a community."

"You traveling east?"

I nodded.

The keeper jerked his head. "The community is a kilometer

farther. It's an Avalon Society though, so regular folks, they stay here. Once a month, I open a new barrel of mead, and even the people from Chester come. Want a pint?"

I shrugged. "I haven't had mead in years."

The keeper grinned and pulled a pint. "My bees are generous, and there's only so much honey you can eat. Sit over there, and I'll bring you your meal. What's your chap want?"

I shrugged again. "Whatever you have."

Charcoal searched my face.

"He's partial to a marrow bone," I admitted.

"He's in luck. We don't stew until Fridays."

"What's today?"

"Wednesday."

I picked up the sweating glass and pointed at the table. "There?"

The keeper nodded.

I wandered to the table and slumped into a chair, setting my saddlebags on the floor.

Charcoal panted at my knee until I pulled a chair out for him.

The dog jumped onto the chair and sat, surveying the room.

I snorted at him, looking around without interest.

More people, more noise.

The mead was cold and slightly effervescent. Though it wasn't sweet, it had a pleasant floral scent. The alcohol warmed my empty stomach, and a deep languor spread through me.

A table of young women eyed me, and I ignored them, pretending I hadn't noticed.

Leave me alone. I have nothing to offer.

CHAPTER FORTY-EIGHT

Rain drumming on the roof woke me. So much for traveling. Sleep beckoned, but my stomach rumbled. For the first time in weeks, I was famished, ravenous.

"Hush, child. He'll wake when he wakes," said a low voice outside my door.

The keeper's boy.

I swung my legs over the side of the narrow bed and let them hover over the floor.

"Father, he's awake!"

"Tell Barnaby to ready the morning meal."

Small feet stamped away, and I flexed my own. Experimentally, I touched the floor with my left foot.

Icy.

My toes curled involuntarily, and I fought the temptation to slide back into the warmth of the blankets.

The floors of the abbey were always cold. I smiled, remembering the myriad ways we'd tried to fight the early morning chill in the magnificent stone building. They heated only the corridors and class-rooms with under-floor steam lines. When I was young enough to bunk with the others, we'd concocted an elaborate obstacle course to climb from the farthest cot to the edge of the dormitory corridor. Older boys with private rooms tried to paint rugs, but these were rarely an improvement in either warmth or comfort from the austere stone floors.

Cara has cold feet in the morning.

My chest clenched, and I tightened my jaw. Resolved, I stood on the smooth floor, pushing away thoughts of Cara. I needed a distraction.

Charcoal sat on the bed and watched me dress, his stomach rumbling in time with mine. When I opened the door, a small boy jumped backward with a surprised expression.

"What were you doing?"

He stared at me, his face blank.

"Breakfast?"

Mute, the boy pointed down the corridor.

I nodded and strode down the long hallway, Charcoal at my heel. When I reached the doorway, I held it open in invitation to the child.

The boy nearly stumbled over his own feet in his haste to join me, then disappeared into the kitchens with a cheerful wave.

Gray light filtered through a series of rain-streaked windows. With last night's crowd, I hadn't looked around. Someone had stenciled the walls, giving the room the impression of a walled garden. Hidden among the leaves were fantastical creatures. Fairies, trolls, goblins, and unicorns scampered in the curtains of vines.

The keeper approached with a towel-covered wooden tray. I gestured toward the nearest empty table, and he changed course. After I sat, he set it down and removed the towel. On the tray were a plate with scones, a dish of porridge with two poached eggs on top, and a bowl of sliced strawberries drizzled with cream.

I smiled. "Strawberries already?"

"I keep a hotbed. Tea or coffee?" asked the keeper.

"Tea, please," I said. "With honey?"

The keeper grinned. "Honey, I always have. I'll bring a meal for your chap. Come, son."

I broke the chrome orange yolks, watching them spill across the porridge. Sprinkling the eggs with salt, I spooned a large bite.

"Here," the boy said, placing a jar of honey on the table.

"Thanks."

"I like honey on my porridge," the boy confided, "but only if Barnaby hasn't cooked the eggs yet."

"Who's Barnaby?"

The boy looked down. "My uncle."

"Who taught you to draw?"

The boy looked at me with surprise. "How did you know?"

"There are naughty-looking insects riding snails, over there, by the dragon's foot."

"Dragon's foot?" asked the boy.

I took a bite of my porridge and watched the boy try to find the dragon hidden in the vines. The egg yolks coated my tongue like a rich syrup, buttery and savory.

"I told you to leave him alone while he was eating," scolded the keeper. "Here's your tea, and I have eggs for your chap. Oh, I see he brought you honey."

Steam rose from the mug, fragrant with mint and hyssop. I winked at the boy.

The keeper looked at him fondly. "Go. Barnaby said you haven't finished your chores."

"What dragon?" the boy asked again.

"Go," said the keeper. He eyed me. "Dragon?"

"Aren't we in the beast's belly?" I asked, adding honey to my mug.

The keeper rubbed his chin. "No one's ever noticed."

"I shouldn't think so. Who started the mural?"

Another man entered the room from the sleeping quarters.

"Excuse me," said the keeper, leaving to speak with the new

arrival. After a quick conversation, the keeper disappeared into the kitchen.

The man nodded at me and sat at a table on the far side of the room.

Sipping my tea, I picked up a heavy scone. I sawed it in half and slathered it with butter. *Not bad.* I broke a piece off and put it on Charcoal's plate, then added a liberal dollop of honey and sampled it again. The honey sparkled with summer flavors, flowers, and cut grass. I demolished the first scone and was partway through the second when the keeper returned with three additional jars.

"Since you appreciate honey," said the keeper. "Try this one."

I paused with the scone halfway to my mouth.

The keeper unscrewed the lid from the jar and took a spoonful of honey from it.

Where the first honey had a light amber color, this one was so dark it obscured the spoon. I popped it into my mouth, my eyes widening.

The honey melted on my tongue, dark and rich. "Mixed with molasses?"

The keeper shook his head and grinned. "Buckwheat."

"And this?" I pointed at the pale amber jar.

"Raspberry. Here, try this one." He pushed a nearly transparent jar with the faintest hint of arylide yellow. He sat, producing more spoons.

I dug into the newest jar. Compared to the other two, the honey had little depth or flavor.

His lips twisted. "Clover."

I set the spoon down and took a sip of my tea. Wrapping my hands around the mug, its warmth seeped into my fingers. "Such different flavors."

The keeper nodded. He picked up the lightest jar and rolled it around in his hands absentmindedly. "Bees really are such clever creatures."

I waited, sensing there was more to this than honey sampling.

"Bees fascinated my wife," the keeper continued. "We moved to this plateau because she wanted to experiment with a longer bee season. She also"—he paused and looked around—"painted." He sat back and didn't meet my eyes.

I twisted the lids onto the other two jars. A woman painter? *Interesting*.

"She taught the boy to draw?"

The keeper shook his head. "No, I lost her when he was born. He paints and draws for hours." He looked at me with a pleading expression. "Does this mean he could be an artist?"

"Do you want him to be?"

The keeper slumped and rubbed the back of his head, eyes still on the jars of honey. "I don't know," he admitted. "His mother would have been so pleased. But an artist..."

I popped the last of my scone into my mouth and studied the walls.

Charcoal sighed, eyes raking my empty plate.

The keeper's voice was heavy. "An artist wouldn't belong here, and I don't know which weighs on me more: pushing my boy into a profession which may not suit him or keeping him from a profession bringing him respect and comfort." He shook his head.

The keeper's dilemma moved me.

Had my parents wrestled with the choice to send me away? A frisson of pain bolted through me, hardening my resolve to restart the search for my family.

"I can test him, and if I think he's a candidate, I'll write a letter of recommendation. But a word of caution. If you decide he should go, you must send him immediately. He's already almost at the oldest age an abbey will accept a candidate."

"How old were you?"

"I was engaged in my studies by four. Your boy is six?"

"Yes, soon." The keeper stared at the walls. "Are you done with your meal? Would you mind testing him?"

I took the bowl of strawberries I'd been saving off the tray. "Yes.

I'm not planning on traveling farther than Chester today, so I have time."

The keeper nodded and stood. "I'll send him when he's finished his chores. The jars are yours."

Smiling, I lined the jars from light to dark. A flight of honey. I considered the gradient of color and flavor and imagined the flowers and bees that had gone into the making of each.

Could I paint the passage of time? Flowers, insects, the quality of light and temperature. Could I paint all three together? Perhaps as three paintings layered one on top of the other?

I looked up, but the boy had not reappeared.

What about the passage of time? For even if I found my parents, I doubted they'd recognize me.

As a boy, I'd longed for them, but I was no longer a lonely child. Had too much time passed? Could I build a relationship with them as an adult? What if there wasn't enough time left? I didn't even know how old my parents were.

If I could paint time, what then of age?

Maiden, Mother, Crone.

What of youth? Could I erase the lines of age and turn back the clock? Could advancing the clock hasten death?

———

"You the artist?"

Surprised, I looked up from folding the letter of recommendation. "I am."

The man gestured at the table.

He was of middle height and slight; I judged his age around forty. "Please, sit." I put a warning hand on the dog's shoulders and rubbed his stiff neck.

"So"—the man leaned forward—"all is ready, and we march in four days."

"Mmm."

What is he talking about?

"Even so"—the man looked around to ensure no one was within earshot—"Preacher Talbot urges stealth."

"Stealth," I repeated.

Preacher Talbot. Preacher Talbot. Where had I heard the name?

"Stealth," the man agreed. "Though I don't understand the excessive caution. Wakefield's a small community and unlikely to have defenses."

"No," I said, alarms clanging. "I shouldn't think so."

"After the mess in Brookfield, we've learned. Better to bring too many than not enough. Plus, we'll have our own artist this time. Once we have Wakefield, we'll use it as a staging ground for Newfane." He stood and rapped his knuckles on the table once. "Go with God, Brother Artist."

Mind racing and mouth dry, I dug up the peculiar phrase I'd heard in New Bethel. "Peace be with you."

The man bowed and left the filling station. Through the window, I watched him turn up his collar and turn east toward Chester.

Preacher Talbot. Hadn't Akiko mentioned the name? Mess in Brookfield. Wakefield. Preacher Talbot. Wakefield. Newfane. My mind whirled.

Four days.

Horror howled in my ears as I connected the pieces, my mind fracturing. Images of what could be, each more terrible than the last, tumbled through my thoughts in a blood-soaked jumble.

I needed to get back.

My hands shook as I shoved the letter into the envelope. "Keeper. Keeper! Here's the letter for your boy. I need my horse *now*. Make haste, sir!"

"Now? In this weather?"

"Now!"

CHAPTER FORTY-NINE

We raced back the way we'd come. I'd already lost most of the morning; could I reach Wakefield by supper time? Words pounded in my mind in time with the thud of Oxide's hoofbeats.

Talbot. Wakefield. Newfane. God.

Four Days. March.

Wakefield. Talbot. Four.

Preacher. God.

Greasy rain slid down my neck and under the collar of my coat, joining the icy sweat prickling my spine.

Wakefield. Newfane. God. Talbot.

Four Days.

Kilometer after kilometer flew by as we swept over broken pavement through the mists. Oxide's breathing grew ragged, the rasping turning to a roar, and I slowed him to a jog.

We still had such a distance to cover. Once the horse had rested, I quickened the pace.

On we raced through the rain.

A growing awareness of my own aches and pains replaced my

sense of time. Teeth gritted, I tried not to focus on the raw skin chafing on the insides of my knees and calves.

As a distraction, I thought about Akiko and her potential to be an artist. Why hadn't I given her the same assessment I'd given the keeper's boy? As head boy, I'd administered the standard artistic potential tests dozens of times.

Maybe because they'd never accept her at an abbey? Or would they?

Could they make an exception for one exceptional child? If they didn't, could I help her? Akiko's future mattered, and I needed to get her some place safe.

Safer than Wakefield.

Wakefield. Newfane. Four Days. Talbot.

Charcoal barked, and my mind refocused.

We hurtled toward the center of Wakefield.

I didn't remember reaching the bottom of the plateau; I didn't remember turning onto Route 30.

Too slow, I sat back, but Oxide didn't respond. I pulled the reins, but his stride didn't slow or vary, our pace unceasing.

Oxide was running blind, fueled by instinct and panic. Ears pinned to his skull, he was wholly unaware of his surroundings. Desperate, I hauled on the reins, but my efforts yielded no change in his rhythm.

He would kill us both.

Mind racing, I dropped the reins and reached forward to cover the horse's left eye. In response, Oxide shied violently to the right. I was already off-balance, stretched along the horse's neck.

The fall happened in slow motion, the world tilting in fractured moments.

Someone screamed.

The ground rushed toward me, and my face slammed into the sodden grass with a horrific *thud*, filling my nose with mud and grass.

Pain bloomed like a white light.

Can't breathe. Can't move.

366

From a great distance, voices called my name.

Someone turned me over as my chest heaved.

"Matthew! Matthew!" Ben's face loomed over mine. "Matthew!"

I blinked once, trying to draw in a breath.

There was no air.

"Breathe, blast it!" Genevie shook my shoulder roughly, then punched my stomach. "Breathe!"

The weight on my chest lifted, and air flooded into my lungs. Tears leaked from my eyes.

"Hullo," I croaked, my mouth full of blood. I turned my head to the side and spat. The coppery taste mixed with my fear, and I gagged.

Ben's face telegraphed anxiety. He sat back on his heels and shook his head.

"Ass," hissed Genevie. "Why didn't you slow?"

Still laboring to breathe, I swiveled my eyes until I could see her. "Running. Blind."

Josephine nodded. "Horses pushed beyond their endurance lose the ability to see or reason. I'm assuming Oxide didn't bolt?"

I tilted my head.

"Shame on you. He'll recover, but he's shaky."

"Why were you running?" asked Genevie. "What's happened?"

I focused on Josephine and tried to sit up, spitting out blood and grass. "Four. Preacher."

Ben reached forward and helped me sit. "What?"

I shook my head to clear it and tried again, wheezing. "Josephine, Preacher."

She nodded. "Yes?"

"March. Four days. Coming here." I thumped my chest, irritated by my lack of breath. "Talbot," I croaked.

"Preacher Talbot," whispered Akiko.

My eyes flicked to her.

"This Preacher Talbot is coming here," said Ben. "In four days?"

I nodded.

"To what purpose?" Ben asked, his brow furrowed.

I locked eyes with Josephine.

She gasped, a hand fluttering at her throat. "New London," she whispered. "Brookfield. *And then the world died.*"

Genevie sat back on her heels. "New London?"

Josephine nodded. "Preacher Talbot is coming here to take the community of Wakefield."

I closed my eyes, exhausted, my head pounding.

Akiko said, "Whatever it takes."

"Were you in New London, child?" asked Ben.

My eyes flew open as Akiko nodded.

"We didn't find your parents," said Josephine, "among the dead."

A single tear spilled. "They ride for Preacher Talbot. They follow Rudy."

"You. Ran," I whispered. I held my arms out, and the child burrowed into my chest, weeping. I held her, hating her pain.

Blast her parents. Blast this Talbot.

Ben closed his eyes and sighed. "Now they march here."

MINDFUL OF THE CHILD RIDING BESIDE ME, I KEPT FOX'S SPEED to a slow canter. We'd left for Newfane soon after the contentious community meeting, but the late spring twilight was already deepening into darkness.

At least the rain had stopped.

"Why does Ben want to run away?" asked Akiko.

I peered into the deepening gloom. There was no sense in shielding her from the truth. She knew I was taking her to Newfane to keep her from the fight. She wasn't in physical danger if her parents were revivalists, but she didn't need to witness what could happen if Wakefield fought. "He wants to avoid fighting."

"Is he scared?"

"We all should be." Ben and I'd urged the others to abandon the community. With luck, he'd have talked them into leaving by the time I got back.

Lives were infinitely more precious than dwellings.

"What's guns?" Akiko asked.

"What?"

She reached forward and patted her mare's neck. "When the administrator asked Josephine how the people *Before* defended themselves, Josephine said with guns. What's guns?"

I sighed. "Oh, a gun. A weapon favored by the people from *Before*."

"A weapon?"

"Yes, one which threw a projectile fast and straight."

"Like a slingshot?"

"Sure, if a slingshot could puncture metal and wood and fly more than a kilometer."

"A kilometer? No way."

"Way."

"Why don't we have guns?"

I slowed Fox to a jog and glanced at Charcoal. He trotted alongside with a determined look. The dog was indestructible.

My face hurt. "How are you doing?"

"Fine. How far to Newfane?"

"It took under two hours, last time."

"So almost there."

"Yes. Do you need a rest?"

"No. Why don't we have guns?"

I grinned at the tenacious child. "As I understand it, when the world died, people took up arms against each other."

"Arms?"

"Another word for weapons. Which in their case meant guns."

"Oh. Why were they fighting?"

I stretched my back and groaned.

"Does it hurt? From the fall?"

369

"I'll survive. Did anyone ever teach you the rhyme about why the world died?"

"No scholars ride with Rudy."

"Politics, Money, Power, Religion, and Greed. These are the things we never again need," I recited. "The people *Before* forgot how to be human. Or humane."

"Human? What were they? Why did they fight?"

I wasn't handling this well. "Why does Preacher Talbot fight?"

"He doesn't. Rudy does it for him."

"Why?"

"He wants to claim communities for God."

"For God?"

"Yes. They don't want to build; they want to convert people. When they can't, they move in."

"And if the people of the community don't want to leave?"

"I don't know. They disappear."

"Why didn't Preacher Talbot stay in New London?"

"I don't know. I ran away."

"Did your parents come and look for you?"

"I don't know. No one came to the bridge until you did."

My heart pounded. "Was Cara with you?"

"I saw her lying on the logs. I was afraid she fell through the bridge, so I sat down."

"Oh. You didn't know her?"

"Nuh-uh."

She said nothing else, so I let it go.

Stars glittered above us, frog song crescendoing as we passed unseen ponds.

"Matthew?"

"Yes?"

"I see lights."

I looked up. "Right, we're here. Stay quiet." I urged Fox to quicken, and the horse rushed forward.

"Stop!" cried a voice in the dark.

I cued the horse to stop.

Fox danced from side to side, impatient.

"I am Artist Sugiyama, returned from my trip."

"Who's with you?" A bright light blinded me.

I put an arm up to shield my eyes. "My ward! Get that blasted light off us."

The light stayed on, though they redirected it.

We waited for several minutes, and I shivered. What if they wouldn't accept Akiko as my charge?

"Pardon us, Master Sugiyama," said a smooth voice. "Open the gate!"

Noiseless, the iron gate opened.

Fox shied backward, and I swore, trying to keep the skittish horse from dumping me. "I will not hit the ground *again*." As soon as Fox stopped plunging, I swung my leg over the saddle and dropped to the ground.

My body shrieked, but I ignored it.

Akiko moved to dismount, but I held my hand up to stop her.

"Good evening, Artist Sugiyama," said the woman with the smooth voice.

As she moved forward into the light, I recognized the minstrel. "Good evening, Minstrel. I need to speak with your administrator, Ricardo, and Elaina."

The minstrel looked at Akiko on her pony. "The child?"

"She stays with me," I replied.

"Just so," said the minstrel. She studied my bruised face, saying nothing.

Each time I'd visited Newfane, they'd renewed their offer for membership, so I'd hoped they'd agree to my request they shelter Akiko. That the minstrel had accepted her as my ward gave me confidence.

Whether they'd agree to provide Wakefield with aid was another matter.

We followed the main road into the community, and the minstrel stopped before the same inn I'd first met her. "Go in, and I'll send word to the others."

A teenage girl took the reins from me. "I'll take them to the livery. Will you be staying the night?"

"Yes."

"Very good, Sir," she said, leading the horses away.

I watched her and wondered what became of Avalon Society children when they came of age.

"After you," said the minstrel, gesturing at the door. "I'll ask a meal be sent."

I pulled out a chair for Akiko at the long table in the center of the room. She climbed into it and giggled as I pushed her forward with a squeak. Charcoal chose the chair next to Akiko, and I flopped into the chair on the other side of her.

"It's beautiful here," she whispered.

"Yes, it is. I wanted to stay and paint it on my first visit."

The keeper brought two steaming bowls and a small loaf of dark bread.

"I have only split pea and ham ready at the moment," he said, slicing into the loaf, "but I could bring cheese and meat if you don't mind a wait."

"Soup is fine," said Akiko. She waved the slice of bread the keeper handed her. "Can he have some dinner, too?"

The keeper looked at the dog, then at me. He nodded and bowed his head before taking the tray back into the kitchen.

"Eat up," said Akiko, imitating Ben.

I tasted the soup. Like everything here, it was delicious, the smokey ham perfectly balancing the sweet green peas. The surface shimmered, and even the steam rose in a dignified manner, delicious curls of shallot and smoke.

I balled my bread and tossed it over Akiko's head to Charcoal. He caught it and wolfed it down, then looked at the girl. She giggled and stuffed her remaining bread into her mouth.

I smiled at the child. "I bet I can beat you to the bottom of the bowl."

"Not if you tell me why we don't have guns," she mumbled through a mouthful of bread.

I laughed and looked around to make sure no one was within earshot. "Short version?"

She nodded.

"Guns need bullets which use gunpowder. After the world died, the people who had guns used up all the bullets, and then the guns were useless."

The keeper returned with a serving of soup on a shallow dish and set it in front of the dog.

Charcoal huffed politely.

"Why didn't they make more powder?" Akiko asked after the keeper retreated. She dipped her second piece of bread into the soup and sighed with pleasure.

"Gunpowder requires three elements. Saltpeter, sulfur, and charcoal."

"Like drawing pencils?"

"Yes. The charcoal we can make, and saltpeter comes from animal feces, carcasses, or urine."

Akiko wrinkled her nose.

"Quite. But we can make it. The problem is the—"

"Sulfur," she said.

"Yes, sulfur," I agreed. "They used the last of it hundreds of years ago, and we don't have the technology to mine more. Hence—"

"No guns."

"No guns," I agreed. "And I see you've beaten me to the bottom of the bowl, wretched child."

CHAPTER FIFTY

"M atthew!" Josephine hurried to where I was unsaddling Fox. "You missed lunch. Will they come? Will they help?"

Sighing, I lifted the saddle from the horse's back. "Ben didn't convince Wakefield to run?"

Creases appeared on Josephine's brow. "No. The news from Newfane?"

"Not good, but they agreed to harbor Akiko."

Josephine swallowed audibly.

"We could go. We could run."

Josephine searched my face, then shook her head. "We can't."

"Would it be better if I left? What if they're after me?"

"You think Talbot is 'T'?" She frowned. "What if he's not?"

"What if he is? What if all of it has been because of me?" I could barely meet her eyes. "New London and Brookfield—"

She touched my arm. "Don't take this on yourself. They're coming. Even if you go, we won't be safe."

I rested my forehead against Fox's neck. "Things were fine before

374

I started traveling. Maybe I should have done as the masters told me and picked a community."

"If you left, where would you go?"

I looked around Wakefield. "I don't know. Perhaps an abbey. Everything could go back to being perfect."

"Things have never been perfect."

Star Creek and the quiet life I'd rejected flashed on my mind's canvas. "It can't be true. I can't cause any more death."

"Whatever is happening is bigger than you. Bigger than all of us. None of us could leave these people to what's coming. Not even you."

Her truth penetrated deeply, grounding my center. Ben's words surfaced in my memory; *we are stronger together*. My departure wouldn't keep them safe. It would only ensure one less fighter.

It was time to choose. Either I could leave and remain apart from, or I could stay and become a part of—these people, my friends, my *family*.

I slung my arm around her. "You're right, but as soon as we find a moment alone, I need to tell Ben and Sally about 'T'. I've already left it too long."

Josephine smiled at me. "Welcome back."

Picking up my saddlebags, I squeezed her shoulder. "Come. I need to deliver the news about Newfane. Perhaps someone's come up with a plan."

We walked across a corner of the green to the building Wakefield used for community gatherings.

"Why isn't this a pub?" I asked, stepping inside. I held the door for Charcoal, who raised his nose and sniffed the air.

Josephine nudged the dog with her leg. "This is a dry community."

"Dry? Why?" I looked around at the dim space. A single window illuminated a room packed with tables and chairs. The air smelled stale.

She looked at me with the hint of a smile. "Because they have no brewmaster. Why? What did you think?"

I shook my head ruefully. "I don't know. Hullo, Whistler."

Whistler slapped me on the back, his eyes crinkling. "Glad you're back."

When I told my friends Newfane had declined to fight or provide sanctuary for Wakefield, they groaned.

"Blistering cockroach lovers," Sally muttered. "I'll get Carl."

"Carl?"

"The administrator," said Whistler. "And in happier circumstances, Sally's beau."

"She's not too—" I stopped, warned by the expression on Josephine's face.

"Not too, ah... focused on our journey?" I asked.

Genevie snorted. "Nice."

"What's nice?" asked Sally. A small man with round spectacles and a half-dozen people I didn't recognize followed her.

"Newfane agreed to keep Akiko safe while we're focused on—what's coming."

"It's the least they can do." Sally sniffed. "This is Carl."

"Pleased to meet you, sir," said Carl.

He shrank when I leaned forward.

Sally elbowed him. "Matthew. Call him Matthew."

"Sir Matthew," said Carl, bowing.

"This is Nicole and Bao," said Genevie. "Their argument," she said, choosing her words, "is what persuaded the people of Wakefield to stay."

Ah. The people who actually ran Wakefield.

Nicole was tall and sturdy looking, with hard eyes. Bao, a slender man, appeared remote and untroubled. Both were about my age.

"Come, let's sit," Bao said. "The rest will be along soon, but we can start without them."

Everyone sat at the middle table and looked at me.

Charcoal leaned against my leg beneath the table.

"Newfane will not send help. We're on our own."

There were groans and sighs all around me.

"Good," said Nicole. She looked around the table. "We're on our own, so we must make our plans." She looked at Ben. "Newfane has only ever offered us failed applicants, so this isn't unexpected."

Ben inclined his head, his expression neutral.

"We'll fight," said Bao.

Statements of support rang out.

I looked around. If we didn't come up with a plan, we had no hope of defending Wakefield. A memory of the stacked bodies in New London popped onto my mind's canvas, and I swallowed, my mouth sour and sick.

"Where's everyone else? Where's Cara?" I whispered to Genevie.

"It's safer if only a few know the entire plan," she murmured.

"Do any of you know how to fight?" Ben's voice cut through the noise in the room.

Silence.

"Do they?" asked Nicole, tightening her jaw.

Josephine looked thoughtful. "We never found wounds on the bodies."

"How many bodies?" asked a voice.

"Too many," said Ben.

The room fell silent a second time.

"No matter," said Nicole. "We have time. We'll draw up a plan and practice it." The people around the table nodded.

Genevie locked eyes with me.

"What?" said Nicole, catching the look.

Genevie folded her arms and looked at Nicole. "You're assuming they'll make a frontal assault." Seeing their blank looks, she clarified, "You think they'll march into Wakefield with weapons raised."

Nicole nodded, frowning.

"What if they come with smiles on their faces and ask for shelter?" I asked. "Will you still strike at them?"

"Well..." said Nicole, her look of certainty faltering.

"I was told they cautioned stealth," I said, glancing around.

"Do you think he told you the truth?" asked Whistler.

I dismissed his question with a shrug. "He mistook me for another artist, an artist working *with* them."

"What should we do?" asked Bao.

His question unnerved the room. Eyes turned toward me, and my gut clenched.

Josephine nudged Ben, and he sighed and stood. "If I may?"

A muscle in Nicole's jaw flickered, but she nodded.

"A part of their group will come with smiles, well wishes, and they'll ask for simple favors. You, being the good people you are, will agree."

Jeers rang out.

Ben raised his hands for quiet. "As you offered hospitality to us."

People exchanged uncomfortable glances.

"Truth," said Carl, his voice heavy. "What next?"

Ben continued, "As they will smile and pay us compliments, I suggest we do the same."

"What?" a voice in the crowd roared.

Ben waited for their objections to subside. "We'll offer food, shelter, repairs to their equipment, and such per the usual manner. But," he said, quieting the unhappy murmurs, "we'll know they're not our friends. As they plot against us, so too will we plan." He turned and held his hand out to Josephine. She took it and stepped up onto the bench.

I hid my smile; standing on the bench, Josephine was nearly at eye level with Ben.

"We'll offer shelter, but on *our* terms." Her voice rang clear and strong. "We'll split up their group, housing them in ones and twos within our own dwellings. And we'll place hidden locks on the bedroom doors in case we need to incarcerate them."

Heads nodded in agreement around the table.

This was *Josephine's* plan. I leaned forward to listen, stroking the coarse fur on Charcoal's neck.

"Next, we'll put barrels of clean water in the outbuildings — the dairy, the livery. We don't know if they delivered a draught or poison in New London, but knowing we have clean water to drink will help us avoid traps."

Ben picked up the thread. "If they offer a meal, we accept and contribute dishes so we can avoid tainted foods."

"What of those who come with weapons raised?" asked Nicole, her face and voice hard.

Ben and Josephine exchanged glances. "We'll hide sentries in the surrounding wood," said Ben. "Who has combat training?"

Without thinking, I raised my hand. Too late, I dropped it, but everyone had seen.

"Matthew?" asked Sally, her eyes clouding.

To deflect interest, I asked Ben, "Why?"

"We need to learn the basics of defense and attack. Will you train anyone willing to engage in a hand-to-hand struggle?"

I flushed. "Yes."

Charcoal nudged my hands with his nose.

Josephine's eyes lingered on my face. "We'll also need art for defenses."

She'd let me make my decision to stay without telling me she needed my help to implement her plan to protect Wakefield. My chest tightened at her faith in me.

"How do you know all of this?" asked Nicole, her eyes narrowing.

"Josephine studied the engagements from *Before*," said Ben.

Nicole gazed at Josephine, then gave a sharp nod. "I like it," she said.

I shivered with relief. Already, my mind buzzed with ideas of how to implement Josephine's plan.

The people of Wakefield clustered around Ben, Josephine, and Nicole, asking for tasks and assignments, so I tiptoed toward the door.

"Matthew."

I winced, caught.

Charcoal and I turned in unison.

Sally stood behind us, hands on her hips. "When this is over, you *will* explain."

Resigned, I nodded. "When this is over, I will explain."

CHAPTER FIFTY-ONE

The days flew past in a blur of activity. Ben organized the sentries and taught them to use climbing knots and pulleys to ascend and descend from the tree canopy. Sally and Carl worked on a sleeping plan for up to twenty of Preacher Talbot's followers. Genevie designed decorative latches to lock the sleeping rooms, which looked like simple ornamentation, and Whistler and two of the men from Wakefield installed the locks.

I taught four combat training sessions each day. Using a variety of weapons, I showed the correct ways to thrust, evade, and parry. We invited everyone to attend as many sessions as they wished. To my surprise, by the start of the third session, almost every inhabitant of Wakefield, including my friends, was in attendance.

Notably, Cara skipped the lessons.

A gulf had grown between us when I'd refused to share the details of the plan. Furious, she now avoided me. I didn't know what to do about it, so I threw myself into the preparations.

When I wasn't leading a combat session, I fortified Wakefield with improvements, broadening and deepening the river flowing around the community, adding ornamental blocks of stone on our side which made the bank high and straight. The resulting river was too broad and swift to cross, removing all access save the bridge.

"*Substantial*," Josephine had declared upon seeing it.

To armor the dwellings, I thickened the walls with heavy stones resembling a decorative facade.

At Ben's request, I painted a large cave into the hillside on the south end of the community. Ben inspected the cave and made a few suggestions for supporting the space. Once he gave his approval, I added boulders and ferns to obscure the entrance. Remembering the mural's tangle of vines at the filling station, I drew thick brambles at the forest's edge.

Nicole and Bao organized the storage of fresh water and foodstuff, hiding them in the dwellings behind cabinetry I painted based on Ben's designs.

When we'd outfitted the last dwelling, Ben and I shook hands.

"We're as ready as we can be," he said, pulling me into a hug. We clung to each other, our silence speaking volumes.

Ben patted my back. "Come, time for dinner."

Working together, we'd accomplished more than I'd hoped in four days. Our preparations seemed balanced and measured—unlike the disastrous wall I'd drawn around Brookfield.

My stomach tightened. "I wish..."

Charcoal brought me a too-long sanded plank and danced, wanting to play.

"Where have you been all afternoon?" I looked at the plank. "You're going to get us in trouble with someone, dog."

Ben chuckled. "What do you wish?"

My mouth hardened. "I wish we weren't facing a fight."

"Should we have left Wakefield on their own?"

"No, not at all. I wish there was no one to fight. Isn't it why they've taught us politics, money, power, religion, and greed corrupts?" I tossed the plank onto a pile of scrap wood near the carpenter's dwelling.

Ben sighed. "I don't know."

"Don't know what?" asked Josephine, falling into step with us.

"Matthew wishes none of this were happening."

"I do, too," she said.

I punched my palm. "Why is it happening at all, Josephine? We know what happened to the people of *Before*. Why is this happening again?"

She looked at me with pity on her scarred face. "Because we're human."

"But we've improved! Yes, we've lost the use of their technology, but we work and live in cooperative communities. We know our strength comes from relying on one another. Everyone knows the world reborn is better!"

"If that's true," said Josephine, "then why are people following these minstrels? Why is religious conviction rising?"

"Power," said Ben.

"Religion," I said at the same time.

"Mmm," she agreed. "Perhaps greed, too. Oh, *look*."

They had set up long tables in the grass outside of the community building. Small candles winked like fireflies from jars scattered amongst the tables. The white tablecloths floated on the warm spring breeze.

People chattered and murmured, many smiling or nodding as we passed them.

"Matthew! Josephine, Ben, over here!" Genevie called. She was sitting with Sally and Carl at an outer table. I glanced around the tables for Cara, but she wasn't here.

I raised my hand in greeting and sniffed the air—fragrant with fresh bread and roasted fowl. "Hullo, all. Something smells good. What are we having?"

Ben pulled out the bench for Josephine.

I kissed Sally on the cheek and said in a low voice, "We're ready."

She nodded and squeezed my arm.

I sat facing Genevie. "Where's your man?"

"Have you met my husband?" answered Genevie, smirking. "Where would he be before a banquet?"

"Ha! Apologies, Mrs. Canning. Carl, what's on the menu?"

"Fried chicken, mashed turnips, and boiled peas," said Carl.

We groaned with anticipation, and my stomach rumbled. "Fried chicken. I haven't any in ages."

Akiko slid onto the bench next to me.

I stared at her, my mouth dry and sour. "Where'd you come from?"

"Newfane."

Josephine leaned forward. "Did someone bring you? Are people from Newfane here?" She craned her neck, looking for new arrivals.

"No."

"How did you get here?" I asked. My skin prickled as though spiders crawled up the nape of my neck.

It wasn't safe to leave. How was I going to get her back to Newfane?

Akiko shrugged. "Pony knew the way. Can I have some water?"

Silent, I poured the girl a glass. "I wanted you to stay there," I said, sliding the glass to her.

She took a drink. "I like the changes."

"Changes?" asked Sally, cocking her head.

"Houses, the stream, the rocks, and the bushes."

"Bushes?" rumbled Ben. "Which bushes?"

"The ones at the edges of the grass," she said. She narrowed her eyes, trying to decide if Ben was teasing her. "The ones with the thorns."

Ben looked at me.

"I thought it would be easier to watch two directions than three." I turned to Akiko. "How long have you been here?"

She shrugged. "Pony and I got here at lunchtime, but no one was eating and the kids were gone, so I went to see if the bushes had berries."

Sally clucked her tongue. "Oh, honey, you must be hungry. Look, here comes Whistler."

"Did you hear the news?" asked Whistler, putting a board down on the table in front of us—an artful arrangement of freshly baked bread and a crock of butter.

"Pepper bread!" exclaimed Sally.

"What news?" asked Genevie, stroking his arm.

"They're here," said Akiko.

"Welcome, Travelers. I'm Carl, the administrator. Can I be of help?"

"Thank you, Administrator Carl. We've been traveling for days and seek hospitality."

"Wakefield is a small community," Carl said, "but willing to share what we have. We're about to enjoy a community meal. Join us?"

"Thank you. My name is Rudy Bienville. I'm afraid we have no stores to offer, but we carry a barrel of mead we could contribute."

My ears pricked. Mead? From the filling station near Chester?

"We welcome your mead. Wakefield is presently a dry community."

"Ah, then how fortuitous we arrive this night."

"Quite." Carl turned and raised his voice for all to hear. "Here are Rudy Bienville and his companions. I've invited them to join our celebration, and they've accepted. They've also brought a cask of mead to share should anyone care to partake. Are there open seats?"

Hands rose.

Carl gestured to the travelers. "Please, find yourself seats and enjoy the evening."

Carl sat, and the chatter resumed.

Sally's mouth tightened. "Carl—"

He covered her hand with his. "Yes, I agree. Now, Josephine, tell us why you never volunteer for kitchen labor hours."

Everyone laughed, and Josephine blushed. "It seems Ben has been over-sharing," she said.

I struggled to engage in the conversation, trying not to stare at Rudy's people. None of the new arrivals looked Asian. Where were Akiko's parents?

There must be others elsewhere, waiting in the dark.

Under the table, Genevie laid a hand on my knee to still my restless leg.

"The food will make it easier," whispered Akiko.

"To do what?"

"Pretend things are normal."

"You're wise beyond your years. I'm not as good an actor as everyone else."

She gazed at me. "You've never learned to lie."

"How old *are* you?" I mock-whispered.

She grinned and poked her front tooth with her tongue. "Look, it's wiggling."

"Oh, good, you *are* a kid."

She giggled and then exclaimed, "Ooh!"

A procession of kitchen workers carried platters of food toward the tables. I poked her in the ribs. "Keep those grubby mitts off of my favorite pieces of chicken."

"Be fast," she warned with a giggle.

We piled our plates high and dug in, but the food tasted like sawdust. I pushed my fork around the plate.

How was I going to keep Akiko safe?

"Matthew, we need to sell this meal," said Genevie in a low voice.

"I've no appetite."

"None of us do. Pretend."

"Pretend?"

"Like make-believe," said Akiko, waving a drumstick. "Look, I got the last one."

I pulled a face and snarled at her.

"Keep working on your pretending," she advised, rolling her eyes.

I picked up my drumstick. The skin was crispy and deep brown, flecked with pepper and seasonings. It was warm, and the scent rose, familiar and forgotten. I took a big bite. This time, I could taste the salt and grease. The batter crunched under my teeth, and my mouth flooded. I closed my eyes with pleasure.

Genevie chuckled. "Much better."

With genuine enjoyment, I finished my plate and sat back.

Across the tables, Nicole looked stiff and unnatural.

"I'd like a glass of mead," I announced. "Anyone else?"

Josephine stilled, but Whistler grinned and said, "I'll join you."

We wandered to the cask and nodded our thanks to the traveler handing out glasses.

"To your health," said Whistler.

"And to yours!" I replied.

We clinked our glasses and pretended to drink. The man at the cask relaxed.

"Can I take another back to the table?" I asked. "This is delicious. My friend has never tried mead."

"Why don't we bring glasses to all the tables?" said a voice behind me.

I turned, repulsed by the artificial smile Rudy had plastered on his face.

"Yes," said Whistler. "Very kind."

"What kind of honey did you use?" I asked.

Rudy turned to the man at the cask. "Yes, what kind of honey did you use, Lester?"

"Oh, the pale gold stuff," Lester replied. "You know, straight honey. Not the honey jam some people make."

"I've only tasted mead a few times," I said. "This is delightful. It tastes as though there's a hint of molasses in it."

"Bees are really such clever creatures," said Lester with eminent authority.

"Well, thanks again," I said. "We'll let the others know you'll bring glasses to the tables."

As I guided Whistler away, he asked in a low voice, "What was all that about?"

"I met the man who made the mead."

"So, is it safe to drink?"

"No. If it were safe, they'd have admitted where it came from."

Whistler was silent as we walked back to our seats. He clasped my shoulder and said, "I hope your friend is all right."

The keeper. His boy. The invisible Barnaby. I shook my head and took a deep breath, announcing, "They're bringing glasses for everyone to try."

"Good," said Sally, clapping her hands. "Before everyone gets too merry, perhaps Carl and I should hand out the sleeping arrangements."

Ben looked at her. "Ones and twos?"

She patted him on the shoulder and smiled at us. "Oh, yes."

CHAPTER FIFTY-TWO

The first attack began in the middle of the night. From our hillside vantage, we watched the dim glow of candles move from the bedrooms assigned to Rudy's people into our own.

"I bet they're murdering our pillows," muttered Sally.

"Yes. They'll soon discover the truth," said Josephine.

Within minutes, Rudy's companions gathered in the street and were gesturing when Rudy arrived. He quieted them, and they huddled.

"I wish we could hear what they're saying," said Sally.

Ben nodded. "We'll know when we get the reports." He turned to Nicole. "Is everyone here?"

"Yes, except for the sentries in the trees, and your spies."

"Good. Get everyone into the cavern. The night's dark, but we'll be visible if the moon appears."

Nicole nodded and clasped him on the shoulder before ushering people into the cave. They clambered noisily through the narrow opening between the boulders.

"Spies? What spies?" hissed Sally.

389

I grimaced. "We have someone hidden in every dwelling. They're to listen and report back whenever they're able."

"Every dwelling?" asked Carl with surprise. "But that would mean at least twelve."

Ben nodded.

Genevie, face anxious, turned to Ben. "Whistler?" she whispered. "He's a spy?"

Ben gripped her shoulder. "He volunteered."

Josephine's breath caught in a muffled sob.

"Why?" whispered Genevie. "Why didn't you tell us?"

Ben pulled her and Josephine to him. "They'll be okay. Please go into the cave; I need you to keep everyone calm."

In a thin voice, Josephine asked, "Where are you going?"

"We're joining Bao and the sentries. We'll send a signal when the rest of Talbot's people arrive. You remember the plan?" I asked.

The women nodded.

"Good. Stay safe," I said, hugging them.

Sally clasped my sleeve. "Where's Akiko?"

My heart clenched. "Hidden."

Sally recoiled, her eyes narrowing. "Where?"

Ben sighed. "She's in a dwelling."

The women gasped in unison.

"She's a mole," Ben admitted, scanning the dark.

"A mouse," I corrected. It was the safest place I could think of to stash her. "Go!"

Before the women could argue, we slipped away.

Though I didn't love the idea of hiding in a tree to keep watch, I'd chosen sentry duty over being concealed in a dwelling. I needed to keep my friends safe, and my eyes, accustomed to studying shadows and planes, were better suited to interpreting shapes in the dark than my fellow sentries.

When we reached the thicket of briers I'd painted, we worked our way along the tree line through berry-scented air until we could slide into the forest.

Ben's low voice rumbled in my ear. "When you reach your tree, double-check your knots are tight before you load your rope. Know where you're going?"

The forest looked different in the dark. "You go first."

Ben slipped ahead of me. We'd only traveled a few hundred meters before we heard voices.

"What do you mean they're gone?"

"They're not here."

"No one in any of the dwellings?"

"No, not a one."

There was silence, and I strained my ears.

"Someone's betrayed us," said a third *female* voice.

The hairs on my arms rose. I knew the voice. And I knew why Ben had insisted we keep our preparations secret.

The voice continued, "Get the men. We'll post sentries tonight and reassess in the morning."

"All of them?"

"Yes, idiot," she hissed. "Get them all. Make sure they keep their weapons handy."

We waited an eternity before Ben moved.

My heart hammered as I crept after him, sure they'd catch us at any moment.

Something brushed my shoulder, and I froze, waiting for the blade or blow. It brushed my shoulder again, and I shuddered. Craning my neck to the right, I saw not the hand I'd expected, but a rope.

A rope.

Bao perched in the tree above us.

"Sss," I hissed.

Ben turned, and I pointed up.

Bao lowered the remaining rope, and Ben fashioned a harness, tightening each knot carefully.

Bao lowered a second rope.

Looping the rope under one foot and over the other, Ben climbed, noiseless. Reaching Bao, he swung onto a limb and pulled the rope up behind him.

Preparing to leave, I froze as Bao gestured wildly.

The hairs on my arms rose. Scarce meters from where I stood was a figure in the dark. Pulse thundering, I fought to keep from gasping.

Pushing away my panic, I looked at Ben for guidance.

He flashed his hand four times and pointed at his wrist.

Wait twenty minutes.

The shape was so still. Was it a person or a trick of the light?

My breathing relaxed after counting to twenty minutes. What was it? A stump? A broken sapling?

Just after the twenty-minute mark, the figure sighed, and I went rigid, daring only to move my eyes. My mouth tasted sweet, and I fought to keep from giggling.

Ben signaled Bao, who disconnected from the tree and connected to the line to carry him to the next sentry post.

But as Bao pushed away from the tree, his harness knot tightened and groaned. He swung his head toward me with wide eyes.

For a heartbeat, I dared to hope the shadow figure had heard nothing.

A quick motion on the ground caught my eye, and I looked back in time to see the light fading from Bao's eyes as an arrow plowed through his neck with a wet sucking sound.

Ben was already swinging away from the tree as arrows hissed past him. Catching the next guideline and swinging away in a single fluid motion, he bellowed, "We're under attack!"

I RACED BACK ALONG THE TREE LINE TOWARD THE CAVE. IF WE were already under attack, I needed to protect the people in the cavern.

Ben bellowed again as screams and cries rang out.

In the dark, I'd missed the transition and was on the wrong side of the bramble thicket. I peered through the leaves.

"Was that Ben?" Josephine asked, emerging from the cave. Genevie pushed past her.

"Genevie, don't!" said Josephine, trying to pull the larger woman back.

"Let go!" said Genevie.

I needed to warn the women to quiet.

"Good evening, Genevie," said a voice that made my flesh crawl. "One step more, and you'll find yourself a head shorter."

"Joshua," snarled Genevie, turning.

Joshua and the red-haired woman were sitting on the hillside above the hidden entrance to the cave. Focused on my friends, I hadn't seen them.

If I'd spoken, they would have caught me too.

I shivered in revulsion. Joshua's companions had destroyed New London and Brookfield.

"Joshua. Carol!" said Josephine in a shocked voice. "What are you—"

Joshua jumped down and bowed. "Your humble servant, mesdames."

One last cry of pain rent the night air, and all was still.

"Ah," he said. "We've disabled your sentries, and we're free to move into the community. Why don't you join me?" Sarcasm dripped from his words, and my hands balled into fists.

Joshua shouted into the darkness, "Tobe, come and guard the entrance. If anyone attempts to leave, kill them." He turned back to the women. "You two, move."

Genevie and Josephine stumbled down the hillside in the dark. When they slowed, Joshua prodded their backs hard enough to make them yelp. By the time they reached the lights spilling from every window, the women had bloodstains on their backs.

With a palpable rage, I followed, keeping to the shadows until I reached the edge of the brambles.

Rudy turned toward them as they approached. "Well met, Joshua! How many did you capture?"

I climbed the wall of the nearest dwelling, pulling myself onto the roof with as much speed as I could. The rough roofing scraped my palms and chin as I crawled forward on my belly and peered over the edge.

Joshua was standing with his back to me. "Everyone who went into the cave is there, save these two. The sentries?"

"All dispatched," said Rudy. "How delightful when a plan comes together." He turned to Lester and said, "Send someone to retrieve the artist from the cave."

Genevie and Josephine exchanged a glance.

The young man soon returned. Panting, he wheezed. "No artist."

Rudy frowned. "You're sure?"

The young man nodded. "The only man in the cave was the old fellow, the administrator."

"Where are the men?" asked Joshua.

Rudy paced without answering. Turning to the young man, he said, "Tell Kyle to bring the sentries' bodies here."

The man nodded and walked toward the woods.

"Run!" Rudy roared.

The young man sprinted away.

"Rudy?" asked Joshua again. "What is it?"

"There should have been men in the cavern. That one's husband, the artist, and others I noticed at the banquet."

Joshua shrugged. "Maybe we killed them in the woods."

"Yes, with luck," said Rudy, pacing, "except for the artist. Talbot was clear about him."

"You two sit next to the building," instructed Joshua.

Rudy frowned and resumed his pacing.

Footsteps approached, and a man I didn't recognize stepped out of the dark.

He set down a quiver of arrows. "I confirm twelve dead."

"Of how many?" asked Rudy.

394

The man shrugged. "We knew of ten, so at least two were a bonus. They're bringing the bodies now."

A tear slid down my cheek, and I tasted bitter salt.

Ben.

Men appeared from the dark with bodies slung over their shoulders, dropping them like sacks of grain. From the roof, I could smell the blood. Rudy and Joshua inspected the corpses, muttering to each other.

"Can you see him? Please, tell me he's not there," Josephine begged.

"I can't see—oh!" exclaimed Genevie.

"What? No!" hissed Josephine.

"Bao. I see Bao. The rest are too deep in the shadows."

Josephine choked on a sob.

Joshua's head swiveled in our direction, and I flattened as the women fell silent.

Rudy, Joshua, and Kyle conferred then Rudy shouted, "Search the dwellings, top to bottom! Find them!"

Dread crawled through my body.

Akiko, little mouse, stay hidden, stay safe.

Rudy's followers searched the dwellings and other buildings again and again. Humorless, I smiled; their repeated searches meant they hadn't found our fortifications.

Frustrated, Rudy shouted at his people, purple with rage. He stalked back and forth across the road.

"Preacher Talbot is coming," a woman reported.

Talbot, finally.

My stomach fluttered, and I struggled to slow my breathing.

Rudy masked his temper. The color in his face faded, and he adopted a cheerful, beatific smile. "Welcome, Preacher Talbot!"

"Peace be with you, Brother Rudy, Brother Joshua," said Talbot in a sonorous voice.

From where I lay, I couldn't see him, but Genevie gasped. "He's gorgeous."

"He looks like Matthew," Josephine said at the same time.

Looks like me?

The news slammed my gut. I craned my neck, but the men had moved out of sight into the building.

Talbot looked like me? How? What did it mean?

CHAPTER FIFTY-THREE

Other than Whistler, trapped in a dwelling, I was the only one Rudy's men hadn't captured or killed. It was up to me to save my friends, but to do so, I needed information. Slithering to the other side of the roof, I inched toward the open window.

"Update please, Brother Rudy," said Talbot.

"We've killed twelve of their sentries and have captured twenty-five of the residents," said Rudy.

"Oh?" asked Talbot. "How?"

Rudy snorted. "They had the fantastic idea of trapping themselves in a cave the artist drew for them."

I closed my eyes. What a fool I was.

"And the artist? Was he in the cave?"

"No," Rudy admitted.

Talbot's voice deepened. "You'll be accountable if someone has harmed him."

Interesting.

My eyes flicked toward the woods, where a pair of green eyes shone at me.

Charcoal.

My heart thumped, and I swallowed. Charcoal sank to his belly when I lifted my palm.

"No, sir," said Rudy. "I checked myself."

"He's not in the cave, and we didn't capture or kill him," Talbot summarized.

Silence.

"So, where is he?"

"We don't know," Rudy admitted.

I gazed across the expanse of the community's green. Dawn was approaching, and the darkness was no longer impenetrable. I had to move soon or risk being spotted.

"Do they know?" Talbot asked.

"The women? I don't know."

"Well," said Talbot, "you should probably find out."

I heard someone leave and wriggled back to my first spot, the roofing scratching my chest and belly.

Rudy walked around the corner toward the women. "Lester!" he shouted.

A man trotted into view.

"Take that one into the kitchens in the community building. Ask her where her husband is."

Lester frowned. "And if she doesn't talk?"

Rudy straightened and glared at him. "Be *persuasive.* Kyle, take the ugly one and ask her if she knows where the artist is."

Kyle leered, and my forehead beaded with sweat.

"I can be persuasive," he said, smirking. "Let's go, Ugly."

Josephine cried out, and Kyle backed into view, holding a fistful of her hair. Josephine swung at him until he released her.

"How dare you!" she screamed. "How can you call yourselves men of God when you treat people like this?"

Joshua smirked. "We're doing God's work. What we do in His name, He readily forgives."

"I do not forgive you," she spat.

"As you're not a child of God, your forgiveness is meaningless," said Joshua. He jerked his chin at the nearest dwelling. "Keep her until she tells you something useful."

Kyle grinned. "Aye, Brother Joshua. Move, bitch."

Josephine shuffled toward the nearest dwelling.

My hatred bored a hole in Kyle's head as I followed them with my eyes. I'd make him pay.

"Not there," he said, pointing. "That one."

Glancing at the dwelling he'd pointed at, my heart stopped. Akiko was lying on its roof, mirroring me. I waved at her frantically, and she waved back.

Go back, I pantomimed.

Akiko slid backward, out of sight.

I rolled onto my back, gasping, drenched with sweat. What now? *Move.*

I rolled over and swung off the roof. Lowering myself, I dropped to the ground and crouched, expecting to hear shouts. When none came, I sprinted around the back of the building, stopping at the corner to watch Kyle and Josephine climb the steps to the dwelling.

Charcoal bumped my leg.

I wished he'd stayed in the woods, but I'd deal with him later.

Josephine stopped at the threshold, and Kyle prodded her in the back with something sharp. She yelped, and a red smear appeared through her blouse.

Creeping to the side of the dwelling, I retrieved my sword from where I'd hidden it earlier and crouched under the open window.

"Don't. Even. Think about it." Kyle snarled. "Go, the bedroom there."

"I know nothing," Josephine said.

"Shut up. I've asked nothing." He chuckled. "I don't intend to until we're finished."

Josephine screamed.

Vaulting the porch railing, I slipped inside.

Josephine was lying face down with Kyle on top of her. She struggled, but he pinned his forearm to the back of her neck, slicing through her trousers with a blade.

Josephine's shriek was filled with pain and panic.

"I so enjoy doing God's work," Kyle said, panting as she tried to throw him off.

My anxiety and doubt dropped like stones, and I thrust the sword with all my strength, eyes blazing.

Blood sprayed over Josephine, and Kyle flailed his arms, shuddering.

I pulled my arm back.

He turned toward me, and the red wound gaped and closed wetly on his neck, sending sprays of blood everywhere.

Charcoal's growl rumbled deep and low.

Kyle opened his mouth, dropped to his knees, and fell forward, his head on the bed, eyes wide, mouth open in a silent plea as the clock ticked forward.

His body spasmed one last time, and I wiped my sword on his shoulder, holding my finger to my lips.

Josephine's screams died, and she scrambled off the bed as I beckoned to her.

"He was the man I met at the filling station," I muttered.

"What? Where—"

I shook my head and pointed at the bathroom. "Never mind. Clean yourself up." She needed a moment to compose herself before I asked for the impossible.

Sobbing, she wiped the blood from her face with a wet cloth. Shuddering, she dropped it into the sink.

I hated myself for my words. "I'm sorry to ask, dearest, but I need you to go to the porch and bring more of Rudy's men to you."

"What? Like this?" Josephine asked, looking at her shredded clothes. "You cannot—"

Eyes hard, I nodded. "We need to even the odds. Tell them Kyle will share."

Josephine closed her eyes and shuddered. "I'm bait." She went to the door and peered out. "Benjamin and Joshua are standing with two men I don't recognize. What if too many come?"

"I'll be fine. You get them here, and I'll handle the rest." Closing the door to the first bedroom, I called Charcoal into the bathroom. "Be quiet; no bark."

Slipping behind the door, I watched through the crack.

Josephine took a deep breath and called out in a soft, quavering voice, "Brothers? Kyle asks you to come share in the Lord's bounty."

Josephine turned and walked through the kitchen toward the second bedroom. Moving through the doorway, she disappeared from my view. Three men crowded into the kitchen, chuckling.

"Praise Jesus," one of them muttered.

Benjamin took the lead, walking into the bedroom, followed by the second man. The third stopped in the doorway.

I slipped behind him, my sword moving. He coughed, and Benjamin turned, freezing.

The wounded man looked at his stomach, from which the tip of my blade protruded. He died staring at his spooling intestines.

I wrenched my sword out and sprang at the next man, slicing through his neck. Whirling, I impaled Benjamin.

He groaned.

When I withdrew my blade, he turned toward the bed. With jerking steps, he pulled back the covers and lay down. He stared at the ceiling, occasionally gasping but making no other sound.

"Come," I said. The room smelled of blood and urine as I pulled Josephine out and clicked the hidden lock. "Four down."

"Where'd you get it?"

"Get what? Come, we must go."

Josephine locked her knees and swayed. "Where did you get it?"

"What?" I shook the bloody sword and asked, "This? Where'd I get this?"

She nodded, unable to take her eyes from the bloody blade.

"I hid it in the packsaddle's spine. I've had it with me since leaving the abbey. Josephine, dearest, we don't have time for this."

"Matthew, where's Ben?"

I peered out the window. "Don't know. I haven't seen him since the attack began last night."

Something scraped the floor, and I spun.

Akiko.

Josephine sank to her knees, sobbing and reaching for the girl.

Akiko patted Josephine's head and looked at me. "We must go help."

"I know, my fearless mouse."

Josephine stood. "Genevie," she said, wiping her tears.

Akiko darted through the doorway and paused on the porch, waiting for Josephine.

"Go around back," I said.

They nodded and sprinted away.

I locked Charcoal in the bathroom, waiting for them to turn the corner. Sucking in a sharp breath, I sprang from the dwelling to dissuade pursuers, but no one followed.

Outside, the sounds of fighting echoed off the dwelling's stone facades.

As I sprinted around the corner, Ben's spies tumbled out of the dwellings, attacking Rudy's people.

Rounding the next corner, I glimpsed Whistler swinging a large cast-iron frying pan at an attacker.

Comical under other circumstances, but deadly serious now.

I burst into the community room behind Josephine and Akiko, ready to fend off an attacker.

Genevie stood with her foot on Lester's throat. "Hullo, girls, Matthew. This worm thought he could lay a hand on me." Catching sight of Josephine, she asked, "Are *you* all right?"

"Yes," said Josephine, raising her chin.

"We're here to rescue you," Akiko announced.

Genevie grinned. "My brave girls. Let's find something to truss this worm so we can join the fight."

Our cursory search for a rope or cord yielded nothing.

"I've an idea," said Genevie, lips curving. She frog-marched Lester into the kitchen and pulled open the heavy door to the oven. "Get in," she ordered.

His eyes rolled with fear. "No, please," he whimpered.

"In the oven, or I gut you here," said Genevie.

Lester crawled into the cold oven, sobbing.

Josephine held the door shut while Genevie wedged a heavy iron stake through the handle.

"Not a baker's wife for nothing," she said with a humorless laugh. "You good?" she asked me.

I swallowed and swung my sword, tasting blood and salt. "Let's go."

Through the window, all I could see were strangers in the streets, brandishing weapons and shouting cries of encouragement to God and to each other.

"There are so many of them," said Josephine dully. "And we are so few."

"Get Akiko to safety!" I shouted, wading into the fight.

CHAPTER FIFTY-FOUR

The sting in my calf told me a blade had kissed my skin, and I bellowed.

Thrust, parry, slice.

Watch it!

Careful...

Now!

I lunged forward, striking at the exposed belly of a man who'd raised his long-handled ax. I pushed him back with a kick, and crouching, swung to my left. My blade connected, and I ducked as blood sprayed, painting everything.

Time slowed, and the droplets hung in the air, sparkling in the morning sun.

Automatically, my brain identified the pigment. *Alizarine Carmine.*

I repeated the movement to my right, rewarded with a cry and another mist of blood.

Keep moving. Keep fighting.

From the corner of the building, a blood-soaked figure strode into the street holding a hammer and tongs.

Genevie.

Uttering a soul-shriveling cry, she whirled, and the hammer crushed the head of a revivalist with a sickening *squish*. Genevie looked at me, baring her teeth.

Her eyes widened.

Reading her expression, I ducked.

Turning, I brought my sword around in an arc, cutting partway through the side of another attacker. Spinning, I thrust my blade into a man running toward Genevie. With a nod of thanks, she turned, and we fought back-to-back.

The air was humid with blood and vomit. Screams of rage and pain and fear swirled around us.

Deadly, I struck over and over, incandescent with fury for Brookfield and New London. For the Fruchtmans, Akiko, and the boy I'd been when I had left the abbey.

I fought savagely, punishing anyone within reach, but the blood-maddened soldiers of God seemed endless.

I'd fight until they were dead—or I was.

"We can't keep this up forever!" Genevie shouted as she swung her hammer, cracking bones and skulls.

Sweat stung my eyes and ran down my face. "I know!" I shouted back. "But so far—watch it!—this is the only plan I have."

A woman rushed at me with a raised knife.

I hesitated, and Genevie crushed her head with a heavy blow.

"They are not men or women. They are soldiers!" she yelled.

Genevie was right. These weren't *people*; they were soldiers.

Soldiers driving us into a corner.

On one side of us was a fortified dwelling, and on the other, a high stone wall. This wasn't good; corners were great for defense but useless for attacking. If we didn't get out of here, they'd wear us down until we had nothing left.

"Watch it!" Genevie shouted, throwing her tongs at a man who had darted forward to pike me. I nodded my thanks as I struggled with a man armed with a pitchfork.

Suddenly, a passage opened through the wall behind me.

We glanced at each other, my doubts and suspicions mirrored on Genevie's blood-splattered face. What if their artist was attempting to trap us? A woman screamed as she rushed us, and we jumped through the opening instinctively.

The strangled shrieks behind us made me turn. Our attackers had followed close on our heels, but we'd been too quick, and the opening no longer existed. Their limbs stuck out between the stones, faces frozen in grotesque grimaces.

Nauseated, I shivered and shoved the grisly image from my mind.

Racing around the dwellings at the end of the green, we found Whistler and three men from Wakefield fighting Rudy's soldiers.

From the hillside, triumphant screams rang as the women of Wakefield streamed down the hillside. Somehow, they'd gotten past their jailors and joined the fight.

"Here comes help!" I shouted.

Genevie grinned, teeth flashing white through the gore.

Simultaneously, we spotting an archer aim at Whistler, busy bashing someone with his skillet.

Genevie screeched, "Not while I'm breathing!" and threw her hammer, hitting the archer between his shoulder blades.

He slumped forward, releasing his arrow. It pierced Whistler's calf, and his eyes bulged as he roared with pain.

Genevie raced to retrieve her hammer, and without missing a step, she flew to Whistler's side.

"Yell at me later!" she shouted as she dropped to her knees next to his wounded leg. She grabbed the arrow with her hands and simultaneously broke off the head and fletching in a quick motion, leaving the rest in his leg.

"Wife!" Whistler bellowed as he struck a man sprinting toward them.

"Husband!" she shouted back, standing to fight at his side.

I finished the archer and fell backward to avoid a swipe by a long-handled knife.

Josephine ran across rooftops, shouting orders to someone.

Rolling to my left, I skewered the knife-wielding man.

Josephine shouted again, and I followed her gaze.

Akiko sat on the highest roof, sketching. She sat relaxed, as though she sketched merely for the fun of it, taking pleasure from an idle pastime.

The girl can draw.

The girl can create art.

Dark and wild energy rose through me, the hairs on my neck standing. Triumphant, I grinned and raised my fist, my eyes blazing.

Josephine pointed behind me, frantic.

I turned, sword ready, expecting an attack from another maddened revivalist.

Instead, horsemen thundered over the bridge and across the green. At the front of the riders, Ben raced toward us on a white horse, flanked by Ricardo and the keeper of the pub.

My heart lifted.

The Avalon Society.

Ben.

Newfane had arrived to help, and re-energized, I raised my sword and ran at the revivalists attacking my friends. "Newfane comes! Ben comes!" I shouted.

Whoops and cheers rang out as the riders from Newfane swept through the community, weapons flashing.

"Uh," Genevie grunted as something heavy smashed into her back. She fell forward, her hands spasming.

Howling, Whistler whirled and crushed the side of Rudy's head with his skillet.

Rudy fell slowly, dropping his staff as he hit the ground. A woman screamed, long and shrill, as Rudy crashed onto the ground. She dropped to her knees, mouth gaping, her ax falling with a clatter.

The revivalists seemed in unison to realize they'd lost the fight. Their actions switched from attack to defense, and small groups dropped their weapons and fell to their knees, begging God for mercy.

Sword out and ready, I turned a slow circle, but the battle was over.

Together, people from Wakefield and Newfane marched the defeated toward the hillside cavern.

AFTER THE FIGHTING ABATED, OUR WOUNDS SHRIEKED FOR attention.

My sword tip rested on the ground as I bent over, panting. My fighting master would've had my head for treating my weapon like this.

The pain in my leg throbbed, and my shoulders complained like I'd pulled my arms from their sockets.

"We've won," croaked Genevie. She collapsed to the ground, the left side of her face covered in blood from a gash above her eyebrow.

Ben and Ricardo approached, with a tall man between them.

I straightened, breaking into a weary smile. "Ben, Ricardo! Well met. Very well met."

Ben beamed as Sally streaked past us, shrieking, "Thank my stars, you're all right. Slutty dog butler, we are *blessed*!"

Ricardo pushed the tall man forward. "This filth is Preacher Talbot."

Genevie grabbed my hand as my heart twisted. I gaped at Talbot.

Impeccably groomed, his white shirt pristine, and his coat unwrinkled, he waited. Talbot had a strongly defined jaw tapering to a square cleft chin. He wore his dark hair swept back from intelligent brown eyes.

"Wow," muttered Whistler, breaking the silence. "Matthew, he looks like you!"

My knees wobbled as I stared at a man who was at once a stranger and as familiar as my shadow. "Who are you?"

We were the same height, age, and build. Our facial structures were similar, but Talbot was clean-shaven with his hair cut above his collar, whereas I sported a beard and long hair.

Talbot's lips curved into a sardonic smile. "You really don't know who I am? *Who you are?*"

I released Genevie's hand and circled Talbot.

The preacher smiled. "And?" he asked when I stopped in front of him.

"I know you, but how? Who are you?"

Talbot blinked. "It's true. You know nothing. Nothing of who you are or who our family is."

"Family?" asked Genevie.

Talbot's eyes flicked toward her, and his mask slipped for an instant.

From above, Josephine shrieked a warning.

As if in a dream, I turned, mouth filling with bile as a woman screamed, "For Brother Rudy! For the glory of God!"

Whistler fell, eyes lifeless and skull cleaved in half.

CHAPTER FIFTY-FIVE

Ben had tackled Whistler's assassin before Genevie's first wail ended.

"Whistler," whispered Sally, tears streaming down her face. She raced to Talbot and struck him, screaming, "Go suck a tit, you whale beater!"

Talbot easily caught the small woman's fists and smiled at me. "What charming company you keep," he drawled.

"Get them out of here!" roared Ben.

Ricardo summoned two of his men to take Whistler's killer away. She kicked and fought until Talbot spoke to her in a low voice. She ceased brawling, and they left without further struggle.

Josephine raced toward us. "Tell me he's fine, tell me—" Seeing Whistler, Josephine stopped. "Oh," she said, falling silent.

Genevie stumbled toward her, sobbing, and Josephine caught the taller woman in a powerful embrace.

Frozen, the world tilted as I struggled to think of a way to fix everything.

My mouth flooded with bile, and I spat on the ground.

Whistler couldn't be dead. There must be something that someone, anyone, could do.

Genevie broke away from Josephine and dropped to the ground next to her husband.

"Whistler, get up. Get up, blast it!" I said urgently.

Genevie turned her blank face toward me as she cradled her husband's ruined head. She opened her mouth, but no sound came out.

My mind fractured.

The elation of surviving the battle warred with the horror of Whistler's stillness. Nothing was real except the pain in my leg. I clung to the pain, bright and clean, and swiveled my head to find something or someone who could help.

Ricardo misunderstood my expression. "You've nothing to be ashamed of, Artist. Your skill and composure in combat are commendable." He turned to my friends. "You should gather with the others. We'll organize the recovery and find you afterward."

Ben nodded and clasped Ricardo on the shoulder. "Thank you, friend. Please join us when you can."

Ricardo inclined his head and turned to direct his companions to begin the cleanup.

Ben herded us toward the community building, with Josephine supporting Genevie. Josephine's eyes flashed a warning when I tried to help guide the stumbling woman.

I wobbled away. Unsteady myself, I wouldn't have been much help.

"Akiko!" I called, again and again, as I hobbled toward the community building.

Someone had let Lester out of the oven.

Sullen, he sat in a chair, his wrists bound with one of the scarlet sashes the revivalists wore. He stiffened when he saw us enter, then relaxed upon seeing Genevie broken.

"Ladies," he sneered.

In a flash, Nicole crossed the room and slapped him hard across the mouth. "Quiet!"

Lester shriveled in his chair.

My throat closed as Akiko slipped her hand, small and warm, into mine.

She smiled at me.

Beside her, Charcoal panted, his face and fur smeared with blood.

I dropped to a knee to inspect him, the cut on my calf protesting.

"He bit a lady who ran at me after I let him out of the dwelling. He's my hero."

"You saved my life. You're *my* hero," I whispered to the girl.

She shrugged and snuggled into me.

I'd need to speak to Ricardo later to find out if her parents had been located. If we'd killed them, she was as alone as I was. What if we'd captured them?

I couldn't return her to the care of murderous monsters.

My mouth tightened as I wrapped my arms around her. Either way, she was staying with me.

Slowly, blood-splattered survivors filed into the room, each fresh face eliciting murmurs of relief and sad smiles. Everywhere, people sobbed.

When the last of the survivors entered, cries of grief rose as hope died.

I was numb, my eyes caressing Whistler's face on my mind's canvas.

Nicole stepped into the center of the room and cleared her throat. All eyes turned to her.

The air was thick with tears and the scent of blood.

"Our hearts have broken," said Nicole in a quiet voice, looking around the room. "But we have survived." She paused. "We have survived!" she cried, her voice thundering. "We prepared, we executed, and we fought. All of us, young and old, small and large, we fought for our homes, our community, our way of life!"

People shouted words of encouragement.

Quieting again, Nicole continued, "It will take time. We need to mourn our dead and allow room for our grief. But," she pressed on, gathering energy and volume, "we will not merely survive. We will thrive!"

The room resounded with cheers.

Nicole nodded until they quieted. "With the help of our new friends, nay, neighbors *and* friends," she said, bowing to the people of Newfane, "we will heal and rebuild. We will be stronger and more prepared. We will stand united. And we will thrive!"

Akiko tugged on my coat.

"Yes, Mouse?"

"We should draw the portraits," she said. When I didn't respond, she added, "Starting with Whistler."

I closed my eyes, but the image of Whistler lifeless on the ground burned brightly.

How could my friend be dead?

I swallowed and opened my eyes. "You're right."

Sally patted the child's hand. "Carl, too?" she asked, her eyes filled with tears.

"Oh, Sally." There was nothing more to say.

DUSK WAS FAST APPROACHING BEFORE I WAS FREE TO interrogate Talbot. At my request, they had taken him to the dwelling next to ours, and he leaned against the wall as I entered the room.

"I'd like to talk with him alone," I said to Ricardo.

The room smelled faintly of honey from the glowing beeswax candles.

Ricardo frowned at Talbot. "Not a good idea."

I sat at the wooden table with a heavy sigh. "Ricardo, go. Take your men."

He stiffened, but left.

"Anyone else here?" I asked, staring at the table.

"No."

413

Questions whirled in my mind, tumbling over each other. If I didn't play this right, Talbot could keep information about my family from me. Not sure where to start, I raised my head and looked at him.

It was disorienting to see a familiar stranger. "How are we connected?"

Talbot studied me before pulling out a chair. Sitting, he leaned forward on his elbows. "You get to the heart of things."

"No games, Talbot. I want answers."

Talbot pursed his mouth, but said nothing.

"Do you believe in God?" I asked.

His eyes narrowed at the change in the topic. "I'm a trained preacher. A belief in God is a prerequisite."

I sat back. "You didn't answer my question."

Talbot spread his hands over the wooden table. "I may not be *able* to answer your questions."

"Not able, or not willing?" I leaned forward. "Tell me this: did you write letters about me and sign them with 'T'?"

He cocked his head and blinked. "Yes. How did you know?"

Elation flooded through me; I'd been right. "We're connected. I feel it."

Talbot sighed. "We're all connected."

"Don't spout religious crap at me!" I shouted, rising from my seat and leaning forward, my hands planted on the table. "I don't know who you are or why you think it's okay to attack people. I don't know what's wrong with any of you. Maybe at your core, something's rotten. I want to know how we're connected. I want to know if the weakness, spite, and malice in *you* could spread to me." I stopped, breathing hard.

Talbot closed his eyes, but when he opened them, they were clear. "Everything I've done was for *you.*"

"What? For me?" I rapped my knuckles on the table, the pain as loud as the *clunk.*

What was he talking about? How could any of the terrible things done in the name of their blasted god have been for *me?*

414

Struggling to catch my breath, my rage threatened to ignite; a fury that could consume us both. I wanted to wrap my hands around his neck, to see panic in his eyes. My nostrils flared, and my mouth tasted of bitter exhaustion.

Talbot swallowed. "Everything I've done—the obstacles I've created in your path—have been to slow or distract you. All of it was to—"

Footsteps thudded on the porch, and Talbot leaned back in his chair, his face shuttering.

Ricardo stuck his head through the doorway. "Sorry to interrupt, but someone's here to see you, Matthew."

"Now?"

"Yes, I'm afraid it can't wait."

Irritated, I stood, knocking my chair backward. "Be right there."

"Matthew," Ricardo repeated.

"Yes." I eyed Talbot. "I'll return soon."

Talbot tilted his head to one side. "Some truths can change the course of one's entire life."

I blinked.

"Be sure you're ready to accept the consequences of knowledge."

I narrowed my eyes to speak, but Ricardo cleared his throat and without uttering another word, I followed him from the dwelling.

Elaina stood with Josephine, Akiko, and a woman I didn't recognize.

"Sorry, but we need to transport the wounded to Newfane. The healer, Kwan, didn't make it," said Elaina.

Ricardo tilted his head. "This is Alma Sanu, the scholar you've been waiting for."

I didn't know how to greet her. "Welcome, Alma."

Alma bowed her head and said, "I'm sorry for your losses, Matthew. What did you need to discuss?"

"I'll get it," said Akiko, slipping down the street before I could protest. When she returned, Alma waited for me to unwrap the painting.

I stared at *Home* before turning it for everyone to see.

What was the point of the secrecy now?

"This looks like the remnants of a ruined depot. And this..." Her fingers brushed a tall, thin structure to one side of the skyline. "I think this is a tower of sorts. I've seen something like this."

"Where?" I asked, my heart pounding.

"Toronto Depot," said Alma. "This could be the old railway tower."

"Toronto," I breathed. For the first time in my life, I had an actual destination, a place to search for my family.

My painting depicted an actual location.

I tilted my face toward the sky, flooded with relief. Talbot stood at the window, watching.

Talbot.

"Thank you." I didn't have adequate words of gratitude.

"I'm happy to help, and sorry I must leave so soon. We now know we're targets, and they've asked me to travel to the nearest communities in our society and warn them about what's happened here."

"Thank you, Alma. This information means a great deal to me." I turned and squeezed Elaina's shoulder. She smiled and drew me into a hug.

"Thank you, Elaina," I whispered.

She squeezed me back and said into my ear, "The Avalon Society is people, people like you and me, and some of us aren't half bad. Remember that and come talk if you need to rid yourself of today's images."

"I will," I promised. Taking a step backward, I nodded at Ricardo. "I need to finish my conversation."

Ricardo's eyes flicked up toward Talbot. "Of course. I'll see you tomorrow."

Armed with my painting and newfound knowledge, I bounded up the stairs, burning with questions for 'T'.

This time, I would get my answers.

416

CHAPTER FIFTY-SIX

"**B**last, blast, blast *him*," I muttered.

The sun was setting, and patches of pink, orange, and gold flickered through the trees.

A cool breeze carrying the fecund scents of spring teased the hair curling around my collar. Impatient, I flicked it away with my hand. The breeze ruffled my hair again, and I struck the side of the door frame with my fist. Again and again, I bludgeoned it until it splintered, ignoring Charcoal's incessant barks.

"Matthew!" Sally cried as she jogged toward me. "Matthew, stop!"

Reaching us, she wrapped scrawny arms of steel around me.

Rigid, I resisted, but the minute I let myself sink into her, my eyes stung with tears.

"I'm here."

My last defenses toppled, and I wept with deep, shuddering breaths.

"Now, now," Sally murmured. "Come, sit with me." She kept her arms around me and rocked gently back and forth while I cried.

The pain was unbearable; my heart pierced over and over, the dagger twisting in a new direction each time.

I cried for my lost friends, for my lost family, for Akiko's misery.

Humiliated, I also wept for Cara's immense betrayal. How could I have trusted her? Believed she cared for me? My throat ached from my sobs, and I clung to Sally, even though her bony shoulder dug into my cheek. Eventually, I caught my breath and pulled away.

"Not so fast," said Sally. "You stay here and talk to me."

Charcoal lay next to me, his chin on my thigh.

I cleared my throat. "I don't know where to start," I muttered and wiped my eyes. They stung and leaked, even as I willed my emotions away.

"Good, I have questions. Why were you striking the door frame like a deranged bear?"

I looked at my bloody hand and flexed it. "It wasn't smart." I cleared my throat and swallowed.

"Sometimes, young man, it hurts less to hit something than to feel your pain."

"Yes." I blinked to prevent more tears. "It's—"

"I know. Tell me what happened."

"I tried to talk with Talbot again."

Her eyes flashed. "Did he say something to you? I'll give that diarrhea bucket a piece of Sally Park's mind."

"No, it's not something he said. Well, it is, but it isn't."

"Go on."

"He confirmed he tried to prevent my traveling."

"To where? Wakefield?"

I shook my head and looked toward the forest. The memory of Bao's death flashed through my mind, and I swallowed again. "He doesn't want me to find my family."

Sally frowned. "Do you believe him?"

"Yes. No. Maybe? I don't know."

"Well... did you ask why?"

"What?"

"Why he wants to stop you?"

I shrugged.

"You didn't ask why?"

"Ricardo interrupted us."

"Let's ask now," she said, slapping the tops of her thighs. "He's in here, right?"

"Yes, but he's not talking. Not a word. I showed him my painting and asked if it's Toronto Depot."

"Toronto?"

"It's what the scholar from Newfane thought, but Talbot clammed up."

"Ah."

I flexed my hand again. "I'm so tired."

"I know, dearest. I know." She leaned against the railing and opened her mouth but closed it again.

"What?"

"Nothing."

"Sally, what?"

She twitched her lip. "I want to ask you something."

"Yes?"

"Are all artists trained in combat?"

I licked my lips. "I shouldn't have told anyone."

"They train artists because you're valuable."

"*Everyone's* valuable."

"But you can create immense change. If they directed art against your will—"

Though I trusted her, I worried at my lip until I tasted blood.

"Matthew, are artists dangerous? To the rest of us?"

Her question resurfaced all the hurt I thought I'd released. "Have I ever made you feel threatened? Unsafe?"

She seemed taken aback by my question. "No. *No*. I'm sorry, I didn't mean to imply anything."

Standing, I helped her up. "I need rest." My thoughts muddled and murky, I craved the clarity I hoped sleep would bring.

She patted my shoulder. "I suspect we could all use a good cry and a long sleep. Good night."

"Sally?"

She turned. "Yes?"

"Please keep this between us." Behind my back, my hands tightened into fists.

She said nothing and searched my face. "I'll keep your secrets, Artist."

Sally turned the corner without looking back, and I knew things would never be the same between us.

As we had in Brookfield, Akiko and I drew portraits of the dead. This time, I didn't worry about anyone seeing Akiko sketch.

No one wanted to come near the fallen; the hurt was too fresh.

I corrected her work from time to time, showing her how to relax the grimace of death so the living wouldn't witness the moment of passing.

Akiko insisted she sketch Carl's portrait, but each time she started, her hands shook, and the paper remained blank.

I put down my work and sat on the grass at her feet. "What is it?"

Her breathing shallow, She lowered her eyes. "I killed him."

"How?"

"I rolled rocks over the people guarding the cave."

"Show me."

She pulled her sketchbook from inside her tunic and handed it to me.

I flipped it open and studied the first few pages. She'd been diligent with her practice and had covered the pages with vignettes of things she'd found in the woods, candid portraits of the people in Wakefield, and scenes from Newfane. I flipped the page.

Here was the start of the battle. I stared at the drawings. The art was unlike anything I'd ever seen. Instead of sketching and changing it as they'd taught me, Akiko had chronicled the events in a story-board type of style.

She watched me, chewing on her lip.

"This work is outstanding, Akiko."

She relaxed and bent to her sketch, her brow smoothing.

Looking at each scene in sequence, I read the fight. The characters depicted were more caricatures than portraits, but I could clearly tell who was who. I flipped the page and read on, fascinated. Here was Ben leaving for Newfane, and here were Rudy's soldiers following Genevie and me through the opening in the wall before being trapped.

Akiko blew the charcoal from her sketch of Carl and handed it to me.

Sally would approve. "Very nice. Start on the next."

I watched the girl examine the next face and begin the portrait before I turned to the last page. "This is how they escaped. You saved them."

She shook her head. "I saw Carl climb out as the first rocks were hitting the revivalists. I tried to scribble out the rock..."

Rubbing the back of my head, I searched for the right words. "We do not erase," I said finally.

Akiko burst into tears.

I ached to hug the girl, but made no move toward her. Life was harsh, and Akiko had learned the truth at a far earlier age than I had. To give the child a moment, I finished the portrait I'd started.

Nicole had insisted the fallen revivalists be burned, not buried. Though I hadn't argued, I'd given instructions for their bodies to be brought to me before being transported to the funeral pyre at the far end of the community green. I was halfway through the revivalists when I found an Asian man. Akiko was finishing the last Wakefield portrait and hadn't noticed.

I debated sketching the man quickly, or even having the body transported directly to the pyre.

Could I spare Akiko this one last hurt? Would she believe her father had reformed and left this murderous group?

But everything in me screamed she deserved to know the truth. I could never put her through the doubt and uncertainty I'd grown up with. She shouldn't grow up wondering what had happened to her family. Knowing would lessen the pain.

Quick and clean.

I cleared my throat. "Akiko, you need to see this man."

She gazed at him, emotions flickering across her face. "My father." After a long pause, she asked, "Will you?"

"Yes."

She wandered the line of bodies waiting for death portraits and stopped at a woman. "Both of them," she said out loud.

To hide my pity, I bent my head back to my sketch. When I looked up again, she was gone.

Endlessly, I recorded the faces of the dead, preserving the features of the men and women who would have killed us given the chance. There were too many. How had someone convinced so many people to harm strangers?

At long last, I finished. Binding the thick stack of portraits with a jute cord, I wondered who would want them. Surely, somewhere, these people had families. Numb and exhausted, I limped back to the dwelling to bathe and sleep.

Ben sat at the kitchen table with Josephine, Sally, and Genevie. A bowl of shelled walnuts sat in the middle of the table.

So much for a bath.

I circled behind Genevie and wrapped my arms around her.

She set the nutcracker down and leaned into me. "It's all absolutely wretched."

"I know." Patting her head, I set the portraits on the table.

Ben eyed the pages. "Anyone hungry?"

We shook our heads.

"I'll start supper, anyway." He gathered the broken walnut shells and rummaged through the kitchen.

"Did you finish?" Sally asked me.

"Yes. Nicole wants to hold the ceremony for Wakefield tomorrow, and the pyre's being lit tonight. Where's Akiko?" I popped a raw nut into my mouth. The meat was bland and slightly sweet, but left my mouth feeling puckered and bitter.

"Oh, barnacle licker! I owe Nicole a report on what professions Wakefield needs now. How much time until supper?"

Ben sliced an onion and answered without turning. "The supper none of you want will be ready in an hour. I haven't seen the child."

"I'll help you, Sally," said Josephine. "Genevie, will you be all right?"

"Yes. I'll go lie down."

"Very sensible," said Sally. "I haven't seen her either, Matthew."

I watched the women leave and studied Ben's back. "Need help?"

Ben turned to look at me. "Actually, I'd prefer my own company. I need time to process."

I clapped him on the shoulder. "Very sensible." The onion fumes stung my eyes and they watered.

Ben smiled sadly.

I grabbed a fistful of his shirt and pulled him toward me. Wrapping my arms around him, I held on until he returned the embrace, squeezing me.

I coughed when he let go. "I've never done that before."

"Hugged a man?"

"Had my ribs cracked by a dear friend."

Ben chuckled. "Supper in an hour."

Weary, I sat on my bed, the energy necessary to draw a bath insurmountable. My painting was on the floor, propped against the wall. I unwrapped its protective linen and looked at it.

Was Alma right? Could *Home* depict Toronto Depot? I took the painting to the window and tilted it to catch the fading light.

Part of me wanted to set out immediately for Toronto Depot. Perhaps I could even goad Talbot into talking if he thought I'd summarily leave for the depot, anyway. Part of me wanted to stay and attempt to sync with Talbot. If I could come to understand him, I might know myself better.

The funeral pyre blazed.

Through the window, I watched the flames leap for the sky.

So much death, so much destruction.

The people here needed my help to repair or rebuild what the fighting had destroyed. Sally was right; communities needed people like us.

Despite what Josephine believed, I knew I'd played a role in what had happened here. If I'd done my duty and picked a community before leaving the abbey, it wouldn't have happened. But done was done, and the question was—what next?

Near the woods, Akiko stood with Charcoal, watching the flames.

Poor child.

I rubbed my jaw and set the painting down. It wasn't too late, and I could still pick a community. Decide to become a part of instead *of* remaining apart *from*. But where? When? How?

I leaned against the window frame and traced the girl's outline on the glass.

She was exceptional. If I settled, I'd require a community who accepted me training her. My hands tingled with anticipation. She could be my greatest work of art, my masterpiece. Rapping my bruised knuckles against the window frame, I made my decision.

Stepping outside to walk to the pyre, I thought about the Avalon Society.

As much as I despised their elitism, I knew by joining one, I'd have better resources for Akiko. I still needed to know what happened to the Avalon Society children when they came of age, though. I couldn't bear the thought of my child being asked to leave if she turned out to be 'less than the best.'

My child.

The thought sent shivers up my spine as the truth of it settled in my bones. I saw it all, now, as plain as illuminating the subject of a painting with light. She was my child, my daughter, my heart. As much a part of me as my breath.

Toronto beckoned, but it would wait until we were ready to depart. Akiko's needs came first. Nothing, *no one,* mattered more than my child. When she was ready, we'd leave together to find the rest of our family.

CHAPTER FIFTY-SEVEN

"What's going on?" I asked, shaking the rain from my coat. All day, I'd been rehearsing the conversation I needed to have with my friends during supper. Akiko and I were going alone to Toronto Depot, and I'd crafted the message to deliver the news in a way I hoped wouldn't damage or sever our ties. However, when I entered our dwelling, my friends were sitting at the large wooden table in conversation with Ricardo and Nicole.

"We're deciding what's next," said Ricardo.

"Next?" My stomach growled.

Ben had been cooking, and the kitchen smelled of lamb and rosemary.

Nicole snorted. "We're discussing what to do with Talbot."

I rubbed my face with both hands. To distract myself from obsessing about what Talbot knew, I'd been repairing Wakefield's buildings. "Has he said anything?"

Ben shook his head. "He's refused to say anything other than prayers. You're the only one he's spoken to. Did he talk to you this morning?"

"No, he ignored me again. What are you debating?"

Frowning, Ricardo leaned back in his chair. "Nicole wants to execute him. In the Avalon Society, our standard punishment is permanent expulsion from our communities. We have no other punishment, no means of incarceration."

I stared at Nicole.

Execute Talbot? Was she mad? I needed him and the answers he could provide.

"Exactly why I say we should execute him," Nicole growled. "We can't keep him here."

Ricardo gave her a pained look and continued, "My suggestion is we take him to Newfane and hold him while I write to the society elders and solicit advice."

I exhaled. "If you're willing, I thank you. I don't know who he is or how we're connected, but I'd like a chance to find out."

"Good," said Ricardo, standing. "Elaina and I are leaving today, but Denver and the rest can bring Talbot tomorrow when they return."

I set the kettle on the stove. "Elaina's leaving?"

"Yes. We've done as much as we can for the injured here. Do you need to speak with her again?"

I'd been toying with asking her to speak with Akiko, but I feared the child wouldn't respond well to Elaina's probing questions. "No, but she's been helpful."

Ricardo inclined his head.

"What about Joshua and the others?" asked Nicole.

My friends fidgeted, uncomfortable.

"What?" I pressed.

"There's something you should know," said Josephine, biting her lip.

"Cara's a revivalist," Sally blurted.

"Sally—" Josephine hissed.

I stared at them. I hadn't seen Cara since the fight, purposely avoiding the cave we'd been using as a jail.

Hers was the voice I'd heard in the dark during the attack.

427

"What? No, you must be mistaken," I muttered, examining the floor. Though I'd long ago realized she'd played me for a fool, I'd said nothing to them about it.

The kettle shrieked, and I pulled it from the burner, pouring steaming water over dried mint leaves.

They didn't notice my insincerity. I'd learned a thing or two about deception since leaving the abbey.

"She's with the others in the cave," said Nicole.

Postponing the confrontation wouldn't help. I took a tiny sip, the mint unfurling across my tongue. "Thank you. I'll go as soon as I finish this."

"Unless you want to stand guard tonight, you'll wait until tomorrow. We've enough to do without orchestrating a reunion for you and your girlfriend."

I scowled at Nicole, the heat from the mug seeping into my hands. "She's *not* my girlfriend."

"Good, then we'll arrange a meeting tomorrow."

Though I didn't want Nicole to know it, I was glad for the delay. Waiting until tomorrow would allow me to sort my thoughts and muster my courage.

Nicole stood. "Sally, if you change your mind, you can stay here. We need an administrator."

"Appreciate the offer, Nicole, but I'm leaving," Sally answered.

Nicole and Ricardo left, slamming the door. I winced and glanced toward Akiko's bedroom as I took Nicole's vacated chair. "Sally, you could stay."

She smiled, her eyes warm. "I love you all, but I leave tomorrow."

"Where will you go?" asked Genevie, her voice soft.

"To spread the news. Communities must know what happened in New London and Brookfield—and what almost happened here." She looked at us. "I've requested a letter of introduction from Ricardo, and he's agreed. He's sending one of his people with me to warn other Avalon Society communities. He's asked if you'll inform any you pass."

What she said made sense, and I pushed away the ache of abandonment.

This wasn't about me.

"I'll miss you. About the other night..."

"We have an understanding," Sally replied.

Rain pelted against the window, leaving greasy streaks down the glass.

"Oh, Sally," choked Genevie. "We are the last. The last of Brookfield."

"Yes, my love, but I wouldn't leave if you weren't in excellent hands."

Genevie hugged her. "Take Whistler's packhorse. You'll need one, traveling alone."

Sally nodded and stood, wiping her eyes. "I must finish packing."

"You're leaving? Sally?" Akiko stepped through the doorway, accompanied by Charcoal.

"Yes, dear. I'm sorry we woke you. Matthew will fill you in. Take care, Josephine, Genevie, Ben. Take care of each other, all of you. Remember me in your travels," she said, slipping through the doorway, eyes bright with tears.

Akiko turned wounded eyes toward me. "Why is she leaving?"

Without answering, I rested my head in my hands. When I looked up, Akiko was holding the painting.

She looked at me. "The scholar said this is Toronto."

"Yes."

Genevie sat back. "We go to Toronto."

"We?" asked Akiko, studying the painting.

"Me," said Genevie resolutely.

"Me," agreed Josephine.

"Aye, and me," said Ben.

"Me, too," said Akiko, daring any of us to argue. "Me, too," she repeated.

"You, too," agreed Genevie. "I can't lose any more of you. This family sticks together from now on."

In unison, my friends looked at me.

The roar of rain increased, and I looked at the ceiling.

It was time.

"I know you want to help, and I love you for it, but it's my fault Whistler is dead. I can't cause harm to any of you, so Akiko and I are going to Toronto Depot alone."

"What?" Genevie stared at me, disbelief written across her face.

"I fell into Talbot's trap and led Wakefield into battle. My naivety caused all of this."

Akiko leaned against me, still holding the painting. "You saved me."

"Me too," said Josephine.

"You've been a pain in my ass, but I don't blame you for any of this," said Genevie. She pounded her fist on the table, and we jumped.

Josephine's eyes narrowed. "This wasn't your fault."

Ben nodded. "We're coming with you."

Akiko set *Home* on the table, nodding.

Their refusals were fierce and unexpected. Unprepared to argue, I took a deep breath and changed the subject. "I need to talk to Cara before I go."

"Can I come with you?" asked Josephine.

"Why?"

"She betrayed all of us. I need to say my piece."

"As do I," said Ben.

Genevie nodded.

I exhaled slowly and gave my friends a small smile. "We face her together. Except you," I said, poking Akiko in the ribs.

"It's settled," Genevie declared. "We talk to Cara, we pack up, we go."

"Good," said Ben. "How soon can we leave for Toronto Depot?"

I shrugged. "We're ready anytime," I said, shaking Akiko's hand in the air.

She giggled and poked Charcoal. "Ready!"

Josephine bit her lip. "I need to get the records to Edward in Warwick first."

"It's the wrong way," said Akiko.

I squeezed Akiko's hand. "She's studied every map I have."

Ben turned toward Josephine. "I could go with you, and we could meet them in Toronto Depot."

"In which case, I'll stay here until you head north," said Genevie to Ben. "I want to finish helping Wakefield... and maybe stay with Whistler a little longer."

"Works for me," said Akiko. "Meet you there."

"Good," said Genevie. "We go to Toronto separately but together."

My heart was full, swollen with love and gratitude. Not only was I free to leave as soon as I could get us outfitted, but I'd also go with the full support of my friends. It would give Akiko and me time to scout and explore Toronto Depot. We could compare what we found to my painting before they arrived. It was more than I'd let myself hope for, and it meant everything.

———※———

Akiko screamed in the middle of the night.

Heart thudding, I ran to her room, expecting to find a revivalist climbing through the window.

Charcoal's nails scrabbled on the wooden floors after me.

The girl thrashed in her bed, gasping and red-faced.

At the door, I froze, unsure of what to do. Her nightmares had grown progressively worse, leaving her pale and listless with violet bruises of fatigue under her eyes.

"Shh, honey, it's all right," said Josephine, pushing past me. She kneeled by the girl's head and wiped the sweat from her brow.

Akiko woke and sat upright, sobbing. She reached for me, and I sat on the bed and held her. She was fire-hot, damp with sweat, and smelling of fear.

I looked over her head at Josephine, who pantomimed rocking a baby.

Awkward and stiff, I rocked back and forth. The child quieted in my arms, and emboldened, I swayed more naturally, listening to rain batter the dwelling.

"Thank you," I mouthed to Josephine.

She pressed both hands to her chest, eyes warm.

Akiko clutched at my shirt, shuddering.

"I'm here; you're safe," I crooned.

Her eyes fluttered, and I laid her back and brushed her hair from her eyes. Go to sleep, little one. I'm here."

Though eerily precocious, she was still vulnerable and fragile. A child needing what all children craved—trust, love, and care.

Charcoal jumped onto the bed and stretched his length along her leg, determined to comfort and guard her.

After I was sure she was asleep, Josephine and I tiptoed from the room. I shut the door partway so I could monitor her.

Thunder rumbled, and the dwelling groaned as a gust of wind hit it.

"Poor little mite."

I nodded. "I'm thinking of taking her to see Elaina in Newfane."

"Elaina?"

"Yeah." I sighed. "She's a healer of emotion."

Josephine nodded. "Good idea. The people from *Before* often sought the advice of emotional healers."

"Do you know what they do?"

Josephine smiled. "Talk, listen, and ask questions."

I frowned. "That's it? They talk?"

"Shh, quiet."

I peeked in to make sure I hadn't woken the child. "Just talk?"

"There's an art to it. They probe for emotional trauma and root causes. From what I've read, the more we recount the things we've experienced, the less power painful memories have."

"I know what the cause is."

"You do?"

I nodded and looked at the sleeping child.

Charcoal lay next to her, his ears pricked and alert.

"We killed her parents. She saw their bodies before the pyre was lit."

"Dreadful. It might not be everything, though."

"What else could it be?"

"Perhaps she feels guilty."

"Guilty? She's eight." Josephine's suggestion was ridiculous.

Josephine shook her head. "She was at New London and had some idea of what her parents were up to. How do you think she felt when she saw what happened to Brookfield? And Whistler?"

"She couldn't have stopped what happened."

Josephine hugged herself. "She couldn't have prevented what happened any more than you could have."

Something inside me uncurled, but I fidgeted, rubbing my wrist. "It's not the same thing."

"I know you don't think so. Still, seeing Elaina is a good idea. The emotional healers from *Before* practiced active listening."

"What's that?"

"A practice where you 'listen' with all of your senses. You listened with your ears, eyes—"

"Yes, I understand. What if someone didn't want to talk?"

"The healers asked open-ended questions, careful not to judge the answers."

"It might work. We'll go to Newfane tomorrow, after I speak to Cara." My stomach tightened at the unpleasant task ahead of me. I pushed away thoughts of Cara and focused on the sleeping girl through the open door. If Akiko refused to speak with the healer, perhaps Elaina could teach me how to help the child.

"You should speak to Elaina, too. As a model for the girl."

I scratched my beard. "I'll consider it, for Akiko."

Josephine crossed the shadowy room and stood on tiptoe to kiss my cheek. "Goodnight, my brother. Sleep well."

"Goodnight."

Akiko was asleep, but moved restlessly.

Charcoal watched me, his brow furrowed.

Covered by the roar of the rain, I slipped into her room and sat in the chair next to her bed, reaching out to lay my hand on her shoulder.

She quieted, and I watched her sleep, soothed by the rhythm of her breaths.

Perhaps I would speak with Elaina.

For the girl.

CHAPTER FIFTY-EIGHT

We were eating breakfast when Nicole's cousin delivered the message. "The cave dwellers are in the community building."

The pancakes turned to sawdust in my mouth. I tried to swallow and inhaled their gummy dough, starting a violent coughing fit.

Josephine brought me a glass of water, which I promptly spilled, creating more chaos. By the time I'd recovered and they'd cleared the mess, the cousin had disappeared.

"Let's go," Genevie said, standing by the door.

Stalling, I coughed. I wasn't ready, but I needed information from Cara. The more I could learn about what the revivalists wanted and why they'd done what they had, the better we could protect ourselves.

Josephine smoothed her hair unnecessarily and joined Genevie.

Ben looked at me. "Matthew?"

I coughed again. "Akiko—"

"I've got her," said Sally. "We've had to postpone a day, so I'll watch her."

"Well." I couldn't think of anything else, so I lied. "I'm ready. Charcoal, stay."

My friends opened the door and waited for me to walk through, as if afraid I'd bolt the door behind them after they left. Truthfully, I might have.

As we marched toward the community building through intermittent sunbursts, our feet squelched through the mud.

Ben clapped me on the shoulder. "Whatever happens, I'm here for you. Try to learn whatever you can but take care of yourself first."

Tears stung my eyes, and I blinked furiously.

It bothered me I'd become a weeper; my behavior would incense the masters at the abbey.

Too soon, we arrived at the heavy door. My heart hammered, but my friends' faces were grim, jaws set, eyes hard. I pushed open the door with all the bravado I could muster. Entering the room, I fully understood the meaning of ambivalence for the first time. Affecting an outward calm, I hoped no one could see the emotions raging within me.

Although the room was darker than the outdoors, I instantly found her. Cara and Joshua embraced, illuminated by the large window. They broke apart as soon as I stepped into the room, but not soon enough.

"Matthew," said Cara.

Though I'd pictured this meeting hundreds of times, I'd never imagined how strong the urge to strike her would be.

Fire flashed through my veins.

Cara stopped speaking, and Joshua moved in front of her.

"Matthew," he growled.

"Joshua." Pleased my voice remained low and calm, I smiled and imagined tearing his lying head from his neck. I yearned to hear Cara scream as I swung his bloody skull at her face. With effort, I kept my face blank, betraying none of my thoughts. I'd never give them the satisfaction of knowing the depth of my hurt.

Josephine stepped forward, and Cara's face darkened, her fists balling. "Don't bother. You have nothing to say we want to hear."

Seeing Cara's anger soothed me. I could do this. "A word?"

"Not without me," said Joshua, lifting his chin.

I ignored him and kept my eyes on Cara. Slowly, she nodded and stepped around Joshua.

"Cara. No."

Her head whipped around. "Yes."

I imagined the look on her face by the way Joshua shrank backward.

She stepped closer to me, her eyes wary.

Scanning the room, I gestured toward the table farthest from the door.

The air in the room was rank with the scent of unwashed bodies. Nicole hadn't given them the dignity of bathing.

Cara nodded and led the way. The revivalists gathered near the table scattered as she approached, giving me a glimpse into the power she wielded.

From opposite sides of the table, we sized each other up. I wouldn't speak first.

Eventually, Cara tossed her head. "What?"

I paused, savoring my win. "You're a revivalist."

She rolled her eyes.

I studied her, looking for confirmation. "Aren't you?"

She said nothing, and I waited silently, watching her.

"I don't like the word."

"Oh?" I leaned forward.

"Revivalist," she drawled, rolling the syllables.

Bitter words hung on the tip of my tongue, and I clenched my teeth to prevent myself from voicing them.

Cara waited, her posture defensive.

Relaxing my face, I tried again. "Cara, what would you rather I called you?"

She looked surprised at my friendly tone and blinked. "Christian?"

I nodded. "Like the Christians from *Before*?"

She narrowed her eyes and squared her shoulders.

My mind reeled, and I groped for the right words. "I didn't know people were practicing religion again."

Her chin lifted. "We never stopped."

Josephine's words about active listening surfaced, and I grabbed them with both hands. "This is important to you."

Cara's face softened. "It's the most important thing of all. My belief in God moves me forward when things get hard, and they are often hard. We haven't all enjoyed the easy life you've had."

Stung, I froze. When I'd told her about my life at the abbey, I'd never imagined she'd use my past as ammunition.

Swallowing, I fought to keep my expression open. "Can you tell me about it?"

Her posture softened more as she searched my face.

I waited.

"My faith is—" She stopped, narrowing her eyes. "Why are you asking?"

She'd see through anything less than an honest answer. "In all the time we spent together, I never got to know the real you, and I'd like to."

Cara's face softened, and our energies synced. Triumphant, my hands tightened into fists under the table.

Unaware, she continued. "My mother taught me about God and His love for us. I come from a long line of preachers, and though we had to hide our faith, we held onto it after the world died."

"Why is faith important?" On the other side of the room, Joshua argued with my friends, but I ignored them, keeping my focus on her.

"Faith is an expectation. A belief that no matter how bad things are, good will come."

"Like hope?"

She shook her head. "It's deeper than hope. Hope is in the mind, a child's star wish. Faith comes from the heart, from the soul, from the knowledge of God's love."

"I know nothing about a god." I reached for her hand, her slim fingers cold.

She squeezed my hand. "Not *a* god, Matthew, but God. The one and only true God. We are his children, made in his image."

I played with her fingers. "How do you know all of this? Josephine studied religious texts but said they kept them secure."

"Josephine's read the Bible? I didn't know. I would have loved to —" She glanced toward the others.

"How did you learn?"

"We studied the stories when I was young."

"About God?"

"Yes, but specifically the Bible."

"I thought the Bible was a collection of stories. You memorized all of them?"

A look of pain flashed across her face. "I'd dearly love to know the whole thing, but no. Each preacher knows one or two of the books, and it's their job to teach the message from the book they know to the faithful."

"How do you hear the complete story?"

"By attending revivals. They spread the teachings of each of the books."

Cara's honesty was absolute.

She hadn't realized I was fully in control of the conversation, manipulating her energy. "I'm right at the edge of understanding. Please help me, Cara. This is important."

Cara relaxed further. "A revival is a living thing. A preacher gathers congregants, his audience, and preaches the word of God. Through the stories, we learn about grace and God's love."

I smiled. "Go on."

"Revivals are exciting. Your soul connects to the word of God, and your faith becomes so strong, you feel you can overcome any obstacle, endure any hardship. I leave a revival filled with the Holy

439

Spirit, marvelous energy I want to share. My entire purpose becomes the finding of people who are searching for God, who need His help. I bring them to His Glory to save their soul and to save mine."

"How do you know where they'll be?"

"We have people in most of the depots who leave messages. There's a symbol we look for. If you find them, they'll know who is traveling in the region and what book they can share." She stopped and looked surprised she'd shared so much.

I believed her. For her, the stories were her truth. They weren't mine, but they were as important to her as my art was to me. "Thank you, Cara. I'm trying to understand."

She leaned forward, eyes bright. "Understand what? It's all about faith. If you let yourself bathe in His glory, if you felt His love, you'd know. You'd feel whole and pure. You wouldn't need to travel; you'd know you'd found your Father."

"But—"

"But what?" She sat back, her eyes wide.

"Would it help me understand why Rudy and the others killed the people of New London or Brookfield? Why they attacked Wakefield? Weren't the people who died souls to save? Children of God, made in his image?"

Cara's brow furrowed.

I released her hand and let the energy between us drop as suddenly as a stone into water. "Would I understand how you could justify the murders? Or how you could whore yourself for your ridiculous beliefs?"

Cara stiffened, her eyes hardening. "Those beside the road are those who have heard; then the devil comes and takes the word from their heart, so that they will not believe and be saved. Luke 8:12."

I shrugged. "What does it mean?"

She looked at me coldly. "It means when a person has been told about God, about His light and blessings but *chooses* not to be saved, they are no longer the chosen. No longer God's children, and we need not share our love with them."

440

I smirked. "And the devil takes those who don't follow your dogma."

"Our beliefs. We only share the light with a person once."

"As you have with me."

Her chin raised. "You've heard the word of God, and you must choose."

"Before I do, a question. How did you end up on the logs?"

Cara froze, blinking rapidly. "We thought I could talk you into joining us, but a board broke, and I fell. I remember nothing else before waking in your camp."

All of this because of a rotten board and my naivety. "What if I don't want to choose?"

She rolled her eyes, and I knew I'd lost her, but I didn't care. I'd extracted what I needed to know.

She glared at me. "The devil has you, Matthew. You are beyond salvation."

My eyes narrowed. "Not worth saving."

"Worse. An impedance to our mission," she hissed, leaning forward, malevolence dripping from her words. "Like all the others who disregarded the Word."

"Of God," I said.

"God?" asked Josephine, paling.

I flinched. I hadn't seen my friends approach.

Cara whirled and glared at Josephine. "Shut your ugly face! You, too," she snapped at Genevie, who'd opened her mouth. "You all think you're so good," Cara sneered. "So noble. So willing to help the little man and rescue an orphaned brat. You're nothing; you're filth."

Josephine flushed. "We found you with the trash, and we should have left you there. Someone obviously did."

Cara glared at Josephine, her hands clenching into fists, again and again. Her chest heaved.

Frozen, I held my breath. I'd been playing a dangerous game with Cara, but I hadn't planned for my friends to be present when Cara exploded.

Violence simmered in the air between the women, as palpable and bitter as smoke.

"Josephine..."

My warning was too late.

Cara swung her arm and smacked Josephine hard in the face. Josephine went white, and she didn't move until Cara hit her a second time.

Blood sprayed from Josephine's nose, and she shrieked.

Ben wrapped Josephine in his arms, turning his back and shielding her from Cara, who, maddened, continued swinging her fists.

Cara's bloodshot eyes bulged, and the veins in her neck popped out.

I vaulted over the table and wrapped my arms vice-like around Cara. She bucked and kicked backward, screaming obscenities at me, shrieking about God.

She was surprisingly strong, and afraid of what she'd do if I let go, I hung on.

Joshua bellowed and tackled me from the side, sending the three of us crashing into the wooden table. I grunted at the shock and tightened my grip.

Tangled, we rolled, and I ended up at the bottom of the pile.

I lay on my back with Cara screaming and struggling on top of me and Joshua on top of her, flailing his fists, trying to bludgeon me.

With their weight on me, I couldn't breathe.

Genevie hauled Joshua off us, and I gasped, sucking in a grateful breath.

"Thanks, Gen—"

Cara threw her head back and smashed my face before flinging her head forward onto the table's edge.

The pain was worse than the fall from Oxide.

I saw stars—and tasted blood anew.

Cara slumped on top of me, not moving.

Releasing Joshua, Genevie leaned over us with murder in her eyes. "Let go."

I released Cara, and Genevie pulled her from me with her hands locked around Cara's throat.

"Genevie," Ben warned.

Cara was limp in Genevie's hands.

Joshua howled for her to release Cara.

"Genevie," I choked, spitting blood and gasping. "It's no use. She's already been saved."

CHAPTER FIFTY-NINE

"Your nose is ugly."

"Thank you, Akiko."

"Your voice sounds funny, too."

Chuckling, I groaned as the movement jarred my ribs.

"Josephine's nose is pretty. You should have fixed your nose too."

"*Thank* you, Akiko." Her no-nonsense attitude endearing, I fought to keep from grinning.

Smiling hurt my face.

She nodded and kissed at her mare.

I clucked to Oxide to keep up. My ribs protested, but the quicker we reached Newfane, the better. This would be my last chance to speak with Talbot before we left for Toronto Depot.

Maybe he was ready to talk.

The late morning sun sparkled on the dew, refracting into tiny rainbows as we rode. They reminded me I'd soon need more pigments; I'd used up most of my stores rebuilding Wakefield.

"Let *me* do the talking this time," said Akiko.

I couldn't help myself and grinned, pain blooming as my bruised face stretched.

When we reached the gate, Akiko shouted, "Artist Sugiyama and his wart Akiko to see Elaina. Let us through, gate man!"

The gate swung open, and Akiko nodded at Barker.

"Thank you."

He smiled, bowing low. "My lady."

Akiko grinned at me; she'd lost another tooth.

"You lose any more of those chompers and you'll live on creamed greens."

Sticking her tongue through the gap, she giggled.

Elaina was waiting for us in front of the inn, as was the girl who had previously taken our horses.

"We'll be staying for one night only," said Akiko before sweeping up the walkway to the inn, trailed by Charcoal. At the porch, Akiko turned and asked, "Did I sell it?"

"Sell what?"

"Princess Mouse," she said with a deep curtsy.

"I'd buy Scullery Maid Mouse," I said with a straight face. "A princess would know to show more grace."

Akiko bounded back down the stairs. "I didn't mean to be rude," she said to the girl holding our horses. "I was playing." She bit her lip and looked at me with enormous eyes, her chin quivering.

"I knew it," said the girl in a haughty tone of voice. "For I am the Duchess of Livery. Come see me for tea tomorrow."

Akiko smiled shyly. "Truly?"

The girl nodded her head imperiously and giggled.

"Come on, wretched mouse," I said, holding my hand out.

Akiko grabbed it and skipped beside me as we walked into the inn.

"Are you hungry?" Elaina asked.

Akiko nodded.

"I'll see what the keeper has. Be right back." Elaina winked and slipped through the door to the kitchen.

"Should I go first or you?" Akiko asked me in a low voice.

"Let's decide after we see what the keeper brings us. If it's sweets, then you go first. If it's more ham and pea soup, I'll go first."

Akiko laughed. "If it's sweets, you go first, to save you from yourself."

"Says who?"

"Sally." Akiko patted my stomach.

"Oh." I looked down. "Looks flat to me."

Akiko tilted her head and considered my torso. "You're three cookies away from looking like the minstrel."

"Oh, *thank you* very much."

"I got you."

Elaina entered with a tray of cheeses, a jar of jam, and a small loaf of brown bread. "The keeper said to start on this while he's preparing lunch."

Akiko and I looked at the tray.

"You go first," we said in unison, bursting into giggles.

"How about I choose?" said Elaina, raising an eyebrow.

Akiko danced, pointing at me.

"I choose Matthew."

Victorious, Akiko squealed and squirmed onto a chair. Sitting on her knees, she reached for the cheese knife. "At eight, I'm fully capable of cutting the cheese."

I chuckled, and she looked at me.

"What?"

"You said you *cut the cheese*."

"Yeah, so?" She waved the cheese knife.

"It means fart," I said in a mock whisper.

She dissolved into giggles. "Well then, I'd rather cut the cheese than have you do it!"

"Oh!" I grabbed my chest like someone had shot me with an arrow as I staggered after Elaina.

Charcoal looked at me with a pained expression, but stayed with Akiko.

Elaina ushered me into a smaller room with armchairs arranged

446

around a small table. On the table was a tray with a tea set and a plate of bite-sized cookies and scones.

"Akiko will regret picking cheese over sweets," I gloated as I sat in a squashy chair.

"Remind me which one of you is the adult?" Elaina asked, eyebrow raised.

"Why? What have you heard?" I asked, piling my plate with treats.

Elaina smiled and poured the tea. "It's herbal; I hope you don't mind."

"Not if there's honey. I can't smell much, anyway."

She smiled. "I'd have thought you had your fill of honey after Wakefield."

"There's *always* room for honey, though I may give mead a miss for a while."

"Understandable." She sat back and stirred her tea.

"Is this how we start?" I picked a cookie from my plate.

Elaina looked uncomfortable. Her stirring became violent, tea splashing onto her saucer.

"Elaina?" I chewed my cookie, enjoying the buttery sweetness, and watched the healer. This was the least self-assured I'd seen her.

"Matthew," she said, putting her cup and saucer down with a *clang*, "it's my unhappy task to apologize to you."

"Go ahead."

"While I wasn't there when it happened, I still feel, as a member of Newfane, responsible."

I put a crispy cookie into my mouth and nodded.

"We've had people out searching for Talbot, but we haven't found a trace of him yet."

Cookie dust exploded from my mouth. "What?"

Elaina looked at me blankly. "Aren't you here about Talbot?"

"Talbot? Where is he?"

Elaina looked uncomfortable. "He escaped. Two days ago. Did you get Ricardo's message? He sent a messenger..." She broke off, and her eyes widened. "Oh, Matthew, I thought you knew. We sent you the message and begged you to come for a personal apology."

I blinked, trying to process the news.

Talbot had escaped?

"Why are you here?" Elaina asked.

"To have you talk to Akiko—and maybe me, too. She's having nightmares, and I wanted to know what to do about them before we leave."

"Oh."

"Talbot escaped?" I asked.

"What?" asked a small voice behind me.

I turned and beckoned to Akiko.

Charcoal followed her, examining the crumbs around me.

"Can you tell us how?" I asked Elaina.

Akiko clambered into the chair with me, and I moved over to give her room.

"He said he needed a daily walk to commune with his maker," said Elaina finally. "He'd been perfectly congenial."

I nodded.

Akiko took a cookie from my plate. "What happened next?"

Elaina looked from the girl to me. "He... left."

I leaned forward. "Did he hurt anyone?"

"No." Elaina flushed. "He walked away."

"He wasn't being watched?" I asked, incredulous.

"Well," Elaina said weakly, "we are a walled community."

"I left," said Akiko, "with my *horse*."

"Yes, well." Elaina shifted and poured a third cup of tea, handing it to Akiko. "Done is done. If Matthew will excuse us, I'd like to talk about the bad dreams you've been having."

I didn't move until Akiko poked me with her elbow.

"Go," she whispered.

I nodded and stood. "Ricardo?"

Elaina's flush deepened. "He asked me to tell you he's busy."

"Grand. Where is he?"

Elaina bit her lip.

"You should tell him," said Akiko matter-of-factly. "He won't let it go."

"In the livery."

"Tending a sick calf?" I asked, sarcasm dripping.

"Bye, Matthew," said Akiko, balancing her teacup.

Charcoal lay next to her, watching me with pity.

Leaving the inn, I took a deep breath.

Talbot strolled away.

I shook my head and hustled to the livery. Stepping inside, I let my eyes adjust to the dim light.

"Ricardo?" I asked the girl.

She stopped brushing Oxide and pointed at a set of stairs.

"Thanks." I bounded up the stairs two at a time. "Ricardo!" I found the healer sitting in a small office with the administrator and minstrel.

"Matthew!" Ricardo jumped to his feet and looked around frantically, like a man seeking escape from fire. For a moment, I thought he might jump out the window.

"Please sit," said the minstrel, sighing. "We thought Elaina was best suited to apologize."

"Apologize?" I asked with a sardonic laugh. "I'm not here for an apology."

"Oh?" Ricardo's chest puffed. "Then what?"

"I'm here for an explanation."

The administrator stood. Bravely, he said, "Believe you me, Matthew, I've tried to understand it myself."

I leaned against the door frame and folded my arms. "Understand what? From what Elaina said, Talbot wandered away while on his *solitary* daily walk."

Ricardo cleared his throat. "Yes, well, we thought we had his word."

I massaged my temples.

"We are a walled community," said the administrator plaintively.

449

"Yes, I've heard," I muttered.

The fight went out of me.

Talbot had escaped, but Ricardo had warned me they had no incarceration facilities. These people were not, nor did they profess to be, jailers.

"Done is done."

"Yes," said the minstrel. "Are you worried he'll try to harm you?"

"No, but I wanted answers. I've so many questions."

"Yes, well." Ricardo shook his head. "It's hard to hold an unanswered question."

Was he slyly alluding to their offer to join the Avalon Society? Now?

"Can I ask a question?" I asked.

"Yes." Ricardo braced.

I walked to the window and looked out over the picturesque community. "What happens to your children when they come of age?"

Ricardo looked at me blankly, and the administrator looked at Ricardo. I found my answer on the minstrel's face.

"Even your own children," I breathed. "You evict your children."

"We give our children the best start we can. But yes, the Avalon Society only extends offers to the best of the best. Including our children," confirmed Ricardo. He patted the minstrel's shoulder, and she clasped his hand with hers.

The administrator cleared his throat. "We find the best placement we can for them. The best. If we must."

I shook my head. "How old was your child?" I asked the minstrel.

She smiled sadly. "They fostered him at fourteen. He was a builder—"

My chest caught.

"In Brookfield," she finished.

"Metallo," I said, my heart full of sadness. "He *was* the best. The very best."

CHAPTER SIXTY

The morning sun warmed my back as I checked our saddles one last time.

"No, we should stick to the plan. We can get a few hours in before we need to stop for lunch." Patting the donkey's neck, I turned. If I couldn't convince my friends we were safe, they'd delay our departure further.

Josephine sighed, her posture stiff and unnatural. "Ben?"

Ben eyed me, but shook his head.

"You should have told us sooner. We would've come with you," said Genevie.

"Matthew planned this," said Ben. He walked to Akiko's mare and reached his hand up for hers. "Be safe, child."

Akiko caught his hand and waved it cheerfully.

Ben was right. When we'd returned from Newfane, I hadn't mentioned Talbot's escape. Instead, I'd gone about the business of getting Akiko outfitted to travel.

By trading a few minor improvements, I'd gathered clothes, toiletries, a bedroll, and even a few instruction books. Because I

451

hadn't found a packsaddle to fit the donkey, I'd traded for a horse-sized harness and pannier set and improved them.

"Matthew, we don't know how old brownishgreyishyellowish-black is," said Genevie, patting the small animal fondly. "Do you think this trip will be too much for him?"

I tied the donkey to the string on Magnesium's tail. The trees shivered in the light breeze, birdsong trilling as birds flitted from branch to branch.

It was a good day to travel.

"Let's let him choose. Master Donkey, do you want to stay here and start your dotage?"

The donkey raised his muzzle and brayed, and Charcoal huffed in response.

I shrugged. "He's keen to go."

Genevie smiled sadly and pulled me toward her. "Why am I always saying goodbye to you?"

I held her tightly, patting her back and swaying gently. She relaxed in my arms, and I smiled.

Rocking soothed girls of all ages.

When she took a deep breath, I released her, keeping my hands on her shoulders. "If you decide to stay, I'll understand."

Genevie stepped back and shoved my shoulder. "The life I had is over. A few weeks here will give me the time to finish what I started and think about what's next."

Josephine tried again. "Matthew, for Akiko's sake, wouldn't it be safer to wait for us?"

I shrugged. "If the girl becomes a nuisance, I'll tie her to a tree and leave her, so what's the difference?"

Akiko giggled. "I'll tie *you* to a tree!"

Genevie chuckled. "Your cooking is punishment enough and what we *should* worry about. Will this child last all the way to Toronto on Matthew's culinary skills?"

Akiko leaned down from her mare and whispered something to Genevie.

Genevie shouted in laughter and looked at me with a mixture of pity and amusement. "The child will be fine," she announced.

Ben extended his hand. "Matthew."

I shook it and pulled my friend into an embrace. "Take care of Josephine," I murmured. "She's more fragile than she admits."

Ben hugged me. "Funny. She says the same of you."

Me? Fragile?

I turned to Josephine last. "Well, sister," I murmured.

With a watery smile, she hugged me.

I rested my cheek against the top of her head. Small hairs tickled my nostrils, and I stretched my top lip and wrinkled my nose to ease the itch.

My nose protested. It had decreased in size but was still purple and swollen across the bridge from where Cara had broken it.

I hugged Josephine tighter, and she relaxed into me. Her bones were very near the skin, but her pulse beat strong and true.

"Don't forget to eat, dearest," I whispered.

"Ben will make sure of it."

I smiled at Ben from across the top of her head. "I know."

"Be safe, Matthew. I couldn't bear it if—" She drew back and bit her lip.

I'd told my friends some of what I'd learned from Talbot. After the meeting with Cara, I'd accepted Talbot was trying to protect me. "Josephine, if Talbot wanted to harm me, he'd have done so."

"I'll protect him, Josephine," said Akiko.

I kissed Josephine's scarred cheek. "You're right; her nose looks better than mine," I called.

Josephine's hands flew to her face...

Several days ago, I'd finally done what she'd asked so long ago. After fixing her broken nose, I'd asked if she wanted any more changes. She had looked at me then whispered, "My scar."

I nodded. "Where should I start?"

To my surprise, she'd pointed to a cut on her forearm. Though healing, the wound was red and livid.

I expanded the portrait to include her arm and painted out the wound.

She looked at it for a long time, turning it back and forth, as if the cut could reappear upon deeper inspection.

"Anything else?"

"Yes." She'd raised her chin and looked at me. "Can you fix this one?" she pointed to the scar on her eyelid. "It droops when I get tired, making reading difficult."

I'd nodded and made the change. "Anything else?"

Josephine had held her hands out for the painting.

"Careful. It's oil and will take time to dry."

She'd nodded, taking the canvas gently by the sides. She looked at her portrait, tears spilling from her eyes. "Thank you, it's perfect."

I'd agreed...

I smiled at the memory and examined my friend. Even with the scars twisting her cheek, she *was* perfect. "You look different."

She rolled her eyes. "The portrait?"

"No, not that."

"Not what?" Ben asked.

"Matthew said I look different."

"Turn around," said Ben. "Let's see."

Josephine stepped around me.

Ben studied her and nodded. "You look different."

"I figured it out," I murmured to her as Akiko backed her mare in a circle around us.

"What?"

"You've learned to wear your scars and no longer hide them."

Josephine's hand fluttered but didn't touch her face. She nodded and raised her chin. "You need to learn to do the same."

"What, this?" I asked, touching the tiny cut on my temple which was healing nicely.

"No, these," she said, pushing on my chest.

Instantly, I understood what she meant. My scars, while not visible, were deep. If I allowed my mind to probe them, agony seared my heart.

It was the hurt of an abandoned child. The uncertainty of a boy wondering if anyone cared. The pain of a man starting out in life lonely and unsure, not knowing what was safe or who to trust.

"Having parents doesn't mean you don't grow up with scars," she said, patting her own chest. "I know where mine are, and I still yearn for nurturing."

"My friend, you're very wise."

"I should be a scholar."

"Mmm, if the baking career doesn't go well."

We smiled sadly at each other, Whistler's smile dancing in our hearts.

"Time to go?" Akiko asked.

Nodding, I released Josephine's hand. I mounted Oxide and breathed in the scent of leather and hay while settling on the warm saddle. I looked at my friends, memorizing their faces—the color of their hair, and the texture of their skin.

My eyes stung, and I squinted at the sun, letting it water my eyes. "Bright today," I said as a tear spilled.

Ben patted Akiko's mare one last time. "You two take care of each other. See you in Toronto."

I swallowed and jerked my chin at Josephine. "Ben, watch her. When no one is looking, she'll beat her apprentice for not cutting kindling sticks to an exact length. She'll frighten the children who collect the eggs, saying that one cracked shell, just one mind you, could mean no cake for Christmas."

"I'll hoard the vanilla and spices collected from the depots," Josephine said.

"And keep all the baked beauties on the shelves while passing out the uglies to your least favorite folk."

"I'll put salt instead of sugar into a child's birthday cookie, and—"

"Bake the smallest puppy into a pie," we said in unison.

Chuckling, I looked at Ben and Genevie's confused expressions and laughed harder as the tightness inside me uncoiled more.

It was time to go.

AUTHOR'S NOTE

On January 21, 2017, my husband and I jumped on a bus to head to Judkins Park to join the Seattle Womxn's March. I'd never joined a protest before and worried about what could happen, but my fears about the Trump Administration were stronger than my anxiety for my personal safety.

Other than voting, this was the single-most political thing I'd ever done.

My husband was also nervous about joining a "women's march" but on the bus, we chatted with a man in his 80s who was also attending his first political protest. He had left his wife, who was in poor health, at home to watch the coverage on the news and said he needed to be present to show his support for women, good-minded people, and the planet.

We joined approximately 175,000 other people to protest the election results and to promote women's rights, assert that Black Lives Matter, and the importance of our actions on the planet. We were also there because we countered religious discrimination, violence against women, and LGBTQ abuse.

It took us several hours to cover the 3.6-mile route, and though typically wary of crowds, I found the time incredibly healing. As we shuffled along, we drew strength from each other, unified and determined to improve our world. The energy of the crowd was peaceful, patient, inclusive, loving, and joyous.

It was during the march that the what-if thoughts swirled in my mind.

What would a world without politics look like? What if there was no money, no greed, no insane grabs for power? What if we lived in a world of community? What if no one used religion to incite division and violence?

What would our society look like if we valued art and *artists*, we practiced empathy, and we all shared an abundance mindset?

Matthew's world rose from these questions.

ABOUT THE AUTHOR

Thank you for reading Oil and Dust. I hope you enjoyed the journey.

Please leave a review to help other readers find the book. Your review really helps me out!

Want a free, signed book plate for your book? Post a picture of the book on your socials! Don't forget to tag and follow me so I can DM you for your mailing address.

Jami Fairleigh is a writer, urban planner, and hobby collector from Washington. She shares her life with a husband, a trio of well-mannered horses, a pair of dubiously behaved parrots, and one neurotic dog. You can find her and more information about her writing at jamifairleigh.com.

THE ELEMENTAL ARTIST

Matthew's origin story is available for free when you sign up for updates on my books and other fiction at jamifairleigh.com.

What would you paint if you could change the physical world with your art?

Seventeen-year-old art student Matthew Sugiyama has his heart set on winning the coveted position of Head Boy, but so have the other thirteenth-grade boys in the abbey. Winning the spot will secure his future after graduation, but is his art magic strong enough to win?

Matthew's story continues in Book 2 of the Elemental Artist Series, Graphite and Turbulence, available March of 2022.

ACKNOWLEDGMENTS

I've always wondered why so many names were included in the acknowledgment sections for books; after all, writing a book is a solitary affair, isn't it? Now, at the other end of the process, I understand that a book *does not exist* without a team of people to question, guide, critique, support, aid, and push the writer.

I'd like to thank my production team. Thank you to my first readers in the Absolute Write's 100-day Book Program for notes on character development. Can you believe we finished our books? Thank you also to beta readers extraordinaire Erik Shimizu and Douglas Fairleigh for providing insight on the story experience and notes on how men react to events.

To the Jamigos, Jami Sheets and Jamie Sogn, thank you for your words of encouragement and notes on plot, pacing, and character motivation. I can't wait to see your books on my shelf. Jami(e)s of the world unite, and write!

To my editors, thank you to Kim Kessler who read my gigantic second draft and helped me narrow down genre and point of view.

Thank you to Charlie Knight who allowed me to take a year to freak out about the book, and would not allow Matthew Sugiyama to *tell* you how he was feeling. Thank you to Annie Jenkinson and Brad Reynolds who helped me to improve the flow of my prose.

Thank you to Ryan Lanz who provided insight on copy writing, and to my cover design team Andrew and Rebecca Brown for my gorgeous cover and for answering my many, *many*, many questions. Finally, thank you to Paul Martin at Dominion Editorial for proof-reading and typo hunting in this monster of a book.

To the toolmakers without whom the crafting of the book would have been much, much harder, thank you for Scrivener, Fictionary, ProWritingAid, BookFunnel, reMarkable, BetaBooks, and Vellum.

I'd like to thank the people who have supported and encouraged me. My mother who is responsible for my love of reading, my sister whose quiet support I could always feel, and my brother who provided enthusiastic(!!!) notes on the plot, prose, and the cover. Also, my stepmother who assured me I was an artist, and my father who has read and widely shared *every piece* of writing I've had published.

Thank you to Deanna Look, my Number One Super Fan, whose dislike of ebooks helped drive me to finish the print version.

Thank you, Sky Family (Dave, Deb, Nico, Jeanna, David, Helen, and Doug) for keeping me going through the long process by asking questions about the story and evolution of the book over great food and many glasses of wine.

Thank you to author Jane Yolen who gave the keynote at my first-ever writing conference. I was in grade school and meeting a "real" author meant so much.

Thank you to my indie author writing mentors. These people who empowered me with answers and information, including Lindsey Fairleigh and Lindsey Pogue who were extremely generous with their time. Also, thank you to Twitter's #WritingCommunity and the #TweetBookClub— you guys rock. Thank you for the cheers, the laughs, and those really, *really* awkward gifs.

Last, I'd like to thank the three people without whom there

would be no book. First, my husband Douglas Fairleigh to whom the book is dedicated. Thank you for your support, your enthusiasm, for being my personal IT guy, for celebrating every milestone, for listening to my fears and self-doubt, and for your constant faith in me and my story. Buckle up, this is the first of many.

Second, Kate Greenawalt who made me face my fears of finishing this project over a bubbling pot of spicy soup.

Finally, former President Donald J. Trump without whom I may have never imagined a world without politics, religion, money, power, or greed.

CPSIA information can be obtained
at www.ICGtesting.com
Printed in the USA
LVHW040916040921
696963LV00015B/737/J

9 781955 428033